CHICAGO
BLUES

Books and stories by T. Lee Harris

Twenty-Seven Cents of Luck (Short)
Cat in the Middle (Short)
Sweet Water From the Rock (Short)
Muddy Waters (Short)
Winter Wonderland (Novella)

In the Miller and Peale Series
San Francisco at Night (Short)
Chicago Blues
New York Nights

In the Josh Katzen Series
Hanukkah Gelt (Short)
The Pecan Pie Affair (Short)
The Case of the Moche Rolex*

In the Sitehuti and Nefer-Djenou Bastet series
To Be a Scribe (Short)
The Scribe Vanishes (Short)
Wanting the Fish (Short)

* Coming Soon

CHICAGO BLUES

T. LEE HARRIS

Per Bastet

Chicago Blues

Published by Per Bastet Publications LLC, P.O. Box 3023 Corydon, IN 47112
Book designed by T. Lee Harris

ISBN 978-0-9899711-0-2

Cover Art and design by T. Lee Harris

For Deb who gave me a place to hide
until this book came together.

CHICAGO
BLUES

PART ONE

"The tree of liberty must be refreshed from time to time with
the blood of patriots and tyrants. It is its natural manure."
~~Thomas Jefferson

"The weed of crime bears bitter fruit."
~~The Shadow

ONE

I like motorcycles. I like the feeling of speed. I like leather and jazz. Rock'n'roll, too. My name is Byron Cyrus Peale. I prefer BC.

This story starts on my motorcycle, I guess. I was riding through the Chicago streets one evening enjoying the feel of the night air on my skin, bound for Julio's Fiesta (We Never Close). I have a . . . sensitivity to light, so as the song said, I wear my sunglasses at night. It's one reason I like bars: nice dimly lit places where it's easy to socialize.

It's also possible to get a good meal with relative ease.

This last is vital since I have rather odd dietary requirements.

I'm a vampire.

Now, don't sigh and mutter, "oh great, another Melancholy Predator of the Night". Nope! You see, I like being a vampire and, while I do have some objections as to how the change occurred, it's generally been a good unlife. However, even a vampire can have bad days — or nights rather.

Let me tell you about a particularly bad one. It all began at a bar. Hmmm. Quite a few of my bad ones have begun at bars. I wonder if there's something significant there? Anyway, it was like this:

***

The last open parking space in back of Julio's Fiesta was between the battered concrete retaining wall and a late-model Corvette parked diagonally in an effort to keep its custom paint job pure. BC Peale glared at it, then rammed his Harley-Davidson Softail into the gap. Flying gravel ponked off fiberglass, leaving a satisfying sheet of grit across the hood. He flipped off the bike's ignition muttering, "Take two, they're free."

Sitting back in the saddle, he savored the engine heat against his legs, and wondered for the hundredth time if the Hunger was too strong to safely socialize. He'd spent the past three nights poring over new charts at the Inferno Jazz Club, where he played piano in the house band on weekends. That left few opportunities to feed, and now the bloodthirst was stronger than expected. He shouldn't have abstained so long. He knew that, but he always lost track of time when he was at the keyboard. He never seemed to learn, either. He smiled at the memory of his eldest brother's opinion of this. Laughing softly, he answered the spectre of memory, "Yes, Charles, I always carry it one step too far."

Okay. The stockyards would be a much wiser first stop. His fingers closed on the key just as the bar's rear door slammed. The rhythm of a racing heart reached him over the loud, pounding music and the faint scent of female wrapped its allure around him. His canines lengthened involuntarily. Uh oh, fella, best be gone.

Unwilling fingers gripped the starter.

From the stoop, a woman called, "Hey, BC? BC! Wait up!"

Bloody hell. He recognized the voice and scent, now. Jay Marquez, and from her heartbeat, she was quite upset.

The hand still clutched the ignition key. Byron Peale tried to make it turn. The Hunger made it stay.

Perched precariously on stiletto heels, Jay jogged unsteadily across the gravel. She was out of breath when she got to him, her chest heaving in a most disconcerting manner. "BC, am I glad t'see you! I just walked out on that creep Mario Hernandez. Shouldn't of agreed to go out with 'im in the first place! That guy's so in love with himself, he oughta date a mirror." She brushed spun gold hair away from her oval, full-lipped face. "I can't walk worth a damn in these heels; wouldja mind givin' me a lift home on your bike? You know where I live, right?"

BC froze. The Hunger was winning, and her pulse roared in his ears drowning out all else. He slowly lifted his head and gazed deeply into her eyes.

"It ain't far, but it's awful dark . . . and . . . ." She faltered.

Her eyes went vacant, then closed, as she leaned into him, head tilted to expose her throat. He pulled her close, drinking in her bloodscent as his parted lips brushed her throat.

Unnoticed, the rear exit reopened, disgorging Alfie Fallon and Chick Boyce, in a brief burst of noise and stale smoke. Glancing over their shoulders, they gently closed the door behind them, an absurd move considering the noise level from inside. They were stiffing Angie, their waitress and Chick's long-time ladylove, for a thirty-buck tab. They both knew she'd been halfway expecting it. They both also knew she'd get it back one way or another.

There was another reason to take a powder just then, too. They (and the rest of the patrons of Julio's) heard the argument between Jay Marquez and Mario Hernandez and saw the lady's stormy departure. Alfie'd been eyeing that particular piece for a while — with no luck. But maybe, just maybe, he could intercept the damsel in distress and console her a little before Hernandez got off his ass to follow. It was a good plan. Too bad someone beat him to it. Fallon stopped short and swore at the sight of Jay in the arms of another man.

Chick sniggered, "Hey look! Jay's with that Peale guy. I seen fast work before, but this beats everything!"

Fallon gritted his teeth. Chick's eyes worked fine, even if his brain had a couple glitches. It was Peale. The guy showed up the year before and the local girls were still sighing over his good-looks, English accent and fancy manners. The local guys just wanted to beat him to a pulp. Now, here he was with Jay. So much for a clear shot at her.

Boyce said, "I dunno, Alfie, Peale's always got a wad of cash on him. Surprised Jay ain't zeroed in on him before now."

Alfie Fallon's expression changed. "Yeah. He's always loaded, in't he?" Drawing a knife from his jacket sleeve, he held it up to catch the light. "Let's see if he'll float us a little loan."

Chick's chuckle was barely audible as he cracked his knuckles, and followed Fallon across the parking lot. Peale was a good-sized guy; Alfie'd need Boyce's muscle to make this work.

***

As Jay's embrace tightened, BC felt as well as heard the enfolding thump of her heartsblood. The tip of his tongue traced the pulsing vein in her throat. Yes. There. Soft resistance as fangs — a hand gripped his shoulder, spinning him roughly around. The sharp prick of steel manifested at the pit of his throat and he strove to reorient himself. Jay's collapse onto the gravel barely registered.

***

The exit opened and shut a final time, releasing the interior noise in another brief burst, but those near enough to hear it, were too busy to notice.

***

Peale's head slowly lifted and Fallon wasn't prepared for what met him eye to eye. The knife wavered. The mouth opened for a scream, cut off before it began by a steely grip that crushed his windpipe and snapped fragile neck bones with a sickeningly small crunch. He was dead before he hit the ground.

Chick Boyce knew death when he saw it. Pulling a pistol from under his jacket, he dropped into a TV cop crouch. Peale swayed, staring blankly at the crumpled body sprawled on the gravel. Tendrils of long, black hair, escaped from the normally neat ponytail, hung in disarray around the pale, narrow face, giving the impression of a wild animal guarding its kill.

A short distance from the gruesome tableau, Jay moaned and rolled onto her knees. Panicking, Boyce clicked the pistol's hammer back.

Peale swiveled in the direction of the small sound. Instinct told him it meant danger, but disorientation made him slow to react. The pistol spat fire twice making feeble cracks against the background of the night.

The shots took Peale square in the chest and erupted out the back of his leather jacket in a spray of gore. He staggered backwards into the retaining wall. Blood ran freely from his mouth and nose as he crumpled down the pebbled surface into the forlorn posture of a discarded rag doll. He didn't move again.

Boyce smiled the wolf-smile of the victor and advanced to roll the body before anyone came to investigate. He wasn't worried. The jukebox was way too loud for anyone to hear the shots and Jay had collapsed again. Very convenient — for him. He briefly wondered if he ought to pop her, too? Nah, she was cold. He was more interested in seeing what Peale had on him. Still smiling, he closed on the slumped form.

The smile froze as Peale lifted his head and wiped blood from his face with the back of his hand. Impossibly, he spoke, blood-filled lungs lending a hideous bubbling quality to the words, "That . . . was a mistake."

At that moment, Boyce understood terror. The lesson came too late.

Peale sprang like a hunting cat. As from a great distance, he noted a scream of raw panic and four more pops and impacts from the pistol. They didn't matter. The Hunger mattered and it raged within him. Blood filled his mouth and he drank deeply.

TWO

I'm a big guy. Used to play football in the pros. L.A. mostly. That was many years and a lot of knee surgery ago. Name's Galen Miller; might recognize me from my football card. I'm a collector's item.

Never dreamed I'd wind up as a cop like my Pop was. That still isn't right, I'm not exactly a cop. I'm with Sentry International: A U.N.-sanctioned law enforcement agency recently incorporated to create a network to investigate international crime. Maybe it's more like Galen Miller, Super Spy. Ain't that a hoot?

I blame Jim Nelson. You grow up with a guy, he knows what you like. Jim's Captain of Special Investigations for S.I. Chicago now, but before that, he was assigned to California; when he needed a jock-type for a sting operation, I pitched in. I didn't do much, but it gave me a taste, and before long, I was good and hooked. Just like Jim knew I'd be. When I retired from football, the bastard was lurking in the wings with a job offer. Of course, I took it. Apart from wrecking my already rocky marriage, it's the best decision I ever made.

That's history. This is the story: Once upon a time there was a case, a real tough one. Interpol turned it first when it looked like a simple money laundering scheme run by someone known as 'The Borgia.' Then it tied into drug trafficking, then weapons procurement and went downhill from there. The links to Borgia were faint, but European officials traced them to the United States. To the state of Illinois. Right into Chicagoland. At that point, Interpol cheerfully dropped the whole mess into the lap of Sentry who cheerfully dropped it into mine.

That was okay, because it brought me home to Chicago. I was born here, my mother and sister still live here. For my cover, I chose the ever popular "quiet retirement in hometown." Worked great. Why not? It's what I want to do. It also let me work with two of my oldest buddies, Jim Nelson and Mick Marquez.

I moved into a basement apartment in a building I'd bought for Mama back in the old neighborhood. Then, I dug, hoping to trace the organization from the bottom up. Good plan, but it didn't work. This Borgia guy was well hidden. I'd find a front company then everything evaporated. The digging got so hard, I came close to blowing my cover. Then, if things weren't bad enough, they got even more complicated when someone started attacking the goons I was supposed to be watching.

These attacks were unusual in that, along with the normal fight injuries you'd expect, there were weird wounds resembling bite-marks. The majority of these were on the throat, or wrists. Some victims were killed outright, their necks broken or throats torn out. That was rare. Most were found wandering near the lake in what was termed a dazed condition. Nobody remembered shit — other than being grabbed from behind or something equally useless. Inevitably, the supermarket tabloids jumped on it with feature articles about the Chicago Vampire. When word got out the unsub was preying exclusively on criminals, the name became the Vampire Vigilante. Before long, it wasn't just tabloids. It was everywhere.

At SI, we called him the Lake Shore Robin Hood. Our hold-back — what wasn't publicized — was that money taken from the hoods was later donated to various charities — anonymously, of course. Our warped individual displayed an equally warped sense of humor; the first contribution was to the Policeman's Benevolent Fund. Talk about *a bunch of red faces! After that piece of generosity got to the higher-ups, pressure built from all sides for SI (in general) and me (in particular) to make progress. The result? I was chasing anything even resembling a lead. It's embarrassing that the actual break was a stupid accident.*

What brought me to Julio's Fiesta that night was the promise of a cold brew to wash the taste of my latest Failure from my mouth. After I'd called in my report to my CO, Jim Nelson, that is. Failure. I hate that word.

***

Galen Miller carefully punched the last digits into the burner phone. Bad enough the damned candy bar things were constructed for munchkins, but most of the streetlights were out and the bar's thin walls barely muffled the music spilling from inside. Well, that was good cover and a pretty good reason to be calling from outside the bar — aside from the prospect of a cold one. There was also the theory that a black man in a dark corner was harder to recognize.

Sighing, he leaned against the rough stucco side of the tavern and listened to the electronic burr that signaled a connection. *Sure. "Harder to recognize." How many six and a half foot ex-linebackers were there in the neighborhood? Dammit.*

Nelson didn't waste any time. He opened with, "Whatcha got for me, Gae?"

At least he'd picked up fast. Having nothing positive to report was bad. Standing around waiting to report it was worse. "Whole lot of nothin', Jimbo. Not a whiff of our friend, Mr. B. and it almost blew up on me in the bargain."

Jim suddenly sounded tired. He should, he was the poor bastard who'd have to pass the bad tidings on to U.S. Sentry International Director, Colonel Brian Black, in New York. There'd been too many dead ends lately, and while nobody was *exactly* angry, the encouraging words were getting a little forced. "Geez, Gae, what the hell went wrong this time? This looked like the best break in weeks."

"Months! It started off big guns but petered out to a cap pistol. I just wasted the better part of a day on it." Over the din penetrating the walls of the building came the sharp crack of gunfire. Miller's head snapped toward the sound. "Shit! There's trouble, I'll call back."

He thumbed the End button as a scream and more shots tore the night. Miller's hand found Beretta .380 as he dropped his shoulder and broke into the determined run that marked his career on the football field. Moving with surprising speed for one so large, he plunged around the side of the building. When Gae Miller had a bad night, it was *bad*!

At the parking lot, he paused behind the ill-trimmed box elder hedge bordering it and scanned the scene — what he could see of it. Someone had used the lot's lights for target practice and tightwad Julio hadn't replaced them yet. A geriatric sulfur-yellow streetlamp to one side of the driveway provided the only light. *Maybe Julio gets a cut from muggers hiding between the cars.* He stepped cautiously into the murky area. Nobody from inside ventured out to investigate. Most likely no one heard the shots over the music. He sidled closer to the hedge wondering why he was there. No, he knew why. Repeated failure made him want to do something and this qualified.

He was sure this was where the commotion was, and thought he caught the faint scent of gunpowder, but then again, that might have been imagination. Motionless against the shaggy hedge, he pressed into the scratchy embrace and blinked, forcing his eyes to accustom to the gloom.

The distinctive deep-throated rumble of a motorcycle engine turning over pulled his attention to the far corner. The bike was jammed into a tight space between what looked like a Corvette and the concrete retaining wall across the back of the lot. The rider was in a big hurry to vacate, but was hindered by an awkward bundle in his lap. Without conscious thought, Miller stepped from the cover of the shrubbery as the rider wrestled his machine out of the narrow slot and toward the driveway. The bike's headlamp swept the gravel-strewn ground. The brief illumination flashed an impression of crumpled bodies and dark spatters that Galen's mind colored a vivid scarlet. Something about the glimpsed spectacle struck an unpleasant chord in memory. Maybe this wouldn't be such an unproductive night after all.

Forcing his eyes from the tumbled forms, he riveted on the fast-approaching motorcycle; no way was he going to let this guy past. This looked to be the break every law officer dreamed of (or possibly had nightmares about). Bracing in the middle of the drive, he leveled the pistol and yelled, "Stop! Now!"

For a heady moment, the driver wavered, then Miller's elation evaporated as the heavy machine aimed directly at him. Certain he'd be run down, he dove aside, rolling as he hit the pavement, coming up determined to get a good look at the driver and the license when the bike passed under the streetlight.

As the retreating bike passed through the sickly yellow glow, Galen stared in shock after it. He hadn't gotten the license number. He didn't need to. He recognized the rider. They'd first been introduced at a holiday party thrown by a mutual friend last December. British guy — he'd remember the name in a minute. *Peale*, yeah. BC Peale. Played piano at the Inferno Jazz Club a couple of blocks over.

Cold clamped his heart as he considered the second part of his observation. Even in the bad light, it was obvious that the back of the man's jacket hung in shreds and the feeble pinky-yellow light revealed ragged holes in the flesh beneath it.

He knelt on the damp grass, staring after the shrinking taillights, his pistol looking toy-like as it dangled from his fingers. The part of his mind where training and discipline lived clamored for supremacy over raw emotion. It took longer than he liked, but discipline won and he pulled himself to his feet. Like it or not, he had no way to chase a motorcycle, but there was plenty to occupy him right here.

Professionalism didn't do squat to keep his hands from shaking as he holstered the pistol and crept toward the shapes on the gravel. Still, no one came out of the bar. Good. That much luck held. Pulling a miniature flashlight from his pocket, he switched it on, relieved to find the fall hadn't broken it. Already knowing what he'd see, he crept in for a closer examination of the victims, then snapped the light off quickly. The bagmen's throats had been torn in exactly the same way. He hated it when he was right.

It wouldn't take another wordy forensic report to tell him there was little blood left in the bodies, either, though there was more than enough everywhere else to make up for it. Swallowing his gorge, he backed away debating who to call first, Captain Nelson or the police. He'd regained the cover of the hedge when the rear door opened, spilling light and music into the night.

A woman, sounding slightly drunk, called loudly, "Mario! Hey, Mario, you catch up with Jay?"

He froze as the door swung shut, muting the music and dousing the light. Unsteady steps crunched across the gravel. Pressing into the twiggy shadows, he fought the urge to stop her. It was a rotten thing to do, but it would be easier this way.

The woman called again. "Mario, I saw ya come out here. Look, forget that bitch an'. . . ."

From the sounds, she'd tripped. From what came next, she'd fallen over a body. "What th' shit? Oh . . . oh . . . omigod."

Her screams ripped at him and he bit his lip against her scrambling footsteps back to the comparative safety of the tavern. The worst was over. Now he'd wait and mingle with the inevitable gawkers and gather as much as he could by watching the police. Later, he'd try to scrub the dirty feeling away with a hot shower.

***

The shattered thing that remained of Mario Hernandez crouched in a hollow of the shrubbery, mindless of the hundreds of tiny scratches from the grasping twiglets and silently sobbing in the miasma of his urine-soaked designer jeans. The animal impulse that first urged him to hide now recognized the opportunity for escape. He took it, slinking off on foot in the vague direction recognized as 'home.'

***

Miller shifted vainly for a comfortable position in the miniature seat of the commuter train. He'd long ago grown accustomed to adapting his extra large frame to a world of medium accommodations. Invariably, the old joke filtered through his mind: "Where does an eight hundred pound gorilla sit?"

Answer: "Anywhere he wants to."

Yeah, but he probably won't be comfortable. This particular gorilla wasn't happy, either. Bad enough Jim wanted a face-to-face, but this crap about taking several trains to throw off a tail was just stupid. Okay, so his car might be recognized if he drove straight out. There still had to be a better way.

The lighting in the car turned the windows into dark mirrors. He absently watched the passing suburban lights make Doppler streaks through his insubstantial reflection as he let his mind wander back to the gravel lot.

Sometimes, being a local celebrity was a useful thing. He'd had a ringside seat as the forensic team arrived. That didn't help much when they erected their screens and set up the lights behind them, though. Still, for the cost of a few autographs and cell phone snapshots, he'd heard all the witness statements first-hand — what there was of them anyway. Mainly, there was the woman who found the bodies. Her name was Terri Leake, and reading between the lines, she'd been trying to catch Mario Hernandez' eye for a while. She thought she'd struck lucky when Jay got mad and took off through the back.

That stopped Miller cold. He almost forgot to breathe as he brought Peale's tightly clutched bundle into stark focus and realized it was Jay.

After that, it took everything he had to force the audio circuits back online to hear the rest. Fortunately, there wasn't much. After Hernandez broke away to go after Jay, Leake had hung back to finish her beer. She didn't see Boyce and Fallon leave, but it was only a few minutes before she went to see if Mario was still around. The rest of her statement was punctuated with sobs and hysterics. He didn't blame her. He'd seen crime scenes before and this one was messy by any standards. He felt like slime for standing back and letting her stumble on the bodies, but at the same time, the cynical part of him noted that, despite all outward appearances, Ms. Leake was enjoying her brief stardom. No doubt there'd be free drinks in her future for while.

Before the performance ended, one other noteworthy detail emerged: Mario Hernandez was *not* among the dead, although he was missing. Coincidentally, the Corvette near the bodies belonged to Hernandez. Not so coincidentally, the blood-spattered and bullet-holed machine was impounded as evidence. The police had more than one reason to look for Hernandez.

Slouched against the stained vinyl cushions of the train, he ran a mental reconstruction. Jay, hot-headed like her brother, blew up and left the bar in a huff; that was fact. Conjecture took over once she was through the door. Once outside, she probably ran into Peale. Miller squirmed against the unyielding seat; unwilling to think too hard about what happened next. It tended to make him antsy.

Sooooo. That brought him back to Fallon and Boyce. They left the building soon after Jay and . . . um . . . interrupted whatever it was that she and Peale were doing. Hernandez must've put in an appearance somewhere between that and the time Galen rounded the corner. What happened then? Where was Hernandez when he'd made his own entrance?

For that matter, where was he now?

He noted his confidence in Jay's safety with a little surprise. He was worried, yes, but mostly about the fact she was unconscious, not what happened with Peale, himself. Odd, since he'd obviously concluded the man was a genuine vampire. That made him a shoo-in for the role of Lake Shore Robin Hood, too. So why wasn't he chewing his fingernails up to his elbows?

Maybe because he'd *met* Peale? They'd talked several times and he'd never once gotten bad vibes from him. Sure, he could be a jerk, but who couldn't? Besides, he was a likable jerk, and that was more than could be said for a lot of folks. With a lopsided smile at his own reflection, he realized he was launching into a philosophical debate over whether or not being a vampire necessitated being evil, and what constituted evil, anyway. This was neither the time nor place for what his family and friends called his gestalt rationalization techniques.

He settled back against the seat back with finality. Rationalization or no, Peale had cradled Jay in a way that read as *protective*, pure and simple. No debate was stronger than that. Past evidence proved that their Robin Hood could easily have left Ms. Marquez lying on the gravel with nothing more than a vaguely pleasant memory. No. As much for his own sake as anything, he'd keep that part to himself for now. *But* he wanted to talk to that undead bastard ASAP.

Just to be on the safe side, though, he'd log onto the network at the office and run a background check on Mr. Peale. He doubted there'd be much there, but you never knew, besides, it was another reason for going in to HQ. He loathed reporting to an office. After trying nine-to-five life in connection with several business ventures, he found it quickly devolved into a well-upholstered cage with a key to the washroom. One selling point for Sentry International was that he set his own structure with minimum inter-ference from the main office. It worked beautifully — at least while the

'Miller Magic' worked. Once the going got rough, he'd spent more and more time at the computer in the cubbyhole office. He wasn't sure which sucked more, failure or becoming a part-time cubicle rat.

What really ticked him off was that, with all the electronic gizmos the agency was known for, he figured they'd provide him with some way to check in from a distance. He already owned a laptop. Okay, he wasn't a technowizard like Mick, but he could use the damned thing for more than solitaire. Could he wrangle remote access to SINet? Noooooo. Trust a bureaucracy to make a simple thing complicated.

Despite the official designation of *Sentry International, Chicago*, the offices were located in nearby Schaumburg rather than downtown Chicago. The upside was that there was a train stop just a short walk from the complex. Seeing the lit sign for the stop in the distance, he had a sudden sense of dread. It reminded him of the way he'd felt when waiting outside the principal's office to be reamed for fighting. It made an odd sort of sense. Jim Nelson and Mick Marquez were two of his oldest friends, but tonight, they were also his superior officers. Superior officers he intended to withhold information from. He sighed wearily. Usually, he'd enjoy kicking back with them, but he wasn't looking forward to this session. Every time he framed his report, he kept running into things he was reluctant to include.

Maybe the feeling of dread wasn't all that surprising. Back when the tabloids first tagged their troublemaker as the Vampire Vigilante, the whole team had a great time with it. They even made up fake news stories some of them were really funny. But that wasn't his problem — yet. *His* fumble came when he casually remarked that if one were predisposed to believe in vampires, it would be an easy leap of logic given the blood loss and nature of the wounds. Big mistake. Now the team were having a great time with *him*.

Well, let 'em. He wondered what they'd do if they knew the truth. Probably feel as chilled and shaky as he did. It was worse knowing Jay was involved. Funny how it was with people you grew up with: the first image to spring to mind was invariably how they looked back then. In his mind's eye, she was still the grubby-faced baby trailing behind big brother Miguel, not the beautiful woman she'd grown into.

He winced. Mick was going to be a problem. As Deputy Director of Special Operations and Investigations, Lieutenant Marquez was now Jim Nelson's second in command. Mick was sure to be there tonight; he always was. Were there words to tell one of your oldest friends that his baby sister was last seen riding off on a motorcycle in the arms of a suspected vampire? He could hear it now. "Hey, guys! Guess what? There *is* a vampire! I saw 'im tonight when he tried to run me over with his motorcycle. Had Jay with 'im, too!"

Yeah. No problem. He'd always liked padded rooms and the color white.

Admittedly, if it were his *own* sister, Opal, he'd be freaking out instead of bitching about a slow train. Not that he was perfectly comfortable about Jay. . . . It was hard because he knew her, but discipline forced the emotional distance he'd needed to realize she'd been limp but not hurt.

If Peale really was their Robin Hood, he needed to learn more before mentioning him to anyone at Sentry. Especially Mick. Even as kids, Mick was first to dive into (or start) a fight, leaving Galen to mop up and Jim to smooth tempers afterward. By this time, CPD would have contacted him and he'd know Jay was involved. He be insane enough without adding to it. It would serve no useful purpose to have him out beating the bushes for the suspect. Especially if he knew who the suspect was. Miller wanted to question Peale, not spend his time sweeping up what was left when Mick got finished.

Chicago's city-glow stained the sky behind him as he stepped onto the train platform and paused to admire the sight before starting the short walk to the office building. He loved this city. He'd lived in many others, but

Chicago was always Home. In spite of the nightmare this Borgia case had become, he was glad it had brought him back.

As he neared the entrance, frustration mounted. This was the first time in either career he'd found himself spinning his wheels. He hated the word failure, but his mind screamed it over and over as his best efforts turned to smoke. As if the going hadn't been hard enough to start with, the attacks on the guys he'd been counting on to lead him to the big players made them even harder. A year ago. Shortly after BC Peale blew into town, if memory served. Well, that much he *knew* he could verify.

Thrusting a hand into his trouser pocket, he pulled his out his wallet and flipped it open. The night lighting from the hall beyond fell across the photo of his teen-aged kids, Jazz and Drew. They were currently living in California with their mother and there were times he missed them so much it hurt. He gazed at his kids for a few more seconds before wiping the sappy smile from his face and opening the compartment behind the picture to withdraw an anonymous keycard. The plastic card he swiped through the slot to the right of the door looked like a matte silver bankcard, blank but for a line of raised numbers on the front and a magnetic strip on the back. The scanner beeped softly and responded with the red-lit request on its screen: "Enter access code now."

Cursing teensy number pads that seemed to be popping up everywhere like toadstools after a rain, he carefully punched in his code and hit enter. The scanner beeped again and the series of asterisks representing his passcode went green. The door clicked open. He despised this part of the security system. Someday he'd key in the wrong code, he was sure of it. The system allowed three chances to get it right before sounding an alarm, but he never really got along with electronic stuff.

Inset fluorescent ceiling lights illuminated the short hall with a pervasive blue-white glare that all but eliminated shadows. His hard leather shoe soles struck a thunderous tattoo against the linoleum and reverberated off the closed office doors lining the deserted passage. Every time he came this way, he fought the urge to tiptoe to the elevator. Only the thought of being discovered in stealth mode by Jim, Mick or another team member made the impulse squashable. He wished they'd carpet this part of the floor. Maybe it was easier to clean this way. Maybe crepe soles. . . ?

The elevator doors opened as soon as he pressed the button and he stepped into the carpeted car with a sense of relief. Selecting the top floor, he leaned against the faux wood panels, watching the indicators light and fade. Exhaustion crashed over him like a tsunami. It had been a tough night and it wasn't over. He'd have to chug some of the toxic waste Mick passed off as coffee as soon as he hit the common room. If that stuff didn't wake you up, you were dead.

The elevator deposited him in front of a pair of imposing glass doors with the Sentry International logo etched into them. Veering away from the fancy glass, he used a smaller passage that dead-ended at a windowless, wood paneled door marked PRIVATE with another anonymous card scanner and damnable number pad. After a moment of careful button mashing, the door clicked open onto a carpeted corridor where a few dedicated people were hurrying about their business. He made his way to the communal room where the coffee pot lived.

A small knot of Special Agents collected around the urn. Frank Tidrow was extolling the merit (or lack) of local sports teams while Kim Zoeller loudly disagreed and Emily Hu rolled her eyes and investigated a nearly-empty donut box. They all glanced up as Miller entered, Tidrow and Hu suddenly took intense interest in stirring their coffee. Not good.

Zoeller, on the other hand, broke into a wide grin and called out, "Hi, Gae! Captain Nelson said you'd be in tonight. Something big going down?"

He regarded Zoeller with open misgiving. She was the type of small, attractive blond that is frequently labeled "perky." When she'd first transferred to Chicago, some of the male agents mistook this for "easy". Galen

had watched in amusement as Kim redefined it for them — a few of them
the hard way. She was the proud holder of a black belt in karate and their
resident covert warfare expert with all the medals, commendations and cer-
tificates to prove it. Now, smiling up at him as he poured steaming coffee
into a mug, he was reminded of an elf or a faerie. The *old* definition: a
mischievous, sometimes malevolent spirit. He muttered, "You could say
that. Anybody seen Mick Marquez?"

Zoeller gestured over her shoulder toward a corridor leading farther
into the offices. "Well, he's here, but he's been holed up with the Cap all
night; something's put a real big burr into his jockey shorts. He stormed by
here a few minutes ago muttering something about documents coming
through. Said to tell you he'd bring them to your desk when they're all in."

The group drifted apart but stayed close to the common room, oozing
nonchalance. Gae had the nasty feeling they were waiting on him. He took
leave of Zoeller and headed for his cubicle, dreading what lurked within its
flimsy Masonite walls. Jaw set, he stepped in. He didn't have to look far.
There, on the desk, sat a folded paper nameplate with laser printed Gothic
script reading:

GALEN VAN HELSING

Just behind, on the blotter, rested a brightly painted wooden mallet
and matching stake, both sporting glossy black bows. There was much
guffawing from the outer room.

Swearing violently, he crushed the nameplate and hurled it into the
trash basket in the corner. Someone called, "Great shot, Gae, you should
have gone into basketball!"

He spun on the new arrival with murder in his eyes. "Real funny,
Marquez."

"You're right. Even if they had a uniform to fit you, the league would
never have agreed to reinforce all the arena floors!"

With a low growl, Miller snatched up the mallet. "I'm gonna make sure they get a *shroud* to fit you, Marquez!"

Miguel Marquez pressed his wiry frame against the partition, holding a thick sheaf of printouts in front of him like a shield. "If you kill me, you'll get blood all over these nice medical reports."

With a sudden chuckle, Gae chunked the offending gifts into the trash with the crumpled nameplate and dropped heavily into the desk chair. From Zoeller's colorful description of his mood, he was sure the police had called Mick about his sister. If he wanted to razz his pal instead of seeking retribution, Gae was all for it. The documents landed on the desk with a thud. "Watch it, Godzilla, or I'll report you for abusing company property."

"Watch your mouth, shrimp, or I'll step on you. They'll cite it as a community service. Were *those* your idea?"

Sliding the well-tailored seat of his trousers onto the desk, Mick declared, "I can't take credit, it was a group effort. Besides, I don't see what you're so pissy about, you brought it on yourself. Never should have started that talk about vampires, man."

"I didn't start a thing, the *media* did! I only said that, given the evidence, I could see where they got the idea."

"Close enough for these bozos. Cheer up. Jim put out the word that he's tired of the gag, too. They have to cool it after this one." Mick planted a finger on the papers, adding, "*And* he wants to see you as soon as you slog through these. Hope you're brushed up on your speed reading."

Galen silently assessed his friend. He seemed calm enough, but Gae didn't buy it. A volatile undercurrent boiled near the surface. He had to be torn between worry for his baby sister, and the desire to hunt her down and ream her about the company she kept. It was a good bet that the only thing holding him back was Jim. Jimbo was always the calm head any storm.

Seeing the DDSOI putting on his Happy Face made him even more determined to sit on certain facts. His ass would land in a red-hot sling later, but better that than the explosive Marquez the Avenger tearing after Peale's hide before the evidence was in. Hell! Before they'd even talked to him. That was the last thing he wanted or needed. What he *needed* was a face-to-face with Peale. With a jolt, it dawned on him Mick was speaking and he'd missed the first part of it. He was all ears for the rest.

". . .out of his normal territory, but the MO's the same. They might have a sample of the unsub's blood this time, too. Off the retaining wall. None of the other bodies were near enough to make that particular smear and the forensics guys say once they fell, they didn't move. The initial take is a pretty serious wound. At least one perforating hit. The lab guys are champing at the bit for our share of the samples. They've got all kinds of genetic shit they've been dying to use. I don't know what they think they're gonna find." He smirked. "Maybe they believe in vampires, too. Anyways, they're gonna have to wait; the officer in charge of the crime scene won't allow our guys on the scene until she's had a chance to go over the area by daylight, too."

"What? Why?"

"Ah, she says the general conditions at the scene are crap and she doesn't want us stomping over anything the artificial lights didn't show. Smells more like a jurisdictional turf war to me, but it's CPD's scene. We'll just have to take a number. take a seat — for now, anyway." His face darkened as he added, "She also had other interesting bombs to drop. Since you were there, I guess you know about Jay."

Shit. Here it comes. Aloud he remarked, "I heard. All I can say at this moment is that I don't think Jay has anything to do with it." *Not an untrue statement.* "If it were me, I'd concentrate on that butthead, Mario Hernandez. I haven't dealt with him personally, but the talk around the neighborhood is that he likes his booze and controlled substances a little too much lately. It's common knowledge that he's been chasing Jay —"

Mick turned purple. "*¡Nombre de Jesús!*"

Oops! Tactical error.

Mick snapped, "God, Gae! Was that supposed to be reassuring? I suppose you also know that so far, nobody has seen either Jay *or* Hernandez?"

"Yes, I *do* know that," Galen backpedaled. "I also know that Jay left a good space before Hernandez built up enough steam to follow. *And* I know Jay.

Mick hesitated. "You seem awfully certain about that, Gae. I wish I could believe you."

"Believe it, buddy. I'll lay odds that when you talk to her, you'll hear she was out of there before any of it happened and never even *saw* Fallon and Boyce."

Oddly enough, he did believe that would be the case, but for reasons best left unsaid. He maintained his wise-man-of-the-world mien as he watched his friend's face.

Finally, with a weary shrug Mick allowed, "You're probably right. What you said was almost verbatim Jim's opinion when the thing first broke. It just doesn't help that Jay isn't answering her land line or cell. I keep reminding myself how little real time has passed since this hit the fan. She's probably off somewhere with a friend doing her best to ditch Hernandez." Not noticing Galen's noncommittal grunt, he switched back to business mode. "That isn't the worst news, though. From official standpoint, the real bad news is: Even though CPD are playing the situation as close to the vest as possible, we have it on good authority that some of the bar patrons have already been interviewed by the press."

This was news to Galen. He thumped the desktop angrily. "Dammit! How do they get in there so fast? Half the time we get an agent over to take a deposition, the media have been there already. We have more news clippings in our folders than we have firsthand statements."

"My guess is that in this instance somebody called them right after calling the police. Maybe Julio, himself. He's a fiend for any kind of publicity."

"*PUBLICITY?* You gotta be a pretty sick puppy to consider this publicity."

Mick slid off the desk. "Ain't that the truth? Anyways, the police reports are still coming in. I'd better stand by the printer to collect them. These jokers are liable to Photoshop pictures of Christopher Lee and Bela Lugosi on them if we leave 'em alone too long."

Galen watched him disappear toward the wire room, amazed at the ability to make jokes in the face of such violence. It wasn't just Sentry International, most cops did it. He found himself doing it, too. Maybe it was a self-defense thing. If things got too bad, you laughed so the badness couldn't reach out and drag you down into it. Suddenly, the hammer and stake in the trash became a palpable presence. Peale.

And Jay. Enough quiet confidence, he'd better call and make damn sure he wasn't spouting shit and she *was* okay. He pinned the telephone handset between his ear and shoulder and punched the button for an outside line, then dropped the instrument like it was hot. Outgoing calls were automatically registered in the logs and he didn't think he had a good enough reason to be calling Juanita yet. Especially since he was sure Mick just tried. Dammit. He could use the burner. He hadn't destroyed that yet. No, better wait.

There was nothing stopping him from looking over past case files for any vampire-like attacks on lone women, though. He didn't remember any, but it was best to be sure. He'd run the check on Mr. BC Peale at the same time. Sweeping the multitudinous print-outs aside, he pulled out his keyboard, dismissed the floating 3-D SI logo with a sharp jab of a beefy finger and began to type.

***

Jay Marquez' tiny apartment was decorated in a style best termed eclectic, exuding femininity without being all ruffles and lace. Ruffles and lace were decidedly not a part of the lady and she'd succeeded in marking these rooms as singularly her own, making up for any lack of taste with exuberance. BC Peale leaned against the sink and surveyed the place while waiting for the small, stainless steel teakettle to fill. He hadn't been in her digs before, though not from lack of trying on her part. No, Jay was possessed of such a vital, animal sensuality, he'd felt intimacy with her would be too dangerous. Tonight's debacle proved how right he'd been.

Turning back to the sink, he topped off the kettle and placed it on the front burner of the ancient gas range with its surmounting plaque reading: "Law of the Kitchen: Cleanliness is next to impossible."

He allowed himself a smile and stole a glance at Jay where she sat at the modest table rooting inside a plastic first-aid kit. She was plainly still fuzzy around the edges. Turning back to the counter, he extracted a tea bag from the cardboard carton and plopped it into the pastel pink mug he'd found in the drainer.

How could things go so terribly *wrong?* He knew better than to let his appetites get so far out of control. Jay could have been seriously hurt or even killed . . . he did kill those two toughs. Remorse gnawed at him and no amount of pleading self-defense made it easier. Killing wasn't necessary for his survival and it was so psychologically addictive to feel the surge of life in himself as his victim's heart faltered. Worse, was how frequently he'd killed since returning to Chicago. Was the Hunger gaining the upper hand? Turning him into a mindless killer? No, he knew better; it was all those guns.

Absently, he rubbed his chest where the bullets had torn through. The damage was healing rapidly because of the infusion of Fallon's blood, but there was a lot of pain. Not to mention the irritation of losing a nearly new shirt, his favorite motorcycle jacket *and* his sometimes-tenuous grip on humanity.

It wasn't new for criminals to carry guns. He knew from painful experience they always had, but these two were so young . . . .

When the Bill of Rights was framed, he'd supported the 'Right to bear arms' and though the original intent of that article was frequently misunder-stood and misquoted, he still did. Unfortunately, nobody in that long-ago time could have guessed there'd ever be such weapons. In any case, it was impossible to legislate conscience.

His own conscience smarting, he gazed into the kitchen window and watched Jay's reflection through where his once would have been. Long blond hair curtaining her face, she bent, busily smearing antibiotic ointment on her scraped knees. It wouldn't be needed. He'd made a point to lick the abrasions when he'd stopped to check her over and change his bloodied clothes for the clean ones he kept in his saddlebags. The coagulant and whatever else there was in his saliva made him the best first-aid kit around. It wasn't exactly a hardship, either, he liked the taste of blood and she had *great* legs … *WHOA*! Don't start that again.

Sometimes even he was disgusted at how easily he slipped into car-nality — not that it was anything new. He'd leaned that way before he became a vampire. Various family members in various generations asserted it was also *why* he was a vampire. He scoffed at this, and prided himself that, reputation as a rake aside, he always made a point of not taking ad-vantage of friends. Unless they were willing, of course.

The shrill whistle of the boiling kettle nearly pierced his eardrums. He hoisted the pot off the fire as much to silence the thing as to pour water over the tea bag. The aroma of brewing tea rose into his face, at once inviting and nauseating.

Soul-searching wasn't going to solve the problem at hand, though. Dunking the bag, and watching rusty brown tendrils swirl through the water, he probed what the real problem *was*. It wasn't that he'd lost control again, it rested with Jay herself: How far under was she when Fallon and Boyce struck? More to the point, could anything she saw in that halfway state resurface? He didn't know, and that worried him.

It worried him more to see how lethargic she still was as he set the steaming mug on the table. She should have come back more by now. Gently pushing the tea toward her, he warned, "Mind it, now, it's hot. How are you feeling?"

Her smooth brow furrowed as she pasted the last plastic bandage across her knee. Without looking up, she answered, "Scratch one pair of pantyhose, prob'ly more the way these Band-Aids snag stuff. I can't figure it, BC, I never fainted before in my whole life!"

He slid into the opposite chair. "That doesn't mean it can't happen. The important thing is that you're all right now. You hit the ground pretty hard. I was quite worried."

She continued regarding the plastic bandage in silence. He pressed, "You were very upset about Mario Hernandez when you hailed me in the carpark, could that have been enough to make you light-headed?"

Stretching her leg full length to test how the bandages flexed, and exhibiting more thigh than was strictly necessary, she considered, "Maybe, 'specially since I had a drink and left before we got dinner; but I've dealt with bigger jerks than Mario and never even felt dizzy."

"There's a first time for everything."

"I 'spose so. Just hope it don't become a habit."

He grinned. "Oh, I don't know, I rather like having beauteous ladies swoon into my arms."

Jay laughed and draped her hair over her face in imitation of a veil. "My knight in black leather armor!"

As she flipped the pale strands back into place, their eyes met. Perhaps he could . . . maybe just a little . . . no, it was too near dawn to even consider it. With an effort, he broke eye contact and stood. "You still sound a little muzzy, I should let you get some rest. Sure you're okay?"

"I'm fine. Hey, do you haveta go already?"

"I'm afraid so, it's getting awfully late — or should I say *early*?"

She shot a glance at the clock hanging on the kitchen wall and yelped,

"Holy Yikes, BC! Why din't ya say something?" Plonking her mug onto the table, she rose. "After all ya done for me, I can at least walk you to the door."

Catching her shoulder, he eased her back into the chair. The flesh was warm and supple against the chill of his palm . . . *unless they're willing . . . BLAST IT ALL!* No. Why couldn't she look like Great Aunt Agatha's pug dog? Forcing a cheerful grin, he insisted, "No you don't! You stay where you are. Rumor has it that I'm an adult and, true or false, I'm nonetheless capable of locking up behind myself. Good night, Juanita."

Delighted laughter followed him to the door, but she watched his retreat with undisguised regret. A deep sigh escaped her as the door clicked shut with finality. He was so handsome with all that thick black hair and pale skin and his accent was *so* sexy. For a minute there, she'd thought he was finally going to stay; it was the closest she'd come, yet. Well, Mama always told her patience was a virtue, and while this situation wasn't exactly the one Mama had in mind, the saying still applied. Maybe next time. He'd wanted to stay. She knew men and she could tell. He never did, though. She wondered why. Maybe it was what they called the English reserve or something.

THREE

Jim Nelson's father had been a custodian for the Greater Chicago School System for many years and hated working nights. Jim, on the other hand, loved it. Being appointed Director of Special Operations and Investigations over this newest region of the fledgling law-enforcement federation was the best thing to happen to him. That his Special Agents usually reported in after regular hours was a distinct plus.

Nelson was a tall, lanky man with a butterscotch complexion and a pencil line mustache adorning a pleasant face. He preferred to work in vest and shirtsleeves. The informal ritual of the Captain divesting himself of the double-breasted suit coat he favored and relegating it to a hanger as soon as he arrived became a sign to the team that all was right with the universe. If the coat hung neatly by the door, it augured well for the peace of the office. However, if the hanger were bare and the jacket still adorned the chief, it was duck and cover time.

Blissfully unaware of the cosmic significance of his working attire, he tugged down his vest, relaxed into his battered desk chair and ran thin fingers over the kinky salt and pepper hair he kept slightly over military standards. The chair creaked comfortably. Nelson smiled. Mick Marquez referred to the chair as "the Ancient Artifact," advocated trashing it and replacing it with a sharp, new one. He insisted it would lend dignity to the Director's position. Jim invariably countered that *he* had to sit in it and the only thing he wanted to lend to *that* position was comfort.

Well, Mick was born that way. Appearance was everything. Smiling, his mind wandered the good times. Geez, they'd been an odd trio: Gae, Mick and himself. Odd, yes, but they had a chemistry. They worked well together, got things done. If only they could get that chemistry working on this case. It needed *something*.

He grunted, unwillingly coming back to the not-so-pleasant present. Ignoring problems didn't make them easier to deal with. Tonight's incident report was on his desk. He needed to finish it before Gae showed. He'd stopped reading when the name of Juanita Marquez leaped off the page. Galen's accounts were usually professionally crisp, giving the reader no clue to the reporting agent's thoughts, but this one was antiseptic even by those standards.

Nelson's own feelings were mixed. In one respect, he was glad for a witness whose character and accuracy were known factors. On the other hand, the same elements making the witness reliable, made his Deputy Director next to useless. The CPD call informing Mick that his sister was wanted as a possible witness in a double murder, launched a frenzy of epic proportions. Understandable, but useless. Jim would have sent him right home if not for the fear he'd go into his infamous Marquez the Avenger act. Mick's attempts to overprotect his willful and self-sufficient sister were legendary and caused endless friction between them. He prayed Galen would talk to him; Mick usually listened to Gae.

It was good that Galen was working this case. In his time with SI, the man had redefined the term Special Agent. Theory ran that his investigation would work better under deep cover, and id did until this Vigilante crap happened. Well, that was the problem with theories, they tended to get shot to hell when reality got involved.

Nelson was thoughtfully fingering the carefully stacked pages of the disturbing report when someone tapped at his private door. He called, "C'mon in, Gae."

Miller stepped in, beaming. "You gone psychic on me or did you have a camera installed on that door?"

Nelson laughed. "Your timing is just too impeccable, Gae. I finish your report, you show up on my doorstep." His smile faded. He folded his reading glasses on the stack of papers and massaged the bridge of his nose. "Man, when you said there was trouble, you weren't shittin'!"

Gae carefully closed the soundproofed door, then said, "Since you aren't frothing at the mouth, I assume Mick hasn't come back to spread his glad tidings. About an hour ago, he told me the media descended on Julio's right after I left. Apparently, someone called them from the bar. By tomorrow morning, this shit's gonna be everywhere we look."

"Ouch. After all that's hit the fan tonight, he probably didn't want to lay that one on me in person. Can't say I blame him. Not much to be done about it, anyway." He looked up sharply. "You say they missed you?"

"By the skin of my teeth." Miller commandeered the visitor's chair. "I understand this is big news, but this coverage is making me twitchy. Bad enough when it was only those supermarket junk sheets, but now . . . it's gotten so I take the paper right upstairs for Mama to clip her coupons without bothering to read it first."

"I hear you, I been considering buying a canary just so I can line its cage with them."

"Not getting my face plastered all over the papers is about the only thing that's gone right lately. I'm coming up empty on this Borgia mess. And these killings tonight? It's our Robin Hood for sure but, this is outside his usual turf and, while the cause of death fits, other elements are way off. These two were strictly small time local thugs. They look more like targets of opportunity. Maybe they tried to mug him or something."

Jim barked a laugh. "Watch out, you'll give our unsub grounds for a self defense plea." After a moment he added, "You sure it's not a copycat?"

"I saw the bodies. I'm sure."

Jim regarded him carefully, then said, "Overall, your report was thorough, as usual — but I found it pretty neutral on one point that I'd like your *personal* opinion on. I'm sure you have one."

Galen steeled himself, the subject was inevitable, but nothing could help the sick feeling that centered in his stomach.

Jim continued, "I imagine you've gone into this with Mick. None of us want to think about it, but we're cops, so we have to." He paused uncomfortably. "From your observation of the physical evidence, could the blood smear on the retaining wall belong to Jay?"

Galen blinked. With the undeclared knowledge he possessed, *that* spin had never crossed his mind. He searched for a way to be reassuring without tipping his hand. He *hoped* he was placing the right spin on it. He'd just spent the last hour searching the database for reported attacks fitting the specified parameters on women, lone or otherwise and turned up a negative. "Oh, man! No! No way. That blood definitely came from the unsub — Robin Hood — whatever you want to call him." He paused as a new thought struck him. "Oh Jesus H. Christ! Is CPD looking for *Hernandez* as the vigilante?"

Jim nodded and leaned forward. Gae's confidence interested him. "You don't agree?"

"Not on your life. I've been studying this guy's M.O. since he started messing in my backyard, and he may be cold-blooded, but he's smart. Hernandez has been a neighborhood fixture for years and of all the things I've heard him accused of, having brains was never one of them."

"According to the police, Hernandez has gotten into drugs pretty heavily."

"Been fryin' what brains he had you mean. No. That guy doesn't have what it takes to be our unsub, I'd stake my reputation on it."

"So Jay and Hernandez are an unrelated incident?"

"I can't say that unequivocally, but that's the best face to put on it. I believe what I told Mick earlier. Jay's gonna turn up safe and sound and won't even know what went down after she left Julio's. Hearing about it is probably gonna scare the hell outta her."

"You're very positive, Gae, I hope you're right."

Gae treated Jim to his All-American grin. "That's what Mick said, too."

Nelson smoothed his mustache in thoughtful silence. He'd known Gae long enough to sense when he was holding back. He'd also known him long enough to know when to let it ride. Friendship aside, Galen Miller was one of the best agents he'd worked with, if he was holding back it was for a good and well-considered reason. Especially if it concerned someone as close to them all as Juanita. He'd wait. Experience proved the payoff would be high. He stepped into official mode. "Still no luck identifying or locating this Borgia?"

"Brick wall, James." Galen said, glad to be on solid ground again. The big man shrugged. "It's spooky the way the dude materialized a few years back and flooded the international markets with all kinds of stuff. Ordinarily, that kind of saturation would give us gobs to go on, but this guy has found the secret of invisibility. Not a photograph, not a description anywhere. Weird. All anyone can say is that such and such was part of Borgia's operations, then they clam up. Fast. Lots of people are very scared of this guy."

"Borgia. The name evokes the proper images at least. Maybe he's a ghost. I imagine the activities of your Vampire Vigilante makes asking questions even harder." He paused with a wicked grin. :Kind of sucked the vein of information dry, huh?"

Galen jumped like a scalded cat, his sledgehammer fist on the desktop made things bounce. "*DAMMIT, JIM!* Not you, too! Bet you even chipped in on that damn mallet and stake!"

Jim laughed. "Gae, if you didn't scream so loud, no one would bug you. Anyway, the mallet and stake were done on the cheap. They came from Tidrow's kids' croquet set, and Zoeller sprang for the ribbons."

Miller spun on his heel and stalked to the plate glass window opposite the desk. Jim spread placating hands, vainly waving toward the seat. "Okay, okay! Calm down. It was a joke. A bad one. Nobody really thinks you believe in vampires."

Thankful his back was to his friend, Gae parted the slats of the closed Venetian blind. Not trusting his face, he gazed toward the Chicago lights. It was still dark, but dawn wasn't far away. He'd have to finish soon to if he were to locate Peale before daybreak. Providing he could. The non-existent vampire had a good head start and wasn't likely to be in a sociable mood. Then there was the minor detail of not knowing where to look. . . .

Behind him, Nelson continued, "C'mon, Gae, nobody blames you — least of all me. We had squat in this file before you started and *anything* we have now came from you. These attacks are getting to you, man. Hell, it's getting to all of us, but you can't take responsibility for this crap on yourself. You aren't the Shadow. You can't swirl your cloak and look into the hearts of evildoers. We've only got plain old detective work."

Time slowed as the glimmer of an idea flickered in the back of his head. Jim spoke again and the glimmer flickered out. "Well at least the cover story's working. It *is* working, I presume?"

He wondered if he'd jumped. Schooling his expression, he turned. "Quiet retirement in my hometown? Why shouldn't it work? It's what I'd really like to do."

"Damn. I'm not looking forward to reporting this to the Colonel. You're positive nobody got an ID on the unsub?"

No one except me and I'm not ready to talk about it. Aloud he said, "No one that's admitting to it, anyway."

***

Huddling in his velour playpen couch, Mario Hernandez cradled a half-full glass of bourbon and looked wistfully at the remaining powder on the glass top of the coffee table. It was no use. No matter what he tried, nothing erased the memories. He'd never seen anything like it and hoped to God he never would again. Damn. He was crying. Again.

Angrily scraping away tears with the mud-stained sleeve of his once-fashionable jacket, he tried to think rationally. That didn't work either.

Ohgodohgodohgod. What he saw. He saw BC Peale kill Alfie and Chick like they were roaches. Then, he picked Jay up off the ground like some kind of doll and took off with her on his motorcycle. She looked funny, too, like he'd done something to her.

He didn't know what Peale was, but he wasn't human, that was for sure. Maybe he did Jay like he did Alfie? Nonono. Monsters didn't kill women right away; he watched the late shows, he knew about this. They cast spells over them, didn't they? Sure!

That was why Jay was giving him the brush-off. That was why she left him at the Fiesta. She was summoned by that monster. She'd never walk out on him otherwise. Not *him*.

The phone rang. It was probably the police again. He'd let the machine take this one, too. No way he'd tell the cops what he saw. They'd never believe him anyway. They'd probably yell at him, just like Jay's brother did all those times on the answering machine. Marquez was a cop and he seemed to think *he'd* hurt Jay. He'd never do that. If Jay was hurt, he knew who did it.

So did that ex-jock. He saw the monster with Jay, too. What was that guy doing there, anyway? Galen Miller. Yeah that's the name. Used to be real big in sports, but dropped out of sight a couple of years back. Must have been a real flash in the pan if he couldn't even get something on TV after. People said he was living in the neighborhood now, said he came from here. Didn't Jay used to know him? Anyway, the guy had a gun and a clear shot at the thing, but didn't take it, why would he do that? Maybe the Monster had the jock under his spell, too. Maybe he should watch Miller's place while he decided what to do.

But what about Jay? *It* took her away. He'd better check on her and make sure the Thing didn't kill her like Chick and Alfie. Oh God. He couldn't think about that. Try her apartment first. Yes, but he had to be careful, and not let on he knew about the Monster. If Jay was under a spell, that would be too dangerous. She wouldn't mean to tell on him, but she'd have to. It was still dark out, better to wait for daylight. Monsters sleep during daylight.

* * *

The Harley cut through the waning night. There was no need for the head lamp, the night was bright as day to him, and having it on would only make him easier to follow. Killing the engine, he leaped off and wheeled the machine toward the gates of the old cemetery, wincing as his feet hit the ground awakening fiery reminders of his wounds.

Stooping to pull a long piece of metal from his boot top, he muttered, "Lord, I *hate* being shot. Hurts like hell and ruins my clothes."

The steel slid smoothly into the gate's padlock, and he looked pleased as the mechanism snicked open in his hand. He stepped through, pushing the cycle before him. It would hurt less to ride, but it would be courting trouble to fire up in the cemetery, rear entrance or no.

Of course, it was also courting trouble leaving Jay Marquez without finding out how the memory overlay was holding, but with dawn fast approaching, he already felt like he was swimming through jam. He hurried toward a large, old crypt set into the hillside, and did his lock-picking thing again. Pulling the bike in with him he closed the door, carefully rearranging the chains and lock through the barred doors so they looked as they had before.

Admiring his handiwork, he allowed another pleased grin. *See, Mama? You thought I'd never learn anything useful from the company I kept.*

The long stairs into the dark crypt below elicited another grimace. This was going to hurt, but there was nothing else for it. Deftly flipping on the headlight and gripping the bike firmly, he maneuvered the cumbersome vehicle down the steep stone stairs. He needed the light now, even *he* couldn't see in the blackness down there.

At the bottom, he leaned the bike out of sight on the far side of a stone sarcophagus, mentally blessing the pomposity of the extinct family who'd constructed the place. The massive lid grated as he dragged it far enough aside to slip in onto the sleeping bag he'd lined the cavity with. "*I'm going to be sorry to leave this bolt-hole, it was made to order. I'll need to move soon, though, I've been sleeping here for a month. It could be getting dangerous. Galen Miller got a good look at me tonight, I'm sure of it. He was carrying a pistol, too. But what to do about it? Nothing, I suppose — just wait.*"

Extinguishing the light plunged the crypt into instant darkness. He lay back on his cushions and slid the lid into place. His last thought as the day claimed him was: *I've gotten very good at waiting.*

***

The sky was going gray by the time Galen emerged into the growing dawn cursing the invention of paperwork. He remembered his father's opinion of it and wondered with amusement if it was hereditary. At least he had a computer to speed things up. Pop had to do it all by hand — he'd never taken to typewriters. Maybe mechanical incompatibility was hereditary, too.

Squinting at the brightening sky, he realized there was no point looking for Peale. Long-postponed sleep tugged at his brain. He wondered what effect the rising sun was having on the as yet unsampled bloodsmear Peale left on the retaining wall. Doubtless he'd find out soon enough. A large clump of shit was about to hit the collective fans, he hoped most of it wouldn't land on the OIC.

At least he could console himself that his hunch about Jay was right. Just before he'd left, a very relieved Mick came to Gae's cubicle to say she'd called. She was crying. Sobbing how she'd been talking to the police, and no, thank God, she didn't see anything, but it was awful!

The amazing part was that she admitted spending a chunk of the evening with BC Peale. According to her, she'd run out of the bar and slipped in the gravel just as he was pulling in. He'd picked her up (literally), and taken her to a diner for coffee giving her time to calm down about "that butthead Mario", before taking her home to clean up. She said she'd passed out. Sure. At least she was unhurt. Of all the gambles he'd made in the last few hours, that payoff was the most precious.

Relief shut off the adrenaline flow, and weariness, previously just a background feature, became an all-consuming thing. The ride home on the train blurred in a fog of half-doze and the short walk to his digs did nothing to revive him.

Sleepily fitting his key into the door, his half-dreaming mind took him back to college and the day he'd gotten the first offer to play pro ball. He was flying high and tore over to talk to Coach Potts about it. It was then Coach gave him the best advice he'd ever gotten on playing pro sports: "Get a financial advisor". He did. As always, Coach was right. While some of his teammates were buying fast cars and women to go with them, he'd invested for himself and his family. Some of those investments were real estate. This building was one of them. It was in lousy shape when he first saw it, but he'd liked it, anyway. He bought and renovated it for his mother, little knowing at the time he'd be living there, too.

His mother fell in love with the old place, and moved in as soon as it was renovated. She was still there in her apartment on the top floor — they'd even built her a roof garden. His domain was the basement with a nice buffer zone of six other apartments with accompanying tenants in between. Entering the stairwell, he mused that it also claimed the dubious advantage of being close to his (and Peale's) hunting ground.

All his telltales were undisturbed, so he confidently doffed his jacket in his tiny foyer and debated scrabbling for the light switch. It was daylight outside, but the basement windows were few and small so the place was always dark. They had trouble renting it for precisely that reason. Galen liked it. He was a night person, and owing to his profession since quitting sports, often worked through the night and slept by day. The pitch-dark inner bedroom was just the way he wanted it. He decided not to bother with the light; he was heading straight for bed anyway. He snorted with amusement. Maybe that's why he empathized with Peale. Same sleeping habits.

The bedroom door snuffed the remaining daylight, and after undressing in the darkness, he fell onto the bed wondering why he had no trouble believing Peale *was* a vampire. It was his Granmama's fault, no doubt. Mama's side of the family hailed from Jamaica and his Granmama was *really* into the Voodoo. She called it Kumina, but it was the same stuff.

Every time he visited, her biggest joy was scaring the willies out of her eldest grandson with all kinds of stories about ghosts, zombies — and of course, vampires. She'd also (over loud, but largely ineffective protests from his mother) dragged him to a number of ceremonies where he saw enough to convince him such things weren't to be shrugged off. Even Mama, for all her dislike for her mother's conjuring believed enough to insist her son wear a charm around his neck at those meetings. She went so far as to make him swear he'd never take it off while they were in Jamaica.

Hey! That was an idea: Mamma wasn't as heavy into the magic as Granmama, but she was great at making charms and potions. A little protection might be the ticket when he went looking for Peale. The guy *seemed* likable enough, but Granmama taught him not to take unnecessary chances.

He extinguished the bedside lamp, rolled over and slept like the dead.

 FOUR

Day was fast ebbing when he rolled out of bed, smacked the switch on the coffee maker, and stumbled to the bathroom for a shave and shower. He was gulping his second cup of scalding brew when he realized he was stalling.

Why was he worried? He and Mama had a great relationship. Yeah, but the problem wasn't the relationship, it was Jasmine Miller's sharp mind and matching tongue. The more he thought about it, the more he dreaded asking her to make a charm. Especially a charm against *undead*. She'd demand why, and he couldn't tell her because she'd either refuse to let him out of her apartment — or worse — insist on going with him. That would be bad news for him and probably worse for Peale. Add her serious objections to his current profession, and it made for an explosive situation. Still, he had to do it. No way he wanted to face down a vampire without an ace in the hole. Squaring his shoulders, he headed upstairs.

Misgiving melted outside his mother's apartment as the heady aroma of roasting chicken seductively enveloped him and his stomach reminded him of its neglected state. He let himself in. "Mama! What *is* that new perfume you're wearing?"

Beaming and wiping her hands on a brightly colored dishtowel, Jasmine Miller bounded from the kitchen. Galen inherited his size from his late father, and the petite lady pulled her over-sized son down for a solid kiss on the cheek. She exclaimed happily, a faint Jamaican accent turning her words to music, "Galen! I'm so glad you're here; I just called your apartment and thought I'd missed you. Should have left you a note to say I was cooking.

Dinner's almost ready." She shot him a worried glance. "You didn't eat one of dem *frozen* t'ings before you come up, did you?"

His mother's disgust for frozen dinners was legendary. Only the most suicidal of his siblings would admit consuming a 'frozen t'ing' and then only at their most argumentative. Galen was thankful to be telling the truth as he answered, "No, Mama, I was too rushed to eat. . . ."

Glaring up at him, she diagnosed, "Bet you was too busy to eat last night, too. Out all night with no word to your Mama . . . it was that Sentry stuff again. You can save the excuses, boy, I know it was."

"Mama, please. I have a job I'm good at and I *like* it."

"Just like your Papa." He knew what was coming. It happened like clockwork and once again he regretted letting her know what he was doing. "That job killed your Papa."

It was useless, but the words came anyway, "The job didn't kill Pop, it was an armed burglar and inadequate funding that delayed backup. I do not chase burglars and whenever I need backup, I got it." He sighed. "Mama, we're doing it again. I came up to see you, you were cooking dinner for me and all we're doing is fighting the same battle and wasting time."

Suddenly alarmed, she whirled and dashed back into the kitchen, throwing over her shoulder, "I made a baked chicken with dressing the way you like it. I hope it didn't get scorched with all this carrying on."

Galen beamed. All right! Baked chicken! She popped her head around the swinging shutter to the kitchen, adding, "Oh, and I made that bean casserole thing, too."

As her silvered head disappeared, so did his smile. Mama hated the green bean casserole almost as much as frozen dinners. The homey apartment suddenly assumed the sinister aspect of a well-baited trap. He swallowed hard knowing it was too late for a dignified retreat and followed her into the kitchen. The same morbid impulse that compelled a person to pick at a scab kept him wondering what it was about this time and how much he would hate it. Numbly, he sat in the usual chair. *The condemned man enjoyed a hearty meal.*

A laden plate slid into his narrowed range of view and across the table, his mother sat with her own. Again the smells rose enticingly. Why waste good food because Mama has something up her sleeve? He was hungry, and though he'd rather die than admit it, she was right, he hadn't eaten last night. Except a handful of the ubiquitous doughnuts, and those didn't count. He lifted the first forkful of the savory bread dressing as she casually announced, "Talked to Fiona today."

Ah ha! That again. Mama never understood why he and Fiona divorced. Using the trouble she and his late father weathered without even mentioning the 'D' word as proof, she insisted if Galen and Fiona could be friends, there was room for more. Why couldn't they patch things up? He no longer tried to explain there was nothing to patch. Part of him wished there were.

Because his dad's police salary wasn't sufficient to send three kids to college, Galen got into Northwestern on a football scholarship. Serious about his education, he'd immersed himself in study and practice, but sometimes his non-sports oriented friends pried him from the books for a little entertainment. It made for an eclectic set of experiences. One night he'd landed at an avant-garde film festival and reception afterward. Usually, the more esoteric the function, the more out of place he felt, so he'd stood in the corner sipping punch from a thimble-sized cup trying to be inconspicuous, until someone at his side asked if he'd enjoyed the program.

The someone proved to be a tall, willowy woman with golden-brown skin and gleaming brass jewelry looking for all the world like an ancient Egyptian queen returned to life. The "Hello My name is" yielded the pertinent details: Fiona Mitchell, President of the Student Film Studies Association.

He'd smiled warmly and engaged her in conversation. Later Fiona confessed that *her* first impression was Smokey Bear in a sport coat. That set the tone for things to come.

They married while still in college, and had a good run with two wonderful kids to show for it. It turned sour after graduation, when he went pro and she launched a career as a film director. They grew apart and in fewer years than he liked to admit, found little common ground apart from the kids and an enjoyment of the physical side of marriage. He hated her long absences on film shoots and she hated his newfound enjoyment in helping Jim Nelson and the brand new agency, Sentry International. They still *liked* each other, but they were strangers sharing a bed. Both hoped his retirement from pro football would make a difference.

Instead, it boiled over when she laid *her* plans for his retirement on the table. He would be an actor. Through her rapidly expanding contacts, she'd lined up several juicy parts for him! Wasn't that wonderful?

Actor? Part of his pro contracts entailed doing promotional appearances. It was *understood* that a player of his caliber would do commercials. He'd done it, but hated every minute of it.

She went ballistic when he announced he hated acting and he was considering a position with SI. Regardless, his career choice wasn't the kiss of death his mother made it out to be, you couldn't kill something that already died of neglect.

A prickly feeling on his skin said he was being examined the way that convinced him Mama could read his thoughts. He turned his undivided attention to the chicken.

She said, "Jasmine took first place in her school photography show."

He beamed. "Yeah? That's great. She didn't know who the winner was when I talked to her yesterday."

"Just found out this morning. Probably didn't want to call and wake you up seeing how you're on a night beat now."

Shit. Walked right into that one. "Mama, we've been through this. I am a special agent with Sentry International, an undercover investigator. I do not walk a beat. I am currently working on a case that requires me to work unusual hours."

"A case you can't even tell your own mother about."

"I'm sorry, Mama."

Fork clattering onto her plate, she scowled across the table. "Sorry? Is that what you're gonna say when they bring you home shot to death? *Sorry?*"

"*Mama!* I'm only an investigator!"

"You carry a gun, Mr. Investigator."

Galen applied the mental brakes. None of this was getting him any closer to that charm. "Mama, I thought we decided not to ruin this nice dinner. The subject is closed."

He bent back to his cooling chicken hoping she'd do the same. She didn't. "It can't be for the money, you have plenty and they don't pay you spit, anyway. If you're looking for things to *do*, you've had at least six business deals offered to you in the last year and wouldn't even talk to them." She shook her head sorrowfully. "Why you couldn't have opened a chain of restaurants is beyond me — and a good lookin' man like you is *made* for TV. Fiona told me the other day—"

"MAMA!"

She was nowhere near ready to stop. "It's that Nelson boy's fault! I never liked you playin' with him, now he's gonna get you killed."

"Aren't you glad your son is one of the good guys?"

The usual impasse reached, mother and son glared across the table, the specter of his father hovering between them like a blue wall. It was no use. He'd take his shot now, any more wasted time and he'd never find his vampire. Folding his napkin purposefully, he made his voice calm and matter of fact. "Look, Mama, I don't have time for supper, anyway. I'm running late. I came up to ask you for one of those charm bags you make."

Jasmine Miller stared in absolute astonishment. "One of my charms?

What kind of charm?"

"I don't know . . . maybe one of those things like you used to make me wear at Granmama's."

Her glower declared she knew exactly what kind of charm he meant, and it was not a welcome request. Drawing herself up, she blazed, "Well, Mr. Don't-Hold-With-Mumbo-Jumbo-Lawman, what do you want *that* for?"

"I can't tell you, it's a matter of security."

"Don't tell me Security! I don't hand over a powerful charm like that 'less I know what you want it for." Then she paused as facts snapped into place with almost audible clicks. Eyes tightly closed against vividly perceived horror, she breathed, "This is about the vampire that's been in the papers."

Uh oh. He preferred the safer ground with Jim who didn't believe in the supernatural, but he *needed* that charm. He fell back on the tenet of childhood and defense lawyers — deny everything. "No, it isn't. Mamma, don't make me beg."

"Not against the Vampire Vigilante? Then tell me since when Sentry International has used charms against the undead as standard equipment?"

"*Please!* I gotta leave!"

Without another word, she opened the cabinet over the sink, took down several ceramic jars and carefully spooned unnamed powders into a hand-sewn linen bag. When it was filled to her satisfaction, she passed hands over it a few times, lips moving in silent prayer, pulled the drawstring and gravely pressed it into her son's hand. It looked innocuous nestling there, but was beyond a shadow of a doubt, anything but — especially to the undead. Her voice was thin as she said, "I surely hope you know what you're doin', Galen."

"Thanks, Mamma." He tucked the bag into his pocket. *I surely hope I do, too.*

***

Amulet tucked safely into an inner pocket, Miller fled the building certain that confronting a hostile vampire was a piece of cake compared to dealing with Mama. Avoiding the ancient elevator and wanting time to think, he swung into the stairwell. Phase one complete. He had the charm. Whether he'd need it for anything more than a security blanket remained to be seen. Phase two was a little harder: concocting a semi-logical reason to be looking for BC Peale.

In his family, Galen was known as Mr. Rationalization and his ability to cover any circumstance with a logical story served well in his current profession. It was with a sense of confidence he approached the task now. Nothing came to him.

He grumped into his coat, pulling it against the night chill as he stalked toward his waiting car. This shouldn't be hard, he'd *talked* to the guy a couple times. He was supposed to be a trained observer, what were the dude's interests? Aside from jazz. Gae was at sea with that kind of music.

Peale liked the ladies, but that wasn't helpful because the ladies liked him back — not to mention that Galen's own love life was a complete morass. There had to be something else. Wait. A lady first introduced them. Sylvia Stone, at one of her holiday bashes. She'd dragged the guy from behind a baby grand piano, and hauled him across the crowded studio apartment to ask Miller about . . . *parking!*

Peale was looking for sheltered parking for that big Harley-Davidson hog of his. He was parking at the jazz club he played at, but that was strictly open air. More than once he'd emerged after closing to find the bike rain-soaked, and said it wasn't only unpleasant to ride on, but played hob with the leatherwork. In her delightfully brassy manner, Sylvia observed Galen's building was within walking distance of the club, and didn't he have some kind of mini-garage in the back? It was and he did, but there wasn't a space available. Then. There was now.

Perfect. Anyone who knew BC Peale also knew his love for his Harley, and wouldn't give the story a second thought. Anyone but Peale himself. Galen was a realist, if *he* got such a good ID, Peale got one every bit as good. Maybe *better*, since he was accepting vampirism as a fact. Hopefully, the guy was cool enough to stick around to see what happened instead of bugging out. He was sure cool enough with Jay; whose story sounded plausible enough to satisfy CPD. It even satisfied her brother (considerably harder), but not Galen, though he felt sure *she* believed it. When he got his mitts on Peale, the first thing he wanted to know was: what really happened?

First stop was the Inferno Jazz Club, Peale's favorite place. Several times a week, he slid behind the piano on the small stage with the resident band, Nosferatu. Miller grinned as the joke registered for the first time. How many were aware that when Peale sat in, they *were* listening to nosferatu? Still smiling, he stepped into the already packed cellar bistro, and checked the stage. The band was there, but the piano bench was vacant. Not surprising, but disappointing.

This would be the best place to leave a message for Peale, but on first glance, there were only customers handy. A 'Please wait for hostess' sign was turned against the wall, so there'd be no help from that quarter. Scanning the room for a friendly face, he instead locked onto the palpably suspicious glower of the club's bouncer, Benny Glissen. Contemplating Glissen in the murky light was a revolutionary experience for Miller. He rarely encountered another person as large as himself. Glissen was bigger. He was also heading in Miller's direction. Galen put on his most pleasant face, and waited.

Glissen listened stone-faced to the spiel, then in a slow and surprisingly high-pitched voice, said, "BC ain't here."

"Any idea when he might show up?"

"Dunno. When he wants to, I guess."

Galen frowned. Considering the bouncer's undisguised hostility, the statement was not wholly believable. Unfortunately, that left two options:

1) Calling the bluff or:

2) Hitting all of Peale's usual spots.

Reluctantly, he decided on option 2. It was a depressingly long list.

***

Four hours, and enough beer to set his tonsils dog paddling later, still no Peale. His interviews also assumed a discouraging sameness: BC wasn't around lately, he played piano at the Inferno, maybe Miller would have better luck there.

Emerging from the last nightclub on page three of his notebook, he stood under the light, checked the time and scratched an exasperated line through the entry. He flipped to the next page then sagged against the stuccoed wall with an agonized groan. It was well after midnight and the damned notepad showed a half dozen places remaining. Make that *nine* counting the three possibles added in conversations inside. He'd been blissfully unaware there were so many late night spots in *Chicago* let alone in his own neighborhood. Maybe he should have ignored Glissen and planted himself at the Inferno to waylay Peale as he came in.

Assuming he came in.

Assuming he was in Chicago.

Resigned, he trudged forward digging the car keys out of his pea coat, moaning, "*Gotta* be dead to survive this kind of life."

"Lookin' for somebody?"

The voice was gravelly, and oddly accented. Almost but not quite French. Alarmed, he wheeled in the direction it came from and found . . . nothing. Sensing more than seeing a presence, he peered into the darkness seeking a solid form. As he watched, a small shadow detached itself from the side of his car, and limped into the circle of light.

The shadow resolved into Jump Veron, owner of the Inferno, last seen on the stage of same playing sax beside a conspicuously empty piano bench. Veron stood four-foot-nothing at best, was of indeterminate age and reportedly of Cajun extraction. Looking into the upturned and placidly smiling face, Miller was reminded of a weather-beaten stump, the kind that firmly resisted any and all attempts to move it. The little man's presence cast more doubt over Glissen's earlier statement — and on the coincidental nature of the band's name.

Veron spoke again, "You been makin' the rounds tonight, no? Mos' tiring an' unproductive. It is difficult to find a person at this rate, Monsieur Miller."

"Then, I'm wastin' my time, unless you have a suggestion how I *might* find somebody?"

The wizened little man gave a dry chuckle, and held out a folded piece of paper. "*Mais oui*! Jus' follow directions."

Galen unfolded the note into the light and read: "See you in Hell. One o'clock."

Rereading the handwritten line, he looked up in confusion to find himself alone. A short distance away, the dark hulk of a van rolled smoothly away from the curb and melded into traffic. The scrawled note had no signature. It didn't need one. It had to be Peale. Great. A vampire with a quirky sense of humor. 'Hell' must mean the Inferno — at least he *hoped* it did.

***

The Inferno Jazz Club was a dark, smoky, clamorous cellar bistro, qualities that didn't recommend it to Miller personally, but made it a good choice for a meeting. It was public enough to be safe for both of them, but still home turf for Peale.

Galen was barely inside before Glissen materialized like a malevolent genie. "BC said you'd come. He's waiting for you back there." In case the pointing ham-like hand wasn't sufficient, he elaborated, "Corner table."

Miller palmed the amulet, nodded politely and threaded his way to the back. Glissen wasn't in a mood to be polite. Galen understood. BC was one of their own, and Miller smelled like the other team. Benny took the lead, parting the crowd, and making certain there were no unexpected detours. Falling in behind the surly guide, Galen wondered again if confronting a hostile vampire was the most dangerous game around.

Peale's table had a bare wooden top scarred by years of hard use, and was tucked cozily into the shadows of the farthest corner. Illumination consisted mainly of a decorative candle placed in the middle. Catching sight of the impromptu procession, he rose languidly with an amused smile, and motioning his guest to a chair. "Thank you, Benny. If you'd be good enough to ask Bob to bring a beer for Mr. Miller on the way back to your station. . . ?"

Glissen balked. "I dunno, BC, Jump told me to keep an eye—"

The good humor became slightly strained as Peale remarked evenly, "Surely you can do that quite well from across the room? Please, Benny."

Unwillingly, the mountainous man returned to his alcove, but kept a laser-like gaze fastened firmly on Miller's back. Galen understood how a jackrabbit caught in fast approaching headlights felt. Peale, on the other hand, pointedly ignored the bouncer, lounged back, and drawled, "Now, then, Mr. Miller, I hope beer is acceptable. If not, Bob can bring anything you prefer. I'm curious as to what you've been so anxious to speak to me about tonight. Benny mentioned something about putting my motorcycle in your garage?"

Miller hesitated. Looking across a perfectly ordinary table in a perfectly ordinary nightclub at this good-looking man apparently posing a perfectly rational question made the logical part of his brain flare with doubt. He told Logic to shut up. He was tired and his head throbbed from the loud music, loud voices and smoke he'd been assaulted with since his interminable search began. The last thing he needed was a verbal sparring match with a smug vampire. Electing the no-frills approach, he demanded, "Does Glissen know what you are? I imagine Veron does, but do any of the others?"

The flawless smile was the essence of polite puzzlement. "What a way to start a conversation! Are you always this baffling or only on Wednesdays?"

Ignoring the patently innocent air, Miller said, "You didn't answer my question."

Pale hands spread in a gracefully apologetic gesture. "I honestly don't know what your question *is*."

"Dammit, I don't have time for this."

Rolling the pouch onto his fingers, Miller pressed it firmly against his tablemate's outstretched arm where the sleeve slid back. He'd never had occasion to use one of his mother's charms before, and while he expected a reaction, the one he got took him by surprise.

The instant the charm made solid contact, Peale yelped and jerked away like he'd been burned. In a fluid move, he leaped back, overturning the chair in his haste to put distance between himself and the amulet. Back pressed against the wall, and injured arm hugged to his chest, the vampire's handsome face contorted in an animal snarl.

Galen, taken aback at how quickly and completely the cultured façade crumbled, was unnerved by what stood in its place across the uncomfortably tiny tabletop. Abruptly, a heavy hand gripped clothing, and hauled him backward. At his ear, he heard a venomous hiss, "Okay, Miller, *OUT!*"

Twisting brought him nose to nose with Benny Glissen, a decidedly unpleasant sight. A glance over his captor's shoulder showed the incident had created a small uproar, but the background noise and location of the table helped mask the commotion. On stage, Veron assured that the band didn't miss a beat, either. He was impressed by the efficient handling, but kicking himself for impatience, he'd pushed things too fast and. . . .

"It's okay, Benny. Leave him alone."

Two pairs of disbelieving eyes swiveled toward the speaker. Peale stepped from the enfolding shadows and to Galen's amazement, took firm hold of the bouncer's arm. Confused, Benny paused but retained his grip on Miller, who was undergoing the novel experience of being held so that his feet were hardly touching the floor. Glissen protested, "But, BC, I saw — you yelled."

Peale said ruefully, "It was not Mr. Miller's doing. It was a stupid accident. I burned myself on the candle." Exhibiting the puffy red mark, he said, "See? Just a burn and no more than I deserve for being careless."

Benny eyed the angry red mark with skepticism. "You sure?"

"Absolutely. Thank you for being concerned, though. Tell Jump to add the complementary drinks to my tab, okay?"

Dividing another doubt-laden glance between Peale and the interloper, Glissen released his death-grip and returned grudgingly to his niche by the bar. Rearranging his clothing in undisguised relief, Miller double-checked the house and was again impressed by the efficiency of the Inferno's staff. As he watched, servers brought fresh drinks to every table in their vicinity. Peale, thoughtfully massaging his arm, resumed the shadows of the corner. Miller didn't like that move, but with a show of ease, settled himself into his seat, declaring, "Thanks for calling off the lord high executioner, I thought the audience was at an end. Sit down."

Tugging his sleeve over the welt, Peale replied, "No thanks, I prefer to stand." Indicating the pouch, he asked, "What is that thing, anyway?"

Miller glanced in surprise at the forgotten talisman, then darkening in embarrassment, slid it into his breast pocket. "Just a little piece of insurance from my mother."

"Remind me to avoid your mother. I think we'll continue this discussion outside."

"I think we won't."

Intense dark blue eyes locked onto Miller's, and a sickening jolt rocked him as another will insinuated itself into his mind and began to usurp his own. The feeling was unpleasant. Indignation rose like a stone wall. Gathering resolution, he shoved back. Hard.

Eyes wide with surprise, Peale staggered as the mental contact snapped. It had been a long time since he'd been thwarted like that, and only one other ever did it with such force. That person now stood center stage tootling his saxophone with a damnably jolly expression that made BC want to spit.

Miller was surprised, too. The assault took him off-guard and his re-action so instinctive he was trembling in its wake. Another moment of wary watching passed before Galen leaned back in his unsteady chair beaming with pleasure. He wasn't in complete command of the situation, but he had more control than before.

Eyeing the dark giant across the table with misgiving, Peale righted his chair, and sat astride it, pointedly keeping the wooden slab back between himself and the last known location of the "insurance". He ventured, "They don't."

"Huh?"

"What you asked before. The others don't know about my — shall we say condition? I think most suspect I'm not normal, but they don't pry and I have never . . . dined here."

Miller leaned his elbows on the table. "You'd been doing a pretty good job of ducking me tonight. Why did you finally agree to meet?"

Peale's eyes flicked toward the pocket where the charm rested and frowned. He didn't want to answer this question He didn't want to answer *any* questions, but as usual, his Cajun Conscience was right. Miller wasn't hostile. He relaxed, and folding his arms across the chair back, replied, "Perhaps, after last night's disaster, I wondered why a retired professional athlete cum local landlord was more interested in chatting with me than someone in a more official capacity."

The big man allowed a slight smile. "Perhaps this interview is more official than you think."

The vampire raised an eyebrow, and mulled over the implications. He didn't believe he liked any of them. At last, he pushed back from the chair. "*Now* I think we continue outside."

***

Standing beside the conservative charcoal gray Volvo, Peale watched Miller fiddle with the car keys and chewed over the shape of things. His motives for agreeing to talk to this man were too complicated to explain easily. Most of the logic was inexplicable to any one else. Simply put, Jump told him to.

It was called various things. Second sight. Precognition. Jump simply called it his "gift". What it boiled down to was that the little guy knew things. BC bitched and protested, but he *always* did what Jump told him to in the end, to do otherwise was to invite disaster. That painful lesson was learned the hard way many years ago in occupied France.

Sunset brought consciousness, and with it, the memory of the previous night like a suffocating cloud. For hours, he sat the pitch-black debating on clearing out. He didn't want to. He liked Chicago and was doing what he liked: playing jazz and partying. Realizing he needed advice, he'd ridden to the club. His heart sank when Benny made for him like iron filings to a magnet to say Jump was waiting in the back office. That non-functioning organ sank even lower when he stepped into the cluttered room, and instead of the usual warm greeting, the first words out of his friend's mouth were: "*Eh bon, mon ami*, you have come, and at last we shall find why a so-famous former athlete seeks so desperately to speak with an undisciplined reprobate."

That and the carefully folded newspaper told all. He should have known, and here he'd worried where to start. Almost unbidden, the whole ugly saga poured out. His mentor listened without comment, assuming the familiar eyes-closed manner, then after the account trailed off, sat listening to his "inner voices". Uncomfortable minutes passed before Jump stirred, shook his head, and to BC's profound distress, insisted on arranging a meeting with Miller.

BC remained reluctant. This looming man with his accidental knowledge worried him, but he'd bowed to Jump's wishes with the unstated intention to alter Miller's memory. He counted it an outgrowth of the previous night's extraordinary bad luck that Miller was strong-willed enough to thwart the attempt. However, the failure went far to explain Jump's enigmatic chuckle when BC finally acquiesced. Probably foresaw the whole thing. Damn.

Miller popped the lock and impatiently pushed the passenger door open against Peale's legs. In spite of (or maybe because of) the other's insistence, still BC resisted, eyes drawn irresistibly to his motorcycle parked nearby. It was tempting, but Jump had extracted an oath barring just such a thing. The man was annoyingly omniscient.

Admittedly, Miller's idea to drive around while they talked, was sound, but he balked at being confined in a moving vehicle with limited avenues of escape. On the up side, Miller shared those restrictions — especially while steering.

There was also that damned pouch. Remembering the charm in Miller's pocket made him dig unconsciously at his burned arm. It was already healing and itching like the devil. The heavy car door nudged again, and shrugging, he slid in. The firm schunk of the power locks elicited a wince and the unconscious thought that at least things couldn't get much worse.

A slim black card case landed in his lap as the engine started and the car rolled onto the street. The vampire opened it and stared numbly at the official badge and photo card. It got worse. Returning the case, he murmured, "Great. I'm in the hands of the high-tech Interpol."

Unexpected anger took him aback as Miller thumped the dashboard. "We are *not* Interpol. Interpol is strictly an information gathering body with no powers of arrest. Sentry International is a United Nations sanctioned law enforcement agency formed to create an official network for the investigation and prevention of international crime."

Wonderful. Thirty seconds into the dialogue and he'd already found a raw nerve. He slouched further into the seat. "Wow. Betcha can't say that three times really, really fast."

Miller maneuvered the Volvo through the sparse late-night traffic. The evening had been a long chain of frustrations, and he was overreacting. He'd wanted to get Peale alone, and grill him about his involvement with the Borgia investigation. Okay, he'd achieved the first part. Unless he wanted to blow the second, he'd better calm down. Taking a deep breath, he asked, "You running a private war on street crime, Peale? I only ask because you've been having such a high old time chowing down on bag men, drug runners and the like for the year. What gives?"

Peale took a while to answer and sounded profoundly tired when he did. "Like any other creature, I have to eat to survive. It's only what I feed on that makes me different from anyone else." Miller made a dubious noise. Ignoring the editorial comment, Peale continued, "My condition gives me little choice in the matter if I wish to survive. I usually target muggers, drug runners, and their ilk because — well, because they're *available*. The nasty bit comes when they do something awkward, like stabbing or shooting me. That's when things get out of hand." He shifted uncomfortably, and added as if to himself, "Seems like that's happening more and more lately."

"I'll bet. You sound real broken up over it."

The pale man fixed him with an angry glare. "You've a lot of room to criticize! I suppose you carry that pistol at the small of your back because you like the way the gun oil mixes with your aftershave?"

"How'd you know about that?"

"You aimed the damn' thing at me last night, or have you forgotten?"

"No, I mean where I keep it?"

Wryly amused, Peale drawled, "I *don't* like the way gun oil mixes with your aftershave."

"You can *smell* a concealed weapon?" Peale remained silent. Miller said, "Okay, man, I'm sorry for the crack. Now let's get back on the subject."

Peale kept his gaze fixed on Miller. In the uneven light-dark-light-dark of the streetlights, it was difficult for Galen to read an expression; for all he knew, the guy was poised to bolt into traffic at the first red light. At least that's where he hoped he'd spring.

The tension built until Peale insisted, "I. Don't. Enjoy. Killing. I never have. I try to avoid it whenever possible, but the down side of preying on those that prey on others is that killing gets hard to avoid. Look, I don't start out to do it, but I won't say I agonize over long about it afterwards, either."

Astonished that a supernatural being found it so important to be believed by a mere mortal (cop or not), Galen gave his unwilling companion an evaluating glance. "You mean like last night?"

Peale winced. "That was an accident. I was taken by surprise and badly wounded . . . I . . . I lost control."

The big man scanned the scattered traffic as the car merged onto Lake Shore. Maybe Peale was a hostile witness, but he was being more forthcoming than Miller had dared hope. Worried that too much prompting might cause him to clam up, Gae kept silent, allowing him choose his own pace.

As if in response, Peale continued softly, "It was a serious mistake to go to the tavern right after rising. I knew I was too hungry. I'd simply been too busy to feed for the last few nights and was getting desperate. I should never fast that long and I *should* have gone straight to the stockyards." Sensing Miller's confusion, he grinned. "Oh, animal blood will sustain me quite well, but I also crave human companionship." He amended wryly, "I'm a very social animal."

"How about Juanita Marquez? Y'know: My good friend? Sister of

Lieutenant Miguel Marquez, Sentry International Special Investigations' Deputy Director?"

"Oops."

"Yeah, oops. What'd you do to her?"

Peale bristled. "I didn't hurt her. I didn't! I don't *do* friends." Frustrated, he added, "Well . . . ordinarily I can stick to that rule, but Jay presented a strong temptation at a weak time. I'd intended to only take a little — enough to tide me over, and I'd have had enough control to do just that if those two *assholes* hadn't attacked. As it was, I ended up killing. The blood from the one I drained should hold me for a couple nights. Longer if I hadn't been shot."

Thick silence fell as the car rolled along a mostly deserted Michigan Avenue, and BC sensed Miller weighing a decision. The third time past the Art Institute, he concluded one of them better get to the point or he'd never get away before daybreak. Looking at Miller squarely, he asked, "What exactly do you want of me?"

Miller told him.

Peale stared for a full minute. "*Partners?* That's crazy!"

"What's so crazy about it, man? We'll make a great team; I work mostly at night anyway."

BC flopped against the leather upholstery. "I can't deal with this. Take me back to the club."

"Hey, come on! Think about it!"

"I am not a policeman."

"Neither am I! I'm a Special Agent."

"On whose side?"

"I'm a good guy. You must be trying to be a good guy, too or you wouldn't be confining yourself to a strict diet of bad guy. Look, there's this big bad guy, calls himself 'Borgia'—"

"I don't want to hear any of this."

"Too bad, pal, you been messing him over. Who do you think most of those punks you were hitting worked for?"

"Dawn's coming. I want my bike."

"No problem. Where do you sleep? I'll drop you off, your bike ought to be safe at the Inferno. I can pick it up later if you want — I wasn't lying about the parking thing."

"I *want* my *bike*."

"You don't trust me."

"I think you're nuts."

Peale lapsed into a monosyllabic sulk that persisted until Miller relented and guided the Volvo back to their starting point.

The car barely stopped before Peale leaped out. He scanned the sky, and was relieved to note he had enough time for the scenic route to the cemetery. Galen Miller didn't read like a hammer and stake type, but Peale never relished being followed. After tonight, he didn't doubt for a second this man could do it. One thing remained unresolved, and leaning on the door frame, he asked, "So. What are you going to tell your superiors, Special Agent Miller?"

"I don't have to tell them anything — yet."

The slender man stiffened. "If that was supposed to be a threat, I'm not impressed."

Miller exited and leaned a massive forearm on the roof of the car. "That's not a threat, Peale. Consider it part of the offer. At least as long as I can keep it open. There are an awful lot of forensic experts at each other's throats over why that nice big bloodstain on the retaining wall suddenly turned to powder this morning. A shitload of folks are howling for everything we have on this case. Jim Nelson gives me a lot of latitude but I can only stall so long."

The vampire remained silent, but he *also* remained standing by his motorcycle instead of riding away. Encouraged, Galen prodded, "You ought to think it over."

Peale shook his head with finality. "It's insane."

"It's unexpected."

"Same thing and nothing will change my mind." Violently, Peale flung himself onto the saddle, and fired the ignition, cursing the nagging voice at the back of his mind that whispered: *"Can you say, 'Famous last words?'"*

***

The City of Chicago sprawled like a supplicant, its buildings, streets and waterways forming the elaborate pattern of an abstract carpet below his window. At least, that was how Francesco Borgia regarded the view from his penthouse. Behind him, he heard the nervous fluttering of his two Vice Presidents impatient to begin the meeting of the board of directors for the Este Corporation. Let them wait. The reasons for calling a meeting tonight were spurious at best; the agitation exhibited by the pair was most unnecessary. As if *he* couldn't easily nullify such competition . . . from behind came the scratch and flare of a match followed closely by the sickly-sweet stench of a cigar. Borgia spun on the offender. *"GAAAH!* Edgar, I thought you had forsworn that filthy habit!"

Eddie Michalson's rounded face flushed as he hastily stubbed out the cheroot in the heavy alabaster ashtray on Borgia's desk. "Sorry, Boss. This thing's got me nervous. I gotta do *somethin'*!"

Gwen Isendamer favored him with a frosty gaze. "Then take up needlepoint, Eddie. Those things are disgusting. If you insist on polluting the air, at least you could smoke something decent."

Michalson rose to the bait. "Lissen, Gwennie, not all of us have your champagne tastes—"

Slamming a palm onto the antique mahogany desk, Francesco Borgia roared, *"Basta!* Enough!"

Both combatants jumped satisfactorily, and Eddie meekly dropped into his seat.

Gwen flashed a warm smile at their CEO. Depressing how Michalson was so predictable and transparent. It was obvious Gwen, herself, made him more nervous than the current troubles on the street. She reveled in it. His position as personnel director with the corporation was superfluous, what Francesco couldn't handle (and that wasn't much), she could. Eddie was nothing to worry about, given the opportunity, it wouldn't take much to sort him out. Still, whether Francesco admitted it or not, there were bigger fish to fry. She said, "Francesco, I know you think this whole thing foolish, but for once I'm in agreement with Eddie. This situation is getting out of hand and is beginning reflect negatively in our earnings statements. You need to look at them."

Icy blue eyes locked onto brown issuing a mute challenge for him to disagree. He wouldn't. Regardless of their personal relationship, business acumen was her strongest suit, and the reason he'd hired her in the first place. She squashed the surge of victory as the striking Italian snatched the statements from Eddie's hand.

Ignoring the impatient glare he shot over the top of the pages, she continued, "As you see by these figures, our profits are down sharply over the last quarter. This drop corresponds exactly with the increase in the frequency of these incidents."

Michalson nodded. "What it comes down to is our people are scared, Boss. It's gettin' to be a toss-up if they're more scared of you or this . . . whoever or whatever the hell this guy is!"

Borgia frowned, but he was listening. Finally. The unconscious smoothing of the white streak in his otherwise ebony hair witnessed that. Gwen nodded. "Sadly, Eddie has a point there, too. What business this Vampire Vigilante hasn't interfered with directly, has been slowed through *fear* of his interference. It hasn't reached the point of no return, though. If we act now, we can't negate the effect of the attacks, but we can minimize the damage."

Michalson snorted, then leaned over and tapped a blunt finger on the newspaper spread on the desk. "I don't agree there. I'm sayin' our guys are *scared*, Boss and gettin' more scared every night. This here paper oughta be scarin' the bejezus outta *us*. You read it, you know there was two more killings last night."

Borgia waved dismissively. "Unimportant. They were not our people."

Eddie's fist slammed into the center of the newspaper. "Don't you mean they weren't our people *for once?* That don't matter a damn! It still hurts us, Boss. Every time this guy gets away with this shit, our power gets chipped away. We can't afford to let this go on and not do anything about it!

"If ya'd just let me cover the routes. A couple guys with rifles and nightscopes — we got the equipment, we got the people."

"I have already said I am opposed to that kind of open display. We cannot afford to advertise our business in that manner."

"We can't afford to have our people hit every time they go out, either!"

"*Ammesso*, Edgar, *ammesso*! I admit this and am not pleased by it. This is a delicate situation and must be handled with the proper care."

Isendamer leaned eagerly forward. She knew the man behind the desk well, and his manner excited her with possibilities. "Unless I miss my guess, I'd say you had a surprise planned for our unwanted friend? One can only hope it's suitably unpleasant."

A slight smile assured she'd guessed right. Francesco Borgia rarely smiled unless it was at someone else's expense. Turning to his city again, he gestured carelessly toward the desktop. "The box. Open it."

For the first time, Gwen noticed a small rosewood box that hadn't been there earlier. Ignoring her co-VP, she paused to enjoy the rich carved surface of the antique box. Francesco's love for beautiful things was an important part of him and one that manifested even in the tiniest details. She admired the casket until she felt Michalson on the verge of another explosion, then lifted the lid.

It was filled with ranks of tightly packed bullets.

Perplexed, Michalson pulled a cartridge out. "Bullets? But we *got* bullets, Boss."

In sudden inspiration, Isendamer took the shell from his hand. "*Silver* bullets, Eddie. Look more closely!"

Suddenly, Michalson understood. His moon face clouded. "But, Boss! If all the guys is runnin' around with these babies . . . ."

"Your concern is commendable and noted, Edgar, but this special ammunition is not for the ordinary rank and file of our organization. That *would* be too much. Our couriers and delivery people are the ones to whom these are to be issued. They are the ones being attacked, they are the fearful ones. Let these be as a lucky talisman to them."

"I still dunno. Ain't this a little radical?"

Borgia gently closed the little chest and took it into his own hands, regarding it thoughtfully before responding. "*Daverro*, but nowhere near as radical as it could be."

Michalson's strident East Coast accents were hushed. "Y'mean there's *worse*? What else . . . ?"

"That, too, is unimportant at this time. Let us simply designate it 'Plan B' and distribute these to our people right away."

Gwen rolled the bullet between her fingers enjoying the warm metal against her flesh. The small object vibrated with possibilities, looking at Francesco from under her lashes she murmured, "But, will they *work*?"

His smile, as he caressed the ornate casket, was not pleasant. "Of course they will, and I hope they perform their function quickly. Chicago is a large city," he paused allowing a pair of gleaming fangs to extend to their full length. "But there is only room enough for *one* vampire and that is Francesco Borgia."

FIVE

Galen hadn't expected a five-page epistle accepting a truce, but neither did he expect Peale to vanish. On reflection, he wondered why not, because that was exactly what happened.

Certain Peale was still in Chicago, though, Miller turned up with annoying regularity at the Inferno to ask after him. It didn't help much. Talking to Veron was like talking to a Cajun Buddha, all serene smiles and no solid answers. Talking to Glissen, on the other hand, was attempted suicide.

Benny Glissen believed Peale had left town, and laid the blame solidly at Miller's door. Oddly, Veron's carefully noncommittal stance kept Gae coming back. He got the idea that the diminutive jazz man was on his side and took encouragement from it. Maybe too much. Before, he'd given voice to the idea glimmering in the back of his head, he'd been able to ignore it. But now that he'd said it, the idea had taken on solidity and a life of its own. More than that, it grew into The Thing. The legendary Thing that would crack a case wide open once and for all.

The complete disappearance puzzled him, though. It just didn't figure that Peale would get the hell out of Dodge when nobody was seriously giving him trouble. At the moment, Miller was the only interested party. Even CPD, satisfied with Jay's story, simply interviewed him the club to verify he gave her a lift home. Given that, tiny details like being interviewed by an international cop seemed unlikely to flap him. Especially since that cop merely offered to join forces in a seemingly common goal.

It *was* a common goal. Galen was sure of that. Glib excuses about availability of the food source be damned. Miller knew a white-hatted do-gooder lurked inside Mr. BC Peale. There was much easier and safer prey around. Prostitutes, for instance. The very nature of their business was private. A vampire could get a meal and a good time all at one go with no one the wiser — especially someone as good-looking and free with money as Peale. Nope. The guy could deny it all he wanted, but attacking street punks was both courting the thrill of danger and an effort to clean up the neighborhood. Look what the joker did with the money. Donating it to charitable organizations instead of keeping or leaving it?

Okay, maybe he pushed too far too fast, but the big picture convinced him Peale was only making himself scarce until the heat died down. He held to this belief until the nights stretched into a week, and one week threatened to consume another. Each passing night, panic nibbled his confidence like a mouse at a cardboard box, and squeaked that this shot at breaking the case was failing too. Characteristically, he refused to accept it.

So what if there were no muggers were attacked since their talk? It only made sense. For Peale to keep a low profile, the first step would be to change his feeding habits. No doubt, Chicago's underworld was safe from Vampire Vigilantism for a while. But, if the guy was still in town, he had to feed somewhere. He'd mentioned stockyards, but which? Chicago was once the largest meat processor in the nation, but that was a long time ago. The Windy City had changed. Still, there *had* to be lots of holding pens. Damn. Too bad he couldn't request surveillance of anything remotely resembling a cattle pen. Even if there *were* enough agents in the city to cover them all, justifying that request would be artistically challenging at least. Not to mention useless. For all he knew, the guy was slipping into the zoo and chowing down on the wildebeests at that very minute.

To be brutally honest, when he tried to put how joining forces would advance the case into concrete terms, he couldn't. On the other hand, anyone powerful enough to bring down two armed thugs with his bare hands (and teeth) had to be able to help *somehow*.

The worst part was, if Peale really had split, Gae was right back at square one. That was a position he did not want to be in.

Either way, it was hard to settle down to the dull grind of plain old legwork. That was bad, since that was all he had left.

Oh, quit belly-aching, he ordered himself. *Get your mind back to business or these punks you're supposed to be following will lose you without even trying.* And they weren't trying. Ever since these two made the drug sale to another undercover agent, they'd led him on a leisurely walking tour of the lakeside warehouse district. Logically, they'd take the money back to home base or to someone higher up in the organization, but they didn't seem to be in too big a hurry to do that. Shadowing their meandering path for the last half hour disgusted him and left him chilled to the bone. He found himself wishing they'd at least lead him to a nice, warm coffee shop. Unfortunately, he might get that wish and little else if the creeps followed the pattern.

It was a pattern he was all too familiar with. First they made the deal. Then they strolled casually to nowhere. Second stage was to head for a high traffic area where they were pretty successful in ditching a tail. The route these two were on was usually the one for Midway airport. Tidrow was positioned at Midway. Good. He was aces at tailing people.

The shapes ahead turned a corner. Bingo. Headed to Midway. Pulling out the newest burner phone, he thumbed a heads up text to Tidrow, then ,checking that the street was deserted, jogged after them on his new soft-soled shoes. He ducked into a shadowed doorway, and let them gain a little distance before following again. The two strolled along apparently without a care in the world.

Sliding onto the street, he flowed along the gritty brick wall, ducking into the next recessed doorway, blessing both his dark complexion and good trainers for the ability to recede into shadows. The subjects still seemed blissfully unaware of him. Their conversation reached him as a meaningless babble echoing off the building fronts, fading as they moved out of range.

Eyes flicking nervously, he scanned the side street, habitually seeking his next hiding place or potential ambushes. So far, nobody was riding shotgun. No way that luck would hold. Borgia wasn't stupid. As the organization was slowly revealed, the intricately layered structure showed a craftsmanship that commanded grudging admiration from even the most jaded law officers. This person might be guilty of many things, but crass stupidity wouldn't be on the charge sheet.

He wondered at the absence of protection, though. Even if Borgia and his people were unaware of Sentry's presence, Peale made no attempt to hide his. If Miller had been running the show, he'd have covered the corridor with a tight lid after the second hit. The oversight was so glaring, it couldn't be one. If he could figure out the reason, he'd know more about the whole shebang than he did. That was the whole— Muscles locked as he caught movement on the rooftop above his targets. Hastily blending with another doorway, he did a slow five count, then cautiously peeked around the limestone facing.

No bullets pinged into the stonework and there were no new holes in him. Mouthing an Anglo-Saxon epithet, he watched the shadowy figure on the roof-edge pace the pair below. So, these guys had pals riding shotgun, after all. Shit.

Straining to follow the overhead movement, he went open-mouthed when the black-clad figure launched, and dropped feet first onto the outside man. The impact bore both to the pavement with the sickening snap of bone. The attacker rolled to his feet, clipped the remaining bagman on the jaw, and caught the body as the knees sagged. Even before the aggressor bent to the limp man's throat, Galen knew he'd found Peale.

Miller didn't hesitate. He'd be a fool to pass up the opportunity to move in while the vampire was preoccupied. What he'd do close up and personal was up for grabs. He'd worry about details later.

He hadn't gotten far before he sensed movement from the man lying on the pavement. Miller froze. The man hadn't twitched since Peale KOed him . . . had he?

It happened again. The guy moved, raising his arm toward the vampire in a jerky, but unmistakable motion.

Adrenaline surging, Miller ran, his weapon in his fist. He bellowed, "*GUN!*"

The vampire's head snapped up the same moment the thug's pistol flared and recoiled. The sharp crack from the unsuppressed weapon reverberated off the buildings. Peale staggered, then slid to the ground next to his prey.

The grinning gunman spun toward Miller and his smile faded. Panic providing more speed than accuracy, he raised his pistol wincing as his collar bone ground against its own broken end. The weapon leaped three more times, each miss worse than the last. Miller hit the pavement, rolled and fired once. The gunman stared dumbly at the spreading stain on the front of his shirt, then collapsed face down against the sidewalk.

Miller circled, Beretta aimed between the two motionless thugs. Kneeling by Peale's dinner companion, he noted the rise and fall of the man's chest. The man was alive, but deeply unconscious. With luck he'd stay that way. He kicked the dropped weapon away, then nudged the other gunman onto his back, meeting only the glass-eyed stare of death. He swore again.

Peale grunted and stirred. The undead were tough, but this one was going to need a little help. Miller's soft-soled shoe grated on a patch of gravel, and the vampire's eyes flew open. He was conscious, but not all there. Indigo eyes locked onto the weapon and he sprang up and ran. The attempt, while begun with surprising speed, ended in disaster, as long legs folded, sending Peale sprawling atop his former victim. Gae stowed his pistol, gripped him under the arms and hauled him to his feet.

A brief, halfhearted struggle followed until Peale dazedly looked at his captor. Recognition sagged him heavily against the supporting arms. "Ah. Miller. I should have known."

Dangerously wobbly, Peale pushed away and snagged the briefcase the thugs had been carrying. Miller objected, "Don't mess with that, we gotta leave everything the way it is until the crime-scene guys get done with it. Besides, you don't look like you're in any kind of shape for minor weightlifting."

Slightly unfocused eyes staring down the street, BC said, "Then, the folks arriving from down there must be yours. Hope you don't expect me to stick around for introductions."

Galen squinted into the dark, straining to hear anything other than the pounding of his own blood in his ears. "No way, man. I haven't called anything in. If you hear somebody headed our way, they ain't friendlies."

The pale man slumped against the brickwork. "Thought these chaps looked a little too nonchalant. It must have been a trap, then. We've sprung it beautifully."

Miller's mind raced. Peale was right, this pair *hadn't* done the usual over-the-shoulder stuff. If he'd been less occupied with private gripes, and thinking more about the job, he'd have spotted it himself. The question remained: which of them was the trap intended for? Didn't matter. They'd screwed around enough, unless they got their asses into gear, they'd get the answer the hard way. "Maybe we sprung it, but no law says we gotta stay in it. Let's haul our butts out of here!"

Nodding vaguely, Peale tucked the briefcase under his injured arm, slid the other around Miller's waist — and leaped straight up. They landed on the roof directly above. Miller managed to stifle an involuntary scream. Barely.

The impact jolted a cry of pain from Peale and the convulsive tightening of his arm squeezed the remaining air out of Galen's lungs in a whoosh. Pausing long enough to gain purchase on the gritty surface, the vampire launched them again and again until they were blocks away from the scene of the shooting. Abruptly dropping his well-shaken passenger to the tar paper, BC leaned heavily against a grimy chimney.

Scrambling to his feet, Miller squealed, "GEEZus, man! You could warn a guy first. Maybe this kinda jumpin' around is normal for you, but I haven't leaped any tall buildings in a single bound for several weeks. . .*months* maybe!"

Weakly, the wounded vampire lifted his head, the stark white of his face against the bruise-like smudges under his eyes was alarming. His whisper was barely audible. "I don't understand. In two hundred years . . . nothing ever hurt like this . . . ." Losing his grip on both chimney and consciousness, he collapsed.

Miller stared, then moaned, "Aw, shit."

***

Cursing himself for an idiot, Galen did the first thing that came to mind: He carried Peale back to his apartment. The vampire was semiconscious when they got there, but too weak-kneed to walk by himself. Just inside the flat, the briefcase he'd clutched like a talisman slipped from his fingers. It bounced to one side, coming to rest partway under the lamp table. Galen absently kicked it the rest of the way under as he groped for the light switch.

Grimacing at the crimson smear across the off-white wall, he dropped his burden into the recliner. The place looked like a murder scene and that expensive washable paint damn well *better* be. Fumble fingered, Miller pulled red-sodden clothing aside to view the damage. It wasn't reassuring. The entrance wound was a jagged hole in the left pectoral that angled up under the clavicle. The flesh beneath his probing fingers was hot with fever. There was no exit wound. That was bad news.

Peale endured the examination in silence. The naked fear on his gaunt, pale face made him more . . . human. Then, he uttered the words that chilled his host's soul.

"I'm going to be sick."

Wasting a nanosecond on blind panic, Miller scooped him up like a game ball, and made a high-speed run for the bathroom.

They made it in time, but Galen was very glad his mother talked him into ceramic tile when they remodeled. He emerged gulping, several shades paler than usual and escaped to the kitchen, where he wrenched the top off a bottle of his favorite dark beer, and downed the contents. He was still leaning against the refrigerator, holding the cool, empty bottle to his forehead when a rustle from behind him said Peale was back. The vampire leaned against the bathroom doorjamb looking unsteady, and gaunt.

One look decided him. With a minimum of effort, Miller lifted Peale and carried him to the bedroom. The normally voluble Peale was too weak to even make a show of protest. Burden deposited unceremoniously on the bed, Galen ordered, "Get that shirt off, I'm gonna get a washcloth and clean you up some."

Long-fingered hands shook as they tugged at stubborn buttons. BC looked up with an apologetic grimace as his host returned with a plastic basin. "Dreadfully sorry, Miller."

Miller dipped a terry cloth square into the warm water and squeezed it well. "Shut up and lay down."

Peale obeyed. Large, gentle hands swabbed the flesh surrounding the wound as the dark man inquired softly, "What gives? Last time I saw you, you'd just shrugged off five .38 caliber slugs through the chest. I didn't get a close look, but what I saw then looked a helluva lot worse than this."

"I don't know. After all the fresh blood I took from the guy on the street, I should be healing. Instead, my chest and arm are on fire. It's like nothing I've ever felt before."

Having nothing constructive to add, Miller continued swabbing and rinsing the cloth. "Where the hell you been all last week, anyway? I kept looking for you to finish our discussion; I was starting to wonder if you'd skipped on me."

"As far as I'm concerned, the discussion is closed. I told you that. Nevertheless, a little bird told me to keep a low profile."

"A little *Cajun* bird, no doubt. I thought he knew more than he was telling."

"He usually does."

Gae dabbed at another rivulet of blood oozing from the wound. It looked bad. He wasn't a doctor, though in BC's case maybe a Medical Examiner would be better, but the inflammation around the ugly hole seemed worse and the bleeding slowed but wouldn't stop. "Well, if you were supposed to be laying low, why'd you come out tonight?"

The smile rueful. "I got bored."

"Bored? Considering how things went tonight, I hope you got enough excitement to last you a while. Any more is likely to kill you once and for all."

"Odd, that sounds rather like something a little Cajun bird might say. Wrong accent, though."

Pressing Peale's hand over the washcloth compress, Miller reached for the big-buttoned bedside telephone (a gift from the kids in response to his kvetching about the tiny keypads on normal phones). He said, "Sorry, I'm lousy at impressions; it's one of my chief failings. Here, hold that and keep quiet a minute while I take care of some business. I gotta in again to see what the score is, then we'll figure out what to do next."

With misgiving, BC watched blunt, brown fingers press the over-sized number keys. Would Miller turn him in right then and there? Considering the alarming number of times he'd lost control lately, it would be the logical — and safest — move. He bit back pain as another wave radiated from the wound. Holding himself immobile until the spasm subsided, he lifted the compress to peek at the puncture. Bright red had already soaked the cloth, run down his arm, and stained his fingers. Weak and wretched, he watched his essence drip off his body and soak into the rumpled bedclothes. At the rate he was fading, he'd doubtless go dormant long before sunrise. Oh Merciful God. Sunrise.

Looking away from the worrying stain, he fixed on Miller. He hadn't heard the soft voice beside him let alone the one on the other end of the line over the ringing in his ears. That never happened before, either. He wondered what it meant. Nothing good, that was certain. Panic threatened to drown him, but he fought it, concentrating on what he *could* hear. Amazingly, that was reassuring.

Miller related a judiciously edited version of the evening and finished by answering an unheard question from the other end. "Yeah, Jim, I'm pretty sure it's only one guy, at least that's all *I* saw at the time. The whole thing happened so damn' fast . . . no surprise Vigilante didn't stick around long when the shooting started. Personally, I thought that was a great idea since the first two had pals around the corner who decided to pay us a visit when all hell broke loose. They were coming on like the cavalry when I split. I didn't stop runnin' except to call you, then I hoofed it back here."

The tinnitus drowned out Nelson's reply, but Miller listened with furrowed brow. "What? Sure, it was dark, but I think I know a gun when I see one. Our guy's combat was strictly hand-to-hand — if you don't count biting as something else. He dropped onto 'em from above and the only ones shooting were me and the guy I popped.

"The punk started firing before anyone knew I was there. The first shot hit the Vigilante hard. When I left, the second guy was unconscious, but alive and other unfriendlies were on the way." After another moment of listening, Miller's next response oozed doubt. "I don't think much of the 'stray bullet' theory. There weren't many strays flyin' around. I fired once and the other guy was tryin' to hit me — not real well, but *still* in the opposite direction from his buddy."

The other voice buzzed. Miller replied, "I don't like it, either. Let me know if the lab wants my weapon and keep me posted on what the crime-scene guys have to say, huh? This is makin' less sense than usual. Yeah, I'll catch you later."

Hanging up, Miller glared at the phone as if it might leap for his throat. Peale observed, "That was a congenial first name basis conversation. Is your Captain Nelson a friend as well as commanding officer?"

"That's a good way to put it. Yeah, Jim and I go way back. Grew up together right here in the neighborhood."

"You didn't tell him about me."

"Of *course* I didn't tell him about you! What was I gonna say? 'By the way, Jim, the Vampire Vigilante had a boo-boo so I took him home and tucked him into my bed!' No way, man. He may be one of my oldest friends, but he already thinks I'm loony for believing vampires exist. Telling him about you in specific would book me into a private rubber room pronto."

Peale gave him a tight smile, then went thoughtful. "That reminds me. Why *do* you believe in vampires. Oh, sure you got an eyeful at Julio's the other night, but most men would have found a way to convince themselves it was bad lighting."

"Blame my Grandmother, but that can wait for another time. Right now, we gotta figure out what to do with you. Is it my imagination or are you getting worse?"

The vampire ignored the question. "What was that stuff about shooting and whether the Vigilante — *I* — had a weapon?"

The dark face clouded as he weighed his words; fewer things made sense than before. He didn't like it when things didn't make sense. "It was about the other guy. The one you . . . uh . . . drank from? He was dead by the time the cops and the SI teams people got onto the scene."

Peale's eyes widened. "But that *couldn't* be! I didn't take that much from him."

Miller shook his head. "The guy didn't bleed to death. Somebody popped him after we left. Point-blank head shot."

Amazement was wiped away as a spasm shot through Peale's body, doubling him up against the headboard. Helplessly, Galen watched the long fingers reflexively clench at the bedclothes, wondering if vampires could take painkillers. There had to be something to do, especially since even SI emergency facilities were out of the question. Even if the doctors weren't required to report all gunshot wounds, bringing an animated corpse in for treatment would raise a few eyebrows.

The spasm ebbed and Peale quirked a weak smile at Miller. "I'm afraid your linens are a loss."

"Shit happens. I never liked the flowered ones, anyway."

"Thanks for not turning me over to your Captain."

"Don't mention it." Abruptly, Galen removed the blood-soaked cloth from the trembling fingers. "This is getting pretty messy. I'll rinse it and get fresh water. Think you'll be okay alone for a few minutes?"

The answering nod was faint, but resolute. In the bathroom, Miller dumped the bloody water, then looked dubiously at the sodden fabric in his hand. He dropped it into the lavatory with a grimace, ran clear water over his fingers, then pulled another cloth from the vanity.

Opening the medicine cabinet for the third time revealed no miracle cure overlooked on the first two inspections. Same old Peroxide, antibiotic ointment, Tylenol, Band-Aids and tiny bottle of Merthiolate. He wondered what effect, if any, they'd have on Peale. Closing the cabinet on the depressingly scant options, he seized the basin of water and hurried back.

Stepping into the room, he was horrified at the deterioration. The lean, muscular form looked shrunken, and was curled into a tight fetal position. Convulsions sent visible shudders through the limbs. Animal terror shot Peale's head up at the approaching footsteps, sending a cascade of blood from the torn shoulder. The red-rimmed eyes were barely coherent, but recognition glittered there. "Thank God it's you — quickly! What time is it? I must get back before I'm caught out in the dawn."

Not fully understanding, but certain the last thing Peale could afford was to lose more blood, Miller shoved him firmly against the pillows. The resulting grimace flashed long, businesslike fangs. Assuming his I-can-handle-this tone, he assured, "Don't worry about that, man, this is a basement apartment. You're in an inside room so the sun can't reach you here. You'll be okay . . . um . . . that is if you don't need some kinda special dirt or anything like that?"

A milk-white hand clamped his shoulder painfully and pulled him down until their noses were almost touching. "If this destroys me, promise you'll scatter my ashes back home. Maryland. I was born in Maryland."

The heat in the viselike fist crushing his shoulder was intense, and with a certain horror, he realized that undead, too, could become delirious. More agitated by the moment, Peale insisted, "Promise me. *Please!*"

"Okay, sure, man, I'll scatter your . . . I'll do it. I promise I'll do what you ask."

The iron grip loosened and the rigid body relaxed, falling heavily against the pillows. Gae stared helplessly. The telephone on the bedside table rang, he startled at the sound. "I'll answer this in the other room. You try to rest, okay?"

The vampire made no reply. Nevertheless, Gae tiptoed out, closing the door gently behind him. "*Ashes.* Man!"

It was Jim, and his opening remark was unfortunate. "Hey, Gae, still believe in vampires?"

"Dammit, Jim! That joke isn't funny any more, if it ever was. I'm too damn' tired for this shit."

Nelson backpedaled, "*Whoa*, Big Fella! I'm not making a joke. That was a legitimate, if badly phrased, question. What I'm trying to say is that someone out there is taking the tabloid stories seriously."

"Huh?"

"I love that snappy repartee, Gae. It's a wonder you aren't in constant demand for the public speaking circuits."

"Gimme a break, Jim, it's been a rough night. Would you please tell me what you're getting at?"

Jim chuckled and rustled through papers. "We don't have the medical reports on your dance partners yet, that'll be tomorrow at the earliest. We do, however, have the crime scene report. The clips were missing from both weapons, but strangely enough, the slugs recovered from the surrounding area were cast from *silver* of all things.

"The logical conclusion is either they were vampire hunting or playing at Lone Ranger. Funny, I always thought silver bullets were what you went after werewolves with."

"Real funny, Jim."

"You said you thought the Vigilante was hit?"

Oh God. Galen's mouth worked, but no sound emerged as the words hit home. Jim repeated, "Hey! Gae! The other guy was hit?"

"Wha — oh yeah, in the shoulder."

"I doubt it'll do any good, but we'll send word to all the emergency rooms to specially notify us of any wads of silver they dig out of anybody. Man, I'm gonna feel like an idiot calling that one in."

A puzzle piece clicked into place. "Betcha the slug in the other dude's head is silver, too."

"No bets, Gae." A pause. "Man, it must be weird to hear this after the jokes and pranks the team pulled."

"You have no idea, James. I better go, like I said, it's been a wild night and it's all catchin' up to me now."

"Yeah, you sound wiped out. Catch some Zs and call me later. If anything happens that falls into the earth-shattering category, I'll call back. Bye."

Galen clutched the buzzing telephone trying to wrap his mind around Jim's news. Slamming the receiver down, he raced for the kitchen remembering his late grandmother's words about silver. About how the metal was hurtful to most supernatural creatures and deadly to others. He was betting there was a hunk of the stuff lodged in Peale's shoulder and if it didn't come out soon, he *would* be scattering the guy's ashes.

Filling his biggest chili pot with water, he set it to boil, and ransacked the kitchen for things to use. By the time the water was boiling, he'd amassed an odd assortment: one working flashlight of the bendable variety, a roll of paper towels, the ginsu fillet knife the kids gave him for Christmas and a pair long-nosed pliers.

Carrying his hodgepodge tools on a scoured pizza pan, he nervously crept to the bedside, swearing fluently at the vision of a small heap of ashes in the middle of the mattress whenever it attempted to raise it's ugly head. He breathed a sigh of relief to find Peale lying as he'd left him. He set the tray down and reached to feel the pale forehead.

Peale's head lolled to one side. Dead.

Miller remained calm, firmly reminding himself that dead was a vampire's normal condition. For peace of mind, he'd take it as a good sign and keep going. Damn. Field triage courses didn't cover this. Hooking the flashlight around his neck, he grasped the fillet knife and went to work.

***

Time ceased to matter long before the pliers clicked against the bullet lodged against the shoulder blade. Carefully, he worked the toothed jaws around, wincing at the additional abuse to already damaged tissue. He gripped hard, and eased the offending metal out. In the glow of the lamp, it looked too small to have caused all that agony.

He dropped the pellet on the tray and turned back to his patient with a cloth dipped in what had once been boiling water. Dabbing at the blood smeared on Peale's chest, he stopped abruptly, and rubbed at gritty eyes. He was tired, but . . . no, he wasn't imagining things.

The gaping wound filled with blood and began to close as he watched.

Guess he got all the silver out, but was it in time? Peale looked very dead, but never having seen a dormant vampire before, he couldn't guess what was normal. He'd have to wait for sundown and see if Peale rose or if he still had a corpse on his hands. He hoped for the former. That undead asshole had a lot of questions to answer.

The LED on the bedside radio-alarm clock read eight-nineteen a.m., daylight even at this time of year. Squinting at the door, he decided against opening it. Not much sunlight got into the apartment, but it still was an unnecessary risk. Putting all the "surgical" paraphernalia aside, he stuffed the doorjamb with paper towels, and tumbled into his big dressing chair.

He didn't remember falling asleep.

SIX

The telephone was ringing. Again. Jay Marquez leaned wearily in the kitchen doorway clutching a flimsy dressing gown around herself. She knew who it was. It was Mario Hernandez. He'd been calling ever since Chick and Alfie got killed. She'd already had to turn the cell off. Uncertain which was worse, to let the thing ring or pick it up and be right, she angrily snatched it up.

Sometimes, she simply hated being right. The painfully familiar whine began, "Jay, it's me, I just want to be sure you're okay—"

"Mario Hernandez, I been telling you for more'n a week *and* at seven, seven-thirty and eight o'clock this morning that the only way I'm gonna be okay is if you stop calling me! You are a *jerk* and I want you to LEAVE. ME. ALONE!"

She slammed the phone down, unplugged it at the wall, then dropped into a chair fuming and fighting tears. "Gotta get an answering machine, dammit."

Sipping strong and bitter instant coffee, she slouched over the breakfast table determined to forget that a jerk named Mario Hernandez existed. Secure in the knowledge of the dead telephones, she spread the Trib over the cluttered surface. The headline blared across the front page:

Chicagoland Underworld Declares War
on Vampire Vigilante

Reading with growing dread, she stopped at a seemingly-inconsequential line noting two small punctures on one victim's throat. That line was common in the Trib these days, but this morning, it jumped off the page. She knew the significance of those marks, and no amount of wishing would change that.

Was it only ten days since Chick and Alfie died? It seemed longer. Mostly because of Mario, but also because of fragmentary memories that bobbed up like tiny bits of cork from under deep water. As days passed, the fragments formed a recognizable pattern that was both alarming and fascinating. When she told the police her version of that night, it was so vivid in her memory it *seemed* true. But the next day, when she finally drummed up the nerve to look at the news, things got screwy. Suddenly, she could see herself and BC sitting at the coffee shop, just like she'd told the cops, but misty in the background, she saw something else. Something not quite so cozy and pleasant.

She crumpled, sobbing softly, "I *did* see it. I *did*! It's so scary! I *saw* Alfie Fallon shoot BC Peale right through the chest. I *saw* the shots come out his back and the blood all over the wall. He shoulda been dead, but he got up and . . . oh god. He ain't human! No way he can be."

Angry with herself for giving in to fear, she sniffed hard, and held her breath against the convulsive sobs that rocked her. Was she dumb or what? Nobody believed that shit anymore. That stuff only happened in movies and dumb-butt books. Vampires weren't real.

At least she didn't used to think so, but in spite of the dreamlike quality of the memory, what she *saw* was real. Lightly tapping painted nails against her favorite pastel pink mug, she ticked off other certainties. Well, maybe BC wasn't "human," but he was good people. When things went to hell at the Fiesta, he could have taken off and left her lying in the gravel with two other stiffs. He didn't. He brought her home and even made tea for her. So okay, she was in some kind of trance and he'd put her in it, but he also protected her. Then when she was groggy, and coming on to him, he left without taking advantage; not many "normal" guys would have done that, and if BC was . . . oh man!

Maybe she had a closer call than she thought. Maybe, but it was Butthead Mario driving her nuts. She'd hardly laid eyes on BC since then. The most he'd done was buzz by Jake's Bar and Grill where she worked a couple times to say hi and probably check up on her. All in all, she preferred that method to Hernandez'. BC had a secret to protect, God only knew what Mario's problem was. Maybe the drugs finally ate his brains out.

Another thing she was sure of: Alfie and Chick attacked first, and if they'd killed BC, she'd be dead, too. Alfie Fallon was pure hardcase; he didn't leave witnesses. Terrifying as it was, BC killed in self-defense. The truth was that what he did and *how* he did it, scared the hell out of her, but *he* didn't. She liked him and all the time she and her girlfriends flirted with him, he'd never hurt anyone. It sounded dumb, but she got good vibes from him. Still, it might be a good idea to keep an eye on him. Yeah, but how?

She smiled. If she worked at the Inferno Jazz Club, it'd be easy. Since their hostess, Norean Chambers just quit to get married, they'd need a replacement. She'd be qualified for sure *and* it might make it a little harder for Mario to find her for a while. Perfect. Now to hustle her butt down there before they gave the job to someone else. Better call first. Where'd she stick that phone book?

***

In his darkened living room, Hernandez stared at the droning telephone receiver. Jay wasn't answering any more, and she sounded real mad when she hung up last time. He slowly released the instrument back onto its hooks, and held the morning paper toward the dim light filtering through the drawn shades to reread the story he'd marked.

The vampire had killed again, though that wasn't what the story was about. The reporter all but ignored the dead guys, concentrating on several silver bullets recovered from the crime-scene. He tossed the paper onto the growing pile on the floor. It was good to know he wasn't the only one fighting the demon. He hoped there were more. As long as the Peale thing died once and for all, he didn't care who made it happen.

If others were fighting the vampire, were there more like Jay, too? It was a sure bet the thing cast a spell over her, why else would she be acting so mean to him when all he wanted to do was help? He needed to break that spell, to do something about the undead thing. What could he do though?

Silver bullets were a good idea, but it wouldn't work for him. He had a pistol, a nickel plated .357 magnum, but it was big and he wasn't convinced the monster couldn't sense silver. After all, it killed the two dealers last night and *they* had silver bullets. Uh-uh. Special bullets were no good, besides, he didn't know where to buy them. If he could find a way to take it by surprise . . . but he needed to know more. Maybe there were books about vampires at the library. He'd look.

He wasn't sitting on his can these last nights, though. He was watching. But, the monster wasn't in any of the usual places. Maybe it went back to where it came from? No, not before it killed Jay. Did vampires always kill their slaves in the end? He'd better look that up, too.

That jock, Miller, was hanging around a lot. Maybe he was looking for the vampire, too. Was he going to hunt it down? Probably not, he didn't try to stop it at Julio's, and he had a gun then. Could the monster be controlling Miller? It might be important to know, he'd watch Miller's place tonight instead of the club.

***

"Hey, Jump! I'm here!"

True to his word, Jump Veron had left the side door to the Inferno Jazz Club unlocked. Opening was hours away, so when she entered the big room, its raised dais was deserted, the piano and drum set shrouded with dustcovers, and the tables shoved aside.

"Jump!" Her voice echoed back through a forest of chair legs overturned onto the tabletops. Stepping farther in, she glowed with pleasure at the stage-like appearance of the old, brick-walled room. No matter how often she saw it, the transformation of a big, slightly scruffy room by lighting, music and infusion of people into a nightclub was magic. Clutching the resume her sister had typed, she perched on the edge of the dais to wait. Jump was probably still in his office, he'd said he was up to his neck in paperwork. She wondered where Benny was, though. He was usually looming somewhere close by. It must be a busy time if he was tied up, too. No problem, she didn't mind soaking up the atmosphere for a while.

In the corridor that connected the back office to the club floor, Jump Veron tugged at his salt and pepper beard, watching his visitor, and letting her emotions wash over him. He wasn't empathic like his friend and partner, BC, but Jay was a projector. Enthusiasm and hope beat from her like a bright melody, yet underneath ran a counterpoint of deeply troubled bass. He hated spying, but since her call, his Gift clamored that there was more involved than a simple job application. Irritatingly, that intuition remained stubbornly silent as to *what* else.

There was the timing, too. The morning paper was full of Vampire Vigilante stories spurred by the deaths the night before. It didn't take a rocket scientist to figure out what happened. He'd surely get the whole story later when BC showed up. And he would. BC always showed up when he was in trouble.

He been reading an article about the silver bullets found at the scene when Jay called. Another voice from Monsieur Byron Peale's recent past. As he listened to Jay's breathlessly anxious questions, his thoughts returned to BC. *What have you done now, mon ami?*

Who could know? If she knew there was more to BC Peale than met the eye, she was cool about it. He liked that. He liked Jay, anyway. From the first time they'd met, he'd admired her strength and amiable competence. It would be a pleasure to count her among the staff of the Inferno.

Whatever her reasons for coming, there was no threat in her. Stepping out, he called, "You make good time, Jay!"

She bounced to her feet and turned on a warm smile. "C'mon, Jump you know I live within walkin' distance. Woulda been here sooner, 'cept I hadda get Anna to type up this resume thingie for me."

Taking the pages, he ambled to the bar, motioning her to follow. Stepping up on his well-used platform, he set two cans of pale-dry ginger ale on the counter, and bent to filling glasses with ice. He made a big show of squinting at the resume. "Like I say on the phone, Jay, the job still open. But why you want to change? You work at Jake's . . . how long it say here?"

"Five years. But, I think that's the best reason, Jump. I mean, five years and I'm still a waitress? Sure the tips are good, but there ain't nothin' else. When I hired on, Jake promised me advancement, but the only advances I seen was suggestions on how to spend the evenin' after work."

Jump laughed, "I can't promise you that won' happen some here, but if you be wantin' the job? Well, Jake he come after me wit' the axe, but, consider youself hired."

"Huh? That's the whole interview an' I *got* it?"

"Unless you wish otherwise. I know you, Jay, an' I know you do good work. What more can an employer ask? Start Saturday, can you?"

"Oh, I sure *can*! Thanks, Jump! You'll never regret it!"

She bounded for the door only to come to a grinding halt short of the stairs. Pivoting, she bapped herself in the forehead with the flat of her hand. "Geez! I'm so excited, I got no brains. What kinda outfit d'ya want I should wear?"

"Come back tomorrow an' I get you one of Norean's dresses by then. It may need a nip there and a tuck here, but I think it will do, no?"

"Sure! My mom, she can sew great!" With a final wave, she ducked out. Listening to the clatter of her heels on the stairs to street level, he regarded her untouched drink with amusement. Taking a sip from his own, he thought, *No, I don't regret it. The little voice in the back of the head tell Jump to hire you on the spot. Hmmm. What more than a desire for a better job is with you Jay and how much do you know about my only slightly dead friend? Time will tell, it always do.*

* * *

Benny Glissen ducked under the kitchen porthole as Jay wheeled to say something else to Jump. He didn't want her to catch him eavesdropping. Trying to watch her was more to the point, but listening was all he could do from there. Every afternoon, he helped Cal, the chef, get the kitchen ready for the evening's rush, today was no exception. While wrestling two fifty-pound bags of onions into the bin, he'd heard someone come through the side door. That was wrong. This time of day, that door should have been locked. He'd dumped the onions, shoved down his sleeves and made for the glass porthole to scope out the intruder.

His breath caught as he recognized Jay Marquez sweeping through the room in a swirl of golden hair and linen skirts. He took his job as watch-dog seriously, and if this were any other unauthorized visitor, he'd have dealt with them pronto. But it wasn't. It was Jay. Jay, who, without trying, always made him feel like his shoelaces were tied together. Seeing her flustered him so much he couldn't force his petrified body through the door to ask if he could help. He couldn't make himself back away from the window, either, when Jump stumped out to greet her. He could only stand with his hand raised to the door plate like one of those dumb concrete jockeys people put in their front yards.

Jay was the new hostess? Oboy. Now he could act like an idiot in front of the whole club. Why not? They all thought he was retarded anyway. Phil Quinlan, the club manager, was gonna have a ball with this. Phil was such a jerk.

As the high-heel clicks faded, he cracked the swinging door and peeked at the bar. Jump sat deep in thought, absently stirring a glass of ginger ale.

He hated to butt in, but he had to. There was for real club business to take care of. Good thing Jay left when she did, or he'd have had to come out and talk in front of her. Yeah, and tripped on his own feet, and started stammering. Pretty girls did that to him, and Jay was one of the prettiest — and most dangerous. He'd seen her snarf guys who hit on her like sardines on toast. If he were handsome and smooth like BC, maybe he could talk to her. But he wasn't. He was just big, slow Benny. Because he was slow, people thought he was stupid. He wasn't stupid. He was more like a big, friendly mutt who just didn't think or talk so fast. Maybe friendly would be good enough.

Glissen coughed softly to get Jump's attention, then pulled a wad of receipts from his pocket. "The laundry come a few minutes ago, Boss, an' Phil needs for you to check the lists. Ummm . . . was that Juanita Marquez? What's she doin' here? She works for Jake Green, don't she?"

Jump smiled as he ticked off items on the slips of paper. Like his blushing assistant hadn't heard every word. Benny was a lousy actor. It was plain as neon that he thought Jay was the most wonderful thing on two legs. Eyes on the list, the Cajun replied, "Used to, but not no more. Come Saturday, she be the new hostess for the Inferno."

"Yeah? That's great!" He paused desperately needing something else to say that didn't involve Jay, then he remembered, "Oh, yeah, Boss! Phil wanted me to ask should he set up BC's piano for the show tonight?"

"No, I don' think so, I think he be busy again."

"Again? Boy, he ain't been in since that night he and that Miller guy talked. That was almost two weeks! Now BC ain't been showin' up and Miller keeps comin' around looking for 'im. What's up? Is BC in some kind of trouble?"

Jump's grizzled head snapped up. "Benny. You been workin' for me too long to be askin' those questions."

The big man was visibly cowed. Jump didn't get mad often, but he was close this time. Something bad was going on, and Benny knew it. Why else would Jump put out the story BC left town? Up until a couple nights ago, even he believed Peale skipped and that it was Miller's fault. Jump finally broke down and told him the truth only to keep him from decking the has-been linebacker. The news surprised him more than the intensity of Jump's order to leave Miller alone. Still, BC laying low was bad. If it wasn't trouble, why would someone that self-confident make himself scarce? No reason he could see and the blame kept landing splat at Galen Miller's big feet. He said only, "Sorry, Boss. I jus' wanted to help. Guess I was thinkin' out loud."

Regaining his benign manner, Jump said, "You wasn't thinkin' at all, Benny, that's the trouble! Now into the back wit' you, you got things to be doin' an' Phil need these receipts. Tell him they look fine."

Watching his aide beat a hasty retreat, Jump wondered if he'd allowed his own worry to find an innocent target. Benny meant well, but to him, things were black and white, not the myriad shades of gray Jump saw. Too bad things couldn't be that simple. BC *was* staying out of sight because of Galen Miller, but in no way Benny would understand.

It would be amusing, had BC not been so genuinely upset. It was his own fault, though. He was far too careless about keeping his secret. It was surprising others hadn't tumbled to it more frequently. The worst shock was finding out Miller was a cop. That shook BC up on a grand scale. He was certain the authorities would soon close in on him. Touchingly, the vampire's chief worry was that Jump and the others at the club might be caught in the fallout.

Jump didn't think the situation was quite that bad. He sensed no danger from Miller. Whenever the man came asking after BC, he sensed genuine concern. That wasn't to say the Agent wasn't genuinely concerned that he might have chased his best lead away, but there was no danger. According to BC, Miller was under deep cover with Sentry International struggling with a difficult case, and wanting supernatural help. It sounded right, but as with Jay, not the whole story. BC Peale as an undercover agent tickled him, though. History repeats itself, no?

Then, there were the slain drug dealers. Certainly the men died from gunshots, but he knew his friend was involved. How like him to break cover in such an audacious way. BC was prone to rashness, always had been. Doubtless, when confronted, he'd once again hang his head and plead cabin fever. *Benny asks a good question. What are you up to this time, old friend? I have a bad feeling for you, and you got the knack for getting into the hot water. That's how I meet you in Berlin, no? So long ago. I think you be stirrin' up trouble again. Well, time will tell, it always do.*

With an effort he shoved the somber mood into a remote corner of his mind. There was no immediate danger, and he needed his pleasant face for the customers who'd soon crowd the club. If he continued these thoughts, they would bleed through into his music and he never liked those dark overtones. Chuckling, he drained his drink, and returned to the office and its lurking mound of paperwork that never got smaller.

***

Galen woke after sunset to find a blanket draped over him and the rumpled bed empty. Staggering to his feet, he searched the apartment. Peale was gone.

He ground his teeth in cold fury. After all he went through, and all he'd done, that undead s.o.b. up and *split*! Angrily, he swiveled to snarl at the blood smear by the door, only to find no sign of it. Instead, he found a brownish powder dusting the hardwood parquet below where it had been. Puzzlement replaced anger until he remembered the row of small windows in back of him. Sunlight. Of course. Exactly what happened to the evidence at the crime scene. Too bad he hadn't shoved the pizza pan out of the bedroom when he'd finished that morning, it would save on cleanup. Maybe it wasn't too late — for the tray, anyway. There were plenty of places sunlight never reached. There was a helluva lot of work ahead, he was afraid to check out the bathroom, last night it looked like a slaughterhouse. Thank God Jim hadn't stopped by — or worse — Mama.

Giving physical vent to anger, he launched into a whirlwind cleanup, muttering threats against undead in general and Peale in particular. He tackled the bathroom first. Vigorously applying a stiff-bristled brush and disinfectant-laced, sudsy water to the hard tiles that played hob with his bad knees.

"You saved my life. Thank you."

Miller started and glared around wildly. The object of his ire leaned casually in the doorway with a white bag clutched to his breast. "Peale! How the hell did you get in here?"

"By way of the front door, it's not locked. Was it supposed to be?" The vampire busied himself replacing the empty Chinese takeout cartons that littered the coffee table with fresh ones. It was a no-brainer to deduce what kind of food Miller would find acceptable. Straightening, he amended, "Perhaps 'life' isn't quite accurate in my case, but 'You saved my undeath' just doesn't have the same ring."

Spicy aromas from the white cardboard containers pierced the disinfectant. Galen ignored it, and concentrated his fury on Peale. "Where the hell you been?"

"*That's* a greeting! I went to pick up my bike . . . and to get a little dinner. I got some for you, too," Smiling impishly, he added, "Not from the same place, though."

"Jumped somebody, did you?"

Peale became defensive. "I didn't hurt anyone, I only took a little."

Miller exploded, "Dammit, Peale!"

"Well, he was trying to nick my Harley, wasn't he? Right outside the stockyard, mind you! I needed the extra, anyway. I lost a lot last night . . . in a number of ways."

"Yeah, I remember, I been cleaning the bathroom in case you didn't notice!"

"What are you so pissed about?"

Stalking to the tray resting on the kitchen island, Miller smacked wads of paper toweling aside, and snatching the long-nosed pliers, thrust the misshapen nugget toward Peale. The vampire instinctively reached for it, but feeling the silver like heat on his flesh, recoiled in surprise. Mildly satisfied, Galen said, "You got it, pal, it's silver. This is the slug I pulled out of you this morning."

"Silver?" Peale stared. "No wonder it wasn't healing." Abruptly his gaze shifted, and jabbed a finger at Miller's hand. "Wait. *Pliers*?"

"What'd you think I was gonna pull it out with? My teeth?"

"You poked around in *my* body with *pliers?*"

"I boiled 'em first!"

Peale sputtered. Miller cut the incipient tirade short. "Listen! Doesn't this bullet mean anything to you at all? These guys came looking for a vampire. They may not know who you are, but they sure as hell know what you are."

The bullet hung between them for a seeming eternity before BC acknowledged, "*And* they know how to destroy me."

"You got the picture, Sherlock."

"And you, Galen Miller, have got a partner."

***

Lounging on the couch like an indolent cat, Peale watched Miller pace. The big man stopped abruptly. "F'chrissakes! Don't sit there like a supernatural couch potato, help me figure out Who, Where and Why."

Peale sat up. "Then, I'd appreciate being told exactly how I'm supposed to do that. The longer I listen to you ramble, the more this sounds like Philosophy 101, and I think it only fair to warn you, I never read that course."

"You think this sounds confusing? Try going over the same crap for a year or more like I have. There has to be something we can learn from your involvement here. For instance: I believed in vampires because my Jamaican Grandmother was into the voodoo, but what about this guy?"

The vampire shrugged. "I've found, no matter how sophisticated a face society puts on, there are always people who believe in the occult. Lately, vampires have become very popular — much to my chagrin, I might add. Maybe that's the way it is with this guy. You said his name was Borgia?"

"Yeah, as in Lucretzia. Anyway, I think more than popular culture is involved here; I mean, why go to the expense of making silver bullets? Most people think sliver is for werewolves, not vampires. Look at the guys in the team. When they were ribbing me about believing in your kind, they gave me a stake and mallet."

"They gave you a *hammer and stake*?"

"Oh, not the real thing, just something from an old croquet set . . . ." Seeing the increasingly wary expression, he exclaimed, "Oh, come off it! I'm gonna go to all the trouble to get you back on your feet, mess my place up and ruin my sheets so I can ram a croquet goal into your chest later? Let's get back to business. There has to be more to this bullet thing."

Peale snapped, "Maybe he's a Hammer film freak. Why does he call himself 'Borgia,' anyway?"

"That's *another* question we need to answer."

"We're getting quite a list."

"Damn straight. Let's try to shorten it. I brought some files home last night, but got too distracted with something else to read them." Shooting the slender man a meaningful glare, he continued, "Your perspective is bound to be different than mine, maybe you'll spot something I missed."

Dismayed, the draftee eyed the pile of varicolored folders streaming onto the tabletop from a deceptively small leather satchel. The satchel caused something to niggle at the back of his mind. What was it? Oh, yeah! Under the hall table.

Gae flopped into his comfy recliner. Big mistake. Sitting reminded him how tired he was. Last night was tiring and sleeping all day in the bedroom chair didn't help. His eyes felt like they were filled with sand. He scrubbed uselessly at them with thumb and forefinger. Closing his eyes was also a mistake. He angrily jerked himself back from the edge of sleep.

Somehow, when he wasn't looking, Miller's dream of smooth sailing with Peale's help had become a magic cure-all. Problem was, the magic didn't happen, he was still sifting through paper. Not only that, but he'd suddenly realized how much more complicated things had become with Peale on board. Now he was not only protecting his own cover, but BC's as well. Scratch that. Miller was only dodging the bad guys. Peale was dodging the bad guys *and* Sentry International. Well, that would only last until he figured out how to tell Jim about the arrangement with Peale and, uh, maybe something else. Dumb. He'd been so hungry for a break, he neglected to think that part through.

Roused by a small click and rustling paper, Miller glanced up expecting to see Peale busy reading files. He didn't. Instead, the vampire had an attaché case open in his lap, hands almost a blur as he sorted and stacked packets of money on the table.

Snapping the locks home, he shoved a stack toward Miller. "Here, this probably belongs to your lot, they'll be wanting it back since it all went balls up last night."

"Say what?"

"These bills have some sort of dye all over them. That makes me think they belong to someone who'd like to keep track of their movements. Somehow, I tend to think of police in such instances. I thought it only proper to give them back."

"Give me that!" Galen snatched the case away. "This is the courier's case from last night. We marked most of those bills."

The suggestion of a smile played around Peale's lips, as he regarded Miller over the pile of bills. Miller looked blank, then amazed. "You can *see* the dye? But that's special stuff . . . oh shit."

BC smiled broadly. "Vampirism comes with a few perks."

"Makes no difference, partner, its all evidence, it *all* goes back."

"Why? I gave you the marked bills, the rest was the dealer's money. I usually use all of it."

"I *know* what you usually do with it, but it's all evidence — the case, too. Believe me, Jim Nelson will ask some pretty pointed questions if I show up without it. Let's get this straight now. The rules changed when you threw in with me, any further charitable contributions come out of your own pocket." He paused. "What ever possessed you to donate to the Policeman's Benevolent Fund, anyway?"

The smile widened. "It was a stroke of genius, wasn't it?"

"We'll discuss your spending habits later. Let's hit the streets and put those vampiric perks of yours to good use. We've got a lot of ground to cover if you're going to get back to your damned hidey hole by dawn."

***

Eddie Michalson churned the carpet, his unhappiness saturating the elegant room. Francesco Borgia settled back in his throne-like chair and waited for the inevitable outburst. The things these mortals found important.

As if the countdown were audible, Michalson burst out. "I still don't get why you ordered Nakamura liquidated. It wasn't *his* fault that Randall screwed the hit."

Borgia sighed heavily. For all Edgar's intelligence and cunning, he was often more like a dull child than a vice president in a global business concern. "I am not in the habit of explaining my actions to anyone, Edgar, but I will go over it one *last* time for you.

"Nakamura was careless. He and Randall were warned what to watch for, yet they were taken by surprise, and my adversary fed from Nakamura.

This made Nakamura a dangerous liability. Also, due to their negligence, the other vampire — and the rest of Chicago — now knows about our special ammunition." He tossed the folded newspaper to Michalson for emphasis. "Consider Nakamura an object lesson in prudence."

Michalson snatched the paper out of the air, and without glancing at it, crumpled and tossed it into the trash. Though he remained silent, Borgia's predatory senses screamed that his lieutenant didn't consider the issue closed.

Francesco Borgia disapproved of such sentiment. *Too much humanity, Edgar, you bleed too easily. However did you make it this far in such an inhumane business?* His eyes fell on Isendamer, her face unreadable as usual. Here was an altogether different sort, one made to order for the business. *What a mask you wear, Gwen, it lends the aspect of humanity where there is nothing human in residence. You hide the madness well, but for one who has tasted your soul, the rot is palpable.*

Tension crackled. This wouldn't do. Though he felt the meeting was unnecessary, it had been called and must run smoothly if they were to get to more important things. "*Basta.* We must move on. What do our people on the police force have to tell us?"

Michalson's brow creased. "Not a lot, Boss. Our guys in CPD say it looks like the Vigilante guy took a round to the body. There ain't much more, other than what we read in the paper . . . except Sentry International is mixed up in it somehow. Our guys said SI was on the scene before they were."

Borgia frowned. "Ah yes. The new international police. They are becoming a true annoyance."

Michalson paused, then added uncomfortably, "I got no info as to what's goin' down at S.I. proper, either. We still got nobody in that Schaumburg office. Not even a janitor."

"It seems odd for Sentry to keep popping up in the same places as our rogue vampire." Isendamer lightly tapped her fingers against the arm of her chair. "Our CPD contact said they stuck their noses in the disturbance at that sleezy bar the other night, too. Could they be connected?"

Eddie said, "Our police guys swear themselves purple they ain't, but I wouldn't rule it out. Those guys we got on the force are real clowns. Too bad the better people aren't for sale."

Mastering his anger, Borgia interjected, "I agree with your sentiment about our hirelings, Edgar, but, not with the other, Gwen. It would be highly unusual for one of my kind to ally himself with the authorities."

Isendamer said, "More unusual for the authorities to *believe* in your kind."

"*Ecco*, Gwen! It gives one a delicious freedom."

Gwen leaned forward hungrily. She was impatient for Francesco to change her so *she* could share that freedom. He could feel it rolling off her even before her eyes locked onto his. She hadn't forgotten the promise. The promise he should never have made.

Witnessing the exchange, Eddie felt the hairs stand up on his neck. He didn't need special perceptions to read the message, and it scared the hell out of him. Francesco Borgia and the concept of vampirism frightened him, but Gwen Isendamer terrified him. The thought of Gwennie the Nutcase with vampiric abilities sent him into a blind panic. He interrupted, "So, Boss, if the media blew our element of surprise, do we ditch the silver bullet thing now or what?"

Borgia tore his gaze away from Gwen, and forced his mind back to the subject. "I think not, Edgar. The bullets are still effective. True, the element of surprise is lost, but it served well enough to strike at the rogue in a small way. Perhaps if he was truly wounded by our silver, the whole point may be moot." He paused thoughtfully. "Perhaps you'd best inform the *impiegati* — our operatives — of this possibility. It might bolster failing morale in a satisfactory manner." His gaze strayed again and he remarked lightly, "Gwen, I shall need you to remain; there are details of that last chemical shipment to the Middle East that I am unfortunately cloudy on."

Gwen folded her notepad. "Of course, Francesco. I'd be happy to go over it again."

Rising with abruptness verging on a leap, Eddie hurried away knowing he'd been dismissed, and glad of it. "That last chemical shipment" was discussed exhaustively the night before, and if anything was left to be unclear about, he couldn't dredge it up. Whatever the Boss and Gwennie were actually going to discuss, he wanted no part of it. Nodding curtly to them both, he exited, closing the door firmly behind him.

Amused, Gwen watched the retreat, then turned. "So, Francesco, why did you want Eddie out of the room? Feeling a little peckish?"

He strode toward her, drinking deeply of her scent. Physically, she was an exquisitely beautiful woman, and he had long been a connoisseur of beauty. Long legged and willowy, her high-heeled shoes made her slightly taller than he as she moved to meet him halfway, coming into his embrace with a small noise of pleasure.

Sharp teeth pierced the soft skin of her throat sending a shiver of ecstasy through her. Ignoring her passionate response with difficulty, he took a small amount from her; desiring only to strengthen the bond. Her all-consuming madness tugged at his sense of self in weak moments, so he let the link fade after each tryst, but now, he needed her amenable. It was risky revealing weaknesses to these mortals, and more dangerous to reveal them to *this* mortal, but another vampire invading his territory left little choice. She nestled tighter against him, murmuring, "The couch, Beloved, or your chambers?"

Cupping her chin, he raised her head, and looked directly into her eyes. He hated going deeper into her mind. Already her madness sucked at him like a vicious undertow. He said apologetically, "Neither, *cara mio*. I need to share a secret that Edgar mustn't learn yet."

Purring, she dragged a nail across the back of his neck. "Damn, and I was so scrumptiously warmed up. What kind of secret?"

"I need you to procure holy water and distribute it among select members of the organization."

Confusion dampening her euphoria, Gwen pulled away, speech slurred by the strength of his thrall. "Holy water? Why?"

"Those of my kind find the stuff unbearable. If it touches our flesh, it burns like acid and as such, it should be quite useful against our adversary."

Hooking both arms around his neck, she playfully kissed and bit him, then beamed into his face.

"Of course, Francesco! I'll get right on it and Eddie won't hear a whisper until you're ready." Knowing her bloodscent was arousing him, she pressed closer, turning slightly so her freshly wounded throat was under his nose. It had the desired effect. As he drew nearer, she whispered, "A good judgment call, as usual, Darling. Once you've changed me, I don't want Eddie holding too much damaging knowledge, either." He pulled away.

"What you say is true, *Cara*, but you must have patience. The time for your change is not right. Whatever would I do without you to be my representative in the daylight hours?" He kissed her throat again barely managing to refrain from taking more blood. Curse the woman's insistence when he needed them both clear headed — and curse his own vanity for thinking that the carrot could be dangled overlong. Alas, it was no exaggeration to say he needed the woman and her peculiar blend of talents. Stroking her hair, he murmured, "Gwen, you are far too valuable and precious to me to change you now. To make a fledgling of you would require a new type of bond that would interfere with *both* of our abilities to respond to this crisis. Once our enemy is vanquished, and we are once again operating smoothly, we can talk of it again. For now, my love, you'd better go lest we become . . . preoccupied until sunrise."

Partially placated, she withdrew, pausing briefly to tidy her rumpled clothing. He watched her go, then allowed the last breath he'd drawn to release as a sigh of relief.

For a moment, he was uncertain she'd go. She became more uncontrollable as time passed, was madness rendering her immune to his influence? He hoped not. She was gifted, homicidal tendencies included, and it would pain him to kill her while she was still useful. No mistake, he held her loyalty only as long as she believed he'd make her a vampire. She needn't know he never intended to create another fledgling.

He'd made only one and that was enough. Truthfully, he wouldn't have done *that* if it not pressed for a special favor by Maeve Donal. How like a child a fledgling was. Like having a son in this case. It didn't hurt Maeve's case that the young man was very beautiful. *And* very drunk. A condition Borgia found cause to regret. He'd known a vampire could become intoxicated on the blood alcohol of the prey, but not that he could be so hungover afterward. He learned differently that night, and he'd never cared to repeat any part of the experience. Maeve owed him a lot for that.

Yes! Maeve did owe him for that service, and he'd never had occasion to call in the debt. He did now. If anything called for her particular supernatural mastery, it was his rival vampire.

Maybe he'd ask after his scion. He'd been a strong-willed lad, and events didn't quite go the way she planned. That was amusing. He so loved to see plans blow up in her face. They did that *so* rarely. Maybe he'd twit her about it — after she'd augured for him, of course.

It was a fine idea, he wouldn't wait for the outcome of the silver and the holy water. Taking his address book from the hidden drawer of his desk, he flipped through its pages. The last letter he'd had from her, was postmarked Milan. Lovely city . . . at least it was in the early nineteenth century. He should get back more often. He lifted the private line and punched in a series of numbers.

SEVEN

The wood-grained steel door swung violently inward, ricocheted off the rubber doorstop, and was pinned back with shuddering finality as Galen Miller stormed into his apartment. BC Peale followed, paused to glare at the offending door, then kicked it closed. Flinging his jacket onto the nearest chair, Peale paced the living room. "This shadowing business isn't working worth a damn! I'm bloody tired of losing these people in rail stations and airports."

"Hmmm. I seem to remember someone saying that recently." Gae continued into the kitchen, and opened the fridge, regarding the contents with open suspicion. "Oh yeah. Me." He added sourly, "Annoying, isn't it? Not to mention the inconvenience of having to take your meals at the stockyards."

Peale snapped, "That is *not* a factor and I wish you'd stop flogging me with it. If you'd simply let me take them by surprise . . . ."

"Sure! And then I get to dig another silver slug out of you, providing they don't pop me first." Anger fled leaving bone-weariness in its place. Popping the cap off a bottle of dark beer, he drained half of it and said, "Sorry. I guess we're both on edge. See why I was so desperate for your help? You've only been at this a few days; *I've* been doing it a lot longer. Too bad that little mind game you tried on me at the Inferno doesn't work, we could sure use something like that."

BC dropped onto the couch with a short laugh. "It usually does work. Unless the subject is exceptionally prepared, strong-willed . . ." Shooting a meaningful glance at Miller, he added, ". . . Or particularly thick-skulled."

Galen shut the refrigerator with thoughtful care. "You mean because I was *expecting* you to pull something funny, I was on guard against it so it didn't take?"

"Something like that."

"Then, if we got the drop on an unsuspecting drug dealer, you could probably zap him and make him spill his guts about his contacts and all that good shit?"

"Under the proper circumstances, yes."

Frustration propelled Miller across the room to loom over his partner. "What, pray tell, *are* the proper circumstances, dammit? Candy and flowers? Candlelight and a table for two must be out, since we had that."

BC rolled his eyes heavenward in the hope of deliverance. Seeing no forthcoming bolt of lightning, he replied, "I have to make solid eye contact with the subject. It takes a few moments to lock in, and it seems to help if I've tasted the individual's blood beforehand."

Gae grew thoughtful, then enthusiastic. "We can do this! Why aren't we doing this?"

"Because, the badguys have bullets that will work on both of us. Did you forget this already?"

"C'mon, man, it might be a minor detail. The way I see it, you got tagged both times I know of because you took on two guys by your lonesome. If you've got company, too, things are bound to go different."

"You're suggesting we double team them?"

"Exactly."

Peale got quiet, chewing slightly at his lower lip. "That might work."

***

Huddled on the limestone ledge of an ancient brick warehouse, BC Peale turned up the collar of his motorcycle jacket in a futile attempt to ward off the cold, fog-like drizzle blown in from the lake. He'd fed well earlier in the evening, but the residual warmth living blood lent to him, was long since used up. The chill lake wind blew more mist down his neck. Spring could be filthy cold in Chicago.

He'd always hated the cold, and though his change had rendered him immune to its ravages, he now seemed to feel it more keenly. He wondered how much was physiological and how much was psychological.

Hearing an approaching car, he leaned eagerly forward to watch. It passed without slowing. He slumped against the bricks cursing both lack of body heat and his partner's insistence they experiment with his mesmeric abilities *immediately*.

Personally, he thought they should wait until SI set up another buy, but Galen was gung-ho. Against his better judgment, he'd been swept along by Gae's assurance that this warehouse was a hotbed of Borgia activity. It'd be a cinch.

The hotbed had gone cold. He'd perched up there for hours and nobody even slowed down to spit. How was it Miller always managed to get exactly what he wanted? BC thought he'd been refusing vehemently only to find himself climbing onto this damnable ledge. In the rain. It was tantamount to a supernatural ability. Galen Miller was perfectly capable of convincing him a relaxing session in a tanning bed would do him no end of good. He'd probably spend his last moments wondering how he'd gotten roped in *that* time — much like now. He shivered ineffectually, and consoled himself by watching Miller's own body heat cool as he crouched motionless behind the dumpster in the alley across the street.

He was thus occupied when a green Lincoln purred to a halt on the street below. Several seconds ticked by before his brain registered the arrival. *Oh God, don't let it be young love in bloom!* Leaning forward, he brought enhanced senses to bear, and heard male voices kvetching about being out in the rain. He sympathized. Two heartbeats; made to order. Raising his hand in the agreed signal, he prayed only Galen saw the movement. Come to think of it, he hoped *Galen* saw it. True to Miller's cynical prediction, the streetlamps were either broken or unlit. It was fine for him, but nearly pitch dark for everyone else.

Holding an unneeded breath, he watched the men slam car doors, and make for the one light on the street: The warehouse entrance. Glancing toward the street, he saw Miller sprint across to crouch behind the bulk of the Lincoln. *Fine*, he thought, *the sooner we get this over with the better*.

Under the bug light illuminating the stoop, the larger of the two sorted a tangle of keys, while the smaller danced from foot to foot trying to keep warm.

The smaller man whined, "Geez, Pete, why cou'n't ya had the dam' things ready before we got outta th' car? I'm freezin' my buns off."

The other glared over the jumbled keys. "Shuddup, Irvin. If you ever opened yer mouth an' anythin' but bitchin' came out, I think I'd drop dead with a heart attack."

"Promises, promises. Open th' door!"

Rechecking Miller's position, Peale was mildly surprised to find him directly behind the pair, his movement unnoticed by either the subjects or himself. He allowed a moment to be impressed, before he made his own move. Hoping nobody lurked undetected on the other side of the closed door, he stepped off the ledge.

He dropped lightly into a crouch on the pavement in front of them. They stared open-mouthed as he straightened, grabbed the smaller one, and sank fangs into the base of his neck.

Welcome, hot blood filled his mouth. The other man made small mewling noises and dropped the keys to scrabble inside his bulky coat for his weapon. The noises ceased so abruptly that Peale looked up. Galen grinned over the man dangling sack-like in his hands. "Pressure points. Gotta love 'em. Went like clockwork, didn't I tell you it would?"

Peale shifted his unconscious prey, tongue flicking a smear of blood from his lips as he replied, "We're doomed."

Miller dragged Pete to a shadowed niche just down from the door, and disarmed him. "You got no confidence. It's good planning. A good plan always goes smooth."

BC shoved sodden hair from his eyes and looked dubiously after his new partner. Somehow "We'll hang around until a couple guys show up, then you jump one and leave the other to me" didn't seem like much of a well-crafted plan. Deciding against a rejoinder, and suddenly aware of his vulnerability under the light, he hoisted Irvin, and joined Galen in the niche.

The uncertain glow from the bulb over the entrance bled into their sanctuary just enough to foul up Peale's night vision. Blinking in a futile effort to adjust, he bent to drink again, thankful for the warmth. He drank from both and they went pliable, waiting for instructions with pleasantly blank expressions.

Unnerved by the front row seat of his partner's activities, Miller moved toward brighter light and busied himself with the confiscated weapons. They were automatics, and he grunted with recognition as he ejected the clips and held them out for inspection. Peale flinched as silver glinted under the feeble light.

Their questioning produced other problems. Irvin and Pete were regulars. They made regular visits to all the warehouses to collect bills of lading for the latest shipments of weapons. They were expected, and already running late. While this was not unusual, it made the going more sticky. Galen swore. "Damn! S.I. would give a lot to lay hands on evidence like that. It wouldn't crack things wide open, but it would help."

Peale looked thoughtful. "We'll need to go in with them, then."

"Are you nuts? How we gonna do that?"

"Watch."

Peale rose and led the two thugs back to the street to stand unsteadily in front of their car. Speaking clearly, he said, "You have just arrived. Pete, you were walking around the front of the car when your foot slipped on the curbing right there. You fell."

Irvin gave an irritating snigger. Peale grinned devilishly. "Irvin laughed at you and you don't like that. Pete, you're brushing the dirt off. Irvin, you're still laughing . . . and the big guy and me? We don't exist."

Peale stepped back into the shadows beside Miller and said, "Now."

To Galen's astonishment, the punks sprang into action as instructed: Pete brushed street grit off his coat while Irvin giggled madly. Without warning, Pete planted a solid punch in the laughing face, sending Irvin sprawling onto the sidewalk inches from Galen's feet. They squared off until Irvin waved surrender, whining, "Hey, we're late enough a'ready. If we screw around any more, Eddie Michalson'll kill us hisself."

Pete considered. "Yea, or worse . . . give us to Isendamer. We better get them papers an' go."

"Don't think this is done, though, I'll take care o' you later."

Pete snatched his keys from the pavement and fitted one into the lock. "Yeah, sure. I'm real scared."

The bickering pair disappeared into the warehouse leaving the door ajar. Miller and Peale followed a short distance back. Galen whispered, "That was spooky."

"I know. I've never liked doing it. It requires a lot of concentration and the more complicated you make the memory, the less likely it is to stick. It's a lot easier to put them under and make them sleep through the whole thing."

"That's why none of the victims we questioned could remember anything."

"Victim is such an ugly word, don't you think?"

***

Hernandez crept from the cover of the loading platform, shivering involuntarily. He was more chilled by what he'd witnessed than by lying motionless, watching the creature skulk for the past three hours. Realization of how powerful the thing was sickened him, and reinforced his determination to keep his distance. As long as It was unaware of him, *he* was powerful. He could destroy It, he was sure. He'd been reading a lot and knew what to do now.

He better keep watching, especially since Miller was there. What were they doing? Why did they follow those men into that building? Whatever the reason, he'd better go, too, he couldn't afford to lose them now.

He slid to the ground and sprinted across the rain-slicked pavement.

***

Comfortable in their assigned roles, Pete and Irvin carried the quarrel into the stuffy warehouse, unaware of the pair gliding fluidly behind them. Inside the building, the argument and a gasoline motor popping nearby muffled anything short of a shout. The pair threaded through high stacks of wood and metal crates toward a brightly lit area near the middle of the floor. Without slowing, they passed a metal stair to a loft that ran the circuit of the building. BC stopped and indicated the overhang.

Miller grinned, and with Peale hard on his heels, ascended swiftly into the gloom closer to the roof. The loft was as crammed with containers as the downstairs, but the pathways between were narrower. Using the indecipherable shouting and engine noise as a beacon, they found a gap between the boxes. It wasn't directly in line with the action on the floor, and Miller's bulk filled most of the available space, but it was the best seat available.

They sprawled between the towering boxes a distance from the edge and surveyed the vista. Below, their unwitting guides stood beside a rumbling forklift, engaged in earnest conversation with three other men. Pete leafed through a sheaf of papers in a clipboard.

Galen observed, "Kind of amazing the bonehead can read. Maybe he's faking it. Hey, BC, I can't hear a thing over that racket, can you make out what they're saying?"

Peale shook his head. "It's even worse for me. We'll be relying on lip-reading unless they move away from the forklift or shut the bloody thing off."

"Damn." Gae surveyed the wall-like stacks, and shook his head with wonder. "Just *look* at all this shit!"

"Y'don't think this is all weaponry, do you?"

"Nah. I bet most of it is legitimate import stuff. Better cover in case of inspections. The other shit is probably buried in the piles until it's time to ship. Truth to tell, it's that other shit that worries me. This isn't the heart of Chicago, but it's near enough to make no nevermind. ATF will not smile, I assure you."

"Nor will anyone else, I'd imagine."

Nodding, Galen returned his attention to the floor. The surveillance wasn't going as smoothly as he'd like, but for a dry run it wasn't bad. Not to mention that turning up something of this magnitude would keep Jim's undesirable question quota to a bare minimum. He settled in for the duration.

The tight squeeze next to Miller was uncomfortable, so Peale wriggled out. Shielded by the Great Wall of Crates, he stood, and on impulse, searched for a way into the stacks. The opening he found wasn't quite wide enough. He wedged his shoulder into it, and shoved. The boxes were heavier than he'd reckoned, and resisted his efforts before grinding back with a screech like a hundred banshees. He froze. Nothing. Not even a twitch from Galen, the cacophony from below swallowed the sound.

Worming in, he saw the boxes inside were vastly different from those on the outside. Probing fingers touched paper that came away in his hand. Impatiently, he glanced at it, identified it as a shipping label in Russian, then tucked it into his inner pocket. Reaching in again, he traced the edge of the crate until he found a wider part of the crack. Smirking, he worked his fingers in and tugged.

The crate was flimsy, and the side gave with a snap and groan of nails against wood, releasing the mingled scent of excelsior, plastic and the faint aroma of oil. Looked like Galen was on the money. Groping through the packing, his smile broadened as he met a solid object wrapped in plastic. Jackpot. A Kalashnikov auto loader complete with extended clip. A quick check verified the other interior crates were identical with the first.

Intent on the pantomime below, Miller had ignored his companion's departure. Grinning, Peale lowered the rifle in front of him. "Happy Christmas. Don't say I didn't give you anything."

Galen stared at the plastic-shrouded object with dismay. "This is a Russian rifle!"

"I know. There are more in a box back there, and a rather large number of the crates were labeled in Cyrillic."

Galen turned the weapon over in his hands. "I heard a lot of military stuff went out on the black market after the Soviet government collapsed. Guess this is some of it."

"Most likely. From what you've said, our Mr. Borgia has quite a purchasing network. Someone like that isn't prone to ignore an advantageous occurrence."

Stretching past his larger companion, he peeked over the edge. "Anything useful happening down there?"

"Not a thing. They've gone over more invoices than I dreamed existed. I thought only the good guys had to deal with paperwork. Let's take exhibit K here and head for home."

Galen shimmied away from the edge before standing. Peale, glad to be quit of the dusty place, moved to follow, then stopped, eyes narrowed on something below. Falling to a crouch, he waved Miller down.

Gae dropped like a marionette with cut strings. "What?"

"I saw movement back toward the entrance. They may have posted a lookout . . .," Peale said. "No. Damn. I see who it is now; it's that Mario Hernandez."

"Y'mean God's Gift to Womankind? What the hell is the local stud doing here?"

"Following us maybe? I hate to mention this now, but I've noticed him hanging around your place a lot lately."

"Why didn't you say something?"

"I figured he was neighborhood and just hanging out."

"That makes me feel real comfortable. If he *is* following us I wonder how long he's been at it? Oh, Lord! You don't think he's connected to the Borgia organization somehow?"

"Don't know. What I *do* know is that if he isn't careful where he's going he's going to be . . . ."

The forklift operator shouted and pointed. The visitor was apparently not welcome. Two others bolted in his direction. Peale winced. "Too late."

Galen backed away in double-time. "Let's get outta here while they're occupied with Mr. Wonderful."

On the floor below, Hernandez froze, gawked in amazement at the angry people hurtling toward him, then ran back the way he came.

Bawling unintelligibly, the forklift operator produced a large automatic pistol, and before anyone could stop him, fired a burst after the intruder. The rounds missed their mark, impacting on the smooth steel sides of a largish crate inside the stack the crew was building. In the split second before his instincts propelled both Galen and himself backward, BC mentally translated the label stenciled on the metal: hand grenades.

The world exploded with an unearthly roar and lurch.

Ears ringing, Peale pulled himself from the wreckage and surveyed what was left of the warehouse. Through the smoke, he saw Miller lying a distance from the edge. Several smaller explosions knocked dust and trash from the rafters as he bulldozed crates aside to reach his friend. Burning debris floated through the air kindling paper, crating and discarded packing materials all around.

Fear choked him. Fire was one of the few things that could destroy him and this place was igniting fast. His shocky brain provided the addendum that the place was also full of munitions. One needn't be two centuries old to know munitions and fire don't mix. He clawed toward the alarmingly boneless Miller with renewed energy.

Kneeling, he forced himself be rational, and look closer. Relieved, he saw that despite a smear of blood from a cut forehead, Galen's chest still rose and fell in a regular rhythm. A large blast obliterated a chunk of flooring, flung him across Miller and rained burning debris. A second shook an immense beam from the roof, it fell across his shoulders pinning them both in place. Flames hissed and sizzled along the wooden beam, filling his nostrils with a mix of smoke and steam.

Startled, he realized he and Gae were still soaked through from the hours in the steady drizzle outside. He'd never been so happy to be wet.

Bracing against blistering-hot floorboards, he shoved upward. With a groan and crash, the charring oak shifted, allowing him to slide out from under. Ignoring heat and growing panic, he searched for a way out. At the rear, across the burning gap, a window had shattered. Before the explosion, a coating of grime rendered it invisible, but now the gaping frame offered the mixed blessing of oxygen for the flames and a means of escape.

Hoisting Miller's considerable bulk in a fireman's carry, Peale got a running start, hoping for enough momentum to carry them across. Eyes screwed shut, he leaped. The force of the heat pummeled him as he sailed over the blaze. Mid-leap, he realized he needed to see where he was landing. Too late.

He lost his grip on Miller as they slammed into a jumble of crates on the opposite side then tumbled through the splintered packaging. A cursory glance revealed that the important things were still attached as he reclaimed his burden. Gae had smacked his head a couple more times, but at least they were closer to the window. Flesh smarting from the intense heat, he locked streaming eyes on the patch of night sky, and ran for all he was worth.

He first noticed the rain. It poured down as if heaven had broken open, plastering his hair to his head, streaming down his face and sluicing away the smells of smoke, soot and blood. The roar of flames awakened memories and drew his eyes to a building engulfed in fire that stained the storm clouds red. He remembered the fire, he remembered running but he had no recollection of getting out, of reaching safety on the rooftop where he knelt.

A short distance away, Galen Miller moaned and sat up. He tried to speak, but the words turned into violent coughing. He finally managed to rasp, "What happened?"

The words snapped BC Peale a little closer to reality. "I'm not completely sure," he said, then memory kicked back in. "The grenades. The Russian hand grenades."

Miller nodded weakly. Peale regarded the pillar of flame lighting the sky and said, "When the bullet hit the crate, I expected something to happen, but this. . . ?"

Miller said, "Hard to tell how old some of that stuff was. A lot of it is unstable as all get out."

As if in answer, something inside the burning building exploded sending a plume of sparks and fiery debris high into the air. Peale pulled himself up against an air vent. "We'd better get a move on. There will be a lot of official people headed this way very soon and I don't think we should be found here." Turning back to Miller, he added, "I don't think this went well, do you?"

Galen tried to rise, but his shaky legs refused to support him. "Shut up and help me stand."

Peale helped him up, but as they limped toward the fire escape, Miller slapped himself in the forehead. "Shit! I'm not thinking straight."

Galen scrabbled in his pocket and swore as the cell phone he'd had there came out in pieces. "Dammit! I need to get Jim to give the firefighters a heads up. Those guys have no idea what they're walking into."

Peale reached inside his jacket and pulled out his smart phone. "Mine's good." He punched a few buttons on the screen and handed it to Miller. "Just enter the number and touch that button there."

Galen punched the number in fast, then paced nervously. "Pick up pick up pick — Jim! One of Borgia's warehouses just blew up. You need to give CFD and CPD the heads up that there's some nasty shit in there. Saw some Russian munitions just before everything went to hell. . . . Huh? Yeah, we're okay, but shit is cooking off." Peale motioned for the phone, Galen looked puzzled, but said, "Just a sec."

BC paged rapidly through applications, then turned the phone around for Galen to see the map with the location marked by a blinking dot. Peale hit another button and the map blinked out. Realization dawned and he said, " I sent the location to you, now I need to get the hell outta Dodge."

Nelson voice sounded hollow against the drum of the rain. "Get in here ASAP, Gae. I need to know what happened."

"Yeah. Yeah, I'll be in. Give me time to clean off—" Another explosion rocked them, shattering the remaining glass in the surrounding buildings. Sirens wailed just at the edge of hearing. Miller said, "Make that call, Jim!"

***

BC Peale warmed his hands on either side of the steaming coffee maker. It was good to have the soot washed off and even better to have clean and dry clothing from the Harley's saddlebags that didn't stink of smoke. Miller's guest bath had about everything else he'd needed, including a shower stall with a nozzle that could probably be used to remove paint. The water in Galen's bathroom cut off at the same moment that the coffee machine gave its last gurgle.

BC smirked as he pulled a stoneware mug from the cabinet. "Timing is everything."

As steaming coffee cascaded into the mug, he heard his partner muttering while the medicine chest opened and closed violently. There was no need to hear the words to get the gist. Galen was still indignant about Peale's offer of first aid after discovering what it entailed. "If I wanted to be licked, I'd have a goddamn *dog*!"

The scent of scrubbed skin, shampoo, and talc preceded the big man as he emerged and collapsed onto a stool at the counter. The line of butterfly closures arching over one singed eyebrow lent him a surprised look. Peale plunked the mug down in front of him. Miller took a deep drink and said, "Oh man, that feels great. I stood under the hot water until I look like a prune, but I'm still cold."

BC quirked a smile. "I know the feeling!."

Galen gave him a look. "Yeah. I bet you do." Setting the mug down, he said, "I phoned Jim. He got the info to the firefighters in good time. Most of it is probably cooked off by now, but it sounds like they have it handled."

He took another sip and added, "He still wants me in for a face-to-face."

Peale frowned, but remained silent. At length Galen demanded, "What?"

BC's frown deepened. "I'm not sure that's a good idea."

"What isn't? Making my report on a munitions dump that went bang at the harbor?"

"That's not what I meant."

"Oh! You want to be sure I don't tell them all about you? Too late, Kimosabe. You should have thought of that, before you whipped out that smartphone. They got your number, pal. Literally."

Peale shook his head. "It had to be done. I'd do it again in an instant. That isn't what concerns me."

"What *does* concern you, then?"

BC regarded him coolly. Obviously, the man was angry, and any excuse for an argument would do. People reacted differently to shock; Galen Miller's response was to be mad at the world that wasn't working right. On the other hand, BC Peale's reaction was more akin to fatigue, a bone-deep lassitude that made flight a more attractive option than fight. "You took some hard knocks tonight. You ought to rest rather than — look, I'd better go. I'll come by tomorrow evening to find out how it went."

Galen cradled the hot drink before draining it, then relented, "Look, man, I'm just edgy. Where are you sleeping now?"

Peale looked wary. "Why?"

Miller snapped, "Because, *partner*, I hoped you could drop me at the office so I wouldn't have to walk through the rain again."

Mollified, Peale refilled the mug and pushed it across the island. "Sure, I can do that. I can still get to my digs in plenty of time — if you can get a way back without me."

Galen hunched on the stool, elbows resting on the island top. "Peale, I thought we were partners."

"We are."

"No we're not." Peale stared blankly as Miller continued, "Partners trust each other. They watch each other's backs."

"I do watch your back! What about tonight?"

"You saved my life, and I owe you a big one, but you still don't trust me enough to tell where you stay during the day."

The vampire shifted uncomfortably, it was hard to overcome years of ingrained paranoia against revealing his boltholes. It was rare that even Jump Veron knew where he slept. "What difference does it make? I'm not very useful after sunrise."

He met the furious glare and, jaw clenched against the emotional onslaught, snatched his jacket from the back of the chair where it had been drying. "Well, if you're ready, let's go."

Miller slammed the counter making coffee slosh over the sides of the mug. "What the hell do you think I'm going to do? Sneak in and drive a stake through your stubborn heart?"

"Well, no . . . not exactly."

"Not *exactly?*"

Peale folded his arms, and dropped his gaze. He was bruised, tired, and too angry to think straight. Looking at Miller merely tempted him to lunge across the counter. "I didn't mean that the way it sounded. It's late, if I'm to take you to the office, we'd best get moving."

"No, thanks. I think I'll walk to the train station after all."

Again, they locked glares over the cooling puddle of coffee, until Peale snapped, "Right. I'm off, then." He slammed the door behind him.

Galen wasted a moment snarling at the recently slammed door, then stormed to the closet to wrench his rain gear from its hanger. If he had to walk to the station, he better go now. Bruised muscles protested as he slid his arms into the slicker. A long series of train rides lay between home and SIHQ, he hoped he wouldn't stiffen up too much on the train, he'd hate to walk in like the Frankenstein monster. To hell with it, he'd take the direct route. It was so damned late and he was so damned tired, once wouldn't make that big a difference.

***

Hernandez crouched in the doorway across the alley from Miller's place. Miller usually used the back way and this shadowy stoop had a perfect view. He shook his head in the gloom. His ears were still ringing from the explosions. He was lucky to be alive. The guys who chased him weren't so lucky. He gulped queasily at the memory of tumbled brick and twisted flesh.

He still didn't know why Miller and the creature were at the ware-house. The demon simply bit the two men then let them go. That was weird. Vampires killed anyone they bit — unless they made them slaves. Was that it? He saw those same guys in the warehouse just before they came after him with guns, and things started blowing up. He didn't see the Monster, though. Or Miller.

At first, he'd hoped the fire would destroy the vampire for him. He'd watched the blaze until his heart sank as the creature leaped from a window onto the next rooftop, then escaped carrying something big over Its shoulder. The sirens came then, and Mario ran. With his record, being found near a fire . . . well it wouldn't be fun. No way he wanted to answer the questions they'd ask. They'd never believe him, anyway.

He headed straight here. As soon as he saw the Monster leap free of the burning building, he knew it would come back here. It took longer than he thought, but he was right. A little while ago, the creature all but carried Miller into the apartment, and nobody came out since. Did it kill Miller, or maybe was going to spend the day there? The only way to know was to wait.

Hernandez reflexively pressed into the darkness as the door opened. The Monster emerged and stomped over to the motorcycle under the carport. Wishing he could follow, Mario watched the creature kick-start the machine, and roar away at breakneck speed. If he could follow to Its hiding place, he could end the trouble once and for all, but the cops impounded his 'Vette, so he had only his two feet. That didn't count for much.

As he stared after the motorcycle, the door opened again, surprising him back into his refuge. He tensed, as Miller, wearing a plastic rain slicker, strode purposefully down the alley to the street. He brightened. Maybe he wasn't out of luck after all.

***

Dog-tired, and preoccupied with concealing the mind-games Peale used to get into the warehouse, Miller would have been hard pressed to notice a herd of elephants boarding the car behind his, let alone a single man. In spite of efforts to reason it away, anger at Peale still seethed. It was a question of trust pure and simple. BC didn't trust him. That hurt. Sure, they hadn't worked together long. . . .

Aw, nuts.

Maybe he'd pushed too hard. Peale had been on his own for a long time, and if he couldn't loosen up so fast — loosen up nothin', the blood-sucking bastard thought he wanted to drive a stake through his goddamned heart. The train shuddered to a halt. Miller hunched into his slicker and strode onto the platform wondering if Mick still had the mallet and stake he'd fished out of the trash. He hoped so. He'd love to toss them into Peale's lap next time he showed up. Enjoying the image, he stalked toward the Sentry building ignorant of his shadow.

***

Hernandez stood by the massive lighted sign in the rolling, landscaped lawns surrounding the walkway. Sentry International? Maybe Miller was walking past it, going somewhere else? Ducking behind the stone support of the sign, he watched. No such luck, the man in the shiny raincoat made straight for the entrance. Oh God. Was Miller a *cop*?

Melding farther into the plantings to mull this over, he spotted another person jogging across the parking lot on an intercept course with Miller. When the runner passed under the glow of the mercury lights, Mario real-ized he knew this one, too. Miguel Marquez, Jay's brother. He used to be with the Chicago police, and he was pretty sure Jay said he quit to work for Sentry International. This was too dangerous. He'd better duck out before someone saw him. If Miller was one of *them*, they'd never believe anything Hernandez said. Worse — what if they already knew?

***

Mick Marquez clutched his bag of aromatic White Castle burgers and sprinted across the glistening asphalt. He'd developed his sudden craving for sliders as a way to escape the office and intercept his buddy on neutral ground and it was about to go all to hell. Unless the Gloucester Fisherman was way off course, the big guy in the rain slicker up ahead had to be Galen Miller. He was early, too. If the girl who built his burgers had been any slower, they'd have missed entirely. He didn't want that to happen. He had a few questions for Gae best asked in private.

The closer he got, the madder and more ragged around the edges Gae looked. For a moment he wondered if it was a good time to bring Peale up. No. There was something that left a bad taste in his mouth, and God only knew when he'd have another shot at Galen alone. He'd been a cop too long to ignore gut feelings, and until he knew what was making his alarms go off, he wouldn't be comfortable. Peale's name was popping up too frequently to let it pass and tonight, it had been Peale's phone Galen used to call in from the scene. Loping up, he fell in step with Miller. "Hey, Gae! Hear one of your guy's warehouses blew up real good tonight!"

Galen smiled ruefully, the stark white of the butterfly bandages glowed in the gloom. "No shit! I was in it when it went. Surprised I'm not still smokin'."

Mick chuckled. "Naw, whoever stomped you out, got it all." Abruptly his manner turned challenging. "Was it Peale who doused you?"

Ignoring the rain dripping into his face from the crumpled hood, Galen stopped, and studied Marquez. "Oh. The penny drops. I knew something was stuck in your craw." Mick was so damned by-the-book, it was only a matter of time before Gae's unorthodox approach got to him. Good thing he didn't know the truth, yet. Talk about unorthodox. "What if he was, Miguel? Peale's been a big help to me on this. You're the Deputy Director, you've read my reports."

"Yeah, I've read the reports and I admit he's turned some good intel, but Gae, this is sensitive stuff. What do we know about him? Can we trust this guy?"

Trust was a bad word choice. Galen jabbed a finger into Mick's chest, making the smaller man stagger. "Yeah! Yeah, I can trust that guy with my life! Good thing, too, or they'd be sifting the ashes of that warehouse right now tryin' to figure out which pieces used to be me."

Mick was stunned, but looking Gae full in the face, he knew it was true. He wondered if Jim knew how close they'd come to losing him. Couldn't. He'd never call a face-to-face if he did.

Jaw muscles twitching with barely suppressed rage, Galen pivoted, and stalked into the building. Finding his voice, Mick called after the retreating slicker, "Okay! So I'm outta line and he saved your butt tonight. Don't forget, 'mano, Peale is a musician, not a cop and we don't know squat about him. Regulations —"

Galen stopped in his tracks, and without turning, growled, "Regulations be damned. Standard procedure got us exactly nowhere on this one. That's why they brought me in, remember? I was told to play it any way it worked. Now, if it doesn't ruffle your delicate sensibilities, I have to make a report, and get home before regular business hours catch up to me, and we all turn into pumpkins."

Galen punched his code into the scanner with lethal force, then marched inside. Mick followed the oil-skinned time bomb into the building, and they rode the elevator up in silence. In the common room, Miller stomped to his cubicle, leaving Marquez standing alone. Zoeller poked her head around her doorway and drew back quickly when the Deputy Director absently waved her away before disappearing into the Director's office.

Inside his own cubicle, dropped into his chair and scrubbed hard at his face as if he could rub the tired away. "Well, that was smart, Special Agent Miller. Dumbass. Think by now, I'd be able to control my temper better." It didn't help he was already white-hot mad at Peale before Mick pulled his chain. Sure, he trusted Peale, it just didn't work the other way around. The only way the night could get any worse would be a direct hit from a meteorite through the office window.

"Gae?"

On the other hand, the meteorite might be an improvement. "Yes, Captain, what is it?"

Jim Nelson stepped into the tiny enclosure wishing it had a door to close behind him. In the stark fluorescent light, Galen looked even worse than Mick said. "Hey, don't get pissy with me because you and Mick mixed it up. I didn't authorize it, you know better than that."

Gae slumped. "Sorry, Jimbo. It's been a ba-a-a-ad night."

"So I hear."

Pulling the visitor's chair around, Nelson straddled it and looked his friend over. He didn't like what he saw. Damn Mick for starting an argument tonight of all nights. Yes, taking on a civilian partner was an unorthodox move, but Gae was infamous for success through unorthodox moves. Jim trusted his judgment. Sure, the partnership with a civilian bugged him, but he intended to let it ride to see if the pair made any progress. He'd kick Mick's ass later, he'd follow his first inclination now. "You look like shit. Have the medics checked you out?"

Galen wasn't tracking well, and this was an unexpected question. All he could muster was a vaguely surprised blink. Jim prompted, "Mick said you were *in* the explosion tonight."

Gae collected himself and said, "Not exactly *in* it, more running like hell on the edges of it . . . it'll all be in the report."

"Forget the damned report for now, Gae. I want you checked over, then I want you to go home. If I'd known about this earlier I'd have sent a doc over and had you phone the report tomorrow. Damn the security arrangements! *Tell* me next time."

Galen gawked. There hadn't been time for Mick to go off about their argument, still he was bound to have vented about Peale even before he approached Galen. Why wasn't Jim mentioning it? To his foggy mind, *pointedly* not mentioning it. Something wasn't clicking, but he ached too much to care. "Okay, I'll see the docs, but I'm fine."

Jim stood. "You don't *look* fine, now get out of here. Call me tomorrow."

Galen gratefully escaped.

EIGHT

Maeve Donal stepped from the debarkation tube into the concourse, reseating the padded strap of her voluminous carry-all on her shoulder. At the end of the ramp she paused to let the pleasurable sights and sounds of constant motion wash over her. She liked big cities, and though Chicago wasn't her favorite, it had much to offer. It was ages since her last visit; she anticipated a pleasant adventure sampling the changes. Brushing an errant wave of red-gold hair aside, her eyes lit on the steward who'd flirted with her since New York. He smiled invitingly. She'd never liked exploring alone.

He was her type, tall, slender, dark haired, and handsome . . . so very like . . . . Oh, damn Frankie for calling in that particular favor. She'd worked hard to get those feelings under control. Stirring them up again was unwelcome, but a debt was a debt regardless of the outcome of the favor granted. She reexamined the steward. No. With old passions reawakening, he just wasn't like enough to substitute for the real thing. Still, he was comely in his own right. She enjoyed blowing a kiss before blending into the throng.

The short walk to the gate was marked by the conspicuous absence of familiar faces, and the assemblage on the other side of the barriers was no different. She frowned. Damn the man again, he was supposed to meet her, and here she'd booked a night flight expressly for that purpose. Easing out of the pedestrian traffic, she took a deep breath, opening all her senses for a glimmer of a familiar presence. She broke off trying. Chicago O'Hare International Airport was a big place, full of distractions, and she *really* needed quiet to find the likes of Francesco Borgia. There was nothing else

for it, but to simply wait for her fellow passengers to disperse, then see who
— if anyone — was left.

***

On the other side of the gate, Carlo Alberti stood at quasi-attention, scanning the stream of disembarking passengers, well aware of the fine figure he
presented in his blue chauffeur's uniform. In spite of his height, he craned to
peer into the roiling humanity, trying to ignore the jostling reunions around
him. He only had an abbreviated description to go by, and felt like he should
be holding up one of those ridiculous cardboard placards with 'DONAL'
scrawled across it. Presently, the crowd thinned, leaving one woman standing on the passenger side of the gate. She turned a heart-shaped, peaches
and cream face toward him. He caught his breath.

Signor Borgia told him to look for the most beautiful woman there.
Carlo had nodded politely. One did not question an instruction *Il Padrone*
gave, it was known to be an unhealthy occupation. He'd chalked it up to a
flattering compliment, and concluded he'd be looking for a pretty woman.
Non è! The description was accurate.

Unconsciously straightening his uniform, he assumed his most charming smile and waved to attract her attention. Speculatively, she approached,
graceful body sinuous under the silk suit. Bowing slightly, he inquired, "*Scusi,
signorina*, would you be Ms. Donal?"

Cool gray-blue eyes swept him from head to foot. *Ah, yes,* she decided, *once again Frankie reverts to type.* No matter where he took up
residence, Francesco Borgia heavily salted his domestic staff with Italian
nationals. She suspected he disliked speaking anything but his birth tongue
unless absolutely forced to. This lad fit every one of Francesco's criteria.
With his stature and fine looks, in previous centuries, he'd have been a
liveried footman. She wondered idly if this youth had other, more intimate,
things in common with past well-favored servants. There was usually at
least one. Dismissing the thought, she smiled graciously.

"I am. And who would you be?"

The lilting Irish accent added to the lady's allure leaving him uncharacteristically flustered. "I am Carlo, Signore Borgia's chauffeur. I am instructed to request the lady to join him for a drink in the upper lounge. I am to collect your luggage and summon you when I have loaded it into the limousine."

Of course Francesco would delegate. It was an integral part of the man. As far as she could tell, it was an integral part of the clan. She had yet to meet a Borgia lacking an imperious glint at the core. Slipping the bag smoothly from her shoulder, she relinquished it, smiling sweetly at his manly attempt to act unsurprised at the weight of it. "Thank you, Carlo, a drink sounds lovely. Now, I have five other bags that match this one, and a trunk. So, if you'll be pointin' the way to the lounge, I'll be on me way and leave you to your job."

Carlo had a way with directions that was the mark of a good driver, so in spite of the maze-like floor plan of the terminal, she soon stood in front of the intimately lit lounge enjoying the inviting sounds of china and glassware. Before entering, she brushed the patrons with her mind, then smiled. There was no trouble finding Frankie at this distance. If one knew what to look for, a vampire always stood out.

He was in the back, absently stirring a drink, apparently lost in thought and unaware of her arrival. He was likely bent on *not* noticing anything. To one with his enhanced senses and solitary nature, being in the midst of a mass of humanity was like drowning.

Weaving through the tightly packed tables, she took advantage of his absorption for a quick inspection. He hadn't changed a whit — but then, his type of undead didn't. From across the room, she admired how the expensive cut of his suit accented the lines of his slightly stocky body, and how the styling of his wavy black hair with its distinctive white streak over the left brow emphasized the strength of his square-jawed face. As always, his appearance told the observer at a glance this was a powerful man.

Francesco's passion for fine clothing and pride in his superb body was a constant throughout the time she'd known him. It *was* a superb body, too. Briefly, they'd been lovers, sharing an intense physical relationship but little else. A romantic entanglement gives those entangled a certain power over each other. Back then, she was very young, and anxious to know all there was to know about the man she found so exciting. Unfortunately, Francesco did not share. He dominated. The more each tried to assert themselves, the more their love-making came to resemble battles until one dawn, Maeve packed her belongings and vacated the palazzo. Francesco thundered and protested, but didn't come after her. They still enjoyed each other's company now and again, but the fiery passion slowly devolved into a strong friendship.

Abruptly, she was awash in a battering sea of memories, and through blurred vision, saw instead of Francesco, a taller, more slender man. As she struggled for breath, the vision lifted a tousled, dark head and the long face split with a roguish smile. She gasped, shook herself angrily, and the irritating apparition vanished leaving her slightly dizzy in it's wake. Well, that hadn't happened in a long time, and she hadn't missed it at all. A pity *some* passions didn't devolve as smoothly as others.

Composing herself, she scanned the crowd. Conversation still buzzed. If anyone noticed her brief seizure, they were hiding it well. More importantly, Francesco didn't notice. She was glad, but it made her marvel at the strength of the barriers he'd erected. They were powerful to block such a sudden and intense burst. Fine. He needn't know she was still troubled, besides, it was his fault for opening old wounds, wasn't it? That blasted enigmatic telephone call triggered it all.

The sooner she got to the table, the sooner she'd learn why the powerful Francesco Borgia needed her to dash halfway around the globe on such short notice. Well, Frankie never cried wolf, if he said it was important, it was. Gliding to his side, she planted a loud kiss on his ear. Enjoying his startlement, she slid into the opposite chair, enthusing, "Francesco, Love, it's so good t'see you! I suppose I ought t'be furious with you for lettin' *eons* go by with no word, then all of a sudden there you are, bein' ever so mysterious with 'Maeve, I need you this instant!' And all the time knowin' it's curiosity that'll do your dirty work for gettin' me here." Lashes lowered coquettishly, she demanded, "Here I sit fair consumed with curiosity. Now tell me. Why am I here?"

His pleasure was genuine, same Maeve as ever. Quicksilver tongue and mind to match. He hadn't anticipated enjoying her company so much. Clucking at her with mock severity, he replied as he signaled the waiter. "*Pazienza, cara mio!* Allow a moment for us to catch up with each other. You would like a drink, perhaps?"

Tapping a lacquered nail on the rim of the well-stirred Bloody Mary in front of him, she said, "I'll have one of those."

Amused, she watched him worry the celery stalk in his glass. Even when buying a drink to appear normal, Francesco still went for red. Too bad she couldn't share this with him, he was notoriously lacking in the sense of humor department, especially where it concerned himself. She chatted idly until the drink came, then waiter safely out of earshot, took a dainty sip. "Frankie, you didn't jet me all the way to Chicago simply to bring each other up to date. That's what telephones and postcards are for."

He winced at the shortened form of his name, he disliked such informality and she knew it. Precisely why she did it. Maeve reveled in irreverence. Protesting was useless, it hadn't helped in three hundred years, it wouldn't make a speck of difference now. With an inward sigh, he answered, "What I need, Dear One, are your special talents for locating . . . an individual."

Blue-gray eyes narrowed over the rim of the glass. "With your own special talents, someone has been able to elude you? There's more to it than that."

"This person seems to be a great deal like myself. In fact, we share the same blood disorder."

Realization flashed like lightning. "That complicates matters considerably, Darlin'. Certain immunities are part of the package and you know that better than most."

Although her outward composure remained unperturbed, he could smell her discomfiture like a heady perfume, and in spite of his own problems, savored the moment. Seeing Maeve shaken was such a rare occurrence, he couldn't suppress a smile. "*Daverro*, as you say, I understand the condition very well, but I have the utmost confidence in your ability to overcome such obstacles."

Eyes swiveling toward the concourse, he exclaimed, "Ah! There is Carlo. We must go." Tossing a large denomination bill onto the table and without leaving space for a reply, he pulled back her chair. "I trust you have not been too fatigued by your journey, Maeve. I've taken the liberty of having a room specially prepared and I would like to begin our project tonight."

She surveyed him with eyebrows cocked in speculation, if he enjoyed her discomfort in learning her quarry was another vampire, the tables were turned now. It was late, and the preparations for her incantations were time-consuming. It would be uncomfortably near dawn before she could begin. Francesco's urgency was crystal clear, he was a territorial creature at the best of times, and this was not the best of times. She eagerly anticipated prying the story out of him in the car; it was bound to be entertaining. She observed dryly, "You want to start tonight? This one must be givin' you a *lot* of trouble!"

Francesco's scowl was quickly quashed, but Maeve considered the point hers. Laughing, she preceded him into the concourse.

***

Galen marveled at his apparent good fortune all the way home. Aside from

Mick, nobody mentioned Peale, and in spite of Doc Klotski's disapproving grunts, his injuries weren't serious. He'd been hurt worse on the gridiron. Regardless, he was happy to put distance between himself and SIHQ. When the Doc released him, he found Kim Zoeller in the waiting room, car keys in hand, offering a lift. He was grateful for both the ride and the companionable silence.

Surprised at how he'd stiffened on the ride home, he swallowed a groan as he waved goodnight to Zoeller from the stoop. In concession to his tortured muscles, he used the elevator rather than face the single flight to the basement. Slotting his latchkey into the cylinder, he wondered how Peale was faring in the aftermath. With his healing rate, the bastard was probably ready to party the rest of the night away. Damn his undead hide, anyway.

"That didn't take nearly as long as I'd feared."

It came from behind him — but the hallway was empty when he entered. He whirled, reaching instinctively for the weapon nestled at the small of his back.

Peale leaned casually against the wall. As he stepped into the wan glow of the overhead light, Galen saw he was damp from the still-falling rain. Miller's anger erupted. "What the hell do *you* want?"

With a visible flinch, Peale paused, then suppressed a flash of temper. "I deserved that." Resolutely, he continued, "Look, I didn't like leaving you to take all the heat tonight. No pun intended. I came back and waited to be sure everything went okay with Captain Nelson."

Twitching with rage, Galen threw the door open and stalked into the flat, flinging over his shoulder, "What are you waitin' for, an engraved invitation? Get your butt in here, I want to talk to you, anyway."

BC grinned. Gae was pissed off, but at least he was talking. Closing the door firmly behind him, he thrust his hands into his jacket pockets, and watched the big man ineffectually struggling out of the wet slicker. There was no easy way to do this. "I wanted to say I was sorry about being such an asshole. I was unnecessarily paranoid."

Victorious over the clinging oilskins, Galen flung the garment onto the linoleum. "That's what you came all the way back here in the rain to say?"

"Sort of." Clenched fists dug deeper in the pockets, knuckles making distinct dents against the damp leather. "Okay! I was scared tonight. Fire can kill me, too, and then when I thought you'd bought it . . . anyway, I've been riding around thinking, kicking myself for giving in to paranoia. It becomes a habit after a while. Damnation! I was staying in an cemetery crypt north of here, but I've moved into an old rail tunnel so as to be closer to your flat."

Galen gasped, "Good God, Peale! Those tunnels are damp and collapsing — and they've got *rats*!"

"Not all of them are damp, just the ones nearest the river. They suit my needs, they're dark, abandoned and once I go down, comfort isn't all that important. Believe me. I've stayed in far worse places." He added thoughtfully, "I'll admit, though, I'm not fond of the rats."

"There's gotta be a better place."

"Well, I certainly can't check into a Best Western!"

"I know, but. . . ."

BC dived aside as the door behind him opened precipitously, and a handsome, elderly woman entered carrying a covered plate. She said, "Hi, honey! I couldn't sleep, an' I was messin' in the roof greenhouse so don't yell about bein' spied on. I saw you comin' in an' thought you might like dinner. This time of mornin' it's breakfast for the rest of the world, but for you — Galen Samuel Miller! What in heaven's name happened to you?"

Eyes widening, she stopped and whirled toward Peale. She jabbed a finger toward the stranger, demanding, "What is *that* doin' in my house?"

Galen silently asked heaven if two escapes in one night meant his luck allotment was shot. He hurriedly relieved her of the plate. Trying to sound conversational, he said, "Mama, I'd like you to meet BC Peale, he's—"

Treating him to a look that announced to all and sundry that her son had finally lost his mind, she exploded, "I don't need to know *who* it is, I know *what* it is. And you do, too, don't you?"

Hands firmly clamped to the edge of the door, BC regarded the woman with an awe that threatened to become terror at a moment's notice. This was Galen's mother? She was powerful to sense his presence without having seen him. Jump Veron was the only other individual who could do that, even then it was an uncomfortable feeling — and Jump *liked* him. To all appearances, he wasn't so fortunate with Mrs. Miller. Verging on panic, he opened his senses to detect any charms of the sort that burned him at the club. No luck.

Charm or no charm, he deemed it advisable to beat a hasty retreat. Edging around as best he could, he stammered, "I think I'd best be off, Galen, we can talk later. Maybe I'll ring you tomorrow evening. Very pleased to have met you, Mrs. Miller."

Wrenching out of her son's grasp, she advanced on the cowering creature of the night effectively blocking escape. "Don't Mrs. Miller me, you walking corpse! With you in this house, it's no wonder I couldn't sleep." She turned on Galen. "Now I know why you wanted that charm: This *is* the vampire from the papers! If I'd known you was goin' to bring it home with you I would have skinned you alive before lettin' you out that door."

Watching his mother's bosom heave angrily, and his terrorized partner pressed against the wall, Galen longed to hide under his bed until it all went away. He didn't have that option, though. Besides, he hadn't fit under his bed since he was ten. Inserting himself between them, he said, "Mama, BC is a friend, and before you say anything else, I want you to know this *man* pulled your son out of a burning building tonight. If it wasn't for BC, I wouldn't be standing here arguing with you right now."

Giving the statement time to sink in, he turned to BC who was eying the now-clear route to safety with open longing. "Don't even think about it, pal. And before you go gettin' cocky, don't forget I saved *your* butt the other night an' I'm gettin' damn' tired of having to defend you to my friends and family!"

Slamming the door with a force likely to pop the veneer off, he turned to find his mother staring at him, her face dangerously gray with shock. "I knew this job would kill you just like it killed your Daddy." She paused to catch her breath then, in a stronger voice, demanded, "What do you mean going' into a burning building anyway?"

BC stirred from his intent study of the denied exit, and interjected absently, "Oh, it wasn't on fire when we went in. It only caught fire *after* the crate of hand-grenades exploded."

"*Hand-grenades?*"

Galen's complexion darkened several shades. "Thanks a lot, partner. I would have had *so* much trouble explaining things to my mother without your help. Don't forget we still have to talk about why you left that rifle behind."

BC's eyes went wide. "Well *you* brought the subject up, not me! As to the rifle, pardon me for having my hands full of ex-quarterback."

"I was *never* a quarterback!"

Peale opened his mouth, then snapped it shut with decision. "Look, we can hash this out later. It's getting toward daybreak. I'm leaving."

Galen was shaking his head vigorously before the statement was completed. "No way. We're not through with this, you'll just have to crash here again."

They'd forgotten the third person in the room until reminded by her agonized shriek: "*AGAIN?* Do you mean to tell me that thing's been sleepin' in this house?"

Startled, BC stepped toward the door only to be brought up short by Galen's fist locked onto his lapel. "Galen, I really must go," he said keeping his voice as even as possible.

Neither Miller was paying him the least attention. He debated shucking his jacket and making a dash for it as Galen informed his mother, "He spent the day here last Saturday."

Mrs. Miller regarded the mismatched duo with undisguised horror. BC didn't need psychic abilities to see what direction she thought her son's association with the vampire was taking. Casting about for a way to assuage her, he blurted, "It wasn't what you're thinking. Galen pulled a silver bullet out of me Friday night. I was too sick to leave."

With a fatalistic mien, Mrs. Miller sat on the couch, then gestured pointedly to the flanking chairs. "You're right, Galen, we're *not* through with this. You boys better sit down and get comfortable, this is likely to take a while."

BC looked from one determined face to the other with a sensation of dread, then sank obediently into the nearest chair.

***

The candles guttered each time Francesco sailed by in the orbit he'd paced since she began the spell. She wished he would stand still. No she didn't. He *did* stop periodically, then spent the time looming. Looming was worse.

Watching him fidget, she knew much of it was because of the sun poised on the horizon. If only it were as simple to explain her own difficulties. Try as she might, she couldn't raise a whisper of Frankie's rogue. Something blocked her whichever way she turned, but she couldn't fathom what it was. Was it that she'd rushed the incantations? Complex spells required the caster to center in preparation for the exchange of energies, and she'd been allowed precious little time for that.

She smiled, wondering what Frankie the Impatient would say if she blamed the failure on jet-lag. The notion so tickled her, she bent her head farther into the smoking incense so he wouldn't notice the wide smile. Sometimes, his lack of humor was hard to deal with. Oh well. Sitting back on her heels, she dropped her hands into her lap with finality. "It's no use, darlin'.

We'd best chuck it and start afresh tomorrow evening."

Halting in mid-step, he fixed her with a stony glare. "You're giving up already?"

She reached for her robe. "I'm not giving up. I'm suggestin' we quit for tonight."

Borgia stalked to where she knelt. "Dammit, woman, this is *important*!"

Maeve leaped up, flashing eyes inches from his own. "An' well I'm aware of it! You've only been regalin' me with the whole sordid saga since I got off the plane. I've no love for the business you've set yourself up in, but I owe you for past favors an' I'm doin' all I can. Trackin' a vampire that's not wantin' to be found is well-nigh impossible and you should know that, Francesco Borgia."

He deflated and scrubbed at his face with both hands. It was near-dawn and everything ached. "*Daverro*, Maeve, I do know. My only excuse is that this is more worrisome than I have words for. Whether you approve or not, I have worked to build what I have, and this renegade has undermined it all in less than a twelvemonth." He treated her to a tired smile as he watched her dress. "It's good to have you here; I cannot truly speak my mind with these mortals who surround me. Until you sat across from me in the restaurant, I had not realized how much I missed such companionship."

Maeve slipped her arms around him coquettishly. "An' th' sun'll be up in a matter of minutes which does nothin' t'improve your disposition. You'd better be gettin' yourself to your restin' place. We'll try again when we're both fresh."

Slipping his own arm around her shoulders, he guided her toward the hallway. "*Ammesso.* I can feel myself slowing even as we speak. We'll take up where we left off as soon as I rise tonight, for now, I have instructed Carlo to put your things in the rooms adjoining my own . . . ."

Maeve interrupted, "You shouldn't have gone to the trouble, Francesco, I've already reserved a suite at the Hyatt. I've been promisin' myself some heavy duty shopping first thing tomorrow an' I'll not put up with trippin' over your security people to be about it."

He froze. She'd expected this. He couldn't stand not having complete control. Trouble was, she couldn't either. The ambient temperature dropped ten degrees as he politely stated, "I would prefer you stayed here, my dear."

She pulled away with a rippling laugh, and patted his cheek. He hated it when she did that. "Of course you would, but I'll be goin' anyway — that is unless you plan to hold me prisoner?"

Attempting to hold Maeve Donal against her will was a dangerous proposition and his security people, good as they were, would be power-less to stop an adept witch without his assistance. She left him no other option. He should have seen it coming. "*Vai via*! I shall instruct Carlo to deliver you to your lodgings and to accompany you on your buying expedi-tion if you so desire."

"Thank you, m'dear. To show m' appreciation, I'll postpone the shop-ping excursion. I'll get some sleep, then spend the day preparing to scry right after sunset."

Leaving Francesco slightly mollified, she sashayed away. *Actually, I'll be tryin' right at sunset, Francesco, but on my own. You're testy enough as it is without my sayin' that I believe your own presence is foulin' this spell as much as the outside interference. I've no idea why that is, but I mean to find out.*

NINE

He rushed for the back room clutching Peale in his arms. They'd talked too long, and the sun was rising. Shafts of sunlight from the windows struck the vampire full on the face, and he writhed, his flesh smoking and melting. Galen tightened his hold but convulsions threw his smoldering burden heavily to the floor. Transfixed by horror, he watched the now-still form dissolve into a vaguely human-shaped pile of ashes.

He fell to his knees trying to remember what to do, he was *sure* Peale told him in case something like this happened. What was it? *WHAT*?

His mother came from behind, shaking her head at the pitiful pile. Galen pleaded, "Mama! What do we do now?"

Mama calmly flipped the switch of her heavy-duty red vacuum cleaner, and began to suck the remains through the nozzle. Galen shrieked, "MAMA! That's BC!"

Mama scolded, "Now Galen, I've told you time and again, if you can't keep your friends up off the carpet, you're just gonna have to play with 'em outside."

***

Galen sat bolt upright in bed, the sweat-soaked covers tangled around his legs. It was a dream. He should have known it was a dream, Mama's vacuum cleaner was blue.

Man! He must still be asleep, why else would he think a dumb thing like that. Lolling in the rumpled bed, he pulled the pillow across his face. The bedside phone jangled unpleasantly. He rolled over, fumbled for it and hauled it under the pillow. "Mmmmmph? Yello."

Two voices cried, *"Happy Birthday, Dad!"*

Coming instantly awake, he exclaimed, "Jazz! Drew! What are you talking about?" Groping for his watch in the darkness, he pressed the light button on its side and squinted at the display. "I got a couple of kids who can't read a calendar, my birthday's a week away!"

Jasmine Miller (the younger) explained, "We know, but we'll be on a plane by two o'clock and on location with Mom tomorrow, so we had to call today. It'll be a bear to put the call through on your real birthday."

Drew excitedly added, "We're going to Tunisia! Mom's directing a made for cable movie there. Coolness."

Galen laughed. "Coolness? Not in the Tunisia I know about. You're talkin' *hot*ness there."

His son groaned in exasperation. Thirteen-year-olds took things very seriously. He said, "Dad! You know what I mean."

The sound quality changed as another instrument was lifted, then Fiona's smooth voice interrupted, "Okay, you two, you've had your turn. Get off the line and let the old lady have a shot at your father."

Jasmine laughed, "Uh oh."

Drew interjected, "Duck and run, Dad!"

The faint click as the other receiver went down barely sounded before she began, "Galen, I'm contracted to do a series of commercials later this year and . . . well, the advertising people want you in them."

Galen rolled his eyes toward the dark ceiling, trust Fiona to get to the meat of the matter. Ordinarily he appreciated directness, but there were times a bit of preamble would be nice. Recent conversations with his ex were a case in point. He adored their two kids and, yes, he *did* still care for Fiona, but lately. . . .

"Gae? Are you still there? Did you hear what I said?"

He sighed, "Yeah, I'm still here and I know about the offer, Mama told me and I told *her* I wasn't interested."

"Uhn hunh, that's what she said, but we hoped I could change your mind."

"Right. Just how were you planning to do that?"

Fiona put on her sultry seductress voice, "I have my ways and wiles."

"All the way from Tunisia! You have talents I was previously unaware of!"

She laughed. "The filming is only scheduled for six weeks, Gae. I thought it would be nice if the kids and I could arrange a stopover in Chicago after that. How does that sound?"

"I sense a definite threat to my physical well-being!"

"You're tough, you can handle it. I'll chalk that up as a yes, now, how about that ad campaign?"

"Tell them to line up another linebacker. I did that scene when I was still playing and you *know* I hated it! I still come across my own face starin' at me over a can of shaving cream from time to time. It's enough to make me grow a beard!"

"Galen!"

"You can still come to Chicago to convince me, if you want."

The muffled voice of an adolescent boy sounded, "Gawd! They're gettin' into the mush now!"

Another muffled, but mortified, voice announced, "Moron! I told you to keep quiet!"

A sharp click was followed by a splutter of laughter from his wife. There were times he missed family life so much it hurt. He said, "The peril of a multi-phone home, sounds like you got a situation to handle. Enjoy Tunisia!"

"Deserter!"

"Yep. Bye!"

Smiling into the darkness, he savored the news. He'd see them in three weeks. That was good, he'd seen them at Christmas, but that was always so hectic, he didn't consider it a *real* visit. He mentally reviewed the roster of tenants. No vacant apartments, damn. He'd have to let Mama know they were coming — if she didn't know already. Unless the situation changed drastically in three weeks, they'd be staying at her place; Fiona liked to keep a distance between them.

That was probably best in the long run, especially in view of his new partner. The nearly-forgotten dream came back. He'd have to tell BC about it tonight, he should get a hoot out of it. Actual events didn't go as awry as the dream, but they came close. The three of them talked until Mama noticed Peale was nearly comatose in the armchair. They'd shooed him to the cot in Galen's spare room while Mama groused how she didn't want him there, but be damned if she'd let a guest be reduced to a pile of dust in *her* house.

He wasn't sure, but Mama *might* be on the way to accepting Peale. He wouldn't put money on it yet. If she hadn't accepted his law enforcement career after all this time, God knew how long it would take before she viewed his vampiric partner as a good guy. Mama didn't give up easily.

Just like she never gave up on the TV thing. She and Fiona were cooking something up to make him change his mind, that was a given. Fat chance. Fiona was always trying to get people in front of her cameras. He wondered what would happen when he introduced his ex to BC. Galen's grin broadened. With Peale's looks and accent, Fiona would probably try to sign him for a commercial, too. Probably for toothpaste.

***

The novel wasn't holding his attention. Snapping the book closed, he flung it aside, and checked his pistol. Again. He hated playing bodyguard, and at this time of day 'body' was accurate. He sometimes wondered why he was working for Borgia in the first place, let alone occupying a top position. He snorted, "What is this, Eddie? Gettin' your pride hurt? Just 'cause you got th' title of Vice-President of th' Este Corporation, you think you're too good for th' job you started with?"

He jammed the weapon back into its holster. Talking to himself now. Geez. That was bad, but pulling daytime duty in the Boss' anteroom always got under his skin. Not that he didn't understand the need. It only took one overzealous employee barging into Borgia's sleeping chamber to gum up the works. He'd consider the measures paranoid if it hadn't happened.

Back when Michalson was a brand-new Vice President, a senior accountant uncovered evidence of embezzlement. Outraged, the man sprinted past the guards, and barged straight into Borgia's sleeping chamber. Finding his employer lying dead on the antique canopied bed sent the idiot running in a panic straight to Eddie who calmed him down, and stashed him away from the rest of the employees until dusk.

He brought the incident to the Boss' attention as soon as he rose. Coolly, Borgia summoned both accountant and embezzler to his office. When all were present, he snatched up the embezzler, and drained him of the last drop of blood. The accountant was high-strung, and the 'demonstration' was more than he could bear. That same night, he flung himself from the roof of the building. Eddie was proud he hadn't tossed — until later when he was alone. He never forgot it, though. He'd *never* forget it. The message *This could be you* was very clear.

No, he wasn't likely to forget the warning, nor was he likely to betray the trust the Boss placed in him. It wasn't a question of fear. Eddie was afraid, no denying that, but more importantly, he *respected* Borgia. Francesco Borgia was a smart guy, and ran a tight organization. Five hundred years of experience was a real advantage in this business.

Regardless, he never got used to Borgia's condition, and now there were *two* vampires. When the Boss first discovered another vampire was hunting on his turf, he went bananas. It was like some kind of personal insult. Eddie remained unconvinced the hits were aimed at them specifically. He tried to explain that to Borgia, but he might as well been talking to a cement block for all the good it did. He stopped trying.

In fact, after studying the pattern, Michalson discovered there wasn't one. The hits were random, and maybe shouldn't even be called 'hits' since the guys weren't always killed. It wasn't *always* their people, either. The Vigilante attacked plenty of non-affiliated people, too. The only common theme was that the victims were breaking a law, dealing drugs, mugging, pimping, that sort of stuff. The Boss wouldn't listen.

That raised Michalson's hair in a big way. A gang war, he could deal with, but a vampire feud? His best plan to date was simply to stay out of the way.

Vampirism wasn't the only thing about this job that made him jumpy. Gwen Isendamer made him more nervous than a room full of vampires. Head cases always did.

Well, you can't choose family or co-workers. Gwennie was a package deal with Borgia. The Boss never gave him the particulars, but Eddie wasn't stupid. He'd done his homework when he hired on as Borgia's lieutenant. The short take was: the Boss met her at a ritzy ski resort several years ago, and recognized true value when he saw it. He wooed and won her loyalties on the spot.

No lie, she had a head for business, and knew at a glance if a deal was lucrative. Unfortunately, she was also a sociopath. *That* was the part that made him nervous. If you knew what to look for, her record was scary — and impressive in a spooky sort of way. If there were doubts about her sanity, her reaction to the execution of the embezzler removed them. Gwennie was so turned on by it, his skin crawled standing next to her. She'd spent the rest of the night in Borgia's private chambers, and according to his sources, left the chamber only once; right around the time the accountant took his flying lesson. Since Borgia never showed any qualms about putting any of her talents to use, he suspected Gwennie helped the bookkeeper find his wings. Spookier still, she'd slept through the whole of the next day almost as soundly as Borgia himself. He shuddered.

Isendamer was inordinately happy about something lately, too. That made him more jumpy. If the Ice Empress had something simmering on the back burner, he was sure *he* wouldn't figure pleasantly in it. She hated him. She hated most men. Most living things, for that matter. Somehow, this new project involved the carrot of vampirism the Boss dangled in front of her. She *wanted* immortality and all the power that came with it.

That was the one part that didn't worry him. Francesco Borgia was scary and frequently unpredictable, but not stupid. While he made frequent use of his pet psycho's skills, he was plainly unnerved at the glee with which Isendamer exercised them. There was no danger of Borgia taking Isendamer for a fledgling.

Lucky for everybody. Gwennie was too wiggy to wield that power. Life would get nasty if she ever did.

Now the boss imported this Donal woman out of the clear blue. God knew why. "For her unique skills," the Boss said. She only came in last night, and no doubt he'd learn more as time went by but, he liked the lady already. She oozed class. Best of all, sparks flew when she was introduced to Gwennie. Ms. Donal was polite as you please, but it was easy to see she loathed Isendamer on sight. Well, the Boss said she was a smart cookie.

Brains aside, the lady better watch her back, because the feeling was plainly mutual. Probably, Gwennie recognized a threat to her security. It was obvious watching the Boss and Ms. Donal together, there were sparks of an altogether different kind between them. Maybe this could work to his advantage. If Gwennie concentrated on keeping her hooks in the Boss, maybe she'd put what was on the back burner even farther off the heat.

Hey, a guy could hope, right?

***

Watching Phil and Benny casually maneuver the baby grand piano to its place on stage, Jump Veron grunted softly and shifted on his high stool. Shaking his head, he resumed trimming the new reed for his sax, and wondered at himself. After all this time, surely he'd reconciled to his physical limitations, yet, sometimes watching "normal" people do things they took for granted, he felt a pang — of what? Envy? No. Not envy. Other things more than compensated for the lacks he suffered. Music, for one.

He tightened the reed, wet it, and tested its tone. Music and *other* things. As his great-grandmother used to assure him, there's *always* a trade-off. She had the gift, too, and she was not only small, like himself, but blind to boot. She, too, endured the bane of small folk, arthritis. He played a riff and silently thanked God the awful stuff hadn't struck his hands. He could make do with Benny and others to be his arms and legs, but if his music were taken from him. . . .

This was no good. He was getting himself down and there was reason to be up tonight, the same reason the piano was being wheeled out. BC would be playing with the band.

BC's visits were short and rare since the Miller thing, and he was being strangely reticent when Jump asked about it. He'd come tonight, though. He promised and BC Peale was good for his word. Sometimes he squeaked, but he always came through. It was Saturday night. Saturdays were big nights for the club and BC was a big attraction, especially among the ladies.

It was always so, even in occupied France he was a *real* hit with the French ladies. He was known by his full name then. Jump was responsible for sticking the BC tag on him. Byron was too stuffy. He was just a kid, then and BC? Well, BC was BC.

They'd both been enjoying the jazz scene in Europe when Hitler happened, and they got stuck behind enemy lines. They made good use of the situation, though. Those were frightening times, but he wouldn't trade them for the world.

They'd saved each other's asses time and time again, yet the thing he owed his friend most for was the club. After the war, they'd come back to the states to find things were rough for everyone, but if you were a colored dwarf with a Frenchy accent, it was worse.

He and BC left Louisiana shortly after returning stateside and headed north. He'd thought about Canada where his accent wouldn't have been too out of place, but something about Chicago snared him and the city had been his home ever since. BC, on the other hand, hopped back on his precious motorcycle and roared off to see the country.

While Jump immersed himself in the jazz and blues scene of his adopted city, BC ranged far and wide, but was never out of touch for long. Not only did he buzz through Chicago frequently, but BC Peale had a love-affair with the telephone. He adored being able to pick up a phone and ring someone up anywhere in the world. He *still* did. When cell phones came about, he was in ecstasy. He'd talk until the battery died.

It was after one of these marathon calls that BC had turned up in Chicago with the idea of going partners in a jazz club and bistro. Jump to run it, he to foot the bills. Veron had been floored. When he'd mentioned in passing that a club was up for sale, and wouldn't it be magnificent to buy it, he'd just been engaging in wishful thinking. The longing in his heart must have traveled down the wire. That club was the cellar bistro that had become the Inferno Jazz Club. If BC hadn't gone partners with him, he could never have afforded it., and if BC hadn't become his partner, he could never have afforded the Inferno Club.

Lifting the top sheet from the stack of freshly-printed handouts advertising upcoming performances, he smiled again at their private joke. The house band's name. Nosferatu. If his old friend's heart had been still beating the night Jump announced the name, it would have stopped at that moment.

Jump was pleased that BC had come back to Chicago. He was always happy when his nomadic friend settled down even for a little while. Everyone needed time to pause and reflect — BC more than most. He got precious little opportunity to do that tearing around the country on that blasted motorcycle. It was as if he were *afraid* to stand still. Before the war, BC had a home base, but prior to leaving for Europe in the 1920s, something happened to change that. Jump could never get the story out of him. Perhaps some day he'd open up, it would do him good to let go of it — whatever it was.

Jump worried what his friend was getting into now. He wasn't sure what that was, but he could make an educated guess. There was little doubt what led up to the current tangle, either.

When the first articles about the Vampire Vigilante appeared, Jump tried to wheedle the stubborn, undead jackass from his favorite diet of mugger. This was in vain. When the thugs started traveling in pairs, he did turn more to animal blood, but BC Peale had never played it safe in life *or* unlife. Jump secretly hoped that the first bullet one of those mob boys put through him would make him stop, rethink what he was doing. In a way it did, but it also got Galen Miller involved. In spite of the fact that losing control and killing was his deepest fear, BC invariably pushed the envelope until disaster was unavoidable. It hearkened back to his first night as a vampire. The word 'disaster' was too tame for what happened then. In many ways, BC asked for *that*, too.

Veron frowned. His Gift kept giving warnings, though. Nasty forces were gathering and he was afraid BC might unknowingly be its catalyst. Should he mention it? BC never scoffed . . . but, no, it was too nebulous. Best he should listen a while longer. No need alarming his friend with un-named worries when there were enough identifiable ones close at hand.

***

She sprang up, chest heaving, scattering bedclothes. It took a few moments to reorient and a few more to convince adrenal glands that the spacious hotel room was nonthreatening. Lying back against the soft pillows, she pressed both palms to her face, releasing an involuntary groan.

It was just a dream. No, it was *another* dream. About Byron again, although this was by far the most disturbing. There'd been more of them since she'd come to Chicago. Was it because of Francesco?

Not that she didn't dream of him anyway. Retrieving the miniature painting from the bedstand, she lightly stroked its edge. She *was* still in love with him and her kind did not fall into or out of love easily. With Francesco, there was no such problem, it was mostly a attraction, and the magnetism easily converted to friendship. But with Byron?

Swinging long legs over the edge of the bed, she pulled on a flowing green and gold caftan, enjoying the feel of silk against her bare skin. She hated admitting it, even to herself, but she handled things badly in 1783. She should have given him a little breathing room before making her move, she knew he was a wild spirit very like herself. It was one of the things that attracted her in the first place, and under similar circumstances, she would've reacted the same way. Anger got the best of her, so she'd listened to her heart and stopped using her head. Her mother insisted that was invariably when she got into her worst scrapes.

She flopped across the bed hissing, "Damn you, Mother! You're *always* so bloody *RIGHT!* Not that I'll ever tell you that. Give you too much satisfaction, it would."

Softening, she cradled the cherished miniature. "Byron Peale, where are you, My Heart? I know you still exist, I'd feel your loss were you destroyed."

She would, too. How or when it happened, she wasn't certain, but they were linked. At least *she* was. She doubted he could be, and still pull those wretched stunts . . . she broke off with a mental growl. At least she knew *why* it happened, the same reason the dreams came. She loved him. If she ever ceased to love him or found another to love, would the bond fade? No way to know. According to her mother and aunts, her predicament was unusual. They'd been around a while, too, so the lack of knowledge on the subject was unsettling.

Replacing the painting, she rose to check her preparations for the approaching dusk. Perhaps her strategy with Byron went awry, but she still owed Francesco a great deal for his part in it. It was ready. No surprise, she'd only checked it a dozen times before allowing sleep to overtake her that morning.

Shedding the caftan, she sat cross-legged on the floor attempting to center herself. Unless she could get her mind off Byron, it was only him her spells sought. An enjoyable notion, but not very helpful to Francesco.

After a moment, she sagged and groaned. "Don't think about elephants! Then all you can think of are the bloody pachyderms. Byron, you're a great deal more pleasing to the eye than an elephant, but leave me alone."

That was pointless. He *was* leaving her alone. That was the trouble. Pursing her lips, she considered past efforts at looking in on him. There were successes, but she'd worked for them. The cockerel was *very* good at closing her out, and his vampirism augmented his innate talent. Nonetheless, it was woefully apparent that she needed to see him, maybe then she could give her undivided attention to Frankie's renegade — not to mention get some sleep. That's what she'd do, then, after the evening's session, she'd return here and look for her lover. She smiled as pent-up tension flowed out of her. *Now, if the rest of it were that easy*, she thought as she passed into her meditative state.

TEN

Pounding rattled the hollow core door dangerously against its hinges. "*DAMMIT, PEALE*! What the hell are you doing in there? The sun went down fifteen minutes ago."

Resigned to his fate, BC stalked out. "Galen Miller, you are the most impatient person I have ever met. It can't have been more than five minutes and I was standing just the other side of that door when you tried to bash it in."

That was true as far as it went. The sun wasn't set more than five minutes, and he *was* standing on the other side — as he had been since just before dusk. He usually rose while the sky was still light. Since it was brilliant as an August midday to him, he tended to postpone emerging until it darkened. He wondered if this was unusual, but not knowing others like himself, had no way to tell. All part of the retribution exacted by the person responsible for his state. Anyway, early riser or not, he awoke tonight in ample time to overhear a heated debate in the next room, and realize uncomfortably the argument was about him. Eavesdropping wasn't a favorite pastime, but he was reluctant to enter the field of battle. Turning toward the second combatant, he nodded politely. "Good evening, Mrs. Miller."

He was rewarded with a scowl and a warning finger wagged in his direction. "You *bet* it's a good evening, but it won't be for long if you don't mind your manners."

"Mama, could you at least be civil to my friends in my own house. How many times do you have to hear this? I am *not* on BC's evening menu!" Shooting a meaningful glance over his mother's head at the flustered vampire, Galen asked, "Hey, BC, you got any plans for tonight?"

BC glanced uncertainly from Miller to Miller before responding. "Uh, why?" Struck by an alarming thought, he sidestepped the object of his terror, to whisper intensely in Galen's ear, "She doesn't have one of those charms with her, does she?"

Jasmine Miller planted herself between them and snapped, "No, she doesn't, because *somebody* took it away as soon as she came in."

The vampire retreated closer to the relative safety of the exit, as Galen said, "'Took it away'? You *gave* it to me and I said I didn't want it." Collecting his composure, Gae pointedly ignored his mother, and returned conversationally, "The reason I asked about your plans was I'd kind of like the two of us to get into the remains of that bombed-out warehouse and dig around a little on our own."

Peale wrenched his eyes from Mrs. Miller. "*What?* Whatever for? Haven't the police had forensic teams all over it by now?"

"Twice! Fire department, SI and several other gangs, too."

"Then, I don't see what good it'll do. What can we hope to find that those amassed techno-wizards with their lab equipment missed or just plain trod out of existence?"

"*Lots* of stuff! Those other guys didn't have your special talents backing them up!"

He viewed Galen in silent skepticism, then, eyeing the unyielding barrier planted between them, observed, "Your son is insane."

Undead abomination momentarily forgotten, Jasmine Miller gaped at her offspring like he'd sprouted wings and a tail. "Don't I know it!"

BC was hard pressed to maintain a serious expression at the face Galen pulled in response. It had been years since he was privy to such intimate family behavior, and recognizing the affection between these two required no special senses. He was envious. It awakened much-denied longing for his own family in his heart. At the same time, his head maintained returning was out of the question. The closest thing to family available was Jump Veron. Oh God. Jump! Two heads swiveled in amazement as he yelped, "*BLAST!* This is Saturday!"

Galen said, "Yeah? So?"

"So, I've got a mind like a sieve. I just remembered, I promised Jump I'd play at the club tonight. I should have been there by now."

Galen shrugged, "No problem. We'll do the warehouse another time. Think Jump'll mind if I put in an appearance, too?"

BC grinned, "Good heavens, I think we've created a jazz fan."

"No way, Kimosabe! I'm still strictly a rock 'n' roll man; I can't follow half the stuff you listen to. I wanna keep an eye on you."

Mama Miller held her peace as long as she could. "Galen Samuel Miller! If you think I'm about to stand back and let you walk out of this house without supper to go to some noisy nightclub with this creature, you got yourself another think comin'."

The word supper struck an uneasy chord with Peale. It was a full twenty-four hours since he'd fed and the frenetic activity between left him depleted. True, he wasn't badly injured in the explosion, but it left him shaky and unprepared for the emotional turmoil of an all-night debate. Alarming pangs clamored for attention, and he wasn't anxious for a repeat of the Jay Marquez debacle. Nervously reclaiming his jacket, he ventured, "Uh, Galen, your mother has a point. Why don't you grab supper and we'll meet at the Inferno later? I need a quick stopover at the stockyard, myself."

The path to freedom was open, and the lithe figure was out and on the stairs before anyone knew he was moving. Angrily, Galen pummeled the nearest piece of furniture. "Dammit, he's fast when he wants to be!"

Jasmine murmured, "What a peculiar child." Turning to her own peculiar child she demanded, "What did he mean with that stuff about the stockyard?"

"I think mentioning supper did it. He's gone for what he calls fast food on the hoof. It seems he doesn't have to take human blood all the time."

Smiling slightly, he continued, "He says that human is more fun, though. Especially *female* human."

"That sounds like something he'd say."

Although fixing the open doorway with a frown, she saw neither that object, nor the respectful step back her son took so as not to intrude on her thoughts. Other things occupied her mind like: Why in heaven's name wasn't Byron Peale behaving like any undead she'd ever heard of? His vital forces were powerful, to be sure, but he projected nothing threatening nor evil. This was her first experience with his type of undead, and she was woefully ignorant on the subject. At times like this she missed her mother. Perhaps her sisters would have some thoughts; if nothing else, it was a good excuse to call. She hadn't talked to Rosemary and Cinnamon in weeks.

***

Hitching up elegant black skirts, Jay Marquez peeked under the doors to the three stalls. Nobody. She had the Ladies' room to herself. Straightening, she twitched long, blond hair over her shoulder, checked her makeup and admired her new uniform. Jump Veron called it a uniform, Jay called it the classiest evening gown she ever wore. Unable to contain excitement any longer, she bounced up and down on her high-heels, hugged herself, and let loose a happy squeal.

She realized how lucky she was for Jump to take this chance on her. Truthfully, her reputation didn't warrant the trust he showed in giving her the job. She'd *be* a good hostess, though, and this was a big step up for her. Now to prove to Jump (and maybe to herself) she was worth the gamble.

She'd been at the club all day, learning how things worked, but officially, she'd been on the clock only a few hours. Regardless, she was already enjoying it more than any job she'd had. She owed BC something for that, she took this job because of him and what happened at Julio's — not that she held him to blame.

Oops. She shouldn't have thought about that. She didn't see much of what happened, except to BC. That was bad enough. What happened to Chick and Alfie was fast and off to one side. Thankfully, all she could dredge up were impressions. Afterward, things were blank until she came to on her own couch with a concerned BC bending over her. Maybe she *did* faint in a way.

Damn, she was going to cry. That was no good, her mascara claimed to be waterproof, but she didn't want to put it to the test right now. She pinched back tears and assumed her pleasantly competent face. She should be seating customers, and only told Benny she needed a pitstop, not a full break. She'd better get back pronto. Besides, Jump said BC promised to be there for the first set; that was fifteen minutes away. He'd be showing up soon, and she was determined to surprise him at the door when he did.

The washrooms were down a short corridor from the main entrance providing a good view of the waiting area. Looking up, her breath caught as BC Peale stepped into the club and hailed Benny. Darting forward, she swore at herself for futzing around in the can. If she'd wasted any more time, she'd have blown it for sure, and what she wanted most was to see the look on that gorgeous face when he realized she was working at the club. Suppressing the urge to giggle, she slowed to a sedate pace to obtain maximum swish from the rich fabric of her skirts, swept up to her station, and called out, "S'okay, Benny I'm back! Hey, BC, they said you'd be in tonight, so I got your regular table in the back reserved a'ready."

The tall Englishman turned, eyes widening as he recognized the leggy lady striding toward him. He exclaimed, "Jay? What are...?" She beamed happily as he saw the formal dress for what it was. He amended, "Of course, you're the new hostess. But, I thought you were working at Jake's!"

Chuckling, Benny bent from his greater height to confide, "She quit early this week. Right after Jump gave her the job."

"Oh. I hadn't heard."

She was close enough that the scent of his cologne blended pleasantly with the leather he habitually wore, and overrode the growing fug of tobacco from the club. Clearly he was shaken, but rapidly regaining equilibrium, and she was glad to note, not unhappy to see her. "This is my first night and I wanted to surprise you. Oh yeah, before I forget: Jump said I should tell you to come back to the office as soon as you can. He said there was a bunch of stuff he wanted to talk to you about."

"Ah. No doubt." He smiled charmingly. "Thank you, Jay. You look lovely, the outfit suits you. If you'll both excuse me, I'd best see what Jump wants." He started away, then turned and added with a mischievous glint, "By the way, someone may be meeting me here later. If he shows, could you send him to my table? Big guy, you'll know him when he gets here."

Feeling vaguely proprietary, she watched him cross the floor. He wasn't as upset at her presence as she'd feared. That was good. Now to work extra hard to let him know she was a friend. Behind her, Benny's breath tickled her ear as he leaned close. "Don't let on that I told you, 'cause they like to keep it quiet, but BC owns half of this place."

Nonplussed, she darted a glance at the hulking bouncer. Pleased, he nodded sagely. "His daddy and Jump was buddies in World War Two. Jump told me."

His daddy, huh? After what she figured out, she had her doubts about the identity of Jump's war buddy. Returning her gaze to the crowded floor, she saw the broad shouldered silhouette disappear through the door marked employees only. Interesting. All the time she'd been checking him out with the other employees, there wasn't a whisper of that. Instead, what she kept finding were stories about how he'd helped this one out of a jam or that one over a rough spot. The general consensus was that, BC was weird, but good people

An impatient cough drew her attention to a growing group of customers. "Uh oh. Duty calls, Benny, I gotta get to work. Thanks for coverin' for me."

Blowing a playful kiss, she bustled to the stack of plastic-coated menus, and the waiting throng. Benny blushed and stammered, "Ummm, no problem."

**

Jump's office door was open when BC entered the hall. Homing in on the warm swatch of light spilling across the worn tiling, he wondered if the rat treated himself to a peek from the safety of the back corridor. Probably. He'd do it if the roles were reversed. Lounging against the doorjamb, he announced, "Sadist. I hope you enjoyed the show."

Veron's rusty chuckle was answer in itself. "Give ya a turn, eh, BC?"

Checking over his shoulder confirmed the hall was empty. He closed the door, then, sprawled across the battered couch. "As if you didn't know it would. Why didn't you tell me who you'd hired to take over for Norean?"

"Prob'ly jus' slip my mind, Maybe if you been around lately, I would have remembered. You have objections?"

"Of course I don't. It's just . . . well, I *told* you!"

"Yes, *mon ami*, so you did, and it was a terrible thing that happened, but I do not see why you torture yourself this way about Jay. You did no harm to her and would *not* have done. You would not have harmed those boys, either, had they not attacked you."

The sensual mouth remained set in a grim line, and although unsurprised, Jump was frustrated. BC was, as ever, his own harshest critic. Jump was familiar with the self-imposed rule against taking advantage of friends, and knew that was precisely what BC felt happened. How foolish! It didn't make it right, but many people used the poor girl in many ways. Few were half as concerned over the consequences. He suspected if Jay were aware of the circumstances, she'd feel the same way. She was a realist, if nothing else.

On the other hand, BC's fears might be well-founded about the fragility of his hastily-crafted memory overlay. If true, it would go far to explain the girl's behavior. She was discrete, but all day, he'd overheard her asking questions about BC. Most chalked it up to the new girl checking out the resident Romeo, but Jump wondered.

Looking deeply into his friend's troubled eyes, he decided against mentioning this. There was no proof Jay was suspicious of BC's 'condition,' and she made no threatening moves. Sometimes, BC felt out of step with humanity and from the look of him, this was one of the more extreme times. If only the damned idiot wouldn't dance so close to the edge — worse, do it so frequently. Aloud, he declared, "All that is beside the point and we will not talk of it. The point is that you went too long without feeding again. If you hungry, you mus' *tell* me. We work around it. You always get in trouble when you ignore your nature."

"I know. Maybe one of these centuries, I'll learn the lesson."

Jump laughed heartily. "I doubt it, *mon ami*." It was time to get to the important things, best not to allow BC too much self-pity, it didn't suit him. "So, we have seen little of you these past nights. What have you been up to?"

The long legs crossed uneasily. He wanted to confide in Jump, he trusted this man implicitly, but Galen made him promise to tell nobody about their investigations. Annoyingly, *nobody* was stressed firmly. Like someone with so much to hide would take out a personal in the Trib. "I'm sorry, Jump, but I'm not at liberty to say. You know how that goes. If it were up to me, I'd have the whole thing laid out in front of you hoping for inspiration." He flashed a roguish grin. "I *can* say I'm definitely one of the good guys."

"You have taken Galen Miller up on his offer, no?"

BC nodded, then, brow furrowed asked, "Is this what you wanted to talk to me about? I assume it was more than giving me a ribbing about our new employee."

"*Mais oui*. It is possible, *mon ami*, your association with Miller has set something in motion. Or perhaps it was already in motion, I cannot tell. All I am certain of is my great uneasiness. It is like a great storm were about to break over you."

Eyebrows meeting in worry, BC suddenly bent forward. "Can you tell me anything more specific?"

"No. *Mon ami, please* be careful! After what you've said — correction: *Not* said — both you and Galen Miller watch your asses."

BC was thoughtful, but nodded, his mind already occupied with how to broach this to Gae. There was no doubt he had to, and after meeting Mamma Miller, he knew Galen wouldn't dismiss Jump's Gift out of hand.

***

Arriving at the Inferno, Galen discovered the Please Wait to be Seated sign was back in service. Obediently, he stopped behind it, waited as instructed and exchanged glares with Benny Glissen. He was off-guard, when instead of giving him a seat, the hostess gave him an energetic bear-hug. Uttering a highly articulate "Hunh?," he looked down into the pixie-grin of Jay Marquez.

Enjoying the dumbfounded expression, she impulsively hugged him again. As a child, following the big kids around, she had a tremendous crush on him and it never completely disappeared. She even learned about football, just to follow his career. When she saw the surprise hadn't faded, her face crumpled. "You really weren't expectin' to see me here, were you, Gae?"

Struggling for words, he stammered, "Jay? What happened to Jake's?"

"That's old news! All the way to last week . . . hey! You mean my ditz-brained brother didn't tell you? And here I hoped you'd come for my first night on the new job."

She was so hurt, he resolved to kick Mick's butt solidly downfield at the earliest opportunity. He penciled Peale in for that flight, too. With his connections at this nightclub, BC had to know about the new hostess. It was puzzling, that as torn up as the asshole was over how he'd almost hurt her, he'd keep quiet about working with her. Then again, you never knew which way Peale would jump. Raising the three-fingered Boy Scout pledge high, he vowed, "Cross my heart, and have mercy on a poor decrepit ex-jock, I didn't hear a thing! Mick didn't say a word about it *and* neither did BC Peale. Oh yeah, I'm supposed to be meeting him here tonight. Peale, that is."

Jay perked up. "So *you're* who he meant! I didn't know you knew BC. Hey, that's great!"

So, BC and Gae were friends? She took this news as further proof that BC Peale was okay. Gae Miller's instinct for people was good, and that was enough for her. Gesturing toward the band on the dais, and BC at the keyboard specifically, she said, "He's onstage right now, and if things go like they're supposed to, the set will last for another twenty minutes or so." Swinging back, she waved an admonishing finger at him. "Now, you can ream Mick all night long if you want to, but I don't want you to get pissed with BC, okay? He didn't know I was workin' here until a little while ago, either. It was a surprise."

Suddenly suspicious, he reassessed the gnarled figure manipulating the gleaming horn with practiced ease on stage. Veron and Peale were longtime friends, that much he knew. He also knew the pint-sized Cajun orchestrated the meeting at this very club. Beyond that, his knowledge ended. Not that BC was particularly closed-mouthed about things, it was simply that, so far they'd had little opportunity to sit back and shoot the breeze. They'd have to fix that, a partnership worked best when the partners knew each other well. Fixing his features into a blandly interested arrangement, he remarked, "I bet he was *real* surprised. Jump Veron's idea?"

She guided him to a familiar corner with an even more familiar table. "Yeah, it was! Do you know Jump, too?"

Uh hunh. Thought so. The glare of the stage lights against the relative gloom of the house, caught the flash of his sudden grin, lending it a sinister aspect. "No, but I'm beginning to develop a true appreciation for the little guy."

Jay laughed and slipped a menu in his hands. "Jump's a sweetheart. This is BC's usual spot, he asked me to seat you back here. Just pull up a chair, I'll have Bob send over a beer. I know, dark and German. Check out the menu, too. Jump said Cal, that's our chef, outdid himself tonight."

He watched her swing by the bar to deliver a quick order, then veer toward the door to take charge of a growing cluster of customers. The place was busier than he expected and Jay seemed right at home in the midst of it. He rarely saw her at work, but she'd never looked so happy. He was glad. Veron wasn't the only sweetheart around the place.

A waitress materialized, placed a bedewed glass and bottle on a napkin before him then vanished into the hazy darkness with a smile. Fast service, too, although being associated with one of the house favorites, might gainsay him more attention than normal. He sipped his beer, turning his attention to the stage and his new partner.

It was a revelation. If he rarely saw Jay at work, he'd never seen BC in action. With a pleasant shock he realized that for the first time, he was seeing Peale in his true element, surrounded by people, music, and enjoying the hell out of unlife. Watching the easy familiarity between Veron and Peale, he wondered again how long they'd been friends, and what understanding there was between them. He also wondered if he'd get a straight answer if he asked Peale. Smiling to himself, he decided that newfound trust or no, he'd do better to ask Veron.

He saw someone approaching out of the corner of his eye. It was Jay sailing through the crowd toward him like a proud ice-breaker. She was elated, and for a moment, he couldn't figure why, until he looked past her. Following in her wake, was big brother Mick, but it was doubtful the man knew where he was going, he only had eyes for the piano player. They weren't friendly eyes, either.

Galen winced. Mick was fiercely protective of his baby sister, more so since the Fiesta slayings. He should have expected Mick to put in an appearance. His only excuse for being caught flatfooted was, that he was so surprised to see Jay, his brain was simply immobilized. It was plain from the new arrival's expression, the surprise was mutual. Mick's body language screamed that he hadn't made the connection between Peale, and Jay's new job until he actually saw the object of his ire on the dais.

The new hostess seated her brother with a flourish, then hurried off to order another round of beer, too euphoric and busy to notice the arctic conditions that suddenly swept the corner. Mick was sullenly silent until their teleporting waitress deposited beer, and warped to another part of the house. "When I saw Peale on stage, I should've known you'd be close by."

Galen smirked and said, "Hey! It's great to see you, too, pal! Shut up and drink your beer."

***

At the end of the set, BC stood for a moment with Jump and the band, reveling in the hearty round of applause from the audience. He loved performing before an audience, and though he'd only been away a short time, he'd missed this a lot. Grinning at his Cajun cohort, and shunning the regular stairs, he leaped from the dais, and made for his regular place.

Earlier, he'd been pleased to spot Galen, but then puzzled when a short time later Jay seated some else at his table. From Jay's manner, and a superficial resemblance, he had a pretty good idea of the man's identity, but was burning with curiosity to know for sure.

Curiosity aside, he was also a trifle put out. He'd planned to use the time between sets to tell Gae about Jump's premonition. Oh well, Jay couldn't know, and these things simply happened. If indeed, the man were Mick Marquez, there was ample reason to seat him as she did. Besides, Jump didn't stress urgency, there'd be plenty of time to talk to Galen later. Providing Mrs. Miller permitted it. He idly wondered how Galen got away from her tonight, he didn't need Jump's gift to know that the lady didn't trust him. Well, why should she?

Tension that increased with every step toward his table crackled over his senses. Instinct screamed to make for the bike, but he was committed now. Anyway, he was half-convinced that if he bolted, Galen would tackle and retrieve him before he made the exit. Assuming a mask had become easy over the years, if not always palatable, so he smiled, exclaiming, "Hey, Gae! I'm glad you could make it."

Galen grinned back. "Wouldn't have missed it for the world! Now I know what caused the brain damage. I always thought it was because your mama dropped you on your head. Maybe it's cause and effect." Grinning more broadly at Peale's good-natured sneer, Galen continued. "BC, I'd like you to meet Miguel Marquez, my old buddy and Jay's big brother. Mick, this is BC Peale."

Peale extended a hand and Mick reluctantly shook it. BC said, "I'd wondered if you were Jay's famous brother when I saw her bringing you over here. After hearing so much from Galen, I'm pleased to meet you at last."

Mick eyed the suave musician with reservation. "I've heard a lot about you, too, Peale."

The bare bones nature of the statement was not lost on either of Mick's tablemates. BC gleamed wickedly at the tacit challenge. Galen winced and quoted Bette Davis sotto voce, "Fasten your seatbelts. It's going to be a bumpy night."

Over Peale's shoulder, Gae noted the approach of a cavalry relief unit. He beamed as Jay slid a tray bearing two more beers and a brandy onto the tabletop. "You guys should consider yourselves VIPs! I came back to make a personal check on my three fellas and to deliver drinks compliments of the management."

Pleased with her own private joke, she winked broadly at BC and turned a placidly happy face upon the trio. Peale returned the wink, responding, "*My* compliments to the management on the improvement of the decor."

Laughing, she set the glasses before them, and swished provocatively away. Mick was getting madder by the second, and BC noted that with amusement. There were few brothers that had approved of him through the years, but the emotion in the air had been intense even before he sat down. He couldn't fathom what could have gone so wrong between these long-time friends in so short a time. True, Galen told him about the recent argument, and he was uncomfortably aware of how he figured into it. By all accounts, Marquez was a bug on regulations, but still, he was *so* angry. Too angry.

His thoughts were interrupted by a mild hubbub caused by the drummer cum club manager, Phil Quinlan hurrying toward them. Seeing he'd caught BC's eye, the chunky young man gestured wildly and plunged on. BC commented mildly to nobody in particular, "We're going to need a bigger table."

Phil skidded to a stop beside BC where he hyperventilated and ran agitated fingers through his shaggy sideburns. "God, BC. Is your bartending license still good? Bob just got the call that his wife is at the hospital in labor and he's gotta go. I know we got another set comin' up, but could you fill in?"

"Sure, I can take over. Isn't this early? I thought the baby wasn't due for at least a month."

"Too true and Bob is fit to be tied."

BC stood. "In that case, the last thing we should do is send him off on his own. You'd better ask Benny to drive him to the hospital. I'll tell Bob."

Phil nodded darted away. Apologizing to his tablemates, Peale sped off, privately grateful to escape the emotional barrage. He hoped for Galen's sake the trouble could be smoothed out. Marquez was a valued friend. Seeing a lifetime of friendship end over something trivial would be sad, and knowing he'd been a catalyst would be worse. He frowned. He, of all people, understood the value of friendship, *and* how easily trivial things could trigger cataclysmic events.

As Galen watched the slender figure gracefully navigate the busy room toward the elaborate counter, something about the bar setup niggled in the back of his head. A vague wrongness somewhere. Sipping his drink, he ignored the grumbling beside him as he studied the problem, then realized what was missing. There were no mirrors behind the bar. There were *always* mirrors behind bars. There seemed to be an unwritten law to that effect.

Bemused, he surveyed the rest of the room and discovered there were no mirrors in the entire place. In fact, most surfaces that were normally reflective, were matte or brushed metal; maybe he didn't *need* to ask Veron any pointed questions after all, except maybe how long. He kicked himself for being dense. Of course other folks knew before him. Peale said he was over two and a half centuries old. Two hundred sixty-two to be exact. He was very insistent on the exact number, and got real pissed-off if you rounded up. Imagine a *vampire* being sensitive about his age. Geez, what would he be like when he hit three hundred?

Galen turned back to the grumbling to find that the imprecations were not being directed at him, but rather toward the bar. Following the dark gaze, he saw Jay leaning coquettishly over the oak and brass partition delivering drink orders to the substitute bartender. The fill-in mixologist was responding in kind much to the delight of the surrounding customers. Glancing at Mick's wrathful face, he jibed, "They make a lovely couple, don't they, Miquelito?"

Mick swung on him. "Don't call me that, and that two-bit Lothario pal of yours better stay away from my sister or I'll kick his ass right back to England."

Galen expected a snarl, but the violence behind the words rocked him. "Take it easy, Mick! Anyone can see they're only kidding around. You'd better get a grip on it before Jay sees you like this, I don't think she'll appreciate your attitude."

"Peale will appreciate it less. If he touches her . . . ."

Galen set his glass on the tabletop with a firm clunk. Using the even tones that warned of imminent danger, he said, "Listen to yourself, man, what is wrong with you? BC Peale hasn't got any designs on your sister, and even if he did, it should be up to Jay to decide. Whether you like it or not, Jay's a big girl and she can take care of herself pretty well."

"Listen to *you*! I've seen you deck a few of *your* sister's dates."

"Miguel, I swear, BC will *not* hurt your sister. They're just goofing around. You're getting dug in over nothing, man. Back off and breathe."

Suddenly, Mick sagged in his chair. "Sorry, Gae, I'm wound up tight lately. This Vampire Vigilante shit has me bugged. Now there's this crap about disintegrating blood spatter evidence. I tell you true, 'mano, that one has *everyone* weirded out but good!"

"Don't I know it! I was on the phone with Jim for better than an hour about that. Let it go, man, this is supposed to be Boy's Night Out, right? Good advice bears repeating, pal: Shut up and drink your beer."

Mick made a mock salute with the pilsner and followed the advice. Wiping foam from his lip, he retorted, "If Miss Manners ever decides to retire, people won't be beating your door down as a replacement, Gae."

Miller chuckled, and shot a glance toward where his off-the-record partner was busy mixing, and filling orders. Too bad Mick brought the Vampire Vigilante stuff up, he'd almost managed to put it out of his head. With Peale working so closely with him, there hadn't been any high profile attacks on street criminals. Without that fodder, the papers moved on to other more immediate concerns, and the VV was all but forgotten. No two ways about it, Peale loved attention, but that kind of notoriety was more than even *he* was comfortable with.

Gae wondered what Mick would do if he leaned over, and informed him he'd been sharing a table with their unsub. He'd probably leap across the table, and go for Peale with a sharpened chair leg, amusing, but dangerous and nonproductive. Concern crowded out all else as he watched Marquez breathe deeply in an attempt to calm himself. Though it smacked of carrying tales, he maybe should drop a word to Jim about how edgy his Deputy Director was. Jim wasn't unobservant, but Mick was on snap-to behavior around headquarters, it was possible Jim hadn't seen. At least, he might be able to head off a real blow up before it happened. If only he knew what the trouble was.

Peale was a part of it. He wished like hell he could tell *both* Jim and Mick about Peale, not only because they were superior officers, but because they were friends. If they knew the truth, things would be so much easier. On the other hand, it could also make things a damn sight more uncomfortable. Sensing more than seeing Mick fidgeting beside him, he had the nasty feeling the second possibility was the most likely.

Damn it. Life could get more complicated than he liked. He frowned and silently ordered himself: *Ah, shut up and drink your beer*.

PART TWO

"How sharper than a serpent's tooth it is
To have a thankless child!"

~~ William Shakespeare

"Yakety yak
Don't talk back."

~~ Jerry Leiber and Mike Stoller

ONE

I'm Juanita Marquez. My friends call me Jay. Lots of people, including my family, think I'm some kinda tramp. That ain't so. Sure, I like a good time, but I'm picky about who I have it with. That's why I wanted out of Jake's Place so bad. Look, I ain't out to earn my M.R.S. degree, but the class of guys that hang out there . . . ? Let's just say that's why I was interested in BC Peale when I first clapped eyes on him. No guy that gorgeous should be allowed to live. Omigod. I can't believe I said that. See, BC ain't alive. He's a vampire. An honest to God vampire.

Do I haveta say finding out that little item changed things a lot?

A little while ago something bad happened outside another club. Julio's Fiesta? Maybe you read about it, it was in all the papers. Believe me, they don't have the whole story. Y'see it was BC killed them guys. I was there. It was self-defense. I wasn't supposed to see it, he tried to put some kinda hypnosis on me, but he was real shook and it didn't take. Anyways, when I started remembering what really happened, and with the vampire stuff in the papers, I got the idea of keepin' an eye on 'im. BC, I mean. I thought working at the club where he plays piano would be a great way t'do that.

I know, I know, it feels stupid to believe in vampires. If ya know BC Peale, it's even stupider to believe he is one, but that wasn't why I decided against coming right out an' telling him what I knew. I wanted to see if he was as cool about things as he seemed before I did. I only said I felt stupid, not that I was dumb enough to ignore what I saw with my own eyes.

So, okay, I took the job at the Inferno to spy on the guy, but it turned out to be a primo idea. I mean, this job was a big step up for me. The first night decided me, even though I didn't get much BC watchin' done on account of I about ran my legs off. The Inferno is a lot classier than Jakes'. I didn't go home with my butt black 'n' blue from all the pinches and slaps, if that tells ya anything. Maybe it's just different clientele, the jazz stuff makes that for sure.

I still dunno how much I like jazz. Some numbers I like a lot, others . . . ? Jump's tryin' to teach me about it so I'll be at ease with the customers. He calls it on the job training. It's so different, it'd be hard to like all of it — like any other kind of music, I guess.

Anyways, the first night went smooth. The only glitch was when Mario Hernandez slimed in. Ever since the thing at Julio's Fiesta, he gives me the willies. I don't know if it's because I've changed or he has. Irregardless, when I saw him in the lobby, everything in me screamed to run like hell the other way. I couldn't, though, being hostess don't give me that option. I just took him to a table like he was anyone else. He didn't cause no trouble, though, in fact he left real soon after he got there. That was mostly because of my brother, Mick.

Mick's a cop. He's with Sentry International instead of the Chicago Police, but that's still a cop to me. Anyways, I didn't even have to say anything, 'cause Mick was watchin' the door. Usually, I get P.O.ed at how he keeps watch on me like I was this three year-old, but then, I was glad for it. As soon as Mario sat down, Mick strolled over to say how CPD was wanting to talk to him about what happened at Julio's. But, when Mario saw Mick comin', he clammed up, and got real nervous. Not long after, he took off. When he left, it was like a rock lifted off my chest, I was so relieved. Still, it was good to have Benny Glissen close by; he's the bouncer and sits right by the door in case of trouble.

Benny didn't go too far away from me the rest of the night.

Jump warned me the hours at the Inferno were later than Jake's. He said jazz musicians go to bed when most people are getting up, and he wasn't kiddin'. By closing time I was dead on my feet! That and Mario showin' up made me real glad Mick stuck around, and that Galen Miller showed up, too. Turns out Gae is friends with BC. Small world, huh?

What this boils down to is: Mick stayed until the club closed so he could drive me home. Since I got no car and Mario made me real shaky about walkin' home, that would have been great — except Mick had ulterior motives. I shoulda known. He gets this look. I was dog tired, and I just wanted sleep, but as soon as we got to my place, Mick started stalkin' around like some kinda panther. My place is nice, but not so big, and that sort of thing can make you real nuts real fast in a little place. I knew if I was ever gonna get reacquainted with my bed, I better find out what was buggin' him.

***

Jay watched Mick storm around her living room glaring at each piece of bric-a-brac like it was a personal insult. Turning away, she shucked her overcoat and heels, and with a sigh, padded for the kitchen wondering how long it would take *this* time. Mick got mulish when he was this bugged. Experience taught her that it was best to act as normal as possible. Sometimes this was hard. Cool linoleum soothed the burning soles of her feet as she crossed to the cabinets and called over her shoulder, "Thanks for drivin' me home, Mick. Y'want a nightcap?"

He wouldn't. There was something on his mind and bone-tired or no, she had to wait for him to blurt it out. It was a relief when he loomed behind her growling, "You and Peale were all over each other tonight. How long has *this* been going on"

Yep. It was BC. She'd hoped it was about Super Stud Hernandez, *that* she could deal with. She'd been so busy, she'd nearly missed how Mick got all prickly whenever BC was around. BC hadn't been that busy. He'd noticed early on, and had gleefully tossed gasoline onto the bonfire all night. The guy was gorgeous, but sometimes you just wanted to strangle him. Well, maybe he'd done her a favor by getting Mick so worked up he'd gotten to the point in record time. Affecting nonchalance, she withdrew the bourbon and two glasses, uncapped the bottle and asked, "What are ya talkin' about? There ain't anything 'going on.' BC and me work at the same place, and he gave me a lucky lift home a few nights ago."

Please, God, let the pigheaded sonuvabitch accept it! She wasn't up for an argument. So what if she flirted with BC, she flirted with *lots* of guys. Big deal. The only difference was that she knew BC wasn't exactly a normal guy. As long as Mick didn't know that, things would be okay. Would Mick buy vampirism anyway — and if he did, did she want to know what he'd do about it?

She pinned him with a hard look. "Mick, I'm too tired to argue, okay? I been on my feet since four o'clock this — make that *yesterday* afternoon an' I'm needin' sleep real bad. Now, d'ya want a nightcap before ya go or not?"

Matching her gaze, he snatched the bottle from her hand and set it back on the counter. Hard. "No. I don't want a drink. I want to know what there is between you and Peale."

"Well, *mi 'mano*, usually it's a piano between us, but tonight it was a *bar* and a piano."

"Jay, I'm serious."

"I can tell that, I just can't figure why. BC Peale is a guy who works at a club I've worked at for one whole night. According to something I was told on the QT, he might own a chunk of the place, which might make him my boss. We ain't got a relationship. We ain't been around each other long enough. Try me again in a week. *What. Is. Your. Problem*?"

"I don't like him!"

Jay stared. With unfeigned amazement. "Ya don't like him? *¡Por Dios!* As soon as Colonel Black in New York learns this top secret information, Sentry'll issue a warrant for his arrest!"

"Don't get sarcastic. I know it's senseless. Gae and I have been over this all night and then some. I can't ignore the strange feeling I get whenever Peale's around . . . like all the hairs on my body are trying to stand on end at the same time."

"That's even weirder, Mick. You make it sound like he's got high voltage or something."

"Look! I can't explain it, but every time I turn around, it's like I see a sign BC Peale was here! First, he got you out of Julio's before all hell broke loose, then all of a sudden, I find you're working the same place he does. It's kind of an overload."

She folder her arms and narrowed her eyes. This was starting to sound like a rerun of the old I-don't-like-your-boyfriend routine. "If you got a point, get to it."

"You don't know everything that's going on."

Oops, maybe she was wrong. Mick's intuition was a heavy-duty force to be reckoned with. Everyone was talking about the vampire attacks, and as Deputy Director of Special Operations, Mick undoubtedly knew more than the newspapers. Had he put it together? Did he just *know* and was trying to warn her off? With a drowning sensation, she gripped the counter edge and prompted, "Like . . . ?"

Yanking an aluminum tube chair away from the kitchen table, Mick sank onto it running his hands through slightly graying hair. Words tumbled out in an anxious stream. "It's spooky how Peale keeps popping up! Julio's . . . the Inferno . . . Gae's primary informant and now his unofficial partner . . . ."

"*Wha-a-a-at?*"

Mick dropped his head into his hands, muffling his voice as he said,

"Shit! I'm dead on my feet. That's my excuse and I'm sticking with it." He lowered his hands and sat back against the uncomfortable chair back. His expression killed any response on her lips. "Juanita, you didn't hear what I just said. You've always been good at keeping secrets and that was a doozy that your idiot brother just dropped."

Almost afraid to breathe, she let the thunderbolt reverberate in her head. If she understood Mick, the rocky terrain she'd been tiptoeing across had just become a minefield. The hands gripping the table shook as she replied guardedly, "Okay, Mick, I think I getcha. I didn't hear a thing."

He treated her to a weak smile. "Sorry, I'm overtired and overwound. I oughta know better than to try to make sense at times like this. You never know what'll come out of my mouth next."

On the pretext of sisterly concern, she stepped behind him to knead his knotted shoulders. Glad he couldn't see her face. "S'okay, I can keep my mouth shut pretty good, but you better take care of yourself, Miguel. You been working your ass off since Jim gave you this Deputy thing. This is your day off. Just throw yourself into your silly golf game this afternoon, that always seems to help — though God knows why."

"HA! I said you didn't know everything that was going on! In a couple hours, I've got to drag this weary bod out of the sack to act as a parent-chaperone for Beverly's field trip to the Art Institute."

The giggle escaped her before she knew it was coming, Mick wheeled on her. "Yeah, yeah! Laugh now. See how funny you think it is when I call you before I go out the door."

"Is that a threat? I'll lodge a complaint of police brutality. Worse. I'll tell mom."

Laughing, he stood. "¡*Por la cruz*! You're breaking out the heavy artillery. I'd better run before I'm really in trouble." Seeming much calmer but looking tired, he exchanged goodnight kisses as they strolled to the exit. Pausing in the hall, he ordered, "Don't forget to lock up behind me!"

"Do I ever? You worry too much, Miguelito."

He snorted and stalked down the hall. A grin split her face as she flipped the deadbolt. He'd hated that diminutive of his name, ever since a bad guy on a TV western used it. She dropped onto the loveseat to massage her aching feet and think things over.

The first night of a new job should be exciting — she kind of liked that. Bombshell endings left her a little unsteady, though. Gae working for Sentry? Mick as good as said it, *and* he all but said BC was working *with* Gae. Unofficial partner. ¡Jesus! Here she'd been running around like Sherlockita Holmes asking all those brainless questions. She'd keep her trap shut from now on. She never intended to cause the guys trouble. Damn, those two were *good*! She never suspected they were agents.

Agents. Too bad she couldn't razz the "poor decrepit ex-jock". Retired. Suuuuure.

***

Hernandez slid out from the shadowy stairwell, and stared at the just-closed elevator doors. Marquez almost caught him with his ear to Jay's door — for all the good it did him. The door was so soundproofed, all he heard was when someone yelled. Good thing Jay's brother wasn't one of those fitness freaks who used the stairs all the time, or he'd be sunk. He heard Peale's name a couple times. Real loud.. Did he know Its secret? Maybe he should tell. An anonymous letter or phone call would work. Anyway, it was good to know other people weren't so fooled by the Monster.

Damn. He almost forgot Marquez and Miller were friends *and* cops. An ally against the hellish thing would be nice, but it seemed he was fated to fight alone. Waitaminit. Miller *was* a cop. An agent. Same thing. Even worse, the Monster was almost always with Miller. Was *It* playing cop, too?

Why would a vampire do that? For fun? Who could tell? What normal person could think like a demon? It fit, though. Both It and Miller were dropping questions around the neighborhood about somebody called Borgia.

He knew the name. Rumor said he was a big drug lord, but nobody wanted to say more than that. Hey! Weren't the Vampire Vigilante's victims drug guys? The Monster was hitting these guys and feeding off them. *UGGGH.* He trembled violently, gulping the nausea away. There was more to these attacks, then. Maybe if he made out like he knew something about this Borgia guy, he could set a trap.

It would have to be one of the Monster's regular nights at that club. He could get It alone, then. No way did he want Miller to show up. The guy was way too big to take on by himself — like a vampire wouldn't be enough of a fight. Besides, Miller was probably an innocent slave of the vampire's spells, and would be grateful when it was over.

Jay would be grateful, too. He smiled. Without the Monster clouding her mind, she'd see how much *he* cared.

Descending the stairs, and cutting through the alley, he hurried home — or what passed for home these days. He had a lot to do. Then there was that little item he had his eye on in the hunting section of the Wal-Mart. Yes. The time had come for it.

***

Too early to be legal in a civilized country. This thought repeated in an endless loop as, bleary-eyed, Mick Marquez mounted the stone stairs to the Art Institute. Reveling in daddy's presence, Beverly clung to his hand, chattering happily with her fellow eleven year-olds swarming into the ornate building. They were met inside the Michigan Avenue entrance by a willowy brunette tour guide who was too cheerful to be a real human being. Mick concluded she was a sophisticated android constructed specifically for this purpose, and was probably considered a work of art by the museum. Nothing else explained how an actual human could be so damnably perky when faced with thirty sixth graders at half past ten in the morning.

Nudging his fuzzy brain, he tried to remember why *he* was there. Oh yeah, how could he forget? Vera, couldn't get the day off from the hospital, and Beverly gave him the big eyes begging him to fill in. He could never refuse Beverly, she was too much like Vera. They both twisted him like a pretzel with a look. He stifled a yawn. Too bad there wasn't enough time for another gallon of black coffee.

Studying the two adults chatting with the teacher and the tour guide, he grumbled to himself. Originally, there were to be five chaperons, but "unexpected obligations" arose and two canceled at the last minute. The rats were probably playing golf. Maybe he prized his golf more than he ought to, but dammit, he only got onto the links once a week.

He sighed, and closed the gap between himself and the rear of the noisy group, too deep in a funk to notice either his surroundings or the tour guide's spiel. The memory of last night's goof wouldn't go away. Good thing Jim hadn't heard him spill the big one about Gae or there'd have been three unexpected obligations that morning. *Get over it, Marquez.* So what if something about Peale made his cop-sense go zing? That didn't give him the excuse to blow off like that. No one was supposed to know Gae was with SI, let alone that he was working with somebody no matter how unofficial. *Come on, Marquez,* he urged silently, *say the word. Partner. There. That didn't hurt much, did it?*

When they first heard Gae was coming home to take over the Borgia mess, Mick was over the moon. He hoped he'd be assigned to it, too. Instead he was tapped for Deputy Director of the Special Operations and Investigations section. No mistake, being named DDSOI was a great honor and a great job, but he missed the street. As a CPD detective, he enjoyed interviewing witnesses, and all the hands on things. The notion of teaming up with his buddy and the promise of getting back into the gritty stuff appealed to him. Unfortunately, when the orders came from on high for Gae to maintain deep cover, all those dreams hit the crapper.

He was glad he'd never mentioned it out loud. When it was decided Gae would be solo, he was disappointed, but didn't think it mattered much.

Time proved it did. It mattered a lot. It wasn't that he wasn't working with his old pal. He *was*. He was just tied to that damned desk! He was *good* at paperwork, but he hated it with a passion. He was angry as hell about facing a future of life with three carbons.

¡*Por la cruz*! Some adult he was. If he wanted to set a good example for Beverly and her friends, he'd damn well better rouse himself from this mood. He was always after his kids to broaden their horizons and now look at him! Grousing because of missing a lousy golf game by spending time with his daughter in an educational setting. Disgusted with himself he shoved S.I. aside, and turned to appreciate the artwork.

The turn froze at midpoint as he abruptly found himself nose-to-nose with BC Peale.

But, it wasn't Peale. It was only a painting that resembled the current thorn in his side. Man, did it resemble him! He stepped in for a closer look, and became aware of the tour guide looking at him strangely. Shooting her a sheepish grin, he casually sauntered to scan the card on the wall beside the portrait. It read:

"Portrait of Byron Cyrus Peale. Artist: Charles Willson Peale circa 1780"

He was having a nightmare. That was it. He'd fallen asleep on the damned school bus and was dreaming. That'll teach him to keep late nights before early wake-ups.

The tour guide materialized at his elbow and dimpled up at the big canvas. "I see you've noticed Byron. He's one of my favorites in this show; maybe because he's such a mysterious character. About all we know is that he was the youngest brother of the artist, there isn't much about him in any of the histories."

Huh? Mick faltered, "He is . . . I mean . . . was?"

The guide didn't notice the glitch, but gazed up at the painted face. "Yes. This portrait is considered one of the finest pieces Charles Peale made, and he was one of the finest portraitists of the Colonial era. I think a lot of love shows in it, don't you? The Peale family has never lent this painting out before. We're very honored."

"Uhhhh."

This wasn't sinking in. Trying to jumpstart his gray cells, he reread the placard: *Byron* Peale? Same last name. Same initials. The picture was painted over two hundred years ago, but it sure as hell looked like the Peale he knew today. Unaware of the confusion raging beside her, the guide mused, "Such a handsome man, so full of life . . . he looks like he knows some outrageous joke, and is about to share it. Oh well, we'd better move along now. There are postcards of all the works in the show available in our Museum Shop. This one is one of our best sellers. Byron's *very* popular."

"I'm *sure* he is," Marquez managed.

With a bright smile, the guide herded the noisy throng into the next gallery, leaving him alone with the uncanny likeness. It was too bizarre to ignore. He'd buy a postcard to show to Jim — who would probably decide he was nuts. Maybe he *was* nuts, but things were getting strange, and a hunch said this was important. He never ignored hunches.

Offspring safely delivered into her classroom, he drove to Jim's suburban home. Pulling into the blacktopped driveway, he nervously eyed the dashboard clock. It was one in the afternoon, but it might still be too early. Jim was pulling especially long hours since this Borgia shit hit the fan, and as Mick knew too well, no one was sleeping soundly these days. He also knew Liza would have the hide off anyone who disturbed her husband unnecessarily. Well, it *was* afternoon, and he couldn't shake the certainty this was something Jim should see. Privately.

With trepidation, he approached the planter-flanked entry only to have it flung open as he reached for the doorbell. Jim stood inside wearing his self-christened around-the-house-grungies. Fresh garden soil clung to his hands and the knees of his jeans. Jim said, "I saw you drive up and waffle around in the driveway. Whatever you got must be good. Come on in, we can talk in the kitchen; Liza just made a jug of tea."

Obediently, but uneasily, Mick followed to the kitchen. At the table, he accepted the offered drink, and began, "This is bizarre, Jim, I don't know where to start. Maybe I'd better start by showing you this."

The glossy postcard skittered across the table, and Marquez sat back, knuckles white, waiting for the reaction. Odds were even for being laughed out of the room or ordered to visit the staff psychiatrist. The silence of the kitchen was broken by the schunk-rattle of the refrigerator's built-in icemaker as Jim stared at the photo, then slipped on half-glasses to read the tiny print on the back. Placing the card carefully in the center of the table, he said, "I've only seen the file photos we've accumulated since he started working with Galen, but I'd say that could pass for our Peale. The name Byron Cyrus fits with the initials he's using here in Chicago. What else do you have?"

Marquez was floored. "You looked at the date, right?"

Jim nodded.

A pause. "So . . . you aren't going to order me to get my head examined?"

"Nope. There's too much weird shit happening, and I have too much respect for your instincts, Mick. You've been jumpy about Peale since he came on the scene, and it's interesting we don't have any pictures taken by daylight, isn't it? I can't say this constitutes an ironclad probable cause, but it's a start. I repeat: what else do you have?"

Mick exhaled the breath he'd been unconsciously holding, dug into his pocket and produced the folded show catalog with his scribbled notes about what the guide had told him. With a gravity that made Mick want to squirm in his seat, Jim read the scribbled notes then placed the booklet beside the postcard. Massaging the bridge of his nose, the Captain said in a tired voice, "Okay. I'm authorizing a background check using the name Byron Cyrus Peale. Tie into the New York mainframe and do a global search for any records containing that name or parts of it. Don't bother to specify dates, I think that will get in the way."

Mick didn't want to be ridiculed, but this response left him jogging to catch up. He slowly absorbed the orders, then declared, "My God, Jim, you aren't thinking . . . but that's impossible!"

"I don't know *what* I'm thinking yet, how about you?"

"I think I don't want to think about it."

"I hear you. Let's see how this grabs you: The lab reports on the samples taken from the parking lot came in this morning. The reddish dust from the retaining wall was desiccated blood. Human. There were traces of hemoglobin still detectable. The OIC swears blue that the smear was *wet* when she got to the scene and just fried when the sunlight hit it. She's an intelligent investigator and a good cop. I'm inclined to believe her."

"Holy shit, Jim. Just what are we talking about here?"

"I'm not exactly sure, but I think we'll get interesting feedback on Peale. Another thing, this remains between the two of us. I don't want anyone else in the team — *especially* Gae — to know about this."

Mick nodded. "He'll be pissed that we bypassed him for a background check on his new pal."

"I know, but by keeping Gae out of the loop, we reduce the chance of Peale discovering we're checking on him. Gae wouldn't tell him flat out, but when he gets mad about something, the whole world knows it. Peale couldn't help but figure something was going down. Besides, if this is what it looks like, Gae has bypassed us on more than a simple background check." After a moment, he continued, "How do you feel about the two of us going into the office early today? Say in about as much time as it'd take me to change clothes?"

TWO

Jay put the finishing touches on her makeup in the glare of the dressing-table lights, examining the results critically. Outside her window, she noted the sky darkening and smiled conspiratorially. Somewhere out there, BC Peale was waking up. Or was he already awake? Speculating on the sunset-stained clouds, she ached to tell him she knew his secret. There were gobs of questions to ask. His true age for starters — or would that be too personal? She shrugged at her reflection. Friends kindly referred to her as candid and inquisitive. Mick and her five other siblings used the term nosy. She had the uncomfortable feeling her family was closer to right.

The doorbell rang and, as she rose to answer, her eyes lit on her bedside clock. Oh geez! She'd futzed around daydreaming so long she was going to be late. Well, whoever it was could just come back later. Grabbing her pantyhose, she plopped back onto the vanity bench — the bell rang again. Then again. Another ring, then someone started pounding on the door. Jay spat a curse and, wrapping a dressing gown over her lacy chemise, she sprinted through the apartment to peer out the spy hole pausing just long enough to drop her cell in the gown's pocket. The fish-eye lens revealed a distorted view of Mario Hernandez. If his behavior was odd before, it was downright spooky now with constant fidgets, nervous glances over his shoulders, and plucking at the strap of the backpack slung over his shoulder. Hands clumsy with anger, she fastened the security chain, then demanded through the slitted door, "Mario Hernandez, what the hell are you doing here? Clear out before I call the cops."

The door caught her on the temple, knocking her backward across the loveseat. In slow motion, the chain-lock jerked taut, held, then snapped as the cheap wooden doorjamb splintered and gave way. A black shape blotted out the overhead light, and she yelped as large hands grasped her arms to draw her upright with exaggerated tenderness.

A rough hand stroking her hair broke her daze and she ducked away, clutching her dressing gown closed protectively. She defiantly met his gaze — then froze. Only the hurtling freight train of pure insanity looked back.

Retreating another step, she knew too late she should have used the phone before she opened the door. Now her only option was damage control. If only she could remember what Mick did in these situations. Unfortunately, all she could dredge up was the need to calm the subject down, but Mario wasn't agitated, if anything, he was unnaturally calm.

He regarded her with earnest solemnity as he pronounced, "I know about Peale."

Her heart skipped a beat. "What the hell are you talking about, Mario? What's there to know about BC?"

He only stared with the same compassionate intensity, if not for the chilling madness spilling from his eyes, she might have softened. Mario had never been poster child for mental stability, but he'd begun an alarming downward spiral since she'd left him at . . . *Julio's*. Oh God, did he follow her out?

She stammered, "Mario, you better go. I gotta get to work. I'm late already an' that ain't a good way to start my second night. Maybe you could come by the club later so's we can talk. If you want, I bet you can talk to BC, too."

He wasn't listening, until she mentioned BC. "It's calling you, ain't it? That's why you quit Jake's so sudden and went to that club, so you could be where It is. Don't look so shook up, you know what I'm talking about. But, it's okay, I know you couldn't tell me if you wanted to because that

Monster has you under his spell."

"Mario, don't be ridiculous—"

Fingers dug into her shoulders, and he hauled her up so roughly, she scrambled on tiptoe to stay upright. His breath was hot and sour against her cheek. "*NO*! It *isn't* ridiculous, but don't worry, I'm going to free you from his power tonight. This *Thing* that calls Itself BC Peale is a demon. A creature from Hell. I'll free you *and* Galen Miller tonight. I've been studying up on how to do it and I'm all ready."

She'd heard madness had its own strength, now, struggling against the bruising grip, she knew it was true. How much *did* Mario know? It sounded like he knew about BC's vampirism and maybe even that he was working with Gae . . . but he had everything backwards.

She insisted, "N-no, Mario, you don't understand what's going on."

"I understand better than you do. I saw that Thing kill Alfie and Chick the other night. I saw It put you under a spell and I know It's been feeding off of you. I know *everything*!"

Without warning, he released her. She bounced hard against the rough carpet, then scrambled closer to the door. "No, you got it wrong. BC isn't evil, he's a good person . . . ."

"That *Thing* you call BC ain't a *person* at all! It isn't human and It has to die once and for all." He knelt beside her, and showing the first excitement since he'd burst in, opened his pack revealing an anodized metal crossbow and two rough-carved wooden bolts. "See? I told you I knew what to do. Tonight you'll be free. I'll lure It to the Savoy Hotel — it's deserted, so no real people will be bothered."

Jay saw her chance to escape while he was absorbed with the ugly wooden shafts. Once she reached the hall, she wouldn't bother with the elevator, there were places to hide and the fire escape was close by, too. She had to warn BC. No. Galen would be easier to find. Keeping a wary eye, she fumbled for the knob, managed the latch and turned to run.

Brutal fingers tangled her hair, yanking her back to bounce unceremoniously on the floor. Growling deep in his chest, Mario threw his weight against the door, slamming it shut. Damn. It was so quick, she couldn't even scream. Part of her regretted the soundproofing of these apartments.

Nose bare inches from the carpet, she was astonished to see a bead of sweat roll down her nose and drop onto the nubby pile — or was it a tear? She couldn't be certain. Fearfully, she turned to look at him just in time to see the clenched fist hurtling toward her. Reflexively, she jerked, trying to dodge the blow that landed squarely on the point of her jaw. Stars showered briefly before darkness claimed her and she sagged into Hernandez' waiting arms.

***

Cal Reilly liked the Inferno's kitchen. *His kitchen.* It was efficient, but due to architectural constraints, more compact than luxurious. In other words, there was no room for extraneous personnel. That included the club's owner, who currently perched atop a step-stool deeply inhaling the aroma of the soup of the day. Cal ground his teeth and resumed dicing onions with increased ferocity. The invasion was expected, though. One of the big Jazz societies had reserved several tables for tonight, and Jump was always hyper before those bookings.

"Hey, Cal! Think maybe the soup could use a pinch more sweet basil?"

The cleaver quivered above the pile of minced vegetable. Wheeling, the chef advanced on the gnomish intruder. "That's it, Jump, clear outta my kitchen! Who's the chef here, anyways? When I go out on the stage to tell you what notes to play, then you can come in here and tell me how to cook."

Wizened face split by a mischievous grin, Jump turned, then alarmingly, swayed and clutched at the rail of the step-stool. Pique forgotten, Cal rushed forward to steady the shaky Cajun as he dismounted the ladder. As his feet touched the floor, Veron straightened, patted the chef's arm. "Merci,

Mon ami." Just then, Jump's cell chimed and he drew it out squinting at the screen and his face went gray. Fingers flying over the phone's buttons, he said, "If you will excuse me, there is something I must attend to."

Cal frowned as the doors swung closed behind his employer. He'd been working the club long enough to recognize the symptoms of Jump's premonitions. He'd never seen one hit this hard before.

Jump paused for a moment just outside the kitchen doors, then swore and pressed End on his cell. "Dammit, BC. Why turn off you phone?"

Across the still-darkened club floor by the entrance, Benny Glissen and Phil Quinlan were locked in conversation. Neither looked happy. He called out, "Have either of you seen BC?"

Phil nodded and jerked a thumb toward the door. "Yeah, you just missed him. There was a note for him when he came in. He read it and took off like a bat outta hell."

"Note? Who leave this note?"

Benny said, "It was that Hernandez guy. I thought about tearin' it up, but since it wasn't for Jay . . . did I screw up, Boss?"

"I don' know. Hurry. Try to catch up wit' him."

Benny bolted out the door without another word.

Phil shifted uneasily. "Jump, it doesn't take a genius to see something's wrong and I hate to add to it—"

"Do not waste time. Tell me what has happened," Veron snapped.

"It's Jay. She hasn't showed for work and isn't answering her phones." He tugged at his sideburns. "I just keep thinking about Hernandez. . . ."

Before Jump could respond, Benny returned. His face told the tale even before he said, "Couldn't catch 'im, Boss."

Fear sang in his head. He vaguely felt his knees give and strong hands catch and guide him to the benches that lined the waiting area. This would not do. Taking deep, even breaths, he willed the song to silence. Raising his head, he said, "Then we must do damage control. Benny, get the van. Now."

Benny nodded and was through the doors before Jump pulled himself to his feet. Phil hovered, worry creasing his round, pleasant face. "You sure you're okay, Jump? That was a bad one."

"*Mais oui*, but it will be worse for those the Gift speaks to me about. Come help me fill a box with large bottles." He moved unsteadily toward the bar with Phil right behind him. Control was returning. This was good. He would need all he could muster. He said, "You will have to cover for BC and myself tonight. The Glendale Jazz Society has booked for dinner and all must run smoothly if we are to avoid uncomfortable questions."

Phil nodded and busied himself pulling empty bottles out of the recycle bin. "No problem. I'll just run an open mic night. Those guys never turn down a chance to play."

"*Bon*. That will work well. You will also need to call Noreen to fill in for Jay. It is an emergency, Noreen will not argue."

Phil loaded the box of bottles onto a folding handcart and followed Jump out the back to meet Benny. "Do you know what this is about?"

Jump shook his head. "Not yet. I just that BC is in serious danger — Jay, also."

They busied themselves loading the bottles into the cargo area, then Phil lifted Veron into the van. As he helped the little Cajun into the seat, Jump whispered, "Let Bob open the club, you must get over to Jay's place. Make sure she's all right. There are bad things afoot tonight."

Phil Quinlan's eyes shifted color for a split second before he nodded curtly and shut the door. As the van rolled out into traffic, Jump watched the young man dart back into the club, phone pressed to his ear.

"Where we goin', Boss?" Benny asked.

"We will need supplies. The hardware place where the Inferno has an account should do. When we have that, there will be one other thing." Yes. One other thing. That would come from somewhere else.

As Benny drove, Veron's thoughts kept returning to Mario Hernandez.

The man had until this night been harmless. A narcissist, to be sure — and not a terribly bright one, but still not a threat. This had changed. Why?

He had no idea. The only thing he was certain of was that physical danger threatened his old friend. *That* he could deal with. At least he knew where to go and what to do. Unfortunately, there were things he couldn't handle alone, for that he'd need Benny and Benny's physical strength. Of course, that also meant he'd have to share BC's secret. BC wouldn't mind. Benny had proven himself time and time again. It remained to be seen how Benny would take the revelation.

***

Jay awoke to an extreme close-up of her bedroom rug. Feeble light from the downstairs security lights seeped around the blinds. Discovering she couldn't sit up, she craned her neck to find she'd been trussed up with her own pantyhose.

Damn you, Mario Hernandez, those were new! Curbing her fury, she strained to listen to the rest of the apartment. Nothing. Deciding she was alone, she struggled against the taut nylon. If that louse figured her to lie there and wait for him to come back, he had another think coming. Mrs. Marquez didn't raise no victims! At least he hadn't stuffed a gag in her mouth.

It was so dark, she must've been out a long time, but it was hard to tell. The time didn't matter, anyway. What mattered was getting loose and warning BC and Gae. Oh God! What if BC had already taken the bait — whatever *that* was?

Dammit. The nylon didn't give or even slip a little, and her hands and feet were numb. Maybe she'd work her way to the front door and worry about the latch when she got there. No way she'd simply lie there and yell until someone heard her. Screaming wouldn't do much good, anyway. Wriggling as much in frustration as against the bindings, she caught a flash off the full-length dressing mirror on the closet door. Hey! That was worth a try, it would probably hurt, but it was better than doing nothing.

The carpet burns earned by scooting across the room only fired her determination, but at last, she was in front of the mirror. She rolled over to shield her face and kicked, impacting solidly, knocking the glass from its hangers. It dropped and shattered, raining glittering shards over her. Ignoring the myriad stings of small cuts, she groped for a suitable piece and set to work. It took another eternity to saw through the tough nylon.

Cautiously teetering tiptoe, she flipped on the overheads before gingerly stepping over the puddle of sparkling splinters. Daring a glance at her wrists and fingers, she grimaced at the streams of free-flowing blood. The pain had yet to reach her shock-numbed brain and she wasn't looking forward to when it did. At least she didn't nick anything important.

Her best guesstimate for elapsed time was forty-five minutes. No time to wash up, she dressed quickly, then took a small chromed pistol from the night stand drawer, slamming home a full clip in the same move. Bless Saint Mick the Paranoid for both the weapon and making her practice until she was a decent shot. Sometimes having a cop for a brother wasn't a bad thing.

In the kitchen, she made for the dishcloth drying over the edge of the sink and wrapped the linen tightly around her cuts. She pulled out her cell. Some rhinestones were missing from the pink skin, but she was relieved when the screen lit up. With all the abuse it had taken, she'd figured it would have been toast.

***

Francesco Borgia paced the room like a fractious tiger. The array of flickering candles dazzled his sensitive vision and the billowing incense hung in the air in a choking cloud. The damnable stuff had permeated the entire penthouse.

Trying to ignore the spicy-sweet cloud, he stepped closer to the candle circle to watch Maeve weaving the enchantment. The spell seemed to be proceeding well — that meant nothing, though. They'd all *started* well, they simply didn't work. It *had* to work this time! He shoved his rage down with gritted teeth and clenched fists. Anger here was futile. There was nothing and no one on which to vent it, he certainly couldn't aim it at Maeve. As much as he would have liked a scapegoat, it wasn't Maeve's fault. Throughout the time he'd known her, this was the first time her spells failed to bear fruit. There'd been something odd about this whole affair from the outset. Some vaguely sensed wrongness, even before he learned there was another vampire in his territory. It was an out-of-step feeling that had nagged at him since he set up operations in Chicago.

Maeve was frustrated, too. A witch of her caliber could, if she so wished, shield herself from even the most acute empathic senses. Maeve was drawing the cloak tightly over her emotions now. He was close enough to reach out a hand and brush her hair, but still, she was an empty space in the emotional tapestry of the sprawling penthouse. A Maeve-shaped emptiness outlined by the faintest wisps of frustration seeping around the edges. She'd been casting on her own during daylight hours, too. He knew that as surely as if he'd watched her do it. He knew just as surely that those spells had failed, too. If they hadn't, all the hosts of hell could not have kept her from crowing her triumph. That didn't matter, either, he no longer cared *how* the thing got done, he simply wanted it done.

More was bothering her than the failed spells, but he had no idea what — and Maeve certainly wouldn't tell him. Perhaps he should arrange a quiet time for them both, a retreat to gather thoughts and regain focus. It had been a long time since the two of them had been alone together. Even longer since they had been intimate. He paused, appreciating the graceful movements of her lithe body as she performed the spell. He had no idea where the tradition of casting powerful spells in the nude began, but he approved of it. Yes. He would do this.. Their once overwhelming passion had faded, but they still enjoyed each other physically, and Maeve's blood had a certain power, a tang that . . . .

The supple spine he observed with such keen interest snapped rigid, and her murmured chant changed to a shriek that rent the smoky air of the chamber. Maeve's hands clawed violently at the center of her chest before she collapsed in a frighteningly still heap amid overturned incense cups.

He was at her side before her heart beat again. Yes, it was still beating. Faintly. Stretching his supernatural senses to their limit, he could detect nothing physically wrong. At the same time, those senses screamed that she was near death. He scooped the ragdoll body into his arms and raced into the hall bellowing for Edgar to summon the doctor.

***

Being undercover didn't allow for many nights off — even fewer once things got crazy with the Borgia investigation and Miller had been looking forward to this one. It felt like he and Peale had done nothing but chase their own tails lately, it would be nice to do something different for. Preferably separately.

Apparently, Peale agreed. Miller hadn't seen undead hide nor hair of his partner since he bolted from the apartment just before dawn the night before. His ass was probably glued to the piano bench at the Inferno by now. That was his avowed intention, anyway. To each his own. The idea of sitting under a spotlight on the stage of a smoke-filled nightclub struck Miller as a true slice of hell. Peale seemed to thrive on it.

There. Recliner jacked back as far as it would go. Check. Popcorn and beer within easy reach. Check and check. Sighing his contentment, Galen aimed the remote control at the DVD to start one of the action movies he'd rented and nestled against the pillowed chair back. The telephone rang. He swore artistically and briefly considered letting the machine get it, then snatched the damned thing up, anyway. "Yello."

"Gae? Jay Marquez. You gotta get to the old Savoy hotel as fast as you can, Mario Hernandez is trying to trick BC into meeting him there. He may have already done it, I dunno, he tied me up an' I just got loose."

"Jay?" He sat up violently, slamming the recliner closed. Damn' good thing she'd identified herself, she was so upset he'd never have recognized her voice. She was out of breath and maybe running as she talked. "That jerkoff tied you up? Look, stay where you are and . . . ."

"Gae, I know about BC's . . . uh . . . blood problem. And I know you an' him are agents. Mick told me, he didn't mean to, but he did. I tried to call BC's phone to warn him, but it's turned off, so I called you. We ain't got much time. Mario's setting a trap so he can kill BC with this crossbow thing he's got!"

It took him a second to get his mouth working again and before he could say anything more, she'd hung up.

Numbly replacing the dead handset. He knew without a doubt that BC *would* go to the Savoy. He'd just have to get there first. It wasn't far. Had Peale already left the club or had he even *gotten* there? There was no time to waste on phone tag. Quickly checking his Beretta, he charged out struggling into his jacket as he went.

***

Parking down the block from the dilapidated building, Miller walked the remaining distance with feigned indifference. He needn't have bothered. The street was deserted.

The hotel's once-grand entry was newly boarded in an effort to keep the street people out, the 'NO TRESPASSING' posters were still fresh and the plywood sealing the doors and windows solidly anchored. It would probably hold until the next rainy day. The former landmark was slated for demolition, and had been for longer than Galen cared to remember. Neighborhood wisdom held that the city was waiting for the thing to burn down and save them the trouble of knocking it down.

Without breaking stride, he ducked into the alley along the back of the building. Hernandez was an unknown quantity, but he knew his partner well. BC would shun the front door. Right the first time. BC's Softail was stashed securely behind a battered dumpster, its engine still giving off a little heat. A short distance away, the rear door hung loose on its hinges, swaying in the night breeze. There was no other sign of Peale and none at all of Jay. He was glad for the latter, Hernandez had turned dangerous. With luck, she'd stay far away from this place and Hernandez.

Unweathered wood gleamed through the alligatored paint on the flapping door marking the spot where a lock had been pried off. Hernandez. Peale wouldn't leave that much evidence.

Weapon pointed away and down, Miller slid cautiously inside, pausing just long enough for his eyes to adjust to the interior gloom. It didn't take long, the outside walls were in such sorry shape, the inside light wasn't that different from the outside. Just ahead he discerned the dim outline of a staircase, and carefully picked his way toward it through the refuse, praying that the underlying floorboards were solid. If they weren't, he was gonna be one sorry ex-linebacker.

Soft, scraping footfalls of someone descending spooked him into the deeper shadows. He wasn't fast enough.

"Miller!"

The strangled voice from halfway up the flight wasn't BC, so it had to be: "Hernandez. I was told you'd be here. Where's Peale?"

With a guttural cry and a glitter of panicked eyes, Hernandez hurled himself over the banister and pelted down a side corridor.

Miller spat curses and plunged into the blackness after him. As he rounded the corner, a heavy blow to the side of his head pitched him against the crumbling plaster wall. His pistol clattered to the floor from numbed fingers.

Abandoning his club, Hernandez dived and scrabbled through the trash for the gun. He coaxed uncooperative fingers into the proper positions and raised the weapon. Miller flung himself to one side as the pistol roared in the confined space. Lathe and plaster exploded from the wall where his head had rested a moment before. The flash and explosion momentarily blinded and deafened both of them. Miller had been trained for that. Hernandez hadn't.

Miller snatched the metal thing Hernandez had used on him, and swung. It hooked solidly behind his opponent's legs. Galen grinned in the darkness and yanked with all his strength. Hernandez' legs flew out from under him, crashing him to the deck, loosing a bellow and flurry of wild shots into the ancient ceiling that exploded into a rain of debris.

Galen *hadn't* been prepared for that and caught a faceful of dust. The erstwhile club pinged to the floor, as he dug at stinging streaming eyes. He didn't see Hernandez clenching his hands into a single sledgehammer fist. He felt it, though. The punch sent him reeling backward through a rotting door to sprawl in the room beyond.

Galen groaned, picked himself up and searched for Hernandez through still-flowing tears. The rear door slammed against the building. Something told him it wasn't a passing breeze. Groans became profanity as he raced for the hallway. He didn't have time to chase the idiot through the streets of Chicago, Jim would be better equipped for that — providing he could figure out how to report this without telling all about Peale. Oh, God.

He'd almost forgotten Peale. That was why he was in this dump in the first place. He was worried now. The fight was brief but noisy, and his buddy still hadn't put in an appearance. That wasn't like him. He was there, though. The Harley proved that.

Stepping over the splintered remains of the door, he realized he'd left the flashlight in the car. Stupid. He'd gotten too used to relying on his partner's acute senses lately. Patting himself down produced a book of matches from the Inferno. Wimpy, but there was no time to traipse back to the car. The flaring match caused irritated eyes to resume tearing. Through a lachrymose fog, he searched the trash for his dropped weapon. Missing partner or no, it wouldn't be smart to leave the pistol. The heat from the second match was becoming uncomfortable as he located the 380 half hidden by plaster chunks. He waved the flame out and bent for what he hoped was the right spot. His foot struck the pistol before his questing hand brushed it, sending it skidding and pinging into Hernandez' erstwhile bludgeon. What the hell? He couldn't examine the thing before, he'd simply used what came to hand. Curiosity overcame his aches as he scooped up both items, straining to make out the alien form in the gloom. He wasn't happy when he did. It was a crossbow.

Clutching the bow, he gulped back fear and called, "*Peale*! Where are you?" He ran breakneck up the protesting old staircase ignoring the creaks and snaps of the ancient boards. "*PEALE*! Answer me! This ain't funny dammit!"

At the top of the stairs a door hung off it's hinges making a crazy shape of darker dark against the murk of the hallway. Swallowing hard, he readied his pistol and edged into the room. His voice shook as he called again, "Peale? C'mon, man, tell me where you are, *talk* to me, buddy."

Silence. Not even street noise made it this far into the dusty place. Dry mouthed, he stepped farther in. His left foot landed in wetness and slipped from under him, sprawling him across something soft. Swearing under his breath, he wiped his hands on his jeans and dug out the matches. He struck one.

By the flickering light he found himself kneeling in a pool of thickening blood staring at the end of a shaft of wood that protruded obscenely from his partner's chest.

***

No doubt about it. The big bike was BC's, there couldn't be two hogs in Chicago with that custom leather work. Gae's car was up the block, it was a safe bet both were near, but where? Inside? Ineffectually fanning at the stench of the dumpster, she wondered what *she* was doing there. In the heat of the moment, it seemed like a good idea, but now, after the adrenaline rush subsided, she wasn't so sure. She fingered her cell phone, its pink faceplate and flashy rhinestones looked out of place in the dingy alley. Dammit. She should call Mick. He didn't know about BC's vampirism and it would mean a whole lot of difficult questions, but he was trained for this shit, she wasn't.

The distinctive crack of gunfire from inside jolted through her like an electric shock. Rooted by indecision, she stared at the building until the clatter of running footsteps broke the spell. Instinctively, she ducked behind the motorcycle, peeking through the fork, hoping for an irate BC to loom over her, wanting to know why she was messing with his bike. Instead, she got Mario Hernandez. Eyes wild with terror, he fairly flung himself through the remains of the back door, his velocity slammed it explosively against the grimy brick wall.

Arms flailing, he hit the pavement running and continued past her hiding place without looking anywhere but over his shoulder. He pelted toward the street like he had no intention of stopping until he put a lot of distance between himself and this place. Good. Or was it? Nails dug into palms, she nervously eyed the door to see who emerged next. The black rectangle remained stubbornly empty.

A vision of her friends lying dead in the dark rose up and refused to be dismissed. Finally, she heard Galen's voice deep within the hotel. It was muffled and impossible to make out the words, but proved he was alive. Tentatively, she moved toward the sounds, lighting her electric camping lantern as she entered the blackness. She'd keep her fingers crossed that BC was okay, too.

Galen called somewhere above and ahead of her. Carefully making her way across the ruined hall, her light revealed broad scuffs in the dust leading down a side corridor. Looked like a helluva fight had happened there. She went over to the rickety stairwell and stood with one foot on the bottom step, debating what to do. Part of her hoped the old hotel had swallowed up the sound of the shots. Having a pack of Chicago's finest barging in would be kind of inconvenient. She glanced around, uncertain what to do next. If she stayed put, she had a good view of the back door. If anyone poked their nose in— The thought died unfinished as a crash and an agonized wail tore through the dusty air.

Brain in shutdown, and adrenaline in overdrive, Jay was suddenly at the top of the stairs running toward the sound. It was hard to make out where it was coming from since it had faded to a soft whisper that seemed to come from everywhere. She slowed her pace stepping cautiously until the voice seemed to come through an opening almost directly ahead. The voice said, "I'm sorry. I got here as fast as I could. You should have called me. Why the hell didn't you call me?"

Fear iced her skin. Even through the distortion of the old rooms, she recognized Galen's voice. She'd never heard him sound so sad before. Poking the light around first, she peeked into the room.

The lantern's beam fell across Galen's broad back as he knelt rocking gently, cradling something. Almost against her will, she entered the ruined room, lighting more of the scene as she went. Her knees went rubbery as she recognized BC's leather motorcycle pants. The stillness of the long legs they encased was chilling. She was as prepared as humanly possible for the crude wooden shaft embedded in the vampire's breast, but nothing could've prepared her for the incredible quantities of blood.

Tasting bile, she put the lantern down, forcing herself to kneel to look closer. Fingers trembling, she touched the cold skin. It was supple, but looked like parchment. Most alarming were the long, sharp fangs that gleamed between drawn lips in the glare of the lamp. *¡Madre de Dios!* If she'd only *watched* those stupid drive-in horror movies instead of making out in the back seat, maybe she'd know what to do. Well, she knew one thing. The stake had to come out.

Teeth clenching her lower lip, she wrapped both hands around the shaft and pulled. The withering body shifted slightly, but the stake didn't budge. *It must be jammed between his ribs or something.* She wasn't strong enough. Galen was, though.

The big man was in deep shock, his face vacant as he cradled his friend's head in his lap, stroking the blood-matted hair as he would a sick child's. She had to snap him out of it, or BC was a goner, providing it wasn't too late already. Lacking time for finesse, Jay lashed out with a sneakered foot and kicked. "F'God's sakes, Galen, the stake! Pull the damn' stake out!"

Something stirred behind Gae's eyes as he turned, noticing Jay for the first time. In a faraway voice he said, "Wha . . . Jay?" He focused on her face, then his gaze slid to the blood spattered wooden shaft. "Yeah, you're right! I'm a goddamned idiot. If he's still with us he oughta start healing with that thing gone."

Wasting a second to shake the cobwebs away, huge hands engulfed the exposed portion of the bolt and pulled. Peale's body merely arched off the floor. The stake stayed. Galen swore. Tears cutting paths through the dust caking her cheeks, Jay sobbed.

She threw herself across Peale's body. "Try again."

Galen nodded and pulled. The stake moved. He rearranged his grip and tugged harder. It pulled free with a sucking sound that made Jay wince. Her gaze fell the blood-sodden bandage on her arm. It had slipped, exposing the angry gash that again bled freely. Blood. Vampires needed blood and here was a ready supply.

Cursing Mario Hernandez and his whole family, past and present, she tore off the tape and gauze. Teeth clenched against the pain, she dribbled blood between the vampire's lips. The dim light made the shadows deceptive, but it sure looked like he swallowed.

Galen forgot the gory stake in his hands when he saw her cuts. "Goddam, Jay! Did Hernandez do that?"

"Not exactly, but it was his fault. At least I can say it was for a good cause. I don't think I'd have the nerve to cut myself on purpose — even for BC."

Galen grunted. "I'm still not thinking right. He *will* need lots of blood."

Jay looked up from milking her arm. "You better do it too, he'll probably need more than either of us can give, but maybe we can give him enough to keep him alive."

Fumbling his pocket knife out, he agreed, "Gotcha. Let's see if we can get him stabilized enough to carry back to my place. We're about as close to bein' out in the street as it gets without actually bein' there." Knife blade hovering over his own arm, he returned, "Hey, not that Peale and I don't appreciate the assist, but how did you come to know about Peale's . . . condition, anyway."

"That's a long story, Gae."

He bit back pain as he sliced himself, then leaned forward to join his trickle to Jay's. "Well, start talkin'. I think we've got time."

THREE

"mmmmmrrbrrrgaacnfn nophysical reason for this collapse. Perhaps we shdddremvhr . . . ."

The words echoed down a deep well, coming in and out of focus like someone was wrapping and unwrapping cotton batting around her ears. She swam slowly through the darkness, drawn toward the distant buzz. The softness of a feather mattress resolved itself beneath her, and after a moment, the buzzing became quietly concerned words. A short distance away, Francesco expressed displeasure. An unknown voice insisted the patient be removed to a hospital for proper tests. Since nobody noticed her awakening, she kept her eyes closed. She was weak and needed time to think.

What on earth happened? This had little to do with magic and nothing whatsoever to do with her spells. No. No use fooling herself. She knew exactly what had happened, she was simply avoiding acknowledging it. It was Byron. Dying.

First, there was the agony of something piercing her chest, then a hideous, black cold surged around and through her. It was encouraging that it dissipated as quickly as it struck. A soul-deep certainty told her it was a near thing, but he'd survived. Just as surely, she knew she couldn't tell Francesco anything about it. To him the bond between herself and his way-ward fledgling would be quite an Achilles' heel — not that he ever *wanted* that fledgling. She fought a surge of nausea. *Damn this barrier, whatever or whoever it is! I've never known the like. It wouldn't gall so if it weren't keeping me from seeing Byron, too. I've come closer finding him, albeit only in glimpses. Be damned if I'll settle for glimpses after this. I'll break through if it kills me!*

Deciding was one thing, succeeding was another thing entirely. She had to get away from Francesco, and be quick about it. With his supernatural awareness, her charade couldn't last long. His worry surprised her. Still, it offered her an opening. Concern might provide the wedge she needed to call a hiatus in the spellcasting. She'd need it if she were to find Byron now — and she was going to. Until she knew what happened and how badly he was hurt, she wouldn't be able to keep her mind on anything else.

Knowing it was more effective than a shout, she sighed and stirred. Straightaway, the edge of the bed sank under Francesco's weight. "Maeve! Can you speak, Cara? What has happened?"

How sweet! She almost felt sorry for him. Summoning a weak smile, she replied, "But, Frankie, Darlin', isn't that supposed to be my line?"

He snorted in disgust, and turned to where Eddie Michalson and a stranger stood by the window. "She has recovered. Her impudence has returned unabated." He stood, and bowed toward the stranger. "Thank you for responding so swiftly, Doctor Kampo. Mr. Michalson will see to your fee."

The doctor was not ready to be dismissed, though. He bent over his patient again, fussing and arguing in favor of further tests. When the patient, herself, refused, he shrugged and allowed himself to be shown out

As soon as the door clicked behind Michalson, Maeve flung the coverlet aside and reached for her robe. The room spun as she stood. When it righted itself, she found herself clasped tightly in Francesco's arms. His lips brushed her hair as he murmured, "I hope I have not dismissed the doctor too soon."

She pulled away with a coquettish grin. "You're daft, I'm alright, just tired. You know this kind of castin' takes a lot out of me, perhaps we should take a break. Not a long one, a day or two maybe. Your nuisance seems to be layin' low these past few nights, anyway."

"As you wish, *Preziosa*, I should have sensed . . . I *did* sense your weariness, but I did nothing about it."

With uncharacteristic gentleness, he kissed her fingertips. Exhaustion scented her skin like a heavy musk. How foolish to allow impatience to blind him to her growing weariness. One should never let an ally like Maeve Donal slip away frivolously. He'd been of a mind to take time out and simply enjoy her company, anyway. A pity he hadn't decided before he'd allowed her to push herself to collapse. Returning her smile, he lightly caressed her again. "*Ecco!* It has been a strain for both of us. I wish this renegade found and stopped more than I can express, but you are much more important."

He had more in mind, but Maeve didn't have time for it. She Pulled out of his grasp and slipped into her robe. "Francesco, M'Love, I'm thinkin' I maybe ought to be gettin' back my lodgings. I need rest and there are surely things you've let go beggin' while we were workin'." She added silently. "*And I'll be lookin' for Byron this very night. The last thing I'm needin' is you lookin' over my shoulder.*"

Escaping the charmingly concerned aristocrat and returning to her rooms proved harder than she'd planned. By the time she flopped across the big hotel bed, it was nearly dawn and far too late to begin a complicated spell. If she had to be brutally honest, it was probably too late by the time she regained consciousness. Francesco had never been forthcoming about his vampirism and all it entailed, but she knew enough to know that a severe injury like Byron must have suffered would render him as dormant as he was by day. It was part of the healing process for his kind.

The more time passed, the more confident she was that Byron had survived. The awful chill was fading as she'd regained her senses, and was completely gone now. She hoped that was a good sign. If only she could ask Frankie, but that was out of the question . . . maybe her mother. . . .

She pounded her fists against the mattress, furious at her own timidity. Of course, he wasn't destroyed, she'd *know* if he were, and bother the fine details. Although the concept was ghastly, the sensations she'd felt could mean only one thing. Someone had driven a stake through his heart. He could only survive that mortal blow with quick help from an outside source. Interesting. She smiled. Byron always had the knack of making friends.

Regardless who helped him, the fact remained that it was dawn and she'd have to wait until dusk to have the slightest chance of espying him — if then. As badly hurt as he must be, he might sleep on in spite of the setting sun. There was no way to know. All she could do was to be patient until dusk, then cast again and not stop trying until she'd seen for herself.

Resigned, she rose and folded back the cool sheets. She hadn't exaggerated to Francesco. The kind of sorcery they'd been engaged in was exhausting. The constant effort left her wrung-out, but at the same time, strangely agitated. However, remaining awake wouldn't do Byron or herself any good.

Opening a well-worn leather case, she removed several earthenware jars, expertly mixed a sleeping draught, then drew a hot bath laced with a handful of sweet-scented herbs. Easing her tired body into the steaming potpourri, she smiled as the knots in her muscles loosened. Leaning back, she enjoyed the herbed steam, sipped her draught and allowed the memories to come. They would anyway, she might as well welcome them.

She'd always loved for him to scrub her back. It was such a small thing that gave such great pleasure. Pleasure, that is, until he invariably gave in to temptation and tweaked a sensitive area of her anatomy. Then there'd be a lovely tussle that ended even more pleasurably than a back-scrub.

Those were happy times, at least *she'd* thought they were. She'd surprised everyone (herself included) by falling head over heels in love, and Byron had loved her in return. In the end, that was precisely the trouble.

Witness the day he came to her house, stood by the fireplace bold as brass and announced that it was over. He wasn't ready to accept the obligation of the next stage that their liaison demanded. The dread word marriage never passed his lips, but that's what he'd meant. Well, *she* hadn't been ready for marriage, either, but he didn't give her the chance to say that. That was bad enough, but his reaction when she'd gotten angry and told him that she was a witch and angering her kind was dangerous was worse. He'd openly scoffed . . . worse: He'd laughed. That was the final straw. She'd flung a wine bottle at him. The blackguard ducked, and wine splattered all over the carpet. It had been the very devil to get out. He'd straightway turned on his heel and walked out.

Nobody walked out on Maeve Donal!

It took longer to decide what to do about the black-hearted rat than it did to locate Francesco Borgia. She'd found him in New York City engaged in one of his ubiquitous business deals. Some things never changed. Unfortunately, he hadn't been particularly enthusiastic about her plan. He'd never felt the urge to make a fledgling and didn't care to do so upon request. She prevailed on his carnal nature, coaxing him to Philadelphia to see the intended for himself. As expected, Byron's own dark good-looks were the final persuasion.

A slight frown creased her brow. Perhaps chaining him down after Frankie delivered him into her keeping, was a tactical error. But she hadn't wanted to hold him prisoner, she'd only wanted to hold him still after he rose for the first time so she could instruct him in his new nature.

She chewed her lip thoughtfully. He was quite irate when he awoke and found himself bound to the bed. Byron was so handsome when he was angry and he'd been magnificent up until the time he'd accidentally snapped the chains. She hadn't counted on him doing that. Neither had she counted on him becoming self-sufficient without her.

She sighed and sank deeper into the scented water. There was no way around it, she still loved him even if he loathed her. Draining the last of her tisane, and setting the cup aside, she stepped from the cooling bath into a luxuriously large towel.

A wonderfully warm drowsiness seeped through her as she flicked off the lights and slid between the sheets. Damn, she mixed a good potion! She placed the little portrait of Byron carefully on the other pillow and let sleep enfold her.

***

He'd meant to replace the bulbs in the hall. He even had the new bulbs, energy efficient compact florescent ones, but he just kept forgetting. Truth to tell, he didn't have a lot of incentive to remember, his was the only apartment in the basement and the laundry room was clear on the other side of the building. He cursed his laziness now as he and Jay crept down the badly-lit passage trying not to bang Peale into anything — not that he'd notice if they did. Glancing at the limp burden in his arms he worried again that they hadn't been able to get enough blood into him. For the umpteenth time since they'd left the Savoy, he searched the scarecrow bundle for any encouraging sign. No good. The corridor was too dark to see any difference even if he knew what he was looking for.

His internal alarms went berserk as he approached his doorway and saw the rubber mat lying flat under the door. It was definitely in its usual position *against* the door when he left. He'd been in a hurry and hadn't set the other tells, but he'd certainly kicked *that* into place. Someone entered the apartment after he left. It wouldn't have been his mother, she groused about paranoia, but was careful to reset "his tomfoolery" anyway. He motioned Jay toward the inner wall, then eased his burden onto the carpet beside her.

Weapon drawn, he reached for the knob. The door swung open before he touched it.

He froze, blinking in the wedge of bright light from his apartment, the muzzle of the .380 level with the top of Jump Veron's head. The diminutive jazzman ignored it. "Don' jus' stand there lookin' stupid, get him in here. I got your back room ready an' lots of cow blood in the 'frigerator."

Recovering quickly, Galen thrust the pistol into its holster, reclaimed Peale and hurried through with Jay on his heels. As the mini-procession brushed past, Jump drew a sharp breath at the extent of the damage. BC had been hurt before, but this was more serious than anything he'd seen. Closing the door with trembling hands, he asked in a hushed voice, "How has this happened?"

Jay pulled the crossbow and bloodstained stake from her shoulder-bag, and thrust them into the little man's hands. "Courtesy of Mario Hernandez. We brought them back so we could destroy them."

He stared in horror. "*Mon Dieu*,"

Benny came around the kitchen counter just in time to see Galen Miller carry a filthy mummy into the spare room. The slow realization that the mummy was actually BC Peale was more than he could take in at once. In spite of everything Jump said, the sight of the handsome man reduced to this, and the reality of the jutting fangs stunned him. He wanted to scream, to ask how were they sure he wasn't really dead, but his dry mouth wouldn't form the words.

He watched from the doorway as Jump helped guide the body onto the cot, and started as the little man called sharply, "Benny! Bring two flasks and the tube. Quickly!"

The big blond man tried to carry out the order, but could neither move nor tear his gaze from the scene in the room. Jay, glanced back from her place by the bed, and understood. Taking his arm, she propelled him toward the kitchen, saying, "C'mon, I'll give ya a hand."

With Jay herding him through the tasks, they fell into an efficient routine, and Benny began to relax. He was almost back to normal when, while they were unrolling and cutting the length of aquarium tubing hurriedly bought from a closing pet store, he noticed the cuts on Jay's arms. He froze. "How'd that happen? BC didn't. . . ?"

She shook her head firmly. "Mario Hernandez is responsible for this — hell, that dimwit is responsible for *all* of this!" Uncertain how to respond, Benny concentrated on rinsing out the tubing as she continued, "Damn that stupid sonuvabitch! He found out BC was different and it scared him shitless."

Benny looked up guiltily from drying the tube. "It scares me, too. I mean — damn! I jus' found out an' then to see him like this."

Jay gripped his arm gently. "I know. It ain't an easy idea to get used to. *Vampires?* They're the guys in the movies with the black capes and tuxedos. Then there's BC, leather pants and motorcycle jackets. I wouldn't have believed it myself if I hadn't . . . well, if I hadn't seen some stuff. I ain't sayin' it don't scare me, but I figure ya gotta look at it the same way as a medical thing. Y'know, like if he was diabetic and needed insulin? Instead BC needs blood."

She gathered two bottles of blood and jogged away. Clutching the tubing, Benny followed. He said, "He's always been real good ta me. Other people treat me like I'm retarded because I'm big and kinda slow, BC never did."

"He's one of the good guys, Benny. He needs help now, too."

"I know. It's just . . . ." He reddened. "I hope he don't need this too often. Don't tell nobody, but I don't like blood."

"Really?"

"Yeah. Passed out cold at the butcher's place. Twice."

Jay noted the larger man's pallor with new appreciation. Hugging the bottles closer, she took the tubing from him, saying, "In that case, maybe I oughta take this in an' you should get something to clean him up with. He's an awful mess."

Benny brightened. "Yeah! I'll get soap and water and stuff from the bathroom."

A short time later, Benny emerged from the bathroom juggling towels, a bucket of hot water and a bottle of antibacterial soap as the front door to the apartment opened. He froze as an elderly black woman poked her head into the room and called, "Galen! What in heaven's name you *doin'* down here?"

Catching sight of the blond stranger standing awkwardly in the living room, she slammed the door, marched up and poked an authoritative finger into his face. "Young man, *who* are you and *where* is my son?"

Hastily buttoning sleeves over his newly-dressed cuts, Galen sped in on an intercept and rescue mission. An intrigued Jump Veron followed close behind. Miller assumed his most charming smile and went straight for his mother, sweeping her up for a bear hug. Waving Glissen out of sight, he exclaimed, "Mama! What are you doing down here this time of night? You should be. . . ."

She pushed him away, declaring, "Don't try to put me off Galen Samuel Miller! I want to know what you *doin'* down here. It feels like a psychic fireworks display going on!"

From his unobtrusive post by the back room door, Jump grunted and supplied softly, "That BC fightin' to survive. His will is very strong an' make big ripples aroun' him. Bes' you tell you Mama what has happened. If the lady sense the struggle, she need to know."

Jasmine Miller swung toward the voice, then back with a questioning look at her towering son. Galen said, "Jump's right. I'm sorry, Mama, I'm still too shook to think straight. That damned Mario Hernandez tried to kill Peale tonight by putting a crossbow arrow through his chest. He's in my spare room right now — Peale, I mean, not Hernandez."

She rolled her eyes. She sometimes wondered if the boy suffered brain damage in those football pileups. Brushing briskly past, she strode for the back room. "I *know* who you mean. Like you're gonna bring that bonehead Hernandez into this place!"

Bulling into the room, she stopped short at what met her eyes. For the first time in memory, she was in a quandary. This thing lying helpless and injured before her was an undead creature, but at the same time, an articulate and seemingly well-bred boy. He was also quickly becoming her youngest son's best friend. Shucking indecision like an old coat, she appropriated the pan of water from the blond man. "You call this hot? This is barely warm! What's your name? Benny? Good. Benny, go get another pan of *hot* water. I said pan, mind you. No buckets! We're not swabbin' floors here.

"Juanita, I'm not gonna waste time askin' what you're doin' in this, just keep on doin' what you're doin'." Wheeling, she almost bowled over the amiably homely gnome following her. She ignored him and continued issuing orders. "Galen, go up to my place and bring back my healing things. I don't know how they'll work on an undead, but it couldn't hurt."

Nobody moved. She glared at the stop-action tableau. "Well?"

Benny shot Jump a wild-eyed look, then bolted from the room. Galen followed carrying on an animated, muttered conversation with himself. Jay giggled, then lifting the flask, said, "This one's empty. I better get another one from the kitchen."

She sped out, leaving Mrs. Miller and Jump with the comatose vampire. Mrs. Miller busied herself sponging crusting blood off restoring flesh with the tepid water. Behind her, the little man cleared his throat and began. "I am Augustine Veron. . . ."

She didn't look up. "I know who you are. You own that nightclub this one is always playin' music at."

Jump laid a gentle hand on the vampire's ravaged body, stressing, "I am *half*-owner. BC is my partner and my oldest friend. I am not without skill. I, too, would like to help wit' the healing."

Keen amber eyes sliced through him, making him want to squirm. He resisted the urge, returning her gaze levelly until she turned back to her task, saying, "Suit yourself, but you stay clear of my road, I got work to do here."

"But of course." He agreed readily, then added, "It will be difficult to work together without having a name to call you. . . ?"

Again the penetrating examination, then a slight smile. "My name is Jasmine — and don't you go callin' me Jazz! That's the corrupted nick-name, my son tagged my granddaughter with. What's wrong with calling her by her full name, I don't know."

"*Mais oui*, I shall never commit such an atrocity." He treated her to a wide smile. Such an impressive woman, he'd felt her power even as she was coming down the elevator. *Jasmine*! *Tres magnifique*!

* * *

Peale stirred and was rewarded with shooting pains through his chest. Si-multaneously, a pounding in his head manifested, he discovered his mouth was dry and his throat burned like he'd swallowed lye. He opted to lie still for a while. Yes. That was better.

Waitaminit. This wasn't the tunnel. It was far too warm and there was no dripping water. Concentrating on the scents and sounds of this environ-ment, he noticed that wherever he was, he was lying on a bed. That was nice. Much better than the sleeping bag. Somewhere to his right a door opened and quiet footsteps approached.

He knew that scent . . . yeah . . . it was . . . oh damn if his head would stop throbbing maybe he could think. He tentatively opened his eyes. Jump Veron's pleasantly frog-like face filled his vision.

"*Bien!* You awake finally. You out for a night and a half. We were much worried, *mon ami*." Sweeping a gentle hand over the cool forehead, he smiled and continued, "The fever is gone, too, but I imagine you feel pretty bad, no? Such a wound does not heal so fast."

Drawing breath to reply sent shafts of fire through the vampire's body, and a fit of coughing doubled him up as abused lungs expelled the last of the fluid that had settled there. On the edge of his vision, Galen and his mother burst into the room, the former clutching a bottle and a plastic cup. Jump took the cup and held it under the invalid's nose. A welcome scent rose causing canines to lengthen in response.

Jump said, "Not as good as getting it yourself, *mon ami*, but it will serve until you are stronger."

Peale seized the cup with trembling hands and drained it. Galen stepped forward to refill it, his soft rumble filling the chamber, "This came from the processing place where Jump buys meat for the club. He and Benny have been going there every night to make sure you had fresh when you finally woke up."

Jump commented pointedly, "It is splendid to have friends, no?"

Galen probed, "Do you remember what happened?"

"Not really." Propping himself up on his elbows, Peale's brow furrowed with the effort to recall. "The last thing I remember was meeting Mario Hernandez in an upstairs room at the Savoy Hotel. He was rather incoherent, I don't think he's quite sane."

"You can say that again. Anything else?"

Unconsciously, his hand strayed to his breast. Looking down, he saw he'd been partially stripped and a wide bandage covered most of his chest. "Something hit me here, after that, there's nothing." Regarding the uneasy faces, he asked, "It was a wooden stake, wasn't it?"

Jasmine Miller had stayed by the door. "It was a crossbow arrow, but close enough to make no nevermind." She came forward and busied herself fluffing pillows, shoving him back against them in a manner that would brook no argument.

Galen settled on the foot of the cot making it tilt dangerously. "Why did you go there alone? Didn't you smell a trap?"

"Of course I didn't smell a trap. If I had I wouldn't have gone. I went because Hernandez had dropped off the radar, then he shows up claiming to have information to sell. It sounded like just the sort of thing we've been needing. How was I to know the guy was a looney tune with a crossbow? Normal nuts carry guns."

Jump folded his arms and narrowed his eyes. "An' you turn you cell phone off because you think you get the best of this man. Play a few mind games wit' him. But it backfire, yes?"

Peale squirmed slightly. He didn't have to worry about answering because Miller didn't give him time. "It was dumb! Butt stupid! If Jay hadn't got away from Hernandez to warn me about what was going down, you'd have been dead for good. You're supposed to tell your partner stuff like that, but oh no, we get this Lone-Predator-of-the-Night shit."

"Jay? How did she get involved in this? Oh. My overlay failed, I was afraid it would — but — how did she know what Hernandez . . . waitaminit! Hernandez tried to stake me! He knows I'm a vampire!"

Jump chuckled. "You are a natural born detective, BC. Your powers of deduction are staggering to behold."

"Okay, Jump, you can cut the sarcasm. My head hurts and I'm not thinking real well, okay?" Easing back onto the pillows, he rubbed his temples. "I think I'm having a bad year."

Galen growled, "You better be *glad* things hurt! You're damned lucky you're not a little pile of goddamned ashes blowing around in that goddamned derelict hotel!"

"Okay!" Peale held up a hand in surrender. "Okay! I screwed up and I've paid for it. Did somebody collect my bike? I left it in the alley behind a dumpster."

Galen bellowed in inarticulate frustration, and Jump didn't try to hide his smile. The younger Miller was still ignorant of the fact that his atypical partner was all but grafted to his motorcycle. It was always so, even in the war-ravaged Europe of the 1940's. His amusement was cut short as Jasmine yanked the bedroom door wide and ordered, "*Out*! Galen! Augustine! Out of this room *now*! Byron Peale, you lie down and stay quiet. Your damn' bike is in the storage locker where it's gonna stay until *I* say you are healed enough to take it out."

Levering himself painfully up on an elbow, Peale said, "But I want to know how Hernandez. . . ."

Snatching a handful of her son's shirt, Jasmine Miller hauled him off the bed and propelled him through the door. "This is doing no earthly good and Lone Predator of the Night or not, this boy needs rest."

Before she could turn on him, Jump beat a grinning, strategic retreat. Victorious, Mrs. Miller sealed BC's solitude with a sharp snick of the latch. He sighed softly into the sudden silence. The beef blood had eased his headache, but Mama Miller was right, he felt lousy.

She was on the money on a second point, too. He *wasn't* exactly the Lone Predator, was he? He liked having friends. He'd always liked people. No doubt, that came of being part of a large and very gregarious family. The sudden twinge in his chest had nothing to do with his injuries. He hadn't been back to Belridge in what..? Seventy years? Not so the family knew, anyway. Maybe . . . it had been in the 1920s, surely most of the people involved would be gone after this long . . . . No. He knew better. Nobody in Maryland was going to welcome *him* back with open arms.

Damn and Blast! There he went getting maudlin. Like that ever helped anything. This had come so hard on the heels of the silver bullet thing, he supposed it was only normal that his emotions were on such a roller coaster. Okay, he was scared, why shouldn't he be? People out there not only knew how to destroy him, but were actively trying to do it. Suddenly, the bed felt suffocating. He had to get up, he had to *do* something — anything.

Maybe he'd wander out and see if there was any more beef blood to be had. It was cold and a trifle flat, but Jump was right, it did help. Experimentally, he swung his legs over the edge of the bed. Not bad. The headache had subsided and the pain in his chest wasn't quite so sharp. He'd had worse hangovers.

Elbows on knees, he focused his senses on what was happening beyond the closed door and smiled. Yes, his ears were clearing quite well. Though faint, he heard Mama Miller leaving for her own place. She sounded thoroughly disgusted with the lot of them — himself included, to be sure. Unless his ears were playing tricks, she'd called Jump by his given name. Again. Interesting.

Hmm, Galen was talking. Sounded one-sided. Oh, he was on the telephone. He couldn't hear well enough to here the other side of the conversation, even at full health, it would be difficult. No matter, he'd be out there soon enough.

Reaching down for his boots, dizziness and nausea overwhelmed him, and he sprawled back across the mattress until the urge to toss passed. If he lost it on Gae's carpeting, he'd never hear the end of it. Maybe he was pushing it. Maybe he should just yell for Jump to bring more blood. He'd rather be a pile of ashes than ask Galen. *Lone Predator of the Night my ass!*

Uh uh. He was going to make it out that door under his own power and he was going to do it now. Okay. Who needed boots right now? Socks were good. Levering himself off the cot, he stood, flushed with victory and exertion. He was wobbly and needed to hold onto things to reach the door, but he'd done it without help.

Opening the door, he leaned nonchalantly against the frame, heartily glad he didn't breathe anymore. Casual entrances were *so* badly ruined by gasping for breath. Looking up from the TV Guide, Jump swore fluidly in his native patois. Galen laughed into the telephone, "What can I say, Jay, the dead walk. Yeah, he's up, but not for long by the look of him. Sure come by after closing, the door's open. Bye."

Jump flung the magazine aside. "You are insane! What you want that you couldn't jus' yell for, huh?"

BC's smile broadened, it *was* nice to have friends. The smile was abruptly replaced by loud protests as Galen scooped him up and deposited him roughly on the couch. Jump, still fuming in Cajun-French, stormed into the kitchen.

He came back and thrust a cup into Peale's hands. "Drink that. You are still too sharp and pointy for my liking."

Inviting aromas rose from the cup and, without further prompting, he drank deeply. As he did so, Veron gave Miller a perfunctory nod, then the two sat on either side of him. It was a suspiciously well-choreographed move. Glancing from one to the other, he wondered if coming out had been such a good idea after all.

Clearing his throat, Galen said, "BC, we need to talk."

Nope. Not a good idea at all.

Seeing the wariness, Jump chuckled, "Do not fret, *mon ami*, we do not attack you, we have merely a request."

Measuring his large partner's grim expression, Peale put little stock in the assurance. He set the cup on the table and crossed his arms defensively. "Since I seem to be a captive audience, what is it?"

Galen looked thoughtful and eased back against the cushions. "Well, I suppose you could call it a request, but I think of it more as an invitation. Jump and I thought that under the circumstances, it might be a good idea for you to relocate your daytime sleeping place. Maybe you ought to move in here for a while."

"Say nothing, *mon ami*, but consider the consequences if Jay and Galen had not found you in time?" Jump let the statement sink in before playing his trump. "And what would have happened if Hernandez had traced you to your oh so secret hiding place that you are so unwilling to divulge to your friends without a struggle?"

Peale went silent. Galen sat back to watch the Master work. If he'd known Veron was so good at this, he'd have enlisted him weeks ago. Jump continued, "*Oui*, you would have been destroyed and none of us would know when, where or how."

Shrewd eyes glistening in the weathered face, Veron watched his words impact as unerringly as the wooden shaft. Perhaps it was unfair to press the advantage at this vulnerable time, but when else would the argument have such weight? Powerful forces were arrayed against his friend. At least for a while, he'd have to trade his much-treasured independence for daytime protection. Galen's apartment was a good solution.

After a moment, BC said, "Okay, I see what you're saying. Bear in mind, though, Hernandez didn't find my bolt hole, but he does know where you live."

Galen finished for him. "*And* he got away from me at the Savoy. I know." Shrugging, he continued, "I'm not promising it'll be safe as a bank vault, just that someone is more likely to be around if anyone tried some funny business. If I'm not here, Mama will be."

BC interposed, "That's another thing. Isn't your mother the landlord of this place? I didn't think I'd have to remind you that she isn't exactly enamored of me."

Galen grinned broadly. "I think we can scratch that problem, she's been taking care of you since we brought you in. With Mama, there's nothing like nursing someone back to health to mellow her toward a person. She's gotten positively proprietary about you."

Jump laughed. "Besides, if Jasmine objects, I volunteer to persuade her to a more agreeable line of thought."

BC raised an eyebrow with renewed interest. "Oh?"

Galen shunted the subject aside. "We won't go into that now, what I need to know is: Are you moving in here or not?"

Peale rubbed the bandage over his chest ruefully. "The point has been made. I'll do it."

Galen was nonplussed; Peale never agreed to anything quickly. Miller figured he just *liked* to argue. Veron really knew what he was talking about when he said this thing would scare the hell out of him. It should. All things considered, he was impressed by how well his partner was dealing with it all, if it had been *him*, they'd have to tranq him to the gills. Then again, Peale did look kind of glassy, probably residual shock. Could you sedate a vampire? With luck, they'd never have to find out. Switching on the reassuring bonhomie, he clapped his new roomie on the shoulder. "Glad to hear it, but Mama ain't about to let us do any movin' tonight. You're not up to it anyway. Maybe tomorrow night?"

Jump said, "We will see how our patient is then, no? As for now, drink up, BC, and we enjoy some movies on the TV."

***

He didn't know why he returned to this doorway after fleeing the hotel, and even less sure why he kept returning night after night. Maybe because he had nowhere else to go, especially seeing how everything screwed up so bad. He *still* didn't know why. The trap worked perfectly. He had waited in the dark room with the cocked crossbow resting on a chair back. Then the Monster came and tried to be oh so reassuring, but he knew better. He let the Thing come all the way into middle of the room before he released the bolt. He'd figured right, and by the glow of his flashlight, had looked with satisfaction at the feathered end of the arrow lodged right in the undead heart.

Things spun out when he literally ran into Galen Miller on the way out. The guy was as fast as he was big. Mario didn't want to kill Miller, just knock him down, but the Monster's thrall was so *strong,* Miller was obviously trying to kill him. He'd barely escaped. Watching from here was dangerous, but what else could he do?

Any question about why Miller was there was answered when he saw Jay help carry the Monster's body into the back of the apartment building. He never dreamed she'd get loose by herself. Did Miller untie her? Didn't matter. What mattered was that the vampire was destroyed. But, he still didn't know for sure, did he? The Thing wasn't moving when they carried It in, but It also didn't turn to dust like the books said should happen. Sunlight. He needed to drag It into the sunlight and watch It dissolve with his own eyes. That was the only way to be sure. But then he'd have to know where the Thing slept. He didn't.

The apartment became a regular beehive after the vampire was taken inside. It was mostly Miller and his mother, but Jay and a bunch of people from the Inferno Club were coming around, too. They usually carried boxes full of glass bottles. He heard them clinking. What was in the bottles? He didn't know, but he knew what it meant. The Demon's influence had spread farther than he thought. That was scary. If only he could go to his hiding place in the burned-out building and sleep, but he couldn't. Until he knew for sure the Demon-thing was dead he had to stay where he was.

Peeking in the windows didn't work because the curtains were too thick to see through. When he pressed his ear to the glass, he made out the murmur of voices, although he couldn't make out individual words. He almost ran when a new voice uncomfortably like the Monster's spoke. It had a surprisingly pleasant voice, but he suspected that was all part of Its spell.

He was still trying to calm the frantic pounding of his heart, a car pulled into the alley, then parked. Carefully, he crept around for a look-see. It was the Inferno van. The timed engine fan made small whirring noises as the bouncer and Jay helped the little French guy down. As they locked up and headed in, he debated what to do until they reemerged unexpectedly accompanied by Miller and the *vampire*!

Jay's giggle reached across the lot. "BC, are you *sure* you want to share a place with Gae? I'd think living with grizzly bear would be easier."

Peale answered with a rich laugh, as he lifted Veron into the van with practiced ease. "Speaking from unpleasant experience, Galen has one advantage over bears: He doesn't smell of fish all the time. Now, Jay, if *you* were to offer me a bunk, I might reconsider. I'm certain you *never* smell of fish."

"Oh, sure! You move in with me and it'd be a hard call who'd kill you first, Mick or my mom."

Miller said, "Insults about hygiene aside, will the van be big enough to move all your stuff?"

Peale considered. "I think so." He grinned. "If we run out of room, we can always strap you and Benny to the roof."

Affronted, Glissen objected, "Hey! Who'll drive the van?"

Peale gestured expansively. "I will, of course. Jump *loves* my driving. Don't you, *mon ami*?"

The Cajun made a face. "I can think of more pleasant ways to commit suicide, *mon petite fou*! I think we strap *you* and Galen to the roof."

Galen protested, "Hey! Why am I the constant?"

The heavy door slammed, cutting off the banter. The engine roared, the vehicle pulled away and disappeared from view. Hernandez discovered his fingers convulsively clenched on the corner bricks. The sight of the Creature whole and healed had dissolved him into tremors.

Tasting failure, he collapsed against the roughness of the wall. He'd have to try again, but how? It would be on guard now. He needed time to think. Without further conscious thought, he took to his heels and scurried through the night. When the Monster came looking, he'd be long gone.

***

Eyes closed, Peale relaxed into the seat, allowing the gentle rocking of the vehicle to become a soothing background rhythm. Mrs. Miller had almost refused to allow him out. If Galen hadn't interceded by chucking BC's clothes to him over the obstinate woman's head, he'd still be languishing on the couch swathed in Gae's over-sized bathrobe. Several nights of that made him insanely glad to be out of the house. True, he was still shaky, but his restlessness was assuming a manic edge. That worried him.

He was mortally sick of the apartment, but nobody was inclined to let him go to the club, no matter how fervently he swore not touch to the piano.

He thought he'd go mad watching the time crawl by until Jump and Benny came. It was a pleasant bonus that Jay came, too. Still, they wouldn't reach the blasted tunnel until at least 2:30 — it would be sooner if they'd let him drive. Nobody was inclined to do that, either.

Grinning to himself in the dark, he inhaled deeply of the mingled scents of his friends. Companionable talk made the atmosphere inside the van pleasantly cozy, but he wished the urge for *warm* blood would damn well go away. He was still feeding off what the others gathered for him and it sustained him, but direct contact with life and body heat was lacking. He'd never realized how important these things were, but then again, he'd never depended on secondhand sources for so long before. Maybe later tonight he could get to the stockyard or something. From the wary looks Mama Miller was shooting him, he didn't think it would take much persuasion to get her on his side for *this*.

He opened his eyes as the van slowed and stopped on the nearly-deserted, trash-filled street he'd been calling home for the last few weeks. This was one place he'd not be sorry to see the last of. It was a good hiding place, yes, but mostly because it was so damp and difficult to reach, nobody else wanted to go there. Sometimes, his vampirism dictated choices he'd never consider otherwise.

Leaping lightly onto the pavement, he left Jump in Benny's care as he made his way across the filthy sidewalk to the ugly steel door. The forbidding structure it sealed once housed offices. It wasn't used for anything like that now, as the rude spray-painted graffiti announced. No matter, if they moved quickly, they could easily avoid the notice of the alcohol and drug-sotted current denizens. His goal lay beyond their realms, in the foul-smelling basement where the forgotten access panel to the old rail tunnel was.

Anticipating the reactions that would surely follow, he slid a lockpick from his boot and fell to work on the heavy-duty padlock. The lock didn't do much good, everyone usually went through the windows. He normally would, too, but it would be easier to get his things out through the door. Besides, everyone was bitching about his choice of the tunnels for a resting-place, that would just make it worse. Correction. Everyone was bitching except Benny. Benny took things in stride. That was probably why the liked the big guy so much.

Yep. The "ooooh yuck"s, "my God, Peale"s and "*mon Dieu*"s began on cue. He laughed out loud when even Benny made noises of dismay. So much for the strong, silent image. He didn't see why they were so bugged, sure it wasn't the Carlton, but it was only a temporary bolt-hole. He'd stayed in far worse.

All this fuss for the outside? Wait'll they got a load of the interior! The lock clicked open in his hands as Galen whispered hoarsely, "You *break* in?? Geezus, Peale, why don't you *rent* a place?"

BC slipped the lock into his jacket pocket. "I thought that was what I was going to be doing after tonight."

The commentary quieted ominously as he led them through the tunnels to a new door with a rust-free steel deadbolt lock. Jump was first through. He absorbed his surroundings by the jaundiced glow of a battery operated lantern. "Had I but known of this before, I would have knock you cold wit' the baseball bat an' move you myself."

The vampire huffed, "Oh, come on! It's not *that* bad!" Scanning the wall of implacable faces, he reexamined the fusty room. "Well, maybe it is that bad. All the more reason to get the hell out of here as soon as possible. Anyone want to try that trunk in the corner?"

Wordlessly, Benny hefted the trunk and a toolbox and began his slog back to the van, with a chuckling, duffel-toting Cajun lighting the way.

Thirty minutes later, BC made a final sweep, located the last of his clothing and tossed it onto the sleeping bag he'd spread on a dry ledge. As he bent to roll it up, Jay squawked, "*¡Por Dios*, BC! If that's the way you treat your clothes, it's a miracle you look as good as you do!"

He shrugged. "They're just dirties. I'd have taken them to the Laundromat days ago — if I hadn't been rudely interrupted."

"Don't make no difference," she said as she appropriated the pile and folded them efficiently into a neat stack. "I *saw* the wad of stuff you gave Jump. Gonna hate ta see what the inside o' that trunk looks like!"

Miller snickered watching her snatch and fold clothes. He turned to his friend and asked. "There wasn't a lot here. Is this all you have?"

Peale shrugged. "I try to travel as light as I can, it helps if I have to clear out in a hurry. That happens from time to time. Normally, I keep things like the trunk and toolbox in storage, but I needed them recently. The proliferation of rental storage lockers have been a Godsend to me." He added, "Most of my stuff is still in a rental shed from the last move . . . or was it before that? Honestly, I'm not sure what's there."

Jay bustled past hugging the neatly packed and rolled sleeping bag. "Let's hope it's in better shape than this stuff. Hmmph. Some people, just 'cause they're a little bit dead, think they don't have to be civilized no more."

BC plastered himself dramatically against the wall. "Mercy, O Great White Tornado! Have compassion on a poor undead slattern!"

Jay stuck her tongue out and swept out, head held high. She managed a fair distance before she let her laugh out. BC's sensitive ears caught it anyway. He bent to collect his toiletry case as Galen moved closer and asked in a low voice, "Do you feel up to a little outing? You been going stir crazy these past few nights, I might have a cure."

"Hmmm. Sounds like more than a trip to the cattle pens. What did you have in mind?"

Galen's smile gleamed in the dim light. "Thought that'd grab your interest. How about we wait until everyone — especially Mama — goes home then we head over to the burned-out warehouse?"

"Whatever for? It's been *days* and you said yourself that Sentry, the

Fire Department and Police forensics people have been all over it! Why not read their reports?"

"You forgot to mention the FBI *and* the ATF. They've taken their shot at it, too. I *have* read their reports while I was waiting for you to wake up, I have 'em at home if you want a look. Still, I wanna see if your enhanced senses can pick up something they missed."

"You left out the CIA."

"I didn't get a copy of their report."

"You're *serious*, aren't you?"

"Of *course* I'm serious. I've been telling you all along this was hot stuff, but you never listen to *me*."

Peale raised an eyebrow. Even with supernatural senses, there couldn't be much to find, nonetheless, they possessed one piece of information the others didn't. They knew Hernandez had been there. He murmured, "At least we can try to trace Hernandez' movements. It's been a long time, but a cold trail is better than *no* trail. I *owe* Hernandez."

Galen agreed ominously, "We *all* do, partner."

FOUR

The area was in darkness, but Miller had no trouble envisioning the destruction surrounding him. The explosion of the weapons cache and subsequent fire had reduced a city block of lakeside warehouses to rubble. Vivid scenes of burned and blasted ruins were etched on his mind's eye from the news footage. For almost a week following the disaster, he and Peale had cringed at the unfolding media coverage.

What never made the news was Sentry International's dogged attempts to link the warehouse to the elusive Mr. Borgia. They got no joy. Ownership was finally traced to a company named Parks Properties, Inc. in San Francisco. There the backtrail came to an abrupt and screeching halt in front of a multi-storied municipal parking garage occupying the company's address. Frustrating, but not surprising. For Galen Miller, this added insult to injury. He and Peale had nearly died in the damned place. There was no way he could accept that there was nothing else to be gotten from those ruins.

All this was why Galen Miller found himself picking his way across the rubble, sticking as close to his partner as possible. It was a damned good thing that even overcast moonlight was enough for the vampire to navigate across the cracked and cratered concrete. He was blind as a bat, himself. BC's gliding shadow halted suddenly. Caught unprepared, Galen ran into him. Just as abruptly, he was pulled behind a mound of shattered brick and Peale's breathy whisper brushed his ear. "We have company ahead."

Galen stilled himself and listened. Almost masked by the distant rumble of traffic, the drifting murmur of people speaking in low tones tugged at the edge of his hearing. Just ahead, he glimpsed the elusive phantom glow of flashlights. "CPD?" he ventured. "Nah, they folded their tents days ago. Let's get closer where we can see better." Glancing at the pale smudge next to him in the darkness, he amended, "Make that where *I* can see better."

He caught the flash of Peale's grin, then followed the darting silhouette toward the skeletal building in a low, quick crouch. They dodged from one mound of wreckage to the next moving ever closer to the muted lights.

Alarmingly close to where Peale finally stopped, a blond woman, rendered pale and icy by the dim light, stood in the midst of the destruction directing a small group of men sifting through the rubble. Galen strained to make out what they were doing. HE almost jumped out of his skin when Peale whispered, "They look to be doing as thorough a job as you wanted to."

Miller sensed more than saw BC, scoot into a better vantage point. At length, he dropped back beside Galen, saying, "Hard to tell from here, but it looks like they're sifting through the remains of a safe. Rather good one, too, since it still sort of looks like a safe after an ammo dump went off in the next room." He paused then said, "Oh. Interesting."

"What?" Miller breathed.

After a moment, Peale said, "These men are afraid of that woman. You might even go as far as to say terrified."

Just then, one of the men approached. His manner was diffident. In another age, he would have kept his head down and tugged his forelock before speaking. "Ms. Isendamer, looks like the cops and insurance guys was right. Ain't nothin' left here can be recognized short o' th' safe an' everything in it got burned up. There's just ashes and more ashes here."

The woman regarded him as she would a dog dropping on the sidewalk until he tugged at his tie in discomfort. Finally she replied, "Very well, Nesbitt, but if anything turns up later, Mr. Borgia will not be pleased."

Clutching his partner's sleeve excitedly, Peale whispered, "Jackpot! These lot are Borgia's people, and the guys from the other night mentioned Isendamer."

Galen gestured to his left. "About time we got a break, now let's make one for ourselves. I spy with my little eye a couple of real nervous lookouts over there. Let's flank 'em, clobber 'em, and give the old hocus pocus another shot. Maybe we can bag them and come up with something useful."

BC sighed faintly, but didn't balk. Galen grinned, and trailed by the reluctant creature of the night, pressed soundlessly toward the jittery pair until they were so close even Miller could hear their breathing. The plan went well until, as if warned by some primal instinct, Galen's target shot a nervous glance over his shoulder and found a huge dark shape looming there. The punk managed an incoherent squeak before a sledgehammer fist skidded him senseless across the cindered ground. His fellow sentry noticed none of this. He was too involved with his first up close and personal encounter with a vampire.

Remembering in an unpleasant flash that this was BC's first live meal since his injury, Miller glanced apprehensively at the unnatural intimacy, then relaxed. Although absorbed with feeding, there was none of the primal desperation that had underlain the first cupfuls after awakening in the sickbed. There'd be another entree on the menu as soon as Gae could get his guy out of sight. Easily shouldering the limp guard, he ducked into the cover of a ruined wall. Releasing the burden unceremoniously on the ground, then sensing movement behind him, swung around sharply. Backlit by Isendamer's crew's lights, two vague shapes crept toward where he'd left Peale. He realized with a chill, the noise of the scuffle had alerted another set of watchers. Still, if it was only two of them. . . .

"It's *him*, it's him! It's the Vampire guy!"

Shit. Miller's plans imploded with the shout, he sprinted into the open.

Peale's head lifted, blood making dark smears on his ghostly white face. That was enough for the new guys. Drawing something from the folds of their coats, they broke into a run toward Peale.

They hadn't noticed Miller yet. Good. He let their trajectory bring them into range, let the first pass, then brought the second to ground like a panther pouncing on a rabbit. A single, quick strike and the man was unconscious. The man's weapon dropped from his limp fingers and bounced across the cinders. Galen picked it up it and was puzzled to see a small plastic pump bottle like his mother used on her plants. He watched in confusion as the remaining thug hurtled toward Peale pumping frantically at his own tiny bottle. It apparently didn't have the desired effect. With a wild high-pitched cry, the man wrenched the top off the bottle, and emptied the contents over the vampire's head.

BC sputtered indignation. "What the. . . ?"

Miller was already in motion as the irate vampire lunged, snatched the bottle and solidly slugged his assailant. Snagging a handful of jacket, the flying linebacker dragged his dripping partner away. "There's more where those came from, man! Let's get the hell outta here while they're still making enough noise to cover our retreat."

The dark man sped away. Growling, Peale followed.

***

Good. The blasted smoke detector was disabled. It was *so* bloody embarrassing when one went off in the middle of a spell. Wrecked concentration, too, and she had enough problems without that. How *could* she oversleep? Battering through the nameless barrier drained her, but why on earth hadn't she ordered a mid-afternoon wake up call so she'd be ready by dusk? Careless.

The first night, there'd been only a blank spot where Byron should have been, he was probably too dormant to reach. The blankness scared her. The following night she made contact of a sort. He was unconscious and fevered. That alarmed her even more than the blank spot. She didn't know his kind could be ill. There was no use turning to Francesco for information. He'd called repeatedly and the temptation was great. She managed to put him off, though, claiming she was resting. Indeed. She'd need a rest from her rest if she wasn't careful.

The past few nights were encouraging, though. He was weak, but awake, which lamentably, made the spell harder to hold. It had been nigh impossible last evening. That meant he was strong enough to block her again. Still, she'd kept vigil until she was too tired to hold the enchantment. That proved imprudent. She'd slept as if drugged and only awakened at a quarter to midnight.

The incantation required a lot of groundwork but she was finally ready to begin. The bedside clock read three fifty-four a.m. as she dropped her robe and stepped into the circle. It couldn't be helped, though. If since Byron were up and about, he'd be as accessible now as earlier. Lighting the brazier, she promised herself that if he were still ill, she'd find him and go to him. Damn Frankie and his eternal power struggles, he could bloody well wait!

The comfortable room dwindled as power flowed into her, attenuating the ties of body to spirit. Slipping the last tether, she burst through blackness to find herself hovering over a scene of devastation.

She gazed on the new reality in wonderment. Was this a war zone? There were so many conflicts today, it could be. Scanning the desolation, she sensed nine other entities. Was one Byron? Yes, he was there, directly below. He and another very strong being were moving swiftly toward the center of the destruction and the other psyches.

Savoring the pulse of arcane power from deep within him, she locked onto his vitality, and obediently, her vision shifted as he and the other overcame a pair of less brightly-burning souls. Through their tenuous link, she felt warmth spread as Byron pierced the throat and drank.

His companion, a very large, dark man, ducked out of sight as two others came running. She ached to cry out a warning, but her ethereal state made that impossible. There was no need, Byron heard them and dropped his prey to meet their rush.

The newcomers radiated fear as if they knew what they were facing. Did they see him feeding or was it something more? Byron's companion seized one of the men, and she enjoyed his economy of movement as the big man dealt with his opponent The remaining man ran forward threatening Byron with a weapon of some sort.

Her former lover crouched, preparing to fight. Instead, the man twisted open a plastic bottle, and tossed the contents onto Byron. The shock of cold liquid snapped her link and she awakened sprawled across the plush hotel carpet, gasping and sweat-drenched.

Well. She'd seen Byron.

Adrenaline was still in overdrive and she breathed slowly and deeply for a moment to regulate her pounding heart. He was fit and active, there was no doubt of that. But what had he been up to? And *what* was in that bottle? Obviously, the man wielding it believed it would do something. She wondered what Byron did to him. He really *hated* being wet.

In the bathroom, she applied a damp cloth to her face and neck. It must've been the big man who helped him when he was staked. Dropping the cloth into the sink, she stretched luxuriously, feeling more exhilarated than tired. Maybe she'd cast for Francesco's renegade tonight, after all. It wouldn't hurt to pop over and see what was up.

***

Francesco's wounded bull bellow was audible before she stepped off the lift. Peeking into the lavish office, she saw him storming around shouting into a telephone. Glancing up, he motioned her to a chair.

Wriggling with barely-suppressed glee, she slid into the seat and listened with relish. She did *so* love a good row and it wasn't often one got a ringside seat to see the great Francesco Borgia frothing at the mouth in the bargain. Wait. What did he say about a burned warehouse?

He roared, "*Madonna*, Gwen! Four of our men knocked senseless, and all you say is 'there's been a little trouble?' Surveying the scene of a fire should not. . . ."

He listened briefly, then said sarcastically, "Oh, forgive my misunderstanding! Only *three* knocked senseless. The fourth was bitten by the renegade. That makes all the difference in the world!" He shouted, "Did no one *act? At ALL?*"

Maeve sat breathless as pieces clicked together into an appallingly clear pattern. It was Byron. He was Francesco's renegade! That meant he was right here in Chicago. So close. No wonder she'd felt his pain as her own.

But, why would he target Francesco? Unless . . . *of course!* He'd finally discovered who made him and the willful child was forcing a confrontation. How like Byron to be so emotional and witless. Well, this made all the difference in the world! Happily, she waved to get Francesco's attention. When he learned it was simply his own progeny demanding parental attention, everything would change. "Frankie, y'have t'listen, this is important. . . ."

He didn't listen. Instead he gestured imperiously at her, and snarled into the phone, "You are *certain* the holy water had no effect? *NO!* I do *not* count making him wet! What?" With an expression of infinite pain, he repeated the unheard words, "They took the bottles away with them. You're certain of this, too?"

The pacing resumed as Maeve silently repeated the words: *Holy water*. So that's what was in the bottle and why the man thought it would be effective against Byron. Well it would have had the doused vampire been as unrelentingly wicked as Francesco Borgia himself. But, Byron *wasn't* evil — though Frankie's view might differ. There was the problem. The notion of truly holy things struck fear deep into Francesco's fallen Catholic soul. He assumed it would effect his adversary the same way. Honestly, both of them were so predictable.

A sharp smack on the desk made her jump. "No one got a look at either of them?" His inarticulate roar resolved into, "I want everyone back here! Immediately!"

Slamming the telephone down, he turned to find Maeve struggling against laughter and failing miserably. Arms folded belligerently, he charged, "All right, Maeve. What is so amusing?"

The sight of Francesco Borgia attempting to intimidate her was the final blow to her self control. She burst out in a gale of laughter. "Oh, Francesco! Holy water?" Sobering slightly, she continued, "Frankie, holy things have such a devastatin' effect on yourself because you're so un-abashedly *wicked*. You must remember, one needn't be evil to be a vampire, just bitten in the proper manner. . . ."

He gave her a condescending look. "'Bitten in the proper manner?' You refer of course to that worthless drunken pup you had me beget in the last part of the 1700's? How *did* that work out, Maeve, Dear? I've never known you to be that smitten. So unlike you."

It was Maeve's turn to flare. The arrogant bastard wouldn't be so glib if he knew what that worthless drunken pup was up to these days. But he didn't know, did he? Very well, if Francesco was determined to be offensive, *let* Byron have his fun. If anyone could give the almighty Francesco Borgia the devilment he so richly deserved, it was Byron Cyrus Peale! She'd a good mind to *help* him.

Recognizing the sudden darkening of the peaches and cream cheeks, Borgia regretted the words. He warily watched the play of emotion across her face and braced himself as the montage resolved into a smug smirk. The elegant woman rose and glided to the door, pausing only to comment with terrifying pleasantness, "If that's the way you're wantin' it, Francesco Borgia, that's the way you'll have it. You've no call to be sayin' such things about poor Byron and I'll do no more scryin' for you until you've made amends."

She sailed out leaving Francesco Borgia gaping like a suffocating trout on a riverbank.

***

The argument still raged as they stepped from the stairwell into the gloom-shrouded hall.

"So he got your hair wet. Not like it hasn't happened before! Forget about those damn' bottles and get back to important stuff. I still say this hypnosis thing will work in the field. We just gotta be a little faster and quieter until we get it right."

Peale howled, "*Quieter?* My guy didn't even hit the dirt before you brought half the world down on top of us."

Miller paused mid-stride. "Are you insinuating I made noise?"

Peale flipped a few sodden strands from his eyes, deftly spattering his partner with fine droplets. "Only as much as poleaxing an ox. My mistake, I thought this was a covert operation, not a football scrimmage."

Miller glowered, snatched the bottle from Peale, and sniffed it. It smelled of wet plastic. About a half-inch of liquid still sloshed in the bottom. Even better, they had the unused one from Galen's guy. He wondered if they could get the stuff analyzed on the QT. . . .

His eyes nervously sought the door. With Hernandez running loose, he was leery of leaving the apartment for long. The telltales were still set, though, so he confidently slid his key into the lock and preceding Peale into the apartment, flicking on the overhead lights with sadistic glee.

Peale winced. "Gaaah! Warn me when you're gonna do that!"

Galen chuckled, took a step into the living room then froze.

"If you two hadn't been arguing since you drove up, I bet Peale would've known we were here before you got up the hall." Jim Nelson sat forward in Galen's favorite chair as Mick Marquez leaned insolently across the back. Jim smiled at the dripping vampire. "That's so, isn't it, Byron? Or do you prefer Cyrus Bell? Perhaps Byron Chyme?"

Marquez riffled a paper-crammed folder. With a sense of impending doom, Peale closed the door.

Galen growled, "What are you guys doin' here and what the hell are you talking about?"

Nelson's eyes never left Peale as he accepted the pages from Marquez. "I think you both know what I'm talking about. A curious thing, Peale. With all the aliases you've used, you served in *both* world wars under your true name. We can hash that out later, though." He turned slightly toward Mick. "Mick, would you please show the boys what you came across?"

Giving Peale a hostile glare, Mick thrust a picture postcard at Galen. BC peeked over his partner's shoulder, then lost what color he had. Snatching the card, he flipped it over and read the back. Gratified by the display, Mick illuminated, "It's in a Colonial Artists show that's at the Art Institute of Chicago."

"I don't think Mr. Peale has been to the museum lately." Nelson leaned back with steepled fingertips in his best 'boy's dean' manner. "Do you deny that's your portrait?"

Peale returned the card and dropped onto the couch. "Would it do any good?"

Jim grinned amiably. "Nope. I think the Vampire Vigilante and I are long overdue for a chat, don't you?"

Exchanging worried looks with his partner, Galen sank onto the arm of the couch.

Jim chuckled at their discomfort. "I confess that until this moment, I wasn't convinced we were dealing with an actual vampire. We traced a fairly convincing back-trail into the middle of the 19th century — that *was* you in the Underground Railroad, wasn't it? We filled in the gaps with intuition for the most part. Your problem is that you've never kept a low profile,

Peale. You get into too much trouble and get involved too often to remain invisible."

Marquez took in the stack of boxes and suitcases in the hall. Rifling through a dusty book he observed, "Looks like you've got yourself a room mate, Gae. Were you gonna have a house warming party to let your old pals know?"

Galen snatched the book away before anyone realized he'd moved. "We hadn't decided. Now, let's get to the point of this visit — *if* there is one. If not, you two can head out the same way you came in."

Nelson eyed the slim figure lounging opposite him with the certainty that, though Peale hadn't moved, he was a like coiled snake ready to strike. They weren't going to get anywhere as long as Gae and Mick kept clashing. "*Okay*! Mick. Gae. Sit down and shut up." To Miller, he said, "Mick and I are just a little prickly, we thought we'd been friends long enough for you to trust us with a few secrets."

"Oh? You *wanted* me to tell you there was a real vampire?"

Peale sat forward. "That was my fault, Captain Nelson. Galen knows you, but I don't. It's *my* secret. I asked him not to tell anyone, including you and Lt. Marquez." He smiled broadly. Light glinted off a slightly extended fang.

Jim frowned, wondering who the threat was aimed at. "We understand paranoia, it's an occupational hazard. After a while, I'm afraid, it gets to be a habit."

Galen, who had no doubt where the threat was aimed enjoyed Mick's blanch at the vampire's pointed smile. Apparently, Mick had no doubts, either. Good. He slid satisfied eyes to where Jim was comfortably entrenched in the recliner.

Nelson continued, "I'm warning you both this is worse than irregular. Something will have to be done about it. Fast. When this reaches New York . . . well, let's just say, I'll be ducking my calls for a few days. Maybe

I ought to set Gae to answering them for me. Maybe he'd like to explain it all to Colonel Black."

Not liking the locked gazes, Galen stepped between the captain and his partner. "Look, Jim, this whole thing was my idea. Peale was against it from the first."

Nelson shifted his gaze to Miller. "Gae, I'm not talking to you, I'm talking to Peale. Now get out of the way so I can see him."

With a funeral air Galen stepped back. Jim retrieved a sheaf of papers from the floor. "There were pertinent pieces of information we couldn't find, so you'll have to fill them in yourself, Peale. Let's see . . . how well do you handle a pistol?"

The vampire's face went blank. "What does that have to do with anything?"

"It's purely a formality, but Galen can back me up here. Sentry regulations require certain training and proficiencies from field agents. Special Agents are required to carry a sidearm at all times and to check out regularly with both pistol and rifle. That's no problem, we can set up a session at the range for later this week. Evening, of course. We'll set one up for Gae while were at it, he's overdue and been ducking it for months."

Nelson almost laughed out loud when Mick wheeled to add his stare to the array. It did Mick good to see things done off-the-cuff. Enjoying the universal bafflement, he continued, "Next: there are a few security questions about your activities with the OSS and the other intelligence organizations during. . . ."

Galen furrowed his brow. "Let me get this straight. You're not firing *me*, you're offering *him* a job?"

"You *could* put it that way. I prefer to think of it as the expedient utilization of unique available resources. You've already established a solid working relationship between yourselves; I'm simply offering the opportunity to make it official. If there are no objections. How about it, BC?"

Peale shook his head in disbelief, then turned to Miller. "You're right, he *is* a sadistic bastard."

Jim grinned. "I'll take that as a yes." Tossing a mass of paperwork into Peale's lap, he said, "Sign all three forms . . . here . . . here . . . and here. We'll skirt the physical examination, though. I don't relish telling Dr. Klotski his newest charge's normal condition is dead — at least, not until *I* get used to it."

Mick Marquez seethed. He didn't want to believe in vampires. He prided himself on a logical mind and that didn't lend itself to believing in the supernatural. Throughout their research, he'd nursed the hope Peale was a straightforward nutcase, but that didn't pan out. The deeper they dug, the more apparent it became that there were such things as vampires and this guy was one. Bad enough this undead playboy was his sister's boss, but now Jim waved his magic paperwork and voilà the creep was suddenly his *colleague*. He didn't like it. Well, he couldn't do much about Jim's decision, but he'd sure as hell have a talk with Jay. A guy had to watch out for his family. In light of Jim's action, he wouldn't tell her everything, but he'd warn her off. If he said he knew for a fact Peale was dangerous, she'd listen. Then again, maybe he ought to warn Peale away from *her*. Quashing anger and putting on a stoic face, he turned back to his surroundings.

Jim was saying, "Y'know, guys, Mick has a point, it does look like Peale is moving in. *And* when we raided your fridge for brews, what did we find? Booze bottles full of blood. Taken with all the first-aid stuff in the back room, it adds up to a big what gives."

Galen shot an inquiring look at BC, then a nervous one at the glowering Marquez. "It's a loooong story, but it boils down to a guy named Mario Hernandez used a cheap crossbow to shoot a wooden stake through Peale's chest a couple of nights back—"

Mick abruptly lost his stoicism. "Mario Hernandez?"

"Right. The same asshole that's been stalking Jay," Miller said. "It's all tied together."

BC added, "In fact, it's rather a mess."

Mick planted himself in front of Peale and glared down. "Are you telling me my sister *knows* about all this? About *you?*"

Galen made to intervene, but Jim caught his arm. Uneasily, the dark man's eyes sought his partner who remained seated and outwardly calm. Peale met Marquez' gaze, and answered softly, "I owe my existence to your sister, Lt. Marquez. Without Jay I would be so much ash on the floor of the Savoy Hotel right now." When his words had the desired effect, he stood and extended his hand. "Lt. Marquez, I've never set out to be your enemy. We approach it differently, but I assure you, we are on the same side. Please, let's call a truce, especially seeing how we're going to be working together from now on."

Marquez eyed the outstretched hand, then with a shrug, grasped it firmly. A wicked smile broke as he told Peale, "Okay, truce. But I warn you, it's an uneasy one. I also think you guys better invest in a couple papermills, 'cause you're gonna need to rewrite a shitload of reports!"

Jim nodded. "There's a lot of truth to that. It'll give you two something to do while we're tracking down Hernandez. With that do-it-yourself Van Helsing loose in the city, you both better lay low until we find him. That goes double for you, Peale, he's tried for you once, we don't want to give him another chance."

Peale looked about to protest, when Nelson countered sharply, "No arguments. You guys are in enough trouble as it is." Turning to Mick, he added, "Also, I want Jay under wraps. He's targeted her too and if he knows she helped Peale, he'll be looking upon her unkindly at the moment. Considering the close relationship Byron here has with Mr. Augustine Jump Veron, I don't think much explanation will be necessary for her new boss." Satisfied by Mick's quick nod, Jim turned back to his new agent. "Lastly: Peale, why are you wet?"

***

Peale sat in the darkened living room sprawled unhappily across the couch. Unlife had taken some sharp turns lately and he wasn't certain he liked them all. Suddenly, the overhead lights flicked on, he shied back, shielding his eyes with his hand. "Dammit!"

Miller padded out of the hall wearing pyjama bottoms and an obnoxious smirk. "Oops. My bad. I didn't realize you were still doing your Brooding Predator of the Night shtick in here."

"Sorry, I applied for the Brain-Damaged-Ex-Quarterback shtick, but that one was already taken."

"Linebacker," Miller laughed and continued through to the kitchen. "But you won't get a rise out of me with that one because you only get it wrong when you're pissed about something."

His partner's response was to slouch farther into the couch and jab at his smartphone screen. Pulling the top off a carton of fruit juice, Miller plopped down into the opposite chair. He said, "Beats me why you're in such a rotten mood, anyway. Seems to me things could have gone a lot worse — for both of us."

Indigo eyes narrowed over the top of the phone briefly, then Peale tossed it carelessly onto the cushion next to him. "Oh! Silly me. Everything's just peachyhunkydorykeen! After all, I've had the wonderful experience of being discovered by a brain-damaged ex-athlete cum secret agent and unduly deputized. Then, *then*, I got to be stalked, staked and nearly destroyed by an escapee from a psychotic singles bar. After that, I was found out by the aforementioned athlete turned agent's immediate superiors and *duly* deputized. And the bestest of all, I've got this ever-widening circle of people who know all about me." He retrieved the phone. "Yep. All good."

"Come on, it's not that bad." Miller took a pull at the juice. "I mean it won't *really* get bad until they put up those little green highway signs: Vampire Lair 1/4 mile."

The answering laugh was tired, but genuine.

"Really. We did good, Jim was so happy he almost wet himself over the stuff we had for him tonight. Especially that video you got with your phone. I'm gonna have to get me one of those things."

"Oh, I want to see that! You have enough trouble using those stupid little burner phones." Peale guffawed, then turned serious. "I hope the techs can clean it up enough to get something useful from it. I can see well in that light, but the mobile doesn't have my night vision."

"Mick seemed to think it would enhance just fine. He's sort of the resident techie, so I tend to believe him. Now, the thing that got *me* was when you whipped out that sketch book and drew Isendamer's portrait and sketched the other guys. I didn't know you could draw."

Peale's smile became a little sad. "When you're from a family of artists, that sort of thing is second nature — especially *my* family."

"Drawing — and painting, too? That portrait in the show was by your brother, wasn't it?"

"Yes. Charley — Charles, my eldest brother."

BC became quiet and seemed to stare through the floor more than at it. After a moment, Galen stretched, yawned and stood up. "Looks like you're working on polishing that Brooding Predator bit again. I'm for bed." He paused at the hallway, hand hovering over the switch. "You want the lights?"

Peale startled a little. "Wha? Oh. No need, thanks."

Miller flipped the switch off. Peale listened to him pad down the hall and shut his bedroom door then sat forward and put his face in his hands. He hadn't wanted to let a dark mood take him over and he certainly hadn't wanted Galen to find him in a funk for a lot of reasons. Recent events had him very off balance and being blind-sided at the apartment hard on the heels of the dust-up at the warehouse didn't help. Yes, placating Captain Nelson and through him, other authorities was all well and good, but it only went so far. The problem with the portrait remained. If anything, that was the most worrisome of the lot, but not in any way Galen and the others would understand.

Before he got too bent out of shape, he had to be sure it was *his* painting hanging in the show. Charles hadn't painted any duplicates, he knew that, but he couldn't vouch for anyone else. The whole family was notorious for making copies — well, it *was* a common practice back then. In the eighteenth century, art didn't have the same mystique as it did today. Painting was viewed more as a craft, albeit one that required a great deal of ability. Making exact copies of a portrait was the same thing as making copies of a candle holder: a smart move for an artisan with a popular product.

He only knew of three portraits that were made of him — no — four counting the one Sarah Miriam talked him into. The first was the full-sized one Charley painted (maybe the one in the show), the second was a miniature painted by his brother James for their mother. The third was painted to replace the earlier miniature that had gone mysteriously missing.

That had happened after his change and he snickered remembering James' invective at having to mix his colors by candlelight. Like he'd not done it before. Odd, though, that the first miniature had vanished at all. Stranger still was that Mama wasn't all that upset. She simply requested that James make a replacement. BC suspected she knew *exactly* where the missing miniature went and may even have had a hand in it going there. He couldn't make sense of it and she never admitted to anything other than absentmindedness. Mamma? Absentminded? In a pig's eye!

There was nothing else for it, he'd have to go to the museum. He flipped through web pages on the mobile. There. The museum had extended hours on Thursday. Good. He'd need the extra time.

***

He'd forgotten how hard it was to find a parking space downtown, even for a vehicle as relatively small as a Harley-Davidson Softail. Far later than he found comfortable, he sprinted through the museum entrance. It was nice that it was getting warmer, but the down side to the seasonal change was that the days were lengthening proportionally. That meant less time for him to be up and about.

Once inside, he relaxed. Passing the door lessened the odds against him. They'd be more inclined to *lock* him out than *chuck* him out. He hoped he'd have enough time for a good look, hocus-pocusing his way in after hours didn't seem like too good an idea.

Signs pointed the way to the featured show and, turning up the charm for the pretty girl at the desk, paid admission, bought the catalog book, but declined the taped guide.

Show catalog pinned firmly under arm, he strolled into the gallery, then halted appreciatively. They'd accumulated a fine collection. Too bad he didn't have time to wander through and enjoy the show.

Finding the portrait proved easy. It was a focal piece on a wall dedicated to the Peale family located so as to be seen as soon as the viewer stepped into the room. From the doorway, it certainly *looked* like the one that should have been hanging in his dressing room in the family home, Belridge. He set his jaw and stepped closer. A typed card on the wall identified the lender as Willson R. Peale, Elk Point, Maryland. Bingo.

Two guards kibitzed by the door, they were anticipating quitting time and getting to spend a little sit-down time in their favorite bar. Their practiced eyes noted and examined the latecomer. There was something jarringly familiar about him. The sensation changed to disbelief as the leather-clad stranger strode purposefully up to a particular painting.

The trio stood transfixed for long moments, the tall visitor staring up at his likeness and the guards ogling the portrait come to life. Finally the elder guard broke the spell by deciding to do his job — sort of. He stepped forward, cleared his throat and asked, "Anything I can help you with, sir?"

Peale pivoted toward the voice. *Damn, not paying attention again, Bonehead. A bad habit to fall into. It's a wonder there haven't been more close calls.* He assumed charming smile number three. "The gift shop, please. Where is it?"

"The Museum Shop is at the front of the Institute, Sir. To the right as you come in the main entrance. You might want to hurry, they'll be closing soon."

He swept a hand at the painting. "Would they have a reproduction of this?"

"U-u-uh. Yessir, I think they'd have something."

Still by the door, the other guard muttered, "Why not just look in the mirror?"

Alarmingly, the eerily familiar midnight blue eyes flicked in his direction. After a moment, the stranger's smile broadened. "That only goes so far, I'm afraid. Byron Peale was an ancestor of mine — but, I imagine you'd worked that out yourselves."

Leaving the twosome nodding mutely, he turned back to the painting. The information on the tag removed all doubt: this was his painting. *His* property. Dammit. It wasn't *supposed* to leave the house let alone be loaned to a nationwide tour! Remembering he had company, he reined in his anger and nodded to the pair. "Thank you, gentlemen. I'll be on my way."

They watched the departing figure, then starting galvanically, the elder fumbled for the walkie-talkie on his belt.

His companion asked, "What are you doing, Johnny?"

"I'm calling Shirley in the shop! She's got a heart condition and there's an English cardiac arrest headed her way."

***

Flight booked for the next evening and motorcycle safely registered for shipping, he hailed a cab. Most of his stuff was in the saddlebags of the hog, but he still needed a few things from home *and* to leave a message for

Galen. It would be wise if he wanted to come back to Chicago.

Galen was asleep by the time BC returned to toss toiletries into a duffel, and pen his message. After a great deal of debate, he decided to omit his destination and reasons for leaving. That didn't leave much. Couldn't be helped. With Galen still smarting from Nelson's fusillade about keeping secrets, it was best to be brief. BC grinned recalling the Captain's tirade. It sounded so familiar, it could have been Galen and himself arguing about lack of trust a short time ago. As soon as he was missed, Jim was sure to be all over Galen for an explanation. Gae's loyalty was just as sure to be torn between partner and old friend. Better to simply leave blanks and fill them in later. He was nervous enough of his welcome in Maryland. If it went sour, he wouldn't want to talk about it afterward, and Galen wouldn't let it rest until he'd heard the whole sordid story. He didn't think he could do that. Eighty-some years had passed, but it still hurt.

A big part of him was still reluctant to let SI in on everything. As far as he was concerned, his future with them was as dicey as his reception back home. If time had taught him anything, it was the value of hedging his bets. No, he'd keep Galen clear of it until it was all over, then take the heat, himself. He was used to *that* even before he was changed.

He surveyed what he'd written. Brief, but passable, providing Galen didn't find it before he was ready. As a precaution, he placed it in his new dresser and unpacked a carton of clothing on top of it.

With a grimace, he regarded the daunting amount of unpacking left to do. He shouldn't have stopped at the club before heading home, but self-discipline was never his forte. Ruefully, he dragged more boxes to the dresser and dug in.

***

Dawn threatened as he roared up to the iron gates of Belridge on the Harley, damning flight delays and imbecilic cargo clerks who seemed bent upon treating him to a lethal sunbath. Killing the bike's engine, he trotted it around the back of the sprawling stone house. The concealed entrance to the sub-basement was still there. Abruptly he realized, he'd been holding an unneeded breath. Keying the locks, he slid the well-hidden door back, telling himself softly, "Not so fast. Don't relax until you see the rooms themselves and your belongings are there."

The rooms *had been* intact as of September, 1979. That was when he'd slipped back to retire his stretched fork panhead chopper to the big room with his other bikes. He froze on the ramp. Oh no. If his portrait had been loaned out, how did the motorcycles fare? Some of them were pretty valuable. He closed the door and headed down the incline, headlamp slicing the absolute blackness.

Teeth gritted, he swung wide the storage room door. As it pivoted silently on well-oiled hinges, he was welcomed by the scent of gasoline, oil and leather, but that wasn't proof. Those aromas would hang in the air for a while — at least to him. Groping for the familiar protrusion, he toggled the light and wheeled the Softail in, relieved to see the seven familiar tarp-shrouded shapes crowded together on the far side. Waitaminit. There was no dust anywhere, someone's been tidying. Bemused, he parked the Softail with the others, pulled his duffel off the saddle and flicked off the overhead light.

He hated being in absolute darkness, but he didn't need a light here, he knew the place by heart. It had been his sanctuary for the better part of two centuries. Up until the end of the 1920s, this had been home. Gingerly pushing the door open, he turned the electric switch inside. The light glared painfully in his sensitive eyes, but his sitting room and bookcases were exactly as he remembered.

The bedchamber first. The sun was coming up and he'd be going down soon. The problem of the painting would have to wait until sunset. *Damn*, disappear for a few decades and they forget everything they've promised you. Anger lengthened his canines and he pulled himself up abruptly.

Oops. He'd neglected to feed again. Too busy with all the flight arrangements. Oh, well, it'd just lend him extra force.

A faint, but recent scent hung in the air near the bookshelves. It was strongest in the chair by the reading lamp. Hmmm. Lily of the Valley. Good brand, too. The Jessica thing that sounded like a John Wayne movie. Funny name for a nice perfume.

The room spun and his knees sagged as he caught himself against the back of the chair. *Blast!* Better hit the bed before he simply passed out on the floor. That made for a wretched awakening.

Rubberizing legs gratefully collapsed him onto the mattress, as he murmured thickly, "I'm more tense about this homecoming than I dreamed, but it's good to lie down and . . . hey, the sheets are fresh . . . and smell of Lily of the Valley. *Very* pleasant."

He smiled faintly as the familiar drifting sensation tugged at him. *Seems not everyone has forgotten me.*

FIVE

He awakened to the fug of pipe tobacco mingled with Lily of the Valley and the familiar sound of Peales disagreeing. A deep male voice boomed, "Feh. Our 'long-lost cousin' Byron. Could you *be* any more melodramatic? I tell you, Miriam, there are no such things as vampires!"

A feminine snort answered from the foot of the bed. Weight previously unnoticed shifted as a gentle hand brushed his unruly forelock aside. It was a pleasurable sensation. The woman said softly, "Take a good look and tell me that again, Will."

Will moved farther away. "All right, he *looks* like Byron Peale. So does my son. It proves nothing. Probably some distant relation come to put the touch on us who crawled in here to die, instead. We ought to call the police. From the looks of him, he's probably wanted for something."

The foot of the bed suddenly eased as Miriam launched herself, exclaiming, "Willson Peale, I can't believe you said that. If you hadn't sent the portrait out to be cleaned you'd be singing a different tune. When is that going to be returned, by the way, it doesn't take *that* long to clean one painting? I still don't see why you sent it out. We could have cleaned it in the gallery and had it back by now."

Will's heartbeat gave a satisfying leap. Oh ho! Something he doesn't want Miriam to know, is it? Willson blustered, "I *told* you they had a backlog and had to send it out of the shop. . . ."

A cue if he'd ever heard one! Levering upright with his elbow, Byron challenged, "Yeah! *Way* out of the shop: L.A., San Francesco, St. Louis,

Chicago . . . that's where I saw it, Chicago."

The disputants spun toward the speaker. Miriam beamed with triumphant pleasure. Willson was plainly horrified. He said, "But . . . you were dead . . . you had no pulse . . . ."

Evil smile widening, BC slid off the bed. "I wasn't breathing either, you'll get used to it after a while. I did."

Extracting his copy of the infamous postcard from his jacket pocket, he handed it to Miriam. "Oh, and before I lose my train of thought: Were you aware that sniveling bastard loaned *my* portrait to a traveling art exhibit?"

Uncertainly, Miriam took the card, read the fine print, and promptly wheeled on Willson who was indeed beginning to snivel. "*I KNEW IT!* Willson Raphaelle Peale, how could you? I'd already turned them down twice!"

BC was entranced. When a Peale woman used one's full name, the next step was vaporization.

Willson backed for the door. "Well, I . . . well . . . they *did* clean it. It was part of the deal."

BC flung himself back onto the bed. "Oh God!"

***

Jim Nelson was on the phone again. It was getting so he could almost set hi watch by the calls. Gae said, "Hi, Jimbo. No, I still haven't heard anything from Peale."

Jim grunted. "Not surprised. We got the results on the contents of the squirt bottles. Crazier and crazier."

"What was it? Some kind of esoteric anti-undead potion?"

"Nope. Water. Higher mineral content than normal, but plain old water. Were they trying to melt him or something?"

For the first time that day Galen laughed. "I don't know, but they sure pissed him off. He'd just styled his hair."

"Wish I could have been there. That is one vain sunnovabitch." Jim enjoyed the laugh, then as if the universe might have changed in the hour since his last call, asked, "You're *sure* Peale didn't tell you where he was going?"

"Positive. You saw the note same as I did. If you can make more out of 'Called out of town. Personal stuff. Back in a few. BC,' than me, cryptography is looking for you."

Nelson muttered curses and Galen leaped at the unusual opportunity to needle his pal. Oozing innocence, Miller said, "Well, you *did* tell him to lay especially low, Jimbo."

Nelson failed to see the humor. "If I thought that was the only reason the asshole did a bunk, I'd feel better about it. I don't."

"*OKAY!* It was a joke. A lame one, but a joke." Figuring to head to more solid ground, Miller asked, "Anything on Hernandez, yet?"

"Nothing new. We put a tap on Jay's phones, but he's dropped out of sight as completely as Peale."

"Did you backtrack him?"

"Peale or Hernandez?"

"Both, I guess."

"Yes to both. First Hernandez: We checked out his apartment. He'd been there, but cleared out long before we got there. You should see the place, Gae. Scary. The guy's Looney Tunes for sure. All kinds of books and magazines about vampires. Lots of incoherent scribbling, both on paper and walls, about monsters and Jay. Mick's in a lather. Jay won't be chased out of her place, so he's moved in with her for the duration."

"Sounds like a damn good idea."

"I thought so, too."

"What about Peale? Did you trace the cab?"

"Yeah. We lucked out there. It was a lady cabbie, she remembered him *real* well. Took him to the airport. From there we think he paid cash for a ticket to Baltimore using the name Lawrence Talbot."

"Aw Geez! The Wolfman?"

"He's got a warped sense of humor, Gae, you told me that yourself. Anyway, at Baltimore, he picked up his motorcycle. Seems he shipped *that* yesterday at the same time he bought the ticket. We lose him from there."

Jim paused. Galen knew a question he didn't want to answer was coming. The fact that it was one Jim didn't want to ask wasn't heartening. Finally, Nelson said, "Gae, in your honest opinion, do you think Peale's done a bunk on us?"

Relief unlocked tensed muscles. That wasn't the question he'd been afraid of. He wondered if it was the one Jim *wanted* to ask. "Nah. He said he'd be back in a few days and he's good for his word. I think the painting set him off. He was really in a funk after you and Mick left the other night. The donor's address was in Maryland and the name was Peale if I remember correctly."

"You do, as usual. We're checking on that . . . ."

Oops. Here came the part he hadn't wanted to deal with. "Jim, do me a favor and don't follow it any more. I don't know what he's up to, but I know . . . well . . . let's let him do it in peace. He'll be back."

"Sounds like the wit and wisdom of Augustine Jump Veron."

"Yeah. I called him as soon as I found Peale's note. He got one just as informative."

"Okay, but if he contacts you, tell him to call *me* or I'll have his undead butt in a silver sling!"

"You'll have to stand in line, James!"

***

The air was comfortably cool and the crisply sparkling stars formed a vault supported by towering evergreens. Maeve Donal eased into the cushions of the cedar chair and breathed deeply of the scents of water, pine and drifting tendrils of acrid smoke from Francesco's omnipresent fire. It carried her back to childhood when fifteenth century Ireland seemed such a vast and wild place to an adventurous girl.

She had to hand it to Francesco, getting out of the city was a wonderful idea. It was lovely coming here for a fresh start both personally and magically. She'd no idea such a thing existed as a fishing lodge in the state of Wisconsin or that Francesco Borgia owned one. She should have. Frankie required regular doses of seclusion. It was another reason their romantic entanglement failed. He spent months on end stalking wild animals for fun and prey in his hideaways. Maeve, born into such surroundings, saw no need to commune with the wilds when there were perfectly good cities available. He was right this time, though, with the distracting psychic voices of Chicago's huge population far away, she'd easily regained her focus. The way the reconciliation had happened was fairly enjoyable, too.

After the incident at the penthouse, she'd stormed back to her hotel suite and a ringing telephone. It was Francesco being as contrite as he could without having a stroke. He was stiff, but insistent that old friends should not let temperament come between them. Maeve let him persuade her for several minutes before she melted. She'd expected the call, although not so soon, and had her lines carefully prepared. Allowing tiredness to tinge her voice, she'd told him how upsetting it was when he got nasty about Byron and . . . well . . . she'd paused, counting down to the inevitable outburst of "Dammit, woman! Don't be coy. *WHAT ELSE IS THERE?*"

Then she'd finally told him about the mysterious impediment. That magical equivalent of a stone wall her spells kept breaking against. That there was something or someone powerful near the other vampire. That was the only explanation.

Frankie was predictably dismayed, but didn't doubt her for a moment. Instead, he surprised her by admitting he, too, felt something out of plumb, but had no name for it. Surprise was a mild word for what she felt then. Flabbergasted came closer. No Borgia *ever* admitted that sort of thing. His tone held wonderment as he confessed that it was like something calling to him. His tone became more normal as he said that it had never happened before and he didn't care for the phenomenon.

Well, she knew exactly what that was. It was the child's essence calling to the parent. It wouldn't pay to let Francesco analyze it too closely. If he connected it to his renegade — to Byron — on his own, all her plans were wrecked. She wanted a chat with Byron first.

That was the down side to the retreat, she couldn't do any private spell casting. Francesco was determined to be entertaining and could be *very* diverting when he chose. He was so choosing and Maeve was enjoying the attention. Gwen Isendamer wasn't. The woman had made one visit to the cabin and her hatred was a palpable thing. A snake writhing against the skin. Maeve was revulsed but not afraid. The darkness at the core of the woman's soul was another thing, though. She'd only seen the like twice in her life. Each time, the owner of such a soul was capable of unspeakable atrocities, capable of revolting even Francesco. Nevertheless, the psychopathic wench was loyal to Frankie, and as long as that held, there'd be no trouble.

Francesco said Isendamer wanted to be made a vampire. He didn't have to add that wouldn't happen. Such a thing would be disastrous. Even her fun-loving and romantic Byron could be horrifyingly changed when the bloodthirst overcame him. She'd seen that once, too, and would *never* forget it.

Odd she should think of that, but Byron was the crux of the problem, wasn't he?

How fortunate Francesco that never sealed the bond with him, or he'd have felt the staking more strongly than she. Or *would* Byron and Frankie have bonded? Francesco was far too corrupt for Byron to accept, and Byron's love of wine, women and song grated on Francesco. Both were damnably pigheaded, too. That was probably the most insurmountable obstacle. In that light, it was surprising Frankie felt Byron's pull at all. Perhaps Byron was unconsciously reaching out to his sire as well as actively bedeviling him.

All her hopes hung on Byron and Francesco being reconciled — or at least calling a truce. Then maybe she and Byron would be reconciled, too, but that bridge could wait until she got to it. First, she needed to breach that damned barrier again. Once past that hurdle, there'd be other problems to wrestle with.

At least she had names for them now, and where the name was known, there was power. Unfortunately, Byron was exceptionally adept at locking her out, and there was the additional factor of the blood-link between sire and fledgling. It gave each an odd mixture of protection from and influence over the other. Tomorrow she'd be back in town and could try again.

She sensed more than saw Francesco come down the path from the cabin, his penetrating gaze fixed on her in the darkness. Bright as day to him, though, and she felt his concern run over her like a gentle caress. Considering her train of thought, she was sure her expression was unspeakably bleak. Smiling up into his frowns had the desired softening effect.

He asked, "Will you not come up the house, Maeve? It is so cold out here and difficult to speak openly."

She gleamed mischievously, "You're just wantin' t' compromise an innocent lass by the fire, you wicked creature."

"That is correct," he replied gravely. "However, since I was unable to find an innocent lass in this isolated spot, I am compelled to invite you."

"Devil!" Her laugh was silver against the night. Rising, she grazed his cheekbone with a feathery kiss, then started for the lodge sighing, "You always have the proper words t' melt a woman's heart."

Watching her glide up the path, he frowned. He'd never seen her so preoccupied. He wondered if she were telling all she knew. It would be an historic first if she were. However, he mused happily, there was a wonderful fire in the great room and Maeve offered interesting possibilities for the evening entertainment. How fortuitous that business called Edgar back to Chicago, and they were alone. Maeve's blood had such a wonderful something. . . .

***

Miriam Peale enjoyed watching Byron move. Even prodding the small fire in the drawing room grate, he was extraordinarily graceful. Dancing flames accented the ephemeral ruddiness left from his recent bloodmeal on the neighboring farm's dairy cattle. In her great-great-great-grandfather's papers, she'd read Byron frequently complained how bitterly he felt the cold. Charles, again undertaking his youngest brother's upbringing in the absence of a sire, wrote that he thought it was an unfortunate side effect of his vampiric condition. When she asked Byron, himself, about the observation, he guffawed, then proceeded to entertain them with his own uproarious version of his "instructional evenings" with his family. In all her studies of the family histories those long-vanished ancestors were never so alive and vividly colored. In their first conversation, he'd commented she reminded him of his sister-in-law Rachel, and Willson, of his brother James. From the wicked twinkle accompanying the latter statement, it *might* not have been a pure compliment.

He'd shared that and so much more, but there were volumes that remained firmly closed. So many questions he skillfully shunted aside. It didn't matter, she was as much a Peale as he was. She'd get it out of him. Besides, he seemed to be enjoying talking to her as much as she was to him. He was already ten times more relaxed than when he first arrived. Strange how nervous he was then — almost afraid — like he'd been set to weather a very nasty reception. Curious. Another thing she'd have to work out of him.

She'd have to tread softly, though. In the best Gothic novel fashion, most of the occupants of Belridge were unaware who Cousin Byron really was. Willson's eldest son, James, knew. It wasn't wise or practical to keep it from him. As he grew older, the boy had developed a keen interest in the family legend and spent hours devouring the family documents, both published and private. To his father's delight, the reading spawned a companion interest in the broader history happening concurrently with family history and a talent for thorough research. It looked like Miriam would pass the mantle of official family historian to a male Peale. That was rare. Along with that title came the post of Guardian of the Family Secret, though she honestly couldn't see why. The Family Secret didn't brook much guardianing.

Thinking of James made her glance at the mantle clock. She had some sensitive ground she wanted to cover with Byron before the boy returned from his skating party. The party was an event scheduled and RSVPed long before Byron made his dramatic reappearance. James had been torn whether to stay home with his fascinating cousin or have an evening with Grace Peters. Miriam was amused, but not terribly surprised, when Grace won by a hair. He *was* very like Byron. Even physically. At sixteen, the boy was developing an uncanny resemblance to the portrait downstairs.

Correction: the portrait that *ought* to be downstairs. It would be back soon enough. It had to stay for the duration of the show, because Willson signed a contract, blast his devious hide. Thank goodness the show was almost finished. Currently, her brother was wisely giving their resident vampire a wide berth . . . or *was* he their resident vampire? She hoped so. Though she'd only known him for two nights, she felt she'd known him all her life. In a way she had. She'd heard and read about him all her life. Dry history and dusty papers aside, she liked him. The children adored him. Even the imperious Mrs. Blackburn, their housekeeper, smiled when he was around. That was an accomplishment in itself.

As if sensing her thoughts, he straightened and slipped the poker back into the stand on the hearth. Lounging against the stone mantle in his deceptively lazy manner, he drawled, "Fire away, then. I'll answer all your personal questions before James returns from his party." Mischief danced in his eyes. "Well, most of them, at any rate."

Miriam flung herself against the sofa cushions and hooted. "Are you a mind reader, too, or have I been that obviously champing at the bit?"

Mischief blossomed into a laugh. "I *said* you reminded me of Rachel, didn't I? There are certain unmistakable mannerisms of unsatisfied curiosity in the female Peale — even those who are Peales by marriage. I learned long ago that I disregarded such signs at my peril."

Suddenly, five-year old Titian burst through the double doors all squeals and giggles. He was followed doggedly by a puffing four-year-old Sophie. Titian darted behind Byron and peeked out from the relative safety. Sophie skidded to a halt, planted tiny fists on hips and wailed, "No fair! Everybody else's legs are longer an' I can't catch 'em when I'm It."

BC glanced around where the other toddler crouched. "Y'know, Titian, Sophie has a point. Your legs *are* longer. I think you're much more suited to being It."

So saying, he snatched Titian up and held him squirming and shrieking just off the floor. Gleefully, Sophie darted up, tagged a wriggling leg, and ran. Byron dropped Titian who roared out of the room calling, "I'm It! I'm gonna get you, Sophie!"

As her cousin pattered down the hall, Sophie poked her head from around the door she'd ducked behind. Seeing the coast was clear, she darted into Byron's arms for a hug, whispering in hoarse confidentiality, "Thank you for cheating for me."

"Don't mention it. By the way, if you climb onto the shelf in the hall closet and pull a box in front of you, he'll *never* find you."

Bestowing another quick hug, she slid down and with exaggerated care, tiptoed from the room toward the front hall.

Miriam bit her fist in an effort to keep a straight face. It didn't work.

She gasped helplessly, "Oh, Byron, I'm so sorry. With an instant family of six, this place should be renamed Belvue!"

Smiling, Byron said, "No need to apologize, this has traditionally been a large family. I've always liked children."

"Me, too, but . . . ." She glanced toward the door then back at Byron, whispering, "Are any of them listening?"

He scanned the nearby area giving her a wicked wink. "Preternatural senses are extremely useful when having private discussions at Belridge." After a moment, he said, "For once: no. They're too busy chasing each other around. What deep, dark secret were you going to divulge?"

"Nothing too deep or dark, I was just going to say that, while I love children, too, I more expected to become spinster aunt Miriam rather than default Mommy times six. First came Will's divorce. When he moved back in here with Sophie and James, it wasn't so bad. *Then* the plane crash that killed our brother George and his wife, Glenna! Suddenly there were Elizabeth, Chuck, Maggie and Titian. It's been more than a little overwhelming, especially with Titian and Chuck — but I'd rather die than have any of them overhear and take it the wrong way."

"Understood. It's never easy when responsibility is thrust in one's face. Given my bachelor background, I can't comment on your decision to stay single, either."

Miriam looked teasingly up at him from under her lashes. "You've had your share of near misses, though. I gather you found the one with Katherine Brewer particularly disappointing. She was Rachel's cousin wasn't she?"

Byron dropped his head and stared into the flames, all merriment fading. "I'm impressed. You've been studying up."

Miriam stood and put her hand on the arm that rested across the marble. "I'm so sorry, I didn't mean to get personal. I just — you've fascinated me for a long time. I've read so much, I feel I know you. I was so afraid I'd never get the chance to meet you face to face."

The mischief-laden gleam returned. "That's why you've spent so much time in my lair, huh?"

"Oops." She grinned guiltily. "That and the fact it's a great place to read. You have a very pleasant lair and a good library."

"Thank you. *And* thank you for keeping the place up, I was worried I'd find it full of dust and cobwebs after all this time . . . if I found it at all. When I discovered my portrait on loan to the exhibition, I wasn't sure."

"Don't be silly! Of course your apartments will be there, that's a stipulation of passing the house on to the heirs. That apartment was built expressly for your use."

"I know. I helped build this place. But the painting . . . was unexpected. That blew my cover big time."

"I'm also sorry for 'blowing your cover,' but frankly, since it got you to come home, I'll forgive Will for being a sneak. By the way, whatever possessed you to stay away for so long? Why didn't you write or call? Anything that would let us know you were still with us?"

His initial nervousness returned with a vengeance. He seized the poker and turned back to the fire, worrying the logs in the grate with the hook. The abrupt change puzzled her. "Byron, you're home now. No matter *what*'s gone wrong, I'll stand behind you. Willson will, too. Oh, he blusters and acts all gruff, but he's good-hearted, really. You can tell me what the matter is."

Pain contorting his face/ He finally said, "You said you knew the histories. Surely you know about Lillian Peale?"

Miriam was stunned. Of all the troubles that occurred to her, this one never crossed her mind. The story of Lillian Peale was one of the great family tragedies, but why on earth . . . oh my. "That was *not* your fault! Nobody but you ever thought it was!"

The dark head snapped up, deep-set eyes mocking as he drawled, "You remember the incident well, I take it?"

Ignoring the sarcasm, she replied, "You said it yourself. I *am* the family archivist, Byron, I have the diaries, letters and all that other juicy stuff. I *do* know what I'm talking about."

He regarded the fire in silence.

"According to what I've read, the family felt that if you hadn't been here, it would have happened a lot sooner and nobody would have ever known the truth. I've read her diaries, too, they were singed, but not destroyed — even though that bastard tried hard. You were her friend and confidant. She wrote that without you, she believed she'd have gone utterly insane."

He'd withdrawn somewhere that she wasn't allowed and she had no way of knowing if he'd even heard. An uncomfortable silence loomed as she remained beside him. Giving it a full minute by the ancient clock on the mantle, she resumed lightly, "You said you've just come from Chicago? Is that where you're staying now?"

He roused himself as if from a dream, still distant, but at least aware of her presence. "Yes. I . . . uh . . . oh shit." The dreamy distance was wiped away by what could only be described as a bolt of pure panic. He scrabbled in his pocket, pulled out a smartphone and jabbed at the screen. He closed his eyes and groaned, "Seventy-two missed calls."

She recognized the symptoms. "Forgot to turn your phone on after the flight, huh?"

"Ummm, yeah."

"You probably need to call someone."

"Yeah."

Okay, evasive wasn't what she'd been hoping for, but she'd take it over the deep withdrawal. "You can go out onto the veranda, it's a nice night and no one will interrupt you there."

A broad smile split his face. She had the odd feeling, she was elected to be moral support for something. "No, this will be fine, besides, you'll have to find out sooner or later."

Viewing him with renewed alarm, she said, "That sounds ominous.

You *aren't* in trouble with the law or anything, are you?"

Busy punching buttons, he answered absently, "In a manner of speaking, I suppose I am." Before she could press further, his connection was made. "Hi, Galen! Sorry, I turned the mobile off on the plane and forgot to turn it back on."

Innocence oozed from every pore. In spite of her misgivings, Miriam watched the performance with growing amusement.

He said, "But I *did* tell you I was leaving for a few days. Didn't you find my note? I stuck it to the refrigerator door with that big football helmet magnet. . . ."

She couldn't hear the softly rumbling words on the other end, but the muted tones continued at great length, until finally Byron responded, "But why is he upset? I *am* calling in! That's what I'm doing right now." Again, a disgruntled silence as the rumbling continued, then, in resignation, he replied, "OK, look, I forgot to turn the damn thing back on until this moment! Sue me for having a human memory. I've been busy."

More listening, then firmly, "No, I don't want to say where I am right now." His voice rose as he rebutted the last unheard statement, "I most certainly will *not* tell Captain Nelson, either. It's none of his bloody business, is it? His or Sentry International's."

Stunned, Miriam sank back onto the couch.

Byron resumed his thoughtful expression. "Well, why don't you call him, then? Oh. Said that did he? Right. I'll ring him now. Yeah! Of course I mean *now* now. 'Bye."

He thumbed the End button and flipped through pages on the screen with a sour expression.

Miriam managed, "Byron, did you say Sentry International?"

He nodded and, having found the entry he wanted, punched the screen and held the phone at arm's length. "Got anything handy to catch the ashes? I think I'm about to be disintegrated."

She didn't have to wait long for an explanation as presently the instrument crackled with: "*PEALE!* Where the hell *are* you? What kind of goddamned dumbass stunt are you trying to pull, anyway? I expect my agents to keep me posted on their movements at all times. Why am I not getting that, Peale? Peale? *Peale!* Talk to me, dammit!"

Cautiously Byron brought the instrument close enough to say, "Hi, Captain. I forgot to turn my mobile back on after the plane. Saw I missed a few calls. Anything new on Hernandez since I left?" Quickly, the phone resumed it's safe distance for another, more inarticulate blast of noise. He bestowed a roguish wink on his cousin as he waited for the tirade to wind down.

Fascinated by the show, and perplexed by the revelation, Miriam found herself undecided as to where she came down on the subject. Byron Cyrus Peale, vampire, international agent? No. That was too much to take in at one go. She'd try it on a line/item basis.

Byron Cyrus Peale.

She looked at him hard. Yes, that was definitely Byron. No matter what Willson said, she'd been looking at his portrait all her life.

Vampire.

That one was a bit trickier, but after two days of dormancy and a night and a half of Byron-ness, she was pretty convinced.

International agent.

. . . .

No. Try as she might, his history and the night and a half of Byron-ness made *that* part hard to swallow. Maybe it would grow on her.

An outburst from Byron drew her back, "Of course I know you could ping my mobile! I'd hoped you'd have the decency not to. You *told* me to lay low and I did. Besides, I don't feel all my bolt-holes are Sentry property. I might need them again some day."

This logic didn't impress Captain Nelson. While his reply was better modulated than the previous outbursts, it was still clearly audible from Miriam's spot on the couch. He said, "Alright, Peale. But, *tell* someone the next time! Now, haul your lily-white ass back here ASAP!"

Looking slightly mollified for a reason that escaped Miriam, Byron said, "Since you asked so nicely, okay. It'll probably be sometime late tomorrow night; since day travel presents difficulties."

"I don't care if you have yourself shipped UPS. I need you in Chicago and I need you *yesterday*."

The click of Captain Nelson's disconnect was sharply audible. Byron stood regarding the phone with a sour expression, then slowly slipped it into his pocket. Brightening, he asked, "Hey, Miriam, how much d'you think UPS would cost from Baltimore to Chicago?"

***

The brass brazier lid clapped shut with a furious clank. She'd outsmarted herself this time and lost her first opportunity to pinpoint Byron's location since she'd worked things out with Francesco. How foolish to use an area specific spell. Not only was he not where she'd thought he'd be, he didn't even seem to be in the city. Damn and blast! All that effort and energy wasted.

Bringing herself up short; she heard in memory the long-suffering tones of her aunt Étain admonishing that the most important component in any spell was patience. Right again, dear teacher. She'd simply have to use a *less* specific spell and begin again. Curse it! Where could the blackguard have gone and why leave now? Why did he have to be so bloody elusive? Why did he have to be so bloody *beautiful,* that was the real downfall. Damn him anyway. She'd need more herbs.

SIX

From above, the concourse of the Baltimore-Washington International Airport was a kaleidoscope with knots of people coming together and separating in an infinite variety of color and shape. BC leaned on the rail next to James Peale, and watched the passing show, marveling at the rush and bustle of it all. He ought to be rushing, too. His flight to Chicago would take off soon, but sneaking a sidelong glance at his young cousin, he realized that he was amazingly reluctant to leave his regained family. Their welcome both pleased and surprised him. Maybe Miriam was right: the only one assigning blame was himself. He dismissed the thought; the bottom line was that he didn't want to leave. Sadly, he had no choice. Inescapable responsibilities beckoned him back to Chicago. That was amusing in itself: The most avowedly irresponsible member of the Peale clan being commanded by the call of duty. How Charly would laugh.

He had to admit that it wasn't simply unfinished business that drew him back, either. It had been a long time since he'd done the agent thing, but each passing night reminded him how much he enjoyed the challenge. Moreover, the friendship with Galen Miller was becoming almost as deep as the bond he shared with Jump Veron — his thoughts were interrupted by a whiff of Lily of the Valley and the click of a camera shutter.

"That'll be a good addition to the photo albums."

As one, James and BC pushed off the railing to swivel toward Miriam who did nothing to conceal her amusement. "Wonderful candid shot aside, what are you two doing up here? Will and I have been looking all over for you. You'd better get your things together, Byron, your flight will be boarding in a few minutes. Do you have the receipt for the Harley?"

Patting the zippered pocket on his breast, he replied, "Yep. Right next to my heart, close to the place you occupy. Thank you for shipping it for me, I'm always nervous one of us will miss connections if I ship it as I leave."

She snorted and slipped an arm about his waist. "Flattery will get you everywhere! It wasn't any more trouble to ship a motorcycle than one of the gallery's larger sculptures. Maybe a little easier, most shipping clerks *understand* a Harley-Davidson. But why ship it at all? You have several bikes here, why not use one of them next time?" Pinning the errant relative with a glare, she demanded, "You *are* planning on coming back?"

He laughed, "Of course I'll be back! I simply have to get used to the concept of having a home again."

James said, "But, Belridge *is* your home. You helped build . . . ."

Miriam interrupted, "*James!*"

Trying to ignore Byron's snicker (the rat), James dropped chagrined eyes to his sneakers. "Sorry, it just came out wrong, Aunt Miriam."

Shifting her severity to the smirking vampire, she said, "As I was saying: now that we have you back, you'd better stay in touch. I warn you, I'll systematically dismantle your precious motorcycles if you don't at least *call*."

James interjected, "She'll do it, too, BC."

BC regarded his cousins with wry humor. "I've no difficulty believing it. I solemnly promise, one: I'll use the Electraglide next time I'm home and two: I'll ring you as soon as I get in — oh! You *do* have Jim Nelson's number in case Galen and I are unavailable?"

Miriam nodded. "I have it, but I confess, I'm *still* having trouble with that part."

He grinned. "Me, too."

Willson Peale's stocky figure bulled through the throng. "Ah, Miriam!

You've located them, good!" Stopping in front of them, he turned to Byron and said, "You'd better get a move on, old man, they'll be making the final boarding call any minute."

On cue, the P.A. system crackled to life announcing the very thing. Pleased with proof of his prescience, Will Peale spread his hands to say there you are. Duffel scooped from the floor in a fluid move, BC administered quick hugs, kisses and a final wave, then vanished into the crush of hurrying travelers.

James strained to follow the tall, broad-shouldered form for a few more moments then asked, "D'you really think we'll see him again?"

His father grumbled, "Bad pennies always turn up."

Miriam dug a good-natured elbow into her brother's ribs, then squeezed her nephew's shoulder. "Yes, James, I think we have our Byron back. For a while, at least."

***

The first flush of pleasure at spotting the gigantic figure on the other side of the gate diminished with each step closer. None of the airport's plastic chairs were large, but Miller made the one he occupied look microscopic. As Peale neared, Galen unfolded, his strong face unreadable. Tacking on his most engaging manner, Peale swung his duffel firmly over his shoulder, and said, "Hi, Gae. Thanks for coming down. I've got to collect my bike from freight before we go. D'you mind?"

Falling into step with his partner, Miller strode beside him through the concourse. "I don't mind, after all, Jim told me to meet you and be sure you got to Schaumburg one way or another. Shipped your bike, huh?"

"I needed a way to get around."

"This was a through flight from Baltimore. Care to share anything? With your *partner*?"

Surprisingly, the pale man flinched. "Please, Galen, don't let's get started arguing. I wasn't trying to be secretive, I simply needed a little privacy. I'm sure Jim Nelson could have used the forces at his disposal to trace my movements."

"I had a hard time keeping him from doing just that."

Peale responded sincerely, "Thanks, Gae . . . this was more important to me than I have words to express. I owe you another big one."

There didn't seem to be a way to reply, so the Mutt and Jeff pair shouldered through the crowd in silence until, unable to contain it, Galen blurted, "This was this about the painting, wasn't it? The one Mick saw at the Institute?" His skin darkened with a flush of barely suppressed anger. He subdued it, then added, "I don't mean to pry, don't tell me if you don't want to."

Turning quickly to his friend, BC insisted, "Oh, no! I wanted to tell you and was *going* to tell you after . . . ." He broke off uncomfortably. Not noticing the sudden concern on Miller's face, he amended, "Yes, it was about the portrait — mostly. You see, it belongs to me. My brother, Charles, painted it shortly before I . . . changed. He made me a gift of it. It was never supposed to be removed from my rooms."

"At Elk Point?"

"Belridge, yes."

"This Willson R. Peale is a relative, then . . . uh . . . you were pretty pissed when you left. You didn't do anything to him, did you?"

BC laughed. "No, but I *wanted* to. It's a long story. I thought it could wait until we were at home so we could have quiet. I ought to see Jump, too. I kind of left him unexpectedly piano playerless."

Galen grunted. "Jump was the only one who wasn't worried. He convinced Mama and me this was something you needed to do. He left it to me to convince Jim. I did it by the skin of my teeth, I think."

"Sometimes that little chap knows me better than I know myself."

"Friends are like that. If you let them be."

The bike was prepaid and waiting at the pickup point. He signed the release and hurried outside to check the machine over, then straightened with a smile. "Miriam! I should have known she'd have the last word."

Wordlessly pleased, Peale held his surprise out to Miller. It was a studio portrait of a large family group. It didn't take a rocket scientist to decide they were Peale's family: there was a striking amount of resemblance especially with the teenager at the back. Smiling in spite of himself, Galen asked, "Which one's Miriam?"

His partner indicated a beautiful woman with a calm oval face. "I said there was a lot to tell. Let's head home, I could use one of those wretched Bloody Elsies as you call them right about now."

Miller handed the photo back with a regretful shake of the head. "Sorry, pal, no can do. Jim was more than a little pissed when you bugged out. My orders are to deliver us *both* to the Schaumburg offices ASAP."

"Good Lord, Galen! I'm sorry, why does he want us both? Can't he chew my ass singly and be done with it?"

"I don't think he completely believed I didn't know where you were. Not to mention that you're official now, so you need to meet the rest of the team. *Plus* he wants to review the case files with everybody. That'll take a while by itself. We'll have to postpone talking to Jump and hearing about your trip for later. Maybe tomorrow night."

"Surely there isn't *that* much to review. You told me yourself there hadn't been much to go on before I came on the scene."

"Uh uh, man, I said there wasn't much on Borgia himself. We got shitloads on the operation. Worldwide."

Peale stopped in mid-stride. "Worldwide?"

With a sadistic grin, Miller slapped his shoulder. "Hey, man, international is part of our name. We've got all kinds of stuff on drug smuggling, arms sales . . . the works. The documents go back several years, but until last Spring there wasn't a name to hang it on. There is now."

"And he's here in Chicago."

"*And* he's not real happy with a certain punk I know. C'mon, fire this sucker up and drop me by the car. I'll follow you to Schaumburg."

***

Galen swung the secure inner door of the Special Operations offices wide, but BC hesitated to step through. Miller nudged him saying, "Move your ass, Peale. You waiting for someone to intone 'enter freely and of your own will' or something?" Indigo eyes slid toward his partner and Miller realized that the usually self-assured Peale was actually nervous. "C'mon man, it was a joke."

"I know," Peale said with a shrug. "This is just — you said that Nelson and Marquez told the team about me. How *much* about me?"

Miller suddenly understood. "Not that. Sharing that is up to you. All they said was that I have a new partner and he'll be at the briefing to meet the rest of the team."

Peale hesitated for a moment more, then nodded and entered the hallway. Miller brought up the rear noting with mild surprise that the rest of the team was *not* gathered at the coffee table, their usual place of ambush. The rhythmic rustle of paper and metallic schunk of a stapler from inside went a way to explain this.

Miller poked his head around the corner to find Tidrow stacking papers and Zoeller fastening them together with a punch to the top of a heavy-duty stapler. Zoeller didn't look happy and the punch to the stapler was a little more violent than absolutely necessary.

Tidrow looked up and grinned. He was middle-aged, mouse brown hair graying in spots and thinning in others. His tie was pulled loose and his shirt collar was unbuttoned and askew. There were just some people who looked like they'd been selected for their jobs through Central Casting. Tidrow was one of those. The role description would read: career cop, going slightly to seed, but still on top of things. Tidrow said, "Hey! Lookit, Kim. You ain't the new kid no more!" He advanced around the table with his hand extended. "You gotta be BC Peale. Frank Tidrow. This is—"

The petite blond turned toward him, extending her own hand and interrupting the older man. "Kim Zoeller. Welcome to the team, Peale." Kim Zoeller was a dichotomy. She was tiny and looked more like a teen-aged kid than the decorated soldier she actually was. Her grip, when she shook Peale's hand, was firm.

Tidrow resumed shuffling papers. "And welcome to the Land of Budget Cuts and Limited Funds. This team's so small, we don't rate a secretary, so we gotta do it all ourselves."

Zoeller swept a hand over the table with a sneer. "Tonight's briefing. I almost know it all by heart now. If I staple a few more, I can sleep through the meeting."

Miller snorted and riffled the stacks. "That explains why Marquez got scarce, he's mortally terrified of paper cuts. Where's Emily?"

The door down the hall opened, releasing the spicy scent of pizzas into the office. Tidrow inhaled deeply and released it with a satisfied sigh. "Right behind you, unless I miss my guess. Mick and Emily went on a pizza and pop run." Shooting Peale a glance, he added, "We didn't know what you liked, so we just ordered a couple with extra cheese. That sound good?"

"Thanks, but I can't eat pizza." Peale grinned. "I have some odd dietary requirements, so I take most meals in liquid form."

"That's how you stay so thin," Tidrow said. "Don't tell my wife. She'll put me on the same diet."

"Who stays thin?" Mick asked as he rounded the corner, arms full of fragrant boxes that he slid onto the table with the coffee urn. "Ah! Gotta be you, Peale. Sure isn't Man-Mountain Miller."

"Hey! This is all muscle."

"Yeah, sure it is."

"Here we go again, kids!" A solidly built oriental woman in a pantsuit edged past Miller and Marquez and deposited her load of two litre drinks bottles beside the pizzas. Every move was efficient and economical, yet there was the grace of a dancer behind the motions. She smiled up at Peale and extended her hand, "Lt. Emily Hu. Glad to have you on board. You and Gae, here, have really hit pay dirt on this thing. We're farther along these last few weeks than we've managed to get in all the time SI has been working it."

As he took her hand, a furrow appeared between her delicately arched eyebrows. He said, "Thanks, Lt. Hu. I'm glad to be aboard."

Whatever had happened, passed quickly and she smiled, saying, "Emily. You'll find there's very little formality around here. We'll be going over some of your stuff tonight. It filled in a lot of gaps for us. Lead to some not-so-nice conclusions, but with this unsub, that's been the norm."

After a particularly vicious punch at the stapler, Zoeller looked up and said, "Yeah. Tracing that shipping label back gave us a few other leads to follow. My particular favorite is this one here." Handing Peale the top sheet from one of the stacks, she pointed to a section."

Peale read it and blanched. "*Chemical* weapons?"

"Biological, too — if you have the cash," Tidrow added. "One stop shopping for the discerning terrorist."

Peale was still reading and Galen didn't like the expression on his partner's face. He liked the anger radiating from him even less. Miller nudged him. "Hey! We better get on through to Jim's office. He has your new ID waiting."

"Yes." Peale gave the page back to Zoeller and followed Miller. "Yes. Of course."

Miller rapped twice on the door, then entered all but dragging Peale in behind him. Inside the office, Miller nodded to Jim then turned on his partner. "What the hell happened back there?'

The eyes that met Miller's burned. Peale answered quietly. "Chemical weapons. That's what happened. I had no idea."

Nelson had been standing by the windows and turned to object to the abrupt entry. It died on his lips when he saw the intensity between the two agents. "Is this about Borgia's chemical operations?"

Without taking his eyes off his partner, Galen said, "Yeah. Zoeller gave him one of the info sheets for tonight and this anger vibe just started rolling off him. I didn't know if the paper was gonna burst into flame or the room was gonna ice over."

"Peale?" Jim ventured.

"You both seem to forget, I was *in* the first World War. I'll never forget those gas attacks." Unbidden, vivid memories rolled over him much as the choking clouds had done on those sodden battlefields so long ago. WWI. That's what they called it now, but then it was just Hell. The searing vapor had even hurt him, but unlike his comrades-in-arms, he had the ability to recover.

Without another word, Nelson wheeled a chair over and guided Peale into it.

Peale sat, saying, "That bastard. If I'd known about this, I'd have hit him deliberately. And harder."

"That's our job, BC, to shut this asshole down." Nelson reached to the desk and held a small leather case open in front of him. On one side, a badge gleamed and, on the other, a picture identification card was framed behind a plastic window. "*Your* job."

Nodding, Peale took the case, folded it and tucked it into is leather jacket.

Galen, who had stepped back to let Jim handle the situation, asked, "You okay?"

"I will be," Peale answered.

Nelson tossed him a small plastic card and a slip of paper. Your passcode and keycard. You saw how it works when you came in with Gae tonight?" At Peale's nod, he continued, "Memorize that code and destroy the paper ASAP. Oh, and don't keep that card too close to your cell phone. Plays hob with the magnetic strip."

Peale seemed to be recovering well, so Nelson flopped down behind his desk and grinned up at Miller. "I have a goodie for you, too, Gae. You know that remote access to SINet you've been ding donging for?"

"Ohhhh. Don't tell me they approved it."

"Just this morning."

"YESSS!" Miller punched the air.

Nelson continued, "You'll probably need a new laptop to meet the security specs. They've been buggy about that in the light of these recent hacking attacks on government and law enforcement systems. Besides, I'm tired of listening to you bitch about having to report in to the offices."

"Hey, Jimbo, it came *real* close to blowing my cover several times." After an exchange of uncomfortable glances with his partner, he continued, "Might have actually blown it, if BC's suspicions about Hernandez are as on the money as they sound."

"In that case we may be locking the barn door after the horse is stolen, but I still want you both to be able to log into video conferences. You know how it works?"

"I've done it several times," Peale said with a smile comfortably closer to normal.

"Great. Peale, we need your signature to acknowledge receipt of the ID and key, then we're good." He pointed Peale to some papers on the desk and headed for the door. "Let's get this show on the road, then."

Galen intercepted him and, with a glance back at his partner, murmured, "What about. . . ?"

"I'll handle it," Jim said. "A quick word to Lt Hu that Peale has experienced chemical warfare firsthand will do the trick. These folks understand things like that. That's why we're all here."

Galen quirked a smile and Jim walked out into the common room, saying, "Looks like we're ready to rock and roll, folks. Mick, start a batch of that Mayan poison you call coffee. It's gonna be a long night."

**

The business office of the Inferno bore little resemblance to the images of luxurious opulence portrayed in the movies. Rather, Jump Veron's work area was very like himself, small, forthright and comfortably rumpled. Jump made his last entry, closed the books for the night's receipts and glanced at the clock located to the right of his calendar/blotter half-visible on the battered oak desk. Five twenty-two a.m.. Not as long a night as some, but a respectable session, nonetheless.

Ambling over to the built in bar, he selected a fine single malt scotch whiskey for his nightcap. For health reasons, he abstained from hard drink these days, but allowed himself one per day before hitting bed. He was pouring the amber liquid and admiring the play of light through the stream when a quiet tap came at the door. Without turning, he called, "Come in, BC, I don't expect to see you until tomorrow night."

Smiling broadly, BC stepped in. "I pity anyone who tries to throw a surprise party for you, Jump."

The little man stumped back to the desk, sipping his drink. "I am a great disappointment to such persons."

The tall man draped himself across the scuffed leather sofa occupying the far wall and turned serious. "I'm sorry I took off like that. I should have at least let *you* know."

Jump said, "No need to apologize. It was good for you where you go. Something you been needing to do, maybe for a long time, *non*?"

"Maybe."

"You better now, I can feel all the way over here that you more at peace."

"Yeah? I guess so. I'll have tell you about it when we have more time."

"You know it." Agile hands rummaged through the chaotic piles of paper, extracted musical scores from the tangle and lobbed them to the sprawled figure on the couch. "Take these wit' you an' look them over before you go down. We start workin' wit' these new charts ASAP so we be ready for Saturday night."

BC shuffled through the pages, and announced good-naturedly, "You're a slave driver, Veron."

"Yesterday, we also get a pretty good piano to move into your new place. Even *you* need to practice."

"Galen's gonna love that idea. So will the upstairs neighbors."

"You work something out. Now get outta here, some of us sleep at night."

* * *

Finally! The wretch had stayed in one place long enough for Maeve to track him down, she stood outside the all-night movie theater staring up at the marquee. It read:

Lethal Weapon I, II III & IV

Drawing the light raincoat closed, she continued the internal debate whether to go in and sit down next to him. A theater was such a predictable place to find him, she should have searched them specifically before this. Byron loved entertainment and people. It was what brought them together in the eighteenth century.

It was also what made him a successful vampire.

That success had surprised her. Normally, a fledgling vampire required a period of instruction from the parent. Instruction that Francesco withheld at her specific request. By denying that guidance, she'd hoped to force him to come crawling back to her begging for her help. Unfortunately, her equation included neither Byron's adaptability nor that of his remarkable family. A serious miscalculation, as it turned out. She made a lot of those where Byron was concerned. It was as if his mere proximity made her brain malfunction. Then, why on earth did she desire that proximity so? Silly question. She *knew* why she desired that proximity. The memory brought a glow and a decision. She struck out for the ticket booth. The look on his face when he noticed her would be worth more than gold.

The sight of an imposing and hauntingly familiar figure also striding purposefully toward the theater brought her up short. It wasn't hard to peg him as Byron's companion from the bombed-out warehouse. His presence here *could* be a coincidence . . . oh, not a chance. The big fellow looked *extremely* determined, she wondered what Byron had done this time. Easing back into the shadows, she looked at her watch. She'd give it five minutes, then she'd nip inside and join the fun.

***

Ticket stub crushed in his fist and breathing swear words, Miller pushed through the swinging doors at the back of the theater. As the padded panels whispered closed, he paused blinking rapidly to adjust his vision to the sudden dark. Even after his vision compensated for the flickering light, locating the black-clad vampire proved difficult. At length, he found him toward the front, long legs doubled up against back of the empty seat in front of him and cradling an untouched cardboard container of popcorn.

Sliding in alongside his partner, he whispered, "You have these on DVD at home. How many times can you sit through *one* movie?"

"It's *four* movies and I like them on the big screen." The pale man treated his companion to a gleaming grin. "Besides, the big guy reminds me of you."

"Yeah. Well, the crazy one reminds me of you. Get your ass in gear, Jim wants to see us. Shitload more reports came in today, and since the access isn't active yet, guess who gets to go through them and collate the data?"

Peale groaned, "But we did that *last* night! What with flying in from Baltimore, I didn't even get dinner before I went down."

Miller looked doubtful. "Have you . . . eaten tonight?"

"Yes."

"Then what are you bitching about? Come on! This is the glamorous world of police work."

BC rose and stalked up the aisle. Galen caught him up. "Don't get so huffy! I got a promise we get tomorrow night off."

BC grumbled, "I hope so. I need to be at the Inferno, it's a heavy night at the club and I promised Jump I'd play."

"Nice of you to tell me in advance."

"Give me a break, okay? I just found out, myself."

Stepping into the cool night air, Miller sniffed curiously, the smell of popcorn was still unusually strong. Glancing at his partner, he saw the vampire was leaving a trail of yellow puffs from a brightly colored cardboard container. Rolling his eyes, he started across the nearly empty parking lot. BC trotted on his heels and gesturing across the lot, asked, "My bike's over this way, where'd you park?"

Galen smiled grimly. "Right next to the Harley. That's how I knew for sure you were here. I'm gonna have to enroll you in a class on note writing. 'Going to a movie. Back soon' just don't hack it."

"Sorry, I thought last night cleared the desk."

Halting between their two vehicles, Galen paused to extract his key. "So did I, but Mick called about two hours ago to say we got new shit — all thanks to that shipping label again. Some of it hasn't even been translated yet. You *did* say you spoke Russian, didn't you?"

BC leaned heavily against the side of the car with an eloquent groan. Half-way into the car, Galen paused, saying, "I know it's a bitch, man, but we're on track now. We gotta stay there. Hey! Get rid of that popcorn, you're shedding it everywhere. Why do you buy that stuff, you don't eat it."

"C'mon! I like the smell, besides, it's good cover. If you sit in a movie theater with a bucket of popcorn, nobody looks at you twice. Most of it ends up on the floor anyway."

The slender woman strolling casually between the parked cars stepped into the pinky-yellow glare of the sulfur light. Instead of walking on, she smiled brightly and said, "Good evening, Byron. It's been a while."

Thunderstruck, BC stared at the apparition. Any remaining doubt had just been removed: this was *definitely* a bad year. Possibly vying for worst decade. With barely-controlled anger, he spat, "And I thought things couldn't get worse. Galen Miller, permit me to introduce Maeve Donal. She's the . . . person . . . I have to thank for my sunlight intolerance."

Feeling his partner's sudden anger more than seeing it, Miller's hand sought a comfortable proximity to his weapon, and, treating Peale to a quick evaluation, settled into a 'wait-and-see' stance. Something about this lady that raised his own hackles, too. With unfeigned confusion, he asked, "Your sunlight intolerance? You mean she's like you? But, I thought you didn't know any other —"

Maeve bestowed a charming smile on the big man. "No, Mr. Miller, I'm not a vampire. I'm what you would probably call a witch."

BC leered maliciously. "That's *one* way spell it, I suppose."

Maeve spun, eyes flashing, then reined in. "Byron, I didn't come to fight, I came to ask you to be careful. You're makin' Francesco awfully angry."

"Francesco?" Peale blinked. "What *are* you talking about, Maeve?"

She turned slightly away so that the light glinted on her cascading hair and shadowed her face. This woman knew her stuff, against the glare of the sulfur light, the shadowing would probably make it hard for even Peale to read her expression. "Byron, you don't need t' act the innocent with me. I know you're bedevilin' Francesco Borgia because you've figured out he's your sire."

"Borgia?" The statement jolted through BC like a million volts. "Francesco *Borgia*?"

Too involved with dramatics to notice she'd dropped a bombshell, Maeve continued, "Y'should be honored, not angry! In more than five hundred years, Francesco's never created a single fledgling but yourself. If he hadn't felt you worthy, I doubt he'd have done it even as a favor to me. Forgive me if I'm wrong, but I thought you enjoyed being as you are and 'twas only my little . . . proposition . . . you objected to." She closed the distance, resting her head lovingly on his breast. "He's gettin' close to you, m'love. I'm here t' warn you off until I've had a chance to talk to him on your behalf."

Shock immobilized him while, at the same time, everything inside him screamed. He had *never* known who made him. That was the prime piece of information the woman clinging so tenderly to him in this windy night had withheld that first night in 1783. That night and for many after he wanted to know so badly he could taste it. It was Francesco Borgia? *Borgia's* blood made him?

She mistook his silence for a go-ahead. "I've been puttin' him off. I couldn't very well tell him it was his own fledgling cousin' such an uproar until I'd talked to you, Darlin'. You needn't worry, though, Frankie an' I go back a long way. I can —" Lifting her head to gaze into those well-loved eyes, she found a face shocked into immobility. Breaking off, she backed away stammering, "You didn't know . . . then why? Oh, my. What have I done?"

Miller didn't need to see his partner to know he was on the ropes. He needed to buy time. Stepping between them, assumed his best Jack Webb manner and flipped his ID case open. "What you've done is offer evidence in a very important international investigation. My partner and I would appreciate if you'd come back with us to the Sentry International offices to make a formal statement."

Maeve stared past the dangling identification card and into Galen Miller's gently beaming face. The beatific smile was strangely infuriating. As the witch began to splutter and show signs of dissolving into anger, he produced a pen and business card, and scribbled busily. "Don't decide now. Think about it. These are the numbers where we can be reached. The lower one is our apartment. But, before you think about running to Borgia to warn him about this little incident, let me remind you that Borgia is not noted for kindness. You've just openly admitted deceiving him. How well would he take that? Now, if you'd consider working *with* us, we might be able to help."

She wheeled like a fury. "That's blackmail!"

The dark face split with another placid smile. "More like extortion, actually."

As Gae hoped, the interlude gave BC much-needed time to recover. Wickedly pleased at Maeve's discomfort, he perched on the Volvo's fender, and extended the garish carton toward her. "He's quite good at it. Popcorn?"

SEVEN

Vince Crawford shifted uncomfortably on the jagged remains of the concrete wall. He'd tried padding it with an old blanket, but the smoke-blackened ruin stubbornly insisted on being unsitable. Sipping rapidly-cooling coffee, he longed for his nice, warm living room, but his boss wanted this place watched, so it was being watched. Working for Gwen Isendamer had its drawbacks, but she paid well and success was rewarded. On the other hand, failure was severely punished, and this Vampire Vigilante stuff had Her Ladyship bugged on a major scale. She was *most* unhappy that the guy put in an appearance while she was on duty and she still returned to HQ empty handed.

She was even more P.O.ed that it was her own men who let the Vampire guy and his buddy get away. The rumor-mill said two of them were taken to see Borgia himself. He shuddered involuntarily. Nobody knew for sure what Borgia did to screw-ups, but usually they weren't seen again. He'd even heard . . . he froze as footsteps crunched across the cindered ground. Blending into the dense shadows of the ruined masonry, he firmed his grip on his pistol.

A voice called from the dark, "Hey, Vinny! I got the burgers, ya wanna eat here or in the car?"

Tensed muscles became spaghetti as Vince hissed, "Jeezuz H. Christ, Tony! Where the hell you been?"

Sliding onto the ruined wall, Tony pulled enticingly fragrant bundles from a paper bag. "There was a line, so sue me!"

Snagging a bundle, Vince dissected the contents critically. "These got onions on 'em? I hate onions."

"You tol' me. About a million times you tol' me. There ain't no onions. What's eatin' you, anyways? You ain't usually this persnickety."

Vince viciously chomped the burger and leaned elbows on the impromptu table. "I dunno. Guess I thought for a minute I was gonna have to fight that Vampire guy by myself. Her Ladyship's so bugged, she's got *me* bugged."

"Aw, he ain't gonna come back here. He ain't hit the same place twice since this stuff started, you know that."

"Yeah, it's just so damn' dark and all this burned wood and stuff stinks so bad. Kind of puts you in mind of hell."

With uncomfortable eyes on the grotesquely charred shapes around them, the pair munched burgers in silence until a new set of feet crunched across the clinkers. They leaped up as one. Noticing the white fast-food bag glowed in the gloom, Tony brushed it off the wall. Vinny mimed splitting up and coming at the intruder from opposite sides. Separating, they melded into the night.

***

It was hard to sneak across the rubble, and since he only dared to move around at night it was worse. It wasn't that the people watching the ruins since all the shooting could see him, they couldn't. But the Monster could. Maybe he should find another hiding place? No, no! There wasn't another place as good as this one. Nobody would look for him here. He still didn't know what happened those few nights ago, but from the shouting, he figured the Monster attacked more people. Was It looking for him? If It was, the trouble scared It away, because It didn't come back. The others were still there, though, but that was okay, he'd avoided them so far.

The more he thought about his plans, the more he realized he needed help, but the only enemy the Monster had aside from himself, was this Borgia guy. The guy whose name he'd used to trap the Vampire. Looked like it was also the guy who owned the stuff in the warehouse that blew up, at least he overheard the watchers using the name. They must work for him, but. . . .

"Hey, you! This is a dangerous area, it's closed to the public. What do you think you're doing here?"

Hernandez started, scattering gravel. He was so deep in thought, he didn't notice the men moving in on him. Tensing to run, he caught the glint of moonlight on gunmetal, then swallowing hard, slowly laced his fingers behind his head and lay flat on the sooty ground.

The taller man said approvingly, "Good boy! See that? The guy knows the drill. Get his wallet so we can find out who this smart guy is."

The shorter one switched on a flashlight and advanced to pat him down, but his foot struck the backpack. Metal clanked inside. Hernandez jumped again. "What we got here? Sounds like a couple coffee pots, ain't been lootin' have we, punk?" Tony opened the pack and peered in. He pulled a crossbow intertwined with a braided rope of garlic cloves from the pack. "Hey, get a load of what this guy's carryin'."

Vinny whistled. "Her Ladyship told us to give her a yell if anything unusual happened. I dunno about you, but I think this fits the bill."

Vinny unfolded a cell phone and moved out of earshot. Cold and miserable, Mario lay on the damp ground. The man came back folding the phone as he walked. Looking down on the shivering figure, he said, "She wants to see him right now."

"Okay, be glad ta get someplace warm for a while, but what are we s'posed ta do? Belt him into a baby seat?"

The men examined him thoughtfully, then the short one postulated, "There's always the trunk."

Hernandez whimpered.

Vinny chuckled. "Good idea. There's *always* th' trunk."

*＊＊

He wasn't dead, he was pretty sure dead people didn't hurt so much. He also wasn't in the trunk of a car, although his last memory was being dragged toward the dark bulk of a sedan, and trying to scream through a piece of tape. Painfully turning his head, he realized the tape was gone, and he was lying on a couch. Blinking against the unaccustomed brightness of the lights, he tried to stand, but merely succeeded in sliding off the cushions onto the carpeted floor.

"Ah, Mr. Hernandez, you're awake! Good. I was afraid you'd sleep well into tomorrow and we'd lose our chance for a private chat."

As the owner of the voice came into view, he caught his breath. Standing in front of him was one of the most beautiful women he ever laid eyes on. The light behind her sketched a tantalizing hint of her body against the silvery fabric of her lounging outfit, and turned the wings of white-blond hair framing her face into a halo of gypsum threads. A fairy creature molded from snow. The eyes in the ivory face were icy blue and regarded him with knowing amusement. He opened his mouth, but nothing came out.

The ice-woman was sympathetic. "I'm sorry if my men were rougher than strictly necessary, Mr. Hernandez. They are trained for security, not for social occasions. Now that we have the niceties taken care of, we must get down to business. You never got around to answering the question my men asked: What *were* you doing in that awful place?"

Realizing he was still on his knees, he flushed under the grime and struggled to stand. He'd practically kill for a hit of cocaine right now, but his stash was back at the ruins. Running shaky fingers through greasy hair, he said, "Hey, hold up! Who is it that wants to know? I mean, geezuz, you know my name, but I don't know squat about you."

The only spot of color on her was her mouth, painted a vivid red. This curved into an open smile as she replied, "Don't be so alarmed, Mr. Hernandez, a man who wishes to remain anonymous shouldn't carry credit cards and driving licenses. I took the liberty of looking through your identification while you slept." Ice eyes inspected him briefly, the brain behind making a rapid and accurate calculation of the nature of the animal before divulging, "My name is Isendamer. Gwen Isendamer. Please sit down and be comfortable."

A sly gleam entered his eyes as he lowered himself onto the couch. Gwen winced inwardly at the ugly smudges of soot on the pristine white upholstery. She'd have to buy a new one. The smell would never come out. She sat, waiting for his next move. He didn't look smart enough to make her wait long.

Correct as usual, her back hadn't touched the cushions before he ventured, "You're connected with the guy who owned the warehouse?"

"In a manner of speaking. Now, my turn. Why were you on private property, and why do you have such interesting things in your pack? If I didn't know better, I'd think you were hunting vampires!"

The change was as immediate as it was unproductive. The cunning gleam was erased by a glaze of fear. He closed in on himself, his breathing becoming tortured. "D-don't you read the papers? There's a *real* vampire out there killing people! If he finds me, I want to be ready."

Gwen leaned into him, suddenly interested and conspiratorial. "How brave! I think I'd be too scared to do anything if it were me."

As unpleasant as the proximity was, the gambit worked. A spark of buried braggadocio rose to the surface. "Not me, because I know what to do. He's afraid of *me* now you can bet on it."

"You're hunting him?"

He postured a moment longer, then collapsed onto himself. "I was, but he might be hunting me, now. I almost got him the other night, but it didn't work."

Excitement ran through her, if this human wreckage was telling anything close to the truth, he *knew* who Francesco's rival was. Voice level, she asked, "It didn't work? Why? Didn't you use one of the arrows from your pack?"

"Oh, yes! I used one of the stakes and I put it right square in his chest, but he has too many slaves. He has help. I figured if I'm going to take him, I need help, too." Realizing he'd said more than he intended, he pulled away into a corner of the couch and regarded her in wary silence.

Isendamer adopted a wheedling tone, "Please, Mario, you have to tell me more than that, it's too exciting. Was that what you were doing at the lakefront, looking for help? But why look there?"

Against his will, Mario heard himself answering, "The Monster has an enemy, it's the guy who owned the building, a man named Borgia. I wanted to get a message to him."

Steel crept into the blue eyes inches from his. He recoiled, but was as tightly pressed against the couch as he could get. Her warm breath was moist against his skin as she hissed, "Where did you hear that name?"

"The guy . . . the vampire said it."

"How so?"

Anxiety oiled his tongue and the words tumbled in a rush to appease her. "He was asking questions, how to find him and stuff like that. Cop-type questions. He's hanging out with cops. I don't know why, I kinda hoped maybe. . . ." Fear and the need for drugs became too great, he dissolved wracking sobs.

Mentally kicking herself for losing her advantage, Gwen launched into damage control. She fed him a stiff drink, and cooed comfort into his ear. "No need to fear, Mario. I *may* call you Mario, right? (A panicked nod.) You call me Gwen, okay? (Another less panicked nod.) Do forgive my manner, but you see, Mr. Borgia is my employer, and I had to make certain you meant him no harm. He is a powerful man with many enemies, as you have seen yourself. With a creature like that for an enemy, there is no such thing as too much caution, don't you agree?"

He nodded with more certainty. She took his nearly empty glass and stood with a reassuring smile. Examination of the filthy, smelly creature revealed surprisingly that under the grime was a reasonably attractive man. Forming a hasty plan, she soothed, "Poor Mario, you've had a bad time of it. Tell you what, why don't you get out of those nasty clothes and take a nice, hot shower? I'm sure we can find something else for you to wear. Then, when you get out, I'll have dinner and another drink waiting."

Her caressing hand dropped from his shoulders and began unbuttoning rags that had once been a shirt, she purred, "After that we can *talk* again."

***

The rising sun tinted the clouds brilliant pink and gold. It was astonishing how anything so beautiful could be at the same time so maddening. She cast an angry glare at the bed and the gently snoring figure sprawled across the rumpled sheets. It took all night to get the story, but it was powerful stuff. *Now isn't the time to indulge in impatience, Gwen. Rushing things would be to lose everything. What's one more day in the face of immortality? The time until sunset can be used to best advantage. What a triumph! Francesco was pinning all his hopes on that Irish bitch and now I've discovered more in one night than she has in weeks!* She allowed a satisfied smile. *Francesco Borgia, as much as you've done for me, you'll owe me more after this.*

She frowned. There was one possible glitch. Francesco and the Donal woman had patched things up during that nauseating liaison at the fishing lodge. Damn! If only she'd been at the office when they had their original disagreement, she could have strengthened her position then and there. Instead, she'd been at that accursed warehouse with those *morons*! Nevertheless, her position was strong now.

Hernandez didn't stir when she sat on the edge of the bed and stroked his exposed throat. So weak and foolish. To be so close to such power and merely let the mind be overcome by horror. It would be so easy to kill him. Fantasies of that kept her going all night, but no. This one belonged to Francesco. No doubt he'd reward her loyalty by letting her watch as he killed and drank. Perhaps he'd let her have a taste. She hugged herself in ecstasy at the prospect of future pleasures when she shared Francesco's power and could experience that psychic thrill firsthand.

Disciplining herself, she showered and dressed. The thrill of death had been accidentally discovered at a young age, but patience was a hard-won lesson. She liked that. So many things came easily — almost by accident, one might say. She owed so much to that lovely little book on marine engines she'd found in the boarding school library. How tragic that her parents and hideous brother were killed when their yacht exploded less than a year later leaving her all that beautiful money.

No use dwelling on past glories, there was much to do before dusk. She'd start at the nightclub where this BC Peale played piano. A final check of Hernandez reassured her he wouldn't stir for a while; the drugs and alcohol she'd given him would see to that.

***

Checking the folded playbill in her handbag for the umpteenth time, Gwen blessed her luck again. Everything was falling into place. It was extraordinary good fortune that the club owner kept a box of fliers by the entrance to advertise special shows. Granted, the photograph on the green-tinted paper was far from studio quality, but it was good enough for Francesco to look on the face of his enemy. That there was a name printed below the face was even better.

Pursing her lips, she reflected. Maybe she was rushing things, this Peale was very handsome. Could she afford the time to meet with him and find out if he'd be willing to take her as a fledgling? No. Attractive as the idea and the vampire were, it simply wasn't possible. Her bread was currently buttered on the Borgia side, and the situation was too precarious to allow her to take advantage of an unexpected opportunity to shop around.

Her luck held with Eddie who traded the remainder of his daytime vigil over Francesco with ridiculously little persuasion. It was even easier to discover the Donal woman's hocus pocus had still borne no fruit. She even quit early, leaving Francesco more disgruntled than before. It couldn't get much better! Well, it could, but that was later. Checking the wall clock she sighed comfortably. Very soon now she'd discover how valuable her past twenty-four hours was.

The quiet click of the bedroom latch was welcome when it finally came. With the eagerness of a toddler at Christmas, she bounded into his arms, whispering urgently, "Wonderful news, Francesco darling, The renegade is discovered!"

He exclaimed delightedly, "Has Maeve . . . ? How has she done this during the day?"

"*She* had nothing to do with it." Gwen pulled away angrily. *I* uncovered the name of your rival and *I* am the one who knows where he can be found. That woman has done nothing but take up your time. I told you! I told you that wasn't the way to find your enemy, but you wouldn't listen to *me*!"

He was astounded. Railing inwardly at his blunder, he caressed her throat, tugging at her will through physical contact. She tried to wrench away, but he was insistent. "A thousand apologies, *cara mia*. You found him for me? But this is wonderful! Forgive me that I leaped to the wrong conclusion."

The empathic nudge was working, she leaned into him, complaining plaintively, "I worked for this, Francesco. It's upsetting that you immediately give someone else the credit."

Outwardly contrite, but mentally gritting his teeth, he said, "I will make it up to you in a most pleasurable manner, precious one, but you are punishing me enough by making me wait. Please tell me."

Still smarting, but considerably relaxed, she pressed her forehead into his shoulder. All day, she'd been planning how she'd give him the news and how overjoyed he'd be. It wasn't supposed to happen like this. Nevertheless, the rewards would be rich, no matter how the scene played, and she'd even the score with the Irish whore later. "His name is Peale. He's a jazz musician at a club not far from here."

Curiously, he stiffened. Before she could ask why, a viselike hand pulled her head up. The striking face was a mask of barely controlled rage. "What is his *full* name?"

"I . . . I'm not sure exactly . . . he goes by initials. A nickname. BC Peale."

The painful grip released so suddenly, she collapsed backward against the table. Scrabbling for balance, her hand flailed against the forgotten handbag. She snatched it like a lifeline. "Just a second. I have his picture." Hastily unfolding the flyer, she pointed. "This is Peale. I got this from the club where he works. Do . . . do you know him?"

Borgia stared at the picture, then crumpled the flimsy newsprint and spun toward the window. He was in a dangerous mood, but for the life of her, she couldn't understand why. She'd been expecting triumph, not rage. She advanced cautiously, slipped her arms around him. "Darling, I've upset you. I didn't mean to. I thought you'd be happy. This was what you were wanting so badly for so long."

He pulled her into a fierce embrace. His mind reeled and he couldn't focus on anything except the echoing word *deceit*! Damn Maeve! She *was* deceiving him. The warning signs were there and Gwen had advised him to be careful all along, but her admonishments only served to anger him. Kissing the colorless hair, he whispered, "I should have listened to you, *cara*. How did you discover this?"

He felt her heart lurch triumphantly. She pressed closer. "I wondered why the other vampire — Peale — came to the arms warehouse the night my men and I were searching. Was it a coincidence or did he know it belonged to us? I kept my own people there watching to see who was poking around.

"Last night they caught a man who'd been hiding in one of the ruined buildings. They thought he was a derelict until they searched his backpack." She paused. "He was carrying a crossbow and several wooden stakes as well as a silver crucifix and garlic."

Borgia abruptly pushed away to stare into her face. She hurried on. "He's been hunting Peale. He knows nothing of you . . . anyway, he's been following Peale and . . . it gets real fuzzy here. I'm not sure why yet, but he claims Peale was at the warehouse when the explosion occurred."

He leaned heavily onto the table and though she couldn't see his face, there was anguish in his whisper, "How sharper than a serpent's tooth . . . there, too." Raising his voice he asked, "This derelict; where is he now?"

She'd been waiting for that. "He's at my place. His name is Mario Hernandez. I've been holding him for you."

"*Buona, buona.* Bring him here to my office. Do this quietly."

He remained motionless until the outer door closed and her footfalls receded. Then, he dropped into a chair with a muffled cry of grief and rage. It was beyond belief. Maeve betrayed him after all. True, he'd suspected she knew more than she was telling, but her motivation was murky — until now. Thankful that no one could see how he was shaking, he leaned forward and uncrumpled the flier, smoothing it against the tabletop with unsteady hands. There was no mistake. Maeve's lover was the only fledgling he'd ever made. Whether he was calling himself BC or Byron, that was his scion smiling roguishly out of the wrinkled photograph.

This was how he was repaid for the gift of immortality? With interference and deception? Maeve didn't know at first, he was sure of that, she must have discovered her lover was the renegade *after* arriving in Chicago. But when? The collapse, of course, and there could be only one explanation.

Gwen let herself back into the room, and, affected by his mood, announced quietly, "He was still sleeping, but Vince and Tony will have him here in twenty minutes . . . ." Seeing his tense posture and the advertisement open before him, she stepped closer. Her curiosity was a palpable thing, but she hadn't gotten where she was by being impatient. She perched on the loveseat to wait.

With difficulty, Borgia shut his nostrils to her scent and his ears to the sound of her heartbeat. Emotional turmoil rendered him easy prey to his nature. He should have sent her to get the informant herself, and rid himself of a distraction. There was something she said. Something important. Yes. Abruptly, his head snapped up. "These stakes you told me of, has Hernandez attempted to destroy Peale?"

Gwen was astonished. "How did you know that? Apparently yes, a few nights ago. He says that Peale had help and survived the attack. Everything he says is so confused, Francesco, I think the boy is barely sane. You'll need to ask him these things yourself to get the straight of it, I'm sure you'll be more persuasive than I."

Borgia nodded and stroked his chin, asking reflectively, "Have you told anyone else about this?"

"Of *course* not, why should I tell anyone but you?"

He threw back his head and laughed uproariously. That was just what he'd needed.

***

He was drowsy and comfortable and Gwen was beside him. She wouldn't let anything bad happen. She said Mr. Borgia was wealthy and powerful. It must be true, because he asked for money in exchange for his story and the man agreed without batting an eye. It was a large amount.

He didn't know who the short guy was, Gwen didn't seem to like him much, but Mr. Borgia said he was a friend and Mario could tell all he knew.

He did. It was funny how much he remembered now that he'd relaxed.

He even told them about Galen Miller being a cop. The fact the Undead Thing was working with Miller upset Mr. Borgia. They were talking around the desk now and he couldn't hear what they were saying. They'd forgotten he was there. Suddenly, Borgia gave an order and the other guy left the room like the devil himself was after him. That aroused Mario from his stupor. He had to split, too. Stirring, he whined, "I gotta get outta here. I can't stay in one place too long or he'll find me."

Borgia stood and walked around the desk. He wasn't a big man, but Mario couldn't look away as he approached speaking quietly, "I don't think you need to worry about him any longer."

"But, what about my money? You said you'd pay me."

Erupting into anger, Borgia sprang forward, snatching Hernandez out of the chair as if he were weightless, and snarled around bared fangs, "You'll be paid *all* you deserve."

Terror washed away the residue of mind-numbing torpor as he fought against the grip. "Oh God! You're just like him! You're just like Peale!"

The snarl became a bitter smile, as cold as the reply. "No. He is like me. The *son* takes after the *father*."

Hernandez was dead before he understood.

No so with Gwen. Shock rooted her in place as, before her numbed eyes, Francesco dropped the drained corpse like a fruit rind. Dabbing blood from his lips with a silk handkerchief, he ordered, "Dispose of this debris where my son and his friends will find it. I have planning to do."

Distantly, she watched him disappear into his chambers, then allowed her gaze to return to the upturned face of Hernandez, terror slowly melting under the flaccidity of death.

Peale was Francesco's *son*? Damn.

EIGHT

"Would you guys hold on a minute?"

Infuriated, Miller slammed the front door so hard his framed diplomas bounced, then wheeled on Marquez and Nelson. "What the hell is going on? You assholes knock on my door then run me over when I open it!"

At a signal from Jim, Mick disappeared into the kitchen, then returned dragging two chairs. Jim relieved him of one, saying, "Sorry, Gae, we didn't have a lot of time to waste." He pointed toward BC's closed door adding, "He in there?"

"Of course he's in there. What's this about?"

"Stick close and you'll find out. Is there another exit from his room? I don't want him slipping away. The way things are shaping up, I'm afraid Peale has proved he can't be trusted."

Perplexed, Galen followed the pair into his partner's room. "What things are shaping up how?"

Inside the bedroom, Mick stood by the bed looking down at the motionless vampire. Peale looked *real* dead right now. That wasn't something that immediately sprang to mind when talking with him or watching him in action. Once the sun went down, the man was articulate with moves like a cat. Seeing him like this gave the Deputy Director a case of the heebie jeebies. Behind him Galen and Jim were arguing.

Gae insisted, "You're gonna tell me what's going on, Jim. Commanding officer or not, you can't come in here and hold me and my partner virtual prisoners in our own home without just cause."

"Where was Peale last night?"

"Whaaaat? We took the night off, you know that. He was at the Inferno."

With marked difficulty, Mick tore his eyes away from Peale's lifeless form to ask, "Are you sure of that? Were you with him?"

"*No*! I wasn't with him, but Jump Veron and a helluva lot of other people were. He was on stage in front of the whole place most of the night, if *that's* good enough for you!" Galen rounded on him. "I'm sick of this shit, I think you better tell me what BC is supposed to have done right now."

Marquez's response was cut short as Peale abruptly sat up. Calmly assessing the crowd, he commented dryly, "I thought these were supposed to be *private* accommodations. I see I was mistaken." The emotional tension in the air was high enough to fry his empathic circuits. Looking from face to face, he said hesitantly, "May I ask to what I owe the dubious pleasure of this visit?"

Barely controlled rage hit Peale like a hammer as the Sentry commander snarled, "Look, Peale, I realize you haven't been an agent long, *and* I understand you'd be — upset with Hernandez, but *GODDAMMIT*! You went too far this time, I thought you understood we needed to talk to the asshole."

Curling his long legs under him, BC pressed his bare back against the bed's cool lacquered headboard. Nelson raged on, "If it was an accident, we would have understood, but you could have let us know. *Dammit*! Didn't you learn *anything* from nearly getting killed? *Don't go it alone, Peale!*"

The intervening silence was heavy as BC struggled to make sense of things. "Excuse me? What did I miss?"

"How about Mario Hernandez' impromptu swimming lesson in the Sentry HQ ornamental pond?"

The pale face registered more confusion than ever. Pushed to the limit, Nelson exploded, "He's dead, Peale! Throat torn out and drained of blood.

Does *that* ring any bells?"

Shaking his head vehemently, Peale insisted, "I had nothing to do with it."

Jim slammed his fist on the dresser and swore. "Oh, this is too much! Mario Hernandez was killed by a vampire sometime last night. I suppose you're going to try to tell me there's *another* vampire running around Chicago!"

Peale flinched. "Oh god."

Galen had retired to a post by the dresser; Jim, having forgotten he was there, jumped slightly as the big man said, "I'm afraid there *is* another vampire."

Suddenly weak at the knees, Jim sank onto the bed next to Peale. "Shit." Then, "Okay, what have you guys been holding back *this* time?"

Galen launched into an abbreviated version of the encounter with Maeve Donal and her unwelcome revelations about Francesco Borgia. "So, we were giving Ms. Donal a couple days to get back with us one way or the other." He glanced at his partner adding pointedly, "I kinda doubt I need to add that the news had BC a little upset, too."

"First one vampire, now *two* vampires and a witch!" Nelson groaned. "What's next? Unicorns frolicking down Michigan Avenue? Give me a call if you run into the Mummy and that Black Lagoon Guy. I'm sure Sentry has a place for *them*, too." He turned to his newest agent who was pulling clothes on. "Peale, are you sure this Donal woman is telling the truth? *Is* this the guy who made you what you are?"

With a helpless gesture, BC said, "As sure as I can be. I was attacked from behind in a very dark alleyway. I never got a good look."

In spite of the seriousness of the moment, Galen smiled broadly. "He was drunk as a skunk, too."

BC glared at his partner. "Next thing I remember, I awoke in Maeve Donal's root cellar and she refused to tell me anything more than what I now was. We argued. I left. That was all I knew until the night before last."

Suddenly serious, Galen inserted, "All joking aside, I wonder if Ms.

Donal has any idea what's about to hit the fan. She told us where she's staying, maybe we better give her a shout."

BC grunted. "I suppose it would only be right. *You* ring her up."

Grinning, Galen lifted the extension, called the hotel and asked for the room number. It rang and kept ringing. At length, the desk clerk came back on, but wasn't able to help. Nobody had seen Ms. Donal leave, but she wasn't answering. He couldn't do anymore than that, sir, perhaps the gentleman would like to leave a message?

Galen leaned heavily on the dresser as he dropped BC's extension back into its cradle. He didn't need to look around to know his companions shared the sick feeling now residing in the pit of his stomach.

After a moment, Jim asked, "BC, would Francesco Borgia harm her?"

The vampire gave another eloquent shrug. "I've no idea. I didn't even know the man's name before all this began. Given past data, though, I wouldn't rule it out."

The telephone rang startling everyone. Jim breathed, "Maybe it's Donal."

He snatched the instrument, saying, "Yes?"

To Mick and Galen, the remote end of the conversation was inaudible; to BC it was thunderous. The voice was deep and slightly accented. It said, "I would speak with Byron Peale."

Jim's heart missed a beat before he found breath to ask politely, "Who should I say is calling?"

"Tell him it is his Father."

BC's knees gave out and he sat back onto the bed, a buzzing in his ears drowned the next words. He knew that voice. In a moment, the centuries melted away and he was again lying spent with struggle and blood-loss in a reeking alley of eighteenth century Philadelphia. Again, he felt the press of the freshly gashed wrist against his lips and heard that voice rasping into his ear commanding him to drink of the blood that gushed into his mouth.

With a convulsive effort, he broke free of the memory and forced his attention back to the equally unpleasant present.

Jim Nelson replied smoothly, "I was under the impression that Byron's father was deceased."

A rumbling laugh. "Not quite. I would speak with my son, now. I trust he is nearby. Aren't you, Byron, *figlio mio*?"

As if pulled by wires, BC rose and unwillingly took the telephone. "I'm here. What do you want?"

"Is that any way to speak to one's father? You are an irreverent pup! No matter. Right now I wish to speak of mutual friends. Maeve Donal for instance."

BC struggled to keep his voice level. "Ms. Donal and I parted company quite a while ago."

"That is most interesting, she says differently. In fact, it was from her that I obtained this telephone number. She is in great distress. Would it not be a shame for her to depart this world without having spoken to her true love one last time."

"What are you saying?"

"Merely that you should consider this an invitation for an evening with old friends — and family."

"That's quite an invitation."

"One best not refused."

"Where?"

"Tomorrow evening. It is a small place to the north of here, I will send complete directions to your lodgings. Be sure you come alone, my son."

"I'd've thought you'd be a bit more original."

"Do not mock me, fledgling! Do as I say." The receiver on the other end hung up forcibly.

BC dropped his end into its cradle and scanned the circle of concerned faces. He sagged against the wall. "Shit."

***

Eddie Michalson was back. As a point of fact, he hadn't strayed too far from her since she awoke locked in a set of old-fashioned stocks. This time, he'd brought food, but the drug they'd used made her too sick to eat. To her own ironic amusement, Maeve realized she was too sick to even muster much anger at finding herself in such humiliating circumstances.

Showing odd tenderness for a hireling of Francesco Borgia's, Eddie stood by her, helping her sip a cola through a straw. It tasted foul, but the wetness was welcome. She prodded her fuzzy brain to remember. It began with a call from Francesco saying his meetings were over earlier than expected, and he was ready to begin the nightly spellcasting. She didn't suspect a thing until she got into the car next to him and felt the sharp jab of a needle. That was all she remembered until she awoke here. In the stocks. Frankie had a cruel sense of humor, but at least she was alive. The ease with which she was trapped and bound proved that if Francesco Borgia did not want her to awaken, she wouldn't have. Doubtless, she was a bargaining chip and she had no trouble figuring out who she was being used against.

Francesco must have discovered she'd been protecting Byron. Oh, but the villain was stronger and faster than she'd remembered. The thought gave her pause. The more powerful the parent, the more powerful the fledgling, and Byron had defied her spells on the *first* night he rose. At the time, she chalked it up to strong will, but that might not have been the whole story. Byron was older now, too, and vampires got more powerful with age. If her suspicions were correct, Francesco might be in for a bit of a surprise if he tangled with his child. They'd discover that when — oops — *if* he came to rescue her. There might be a worse surprise in store for her, come to that.

When she spoke, her voice came as more croak than whisper, "He'll likely not come for me, you understand."

Eddie jumped and shushed her. "Not so loud! *He's* out for the day if ya get my drift, but I ain't supposed to take the gag off. If you've known him as long as I think ya have, you know the walls got ears."

She indicated understanding and sipped the drink wondering why he was defying Frankie's orders. That wasn't a safe thing to do. He whispered again, "There ain't no electronic stuff. This is his room an' he don't like that stuff too close to 'im as a rule. I figure in a little while, when ya get your voice back, we can talk . . . kinda soft so we ain't overheard. There's stuff I don't understand and I figure you got a few questions, too. Maybe we can be of mutual assistance, huh?"

She considered, then nodded. He beamed and freshened the cola from a large plastic bottle, saying, "Great! Y'know, you're lucky to still be kickin', the Boss is *real* P.O.'ed with you an' your boyfriend!"

Silently Maeve sipped the syrupy drink. It was as dire as she'd feared. She hoped Francesco wouldn't be *too* angry if Byron didn't rise to the bait. From her former lover's reaction at the cinema, his ire hadn't cooled in the intervening years. There was a distinct possibility he'd refuse to come.

If only she'd thrown in with Byron and his friend right then, she wouldn't be in this fix. Why was her judgment always so poor where that man was concerned?

* * *

It was cold, and foggy on the lake and the shipped outboard motor was gouging Miller in the back. They were close now. They couldn't risk any sound aside from the soft swish of the paddles wielded by Kim Zoeller and Mick Marquez. Galen shifted carefully to evade the offending outboard. His instructions from Mick for this part of the mission were simply to sit still and avoid tipping them into the water. Okay, so he wasn't very good with boats, but he'd been on stealth missions before and knew how to be quiet. The ex-marine simply took perverse enjoyment in treating him like a gigantic toddler and Zoeller was too amused to comment. His companions moved as fluidly as the water they skimmed across in the fog and the darkness.

They were hard to see in the night camouflage — at least for him. Weeks of working with Peale, guaranteed it wouldn't offer much protection from Borgia, but that wasn't their aim. They were more concerned with getting past normal humans.

The goal was to get in and out in a hurry, that's why there were only three of them. Four counting BC, but he was coming via the highway on his Harley and was supposed to contact Galen by his cell when he got close. Gae wondered where he was now. For that matter, he wondered where *he* was now. The fog was a double-edged sword, it protected them from detection on shore, but it also protected the shore from detection by *them*. Well, that was why Kim was there. She was the resident stealth expert. Officially, Mick was in charge of the operation, but in practicality, it was all in Zoeller's hands. Pretty capable hands.

Good thing his companions couldn't see him any better than he could see them. He kept smiling at how script-like the whole affair seemed. In fact, what he was doing now was more like a movie than any script Fiona ever thrust at him. He wished it *were* make-believe and real lives weren't depending on everyone being on their marks and not missing any cues. As unthinkable as a snafu was, there were contingency plans in place with Jim, Emily and Frank sitting off shore in a powerful launch. Nice thought, but he'd worked with a vampire for a while, and doubted even a *supersonic* launch could get there in time to make a difference if things went wrong. He didn't mention that. It was better if nobody thought too much about it, besides, everybody teased him enough about being a worrywart already.

He did worry, though. What if they were aiming all this at the wrong place? From Borgia's directions and mounds of satellite photos, they thought they'd located the lodge, but in this densely wooded area, it was hard to be sure. It would be a true disaster if the extraction team were crouched outside the wrong cabin when BC roared up to Borgia's front door at a completely different location.

He worried about BC, period. Even if his own team performed according to plan, said plan was to extract Maeve and leave Peale to find his own way out. *If* everything went off without a hitch, Borgia wouldn't discover the loss until BC was back on the road. Big if. When did plans go off without a hitch? From the beginning, the worst part of this plan was that his partner was literally putting himself in Borgia's hands.

Like it or not, the strategy made sense. If Peale rode up to the front door alone, they might be less inclined to look for additional people coming from the lake. Might. The monster motor launch docked in most of their photos was the big worry lakeside. Where there was a boat that size, there were usually people taking care of it.

The fog thinned at the water's edge, and the lurch and crunch as the small boat beached on the shaley bank sounded thunderous after the relative silence of their passage. The trio froze, waiting for a smudged shadow from the treeline to resolve into an armed guard. After a few uneventful minutes, they relaxed.

Mick whispered, "Okay, people, so far so good. According to the GPS, we've landed about where we're supposed to. Let's get this thing out of the water and into the undergrowth."

Zoeller took the point on approach. The trees that made it difficult to get good photos worked to their advantage on the ground, thinning only to outline a yard at the back of the log building. Right place or wrong, someone was at home. There were lights in every window and landscaping lights illuminated the lawn. The shadow that was Zoeller swore softly and pulled up short at the edge of the clearing. "Shit! There's a picture window all along the back of the place, looks like it's into a great room. Somebody's pulled the damned curtains open. Room's empty now, but we'll have to be real careful crossing that yard."

Mick grunted acknowledgment. "Okay, let's sit tight to see how much activity we've got. We're close enough to use the parabolic microphone and put Galen's mind at ease that we have the right place. Gae?"

Zoeller watched Miller's big paws deftly assemble the microphone, remarking sotto voce, "The laser is better, these parabolics give you all kinds of collateral noise problems."

Galen chuckled as he aimed the receiver toward the house. "I like the laser, too. Only problem was that when we ran a test with the thing, Peale could see the beam like a lighthouse beacon. If it's like that for him, God only knows how it would be for Borgia, he's a lot older.

"Okay, it's set. Let's see what we've got."

As they fitted their earpieces, Galen heard Zoeller breathe, "I'm gonna have a lot of trouble with that concept."

"You only found out about it today." Miller's smile glinted in the darkness. "Try sharing an apartment with him."

The parabolic rig picked up a brassy New York accent kvetching above the great room in mid sentence, ". . .such a good idea, Boss. After all, even if Peale cooperates right down the line, this place is history. The law knows about it now. It ain't like it was the regular cops, neither, this is *international* shit."

A richly European baritone cut in imperiously, "*Daverro*, Edgar! Why do you think I chose this place for our meeting? After last week, it is already known to Ms. Donal, and therefore an expendable property. At this moment, since the location of our headquarters may also be compromised, Gwen is moving our offices to another location. After all this time, Edgar, do you *still* question my wisdom?"

"Well, no. . . ."

"*Buona*, then we will hear no more about it. Go and prepare for my son's arrival, be sure the fire is burning well, this place is cold as the tomb without it."

Over the softer sound of footfalls on hardwood and the click of a closing door, the voice continued speaking in a gently ironic tone, "You see, *cara mia*, all will soon be in readiness for my wayward son. Are you comfortable? No? Perhaps your situation will improve soon, it depends on Byron. Surely he will be willing to do anything to ransom his beloved."

Reply came in the form of a muffled feminine roar accompanied by sounds of rattling metal against wood and a sharp exclamation in Italian. Then in English, "You *dare* strike at me? This is your own doing, witch. I *never* wanted a scion, but you plead: 'Look at all I have done for you, Francesco! Do this for me and I will be your ally forever.' Then I see the lad. He is graceful and beautiful, and all that a son of the house of Borgia should be. I do this for *you*, you who have come closer to my heart than any other, mortal or otherwise, I give *him* the gift of immortality. In return I receive betrayal. Try my patience no more, Maeve, lest I forget myself and then no longer have a prize with which to tempt my son!"

The resounding door slam put the needle into the red and the three listeners hastily removed their earpieces. Taking a deep breath, Marquez whispered, "I think we've got the right place, don't you?"

Miller said, "On the money. Let's see if we can gauge approximate strength before BC gets here." He replaced his earpiece and resumed his scan.

The listening device only located two other henchmen in the house. They were in the kitchen grabbing a quick game of poker and an unauthorized coffee break. Amused, Miller listened to the flurry of activity as the man called Edgar entered and sent them back to the master bedroom. With the pair they spotted goofing off near the launch, that made four they knew of. Pretty small contingent, although Galen didn't find it surprising. The fewer knowing the truth about Borgia, the better. He'd play it that way himself: Less danger of exposure. This was probably an innate instinct. Even laid-back Peale was getting progressively antsier as more people knew about him and his vampiric condition.

Where was Peale anyway? It was getting damned cold out there. The

Wisconsin woods were not his favorite place in late spring. If anything they were colder and damper than Chicago itself . . . the bluetooth transceiver hooked over the back of his ear crackled to life. "Aries, this is White Fang, do you copy?"

Galen relaxed slightly, touching the send button, he responded, "Yo, White Fang, where are you?"

"Just turned in the gates. There are two guards flanking the road. One had what looked to be a flip phone, so I'm likely being announced even as we speak. Heading toward the house now."

"Gotcha, White Fang, makes a party of eight counting the principle. Signing off."

The shadowy trio strained listening to the night sounds. Presently, the unique roar of a Harley-Davidson engine shattered the peace. Mick grinned and pointed the parabolic receiver back toward the log structure, whispering, "It's showtime!"

***

The façade of the lodge was a mixture of rusticity and elegance that spoke of skillful architects, with a sprawling front porch constructed of intentionally irregular cedar logs. A small parking area occupied by two large, dark boulevard barges was situated to the right. BC pulled the Softail beside the larger of the two and using the engine's rumble for cover, entered the codes that turned his phone into a mic and said, "I'm at the door."

He listened long enough to catch Galen's faint OK then activated the code. He'd tested the function exhaustively to be sure no transmission from the other end came through. Any chatter would be like a shout to Borgia.

Truthfully, he wished he could avoid the whole thing. He had no desire to speak with Francesco Borgia, and the longer he thought about it, the angrier he got. The nerve of that *asshole* calling *him* son. His true father was a good man and a teacher who died just after Byron was born. Francesco Borgia sickened and frightened him. How could Maeve have allied herself with such a vile creature? The thought of Borgia's blood working inside him made him ill. Worse was fear that the taint of that blood could make him as evil as his sire. Even after all this time, he was still too ignorant of his own nature to know what could happen. Curse Maeve and her stupid subterfuges, anyway.

Damn. In a manner of speaking, though, it was his fault she was in trouble. Even *she* didn't deserve to be left at the mercy of Francesco Borgia — if he had any. Resolutely, he shut off the bike's engine, approached the covered stoop, and rapped sharply on the oaken door. The slab door swung inward with a suddenness that assured him he was indeed announced.

Framed in the doorway stood a man who could be none other than Francesco Borgia. BC was riveted by the elder's commanding mien as, for the first time, he looked full upon the face of his sire. The face that gazed back was striking with a square jaw and hawk nose dominated by eyes so dark, the iris was indistinguishable from the pupil. Due to his vampirism, his skin was pale, but still had enough coloring to hint at Mediterranean origins and to contrast elegantly with the well-cut black hair styled to accent a distinctive white streak shot through his left forelock. He was stocky and a full head shorter than his scion, but then, at six feet two inches, Byron had been tall for his time. The casual clothing was obviously expensive, and just as obviously, tailored to compliment the impressive physique.

The two stood transfixed in the open doorway. All the way to the lodge, Byron had wondered if coming face to face with Borgia might bring order to the jumbled memories of his last moments as a mortal. It didn't.

"*Figlio mio!*" Suddenly, Borgia beamed and extending powerful arms in an expansive gesture. "My son, come in out of the damp. We can talk by the fire."

Engulfing the younger man in an inescapable embrace, Borgia propelled him into a richly paneled great room where a fire crackled invitingly in a huge creek stone fireplace. Peale's heart sank as he noticed the drapes pulled back from a depressingly large window commanding an unobstructed view of the path to the lake. Somewhere out there, his friends were concealed. Hopefully, they'd moved into position while Borgia was at the door. Anyway, they had a good view of Borgia's movements — and his own. That was a consolation, albeit a small one. He'd maneuver the older vampire so that his back stayed to the glass and get down to business, he didn't relish staying in Borgia's digs any longer than absolutely necessary. Brusquely, he pulled away and strode across the room. "Alright, I'm here. What do you want?"

Borgia bristled, then immediately smoothed himself. He remembered behaving the same way to his own father. Rebellion was a natural thing with creatures as special as they, he must move slowly were he to win the child's confidence. "Let us not contend with one another, my son. Please, sit down. We have much to talk about."

"I prefer to stand, thank you." Wincing inwardly, he could almost hear Galen swearing at him for being pigheaded. It was a bad idea if he were to buy time for the extraction team to get in and to wherever Maeve was. Moving closer to the fire, he leaned wearily on the warm stone mantle. "I'm sorry, I'm behaving badly. This was all very sudden and I'm a bit on edge. What was it you wanted to speak to me about?"

Mollified, Borgia seated himself in a wing chair, back turned gratifyingly toward the window. "You have made things most difficult for me, Byron. When my hirelings were attacked, I was annoyed, but when they started dying, I became so *angry*! It was unthinkable that another vampire should invade my territory. But now I know who has done this, and all is different, *figlio mio*. Now I ask only 'why.' Was this part of your work as an agent of this international constabulary?"

Byron allowed a rueful laugh. "Actually, I haven't been an agent that long. In a roundabout way, you're responsible for it happening at all." Raising an eyebrow, Borgia motioned him to continue. BC complied. "I only recently returned to Chicago. I like this city and there are several clubs I frequent in the neighborhood. I'd merely been feeding on the criminal population because, unfortunately, they were the most available sources.

"I had no idea most of them worked for any one person, and the killings were accidental. I don't like doing it. It only happened when my dinner guests tried to kill *me*."

"Interesting. Then your presence here is purely coincidental?"

"Possibly. Maeve seems to believe I've been unconsciously drawn here because you'd set up base in the city."

Borgia was intrigued. He'd heard none of this, mostly because Maeve refused to speak to him when he'd arisen that evening. The woman was remarkable. The drug made her weak and ill, but she'd still mustered sufficient strength to lunge and kick at him through the stocks. He hoped he wouldn't have to kill her, he'd miss her. "Do you think this may be true?"

The tall fledgling shrugged. "No idea. I've been in Chicago before, I have friends and business interests here. . . ."

Byron trailed off and stared into the fire. Borgia watched with understanding. "Ah, yes. One of the few disadvantages of our kind. We sense — no, *experience* things more sharply than mortals. Have you realized that warmth is as important to us as the blood we feed on? This is why feeding from living creatures is so much more satisfying than dead blood."

Smiling ruefully, the young vampire's eyes slid from the inviting flames and onto his unwanted sire. "Yes. It took me a while, but I figured that one out for myself." Becoming thoughtful, he asked quietly, "Since we've touched on the subject, could you tell me why I was made as I am, then left to Maeve's tender mercies? Not that I'm complaining, mind you, but there must have been a reason. As a vampire, I have an instinctive understanding how important a fledgling can be to the parent."

For the first time, Borgia looked uncomfortable. He waved dismissively. "That was how Maeve wanted it, and I had no emotional link with you." He finished with a shrug of his own. "But that, too, has changed. It is partly this I wished to speak about."

He felt a surge of pride as his child's handsome head snapped up and he saw the wary intelligence in the dark eyes. Yes, he owed Maeve something for delivering such a fine boy to him. If her death became necessary, he would make it quick.

***

Their objective was a darkened upstairs room on the opposite corner from where Peale and Borgia talked. For as long as they'd been checking, it sounded empty. Galen now pressed his bulk against the rough siding of the house and watched Zoeller assess possible entry.

She and the rest of the team had been briefed about Peale's condition before the mission, but her earlier comment and definite flinch as Peale openly spoke to Borgia about vampirism made him wonder. Perhaps she didn't believe it until then. Perhaps she still didn't. Did any of them? Maybe they thought Peale and Borgia were a couple of nuts they needed to humor to get through the case. Galen was sympathetic with any of those options. It wasn't an easy idea to deal with. It didn't matter, Zoeller was a top agent. She'd do her part whether she believed in vampires or not.

Not for the first time, he wished they had a more solid plan before they'd arrived. When he admitted this to Zoeller, she had a good laugh, then informed him it was *always* like that. She'd participated in several extraction operations around the globe and assured him that no matter how much data was gathered beforehand, it invariably boiled down to off-the-cuff.

Presently, the pixie-like agent was busy with a black nylon rope and a pulley assembly. He grimaced at the rough log sides and seemingly sky-scraping dormer that was their objective. Holding the rope in one hand, she mimed tossing the rope into the tall nearby pine and climbing up. Galen panicked until he realized he was only supposed to toss the rope into the tree. *She* was going to climb it alone. Once aloft, she hooked the pulley in the tree. Lifting themselves to the window and entering the lodge was relatively simple after that.

There was a lock on the window, but not good enough quality to withstand Zoeller. She and Mick slid through first. Both doubted the ex-football player would fit through the small opening, but he did. The room was a bedroom, empty with the exception of someone's messily strewn belongings. The door opened to face its twin directly across a nicely vacant hall that dead-ended at the opposite side of a stairway in another closed door.

Stepping into the hall, they found another door a few feet down, through which issued the noise of water on water followed by the signature k-chunk-whoosh of a flushing toilet. Galen grinned, and without a word exchanged, Mick grabbed Kim and dragged her back into the room. Mick whispered, "Get the duct tape."

Bewildered, she complied, then seconds later, Galen returned bearing on his shoulder a limp man that he eased onto the rumpled bed. Grinning, Zoeller trussed their prize.

Silently, they returned to the hall, then in single-file, swiftly passed the stairs that terminated in the front entry way. Snatches of conversation drifted from below and Galen hoped fervently the remote recorder was catching it all. They hurried ahead. Once they entered the far room, there was no turning back, and speed would be of the essence since they'd be right over Borgia's head. As clearly as they'd heard the voices downstairs, enhanced hearing would be unnecessary to hear a scuffle above.

As they neared, they heard the New York voice saying, "So that's your boyfriend downstairs? The guy that's been causing all the trouble? Don't hardly look like he's capable of that stuff. Too pretty, if ya get my meanin'. But, who can tell with guys like him and the Boss since they ain't regular guys, right? Who woulda guessed the boss *had* a kid, anyways!"

***

Eddie paced before the immobilized woman. He'd only seen the stocks in history books, and never thought of how humiliating they were. To his astonishment, he found that in the face of her discomfort, he was unwilling to take his ease. He wondered why. He'd done plenty of dirty work in his meteoric rise to the top of his profession. Hell, he'd even popped a couple guys on his lonesome! What was it about this business that made him so tenderhearted? Maybe because the Boss and Gwennie had such a lack in that department.

He didn't want to think about that. Maeve's intense blue-slate eyes were following his movements and he longed to remove the gag so she could talk back. He'd enjoyed their illicit conversation earlier. "Sounded like a helluva bike the kid rode up on. I usedta ride a bike. Not one of th' big mothers, though. A little one. They're easier t' get around on in the Apple, y'know. Traffic heavy? No problemo! There's a sidewalk. . . ." He stopped again, then turned to the thinnish young man kicked back in a chair by the door. "Geez, JD! Get off your ass an' go find out what the hell Dirk is doing in the can. If he stays in there much longer, I'm gonna charge 'im rent."

JD leaped to his feet. When Michalson sounded like that it was best to move quickly. "Sure thing, Mr. Michalson."

JD opened the door, then seemed to leap into the hall. Before Eddie could blink and register the dark shape that propelled his henchman into the air, a small woman with a blackened face and tied back hair bounded into the room followed by two men with machine pistols. He opened his mouth to cry out and reached for his pistol. He never completed either move.

***

"You want me to be your *what* in Sentry?"

The elder vampire spat, "I want you to spy for me, boy, what is so surprising about that? What is so different now than what you have done in the past? I have procured your records —"

Byron cut in coldly, "What I did was for the United States against an enemy in wartime! The people you are asking me to betray now are my friends and there is no war."

"But there *is* a war, *caro*."

"*No*. Not like that. Besides, don't you think they'll be watching me pretty closely from now on? *I* bloody well would be, you didn't make any secret of our connection, did you?"

Unimpressed, Borgia waved the argument aside. "Child, you have abilities above the mortals you refer to. Control them, *figlio mio*, they are not an obstacle unless you allow them to be."

"I can't do that. I *won't* do that."

"So much for filial obedience. I feared as much. Then your lover will die."

"So much for paternal affection. Might I remind you that Maeve and I are not lovers. I have no ties with her any longer."

Borgia's smile was slow and sent a chill up his scion's spine. "Yet, you came when she was threatened."

As the sole response was stubborn silence, the aristocrat continued smugly, "Perhaps you would have done as much for any other. Maeve once told me you have a ridiculously noble streak. She found it endearing. However, it may interest you to know that perhaps *she* is tied to *you* more than you suspect, boy." Pleased at the evident confusion, the elder closed the gap between them and thumped his fist squarely into his son's chest. "There, yes? That is where the stake entered your body mere days ago. That is the place Maeve clutched on her own bosom as she fell, that is where she felt your pain."

Whether or not Byron could have found words to reply became moot as, suddenly, the house was rocked by a nearby explosion. A very solid weight smashed against him as the plate glass of the picture window shivered into a thousand shards and strafed the room.

He became aware first of stinging pain on the right side of his face.

Turning his head caused blood to run into his eyes from a gash across the forehead. He impatiently moved to wipe the blinding flow away only to find himself pinned to the floor by a considerable weight. Blinking his eyes clear, he looked again and beheld the bloodied face of Francesco Borgia scant inches from his own. Fear ruled, and the next thing he knew, he was free of the press, kneeling unsteadily on the debris-strewn plank floor a distance from his starting point. Amazingly, Borgia hadn't moved. Investigating, BC found the reason: tangled in the ruins of once fine furniture, his sire hung suspended and unconscious, a large piece of glass embedded in his back from the force of the blast. Reflexively, the younger vampire's hand moved toward the shard, then recoiled. This was *Borgia* and though seriously injured, still the most dangerous thing in the vicinity.

Through the gaping hole of the former window, he saw the end of the dock where the launch had been moored. Now only burning debris floated on the water. That surprised him, from the way his ears buzzed, he'd thought the source was closer. Marveling, he leaned against the shattered frame and wiggled a finger in the worst ear in an attempt to restore hearing, then dropped abruptly to the floor as a pair of shouting henchmen rounded the corner and sped to the lake. Sprawling painfully against the baseboard, he cursed his own idiocy. They hadn't seen him, but it was only a matter of time before someone gathered enough wits to ask where the boss was. This was his exit cue.

The room spun dangerously as he stood and his violent drop had started blood flowing into his eyes again. He impatiently wiped it away wincing against a hundred pinpricks in his face. More glass, no doubt. Making his unsteady way across the great room, he paused at the foot of the stairs for any sign of life above. Nothing. He hoped that was a good sign. Behind him, Borgia moaned, the faint sound stiffened his spine with a flash of unreasoning fear. *Damn. Better haul ass.*

Cold, damp air rushing into his face as the oaken door swung wide helped clear his head as he raced on. He gazed longingly toward the two sedans, then reluctantly flung his leg across the saddle of his motorcycle; there wasn't time to disable both of them. Another smaller explosion from the lake convinced him he'd have no need for such things, anyway. Borgia's people would have their hands full for a while to come. He kicked the Harley to life and hared for the highway wondering why on earth the team blew up the boat. That wasn't part of any plan *he'd* heard.

***

Sounds collided in his head as Francesco Borgia awoke to pain. The basso note of a small gasoline engine separated itself from the other sounds and made him jerk fully awake. "Byron! Byron, my child, where are you?"

Distant pandemonium answered and the agony resolved itself as originating at his back where tentative fingertips discovered the jagged surface of glass. Propelled by fury and sheer strength of will, he hove himself out of the wreckage and dragged himself to the front door. It was open, and he knew before he looked that the motorcycle was gone. Gasping with rage and pain, he vented his ire against the wooden frame of the door until he noticed a smear of blood on the door facing under his hand. He sniffed and tasted it. His son's. Anger surged anew. How could the thankless pup have fled?

Wrenching the brittle fragment from his body depleted the last of his reserves, and it smashed unheeded onto the floor as he clung weakly to the jamb. The scent of his child's blood was tantalizingly close, sending the warning to his sluggish brain that he needed blood to begin healing. That confused organ was also sending alarms that something else was amiss. What was it? *Edgar*! Where *were* Edgar and the men from upstairs?

Summoning the determination that carried him to the entrance, he pulled himself up the steps, pausing at the top to listen. From the master bedroom he heard Edgar struggling and venting inarticulate rage against a gag. Stepping over the young henchman bound with silvery tape on the hall floor, he burst in to find Michalson, locked in the stocks, a swatch of the same silvery tape covering his mouth.

Eddie looked up and deflated. Borgia was here, and from the look of him, their side lost. The stocky Italian limped forward and ripped the tape from Eddie's mouth; it hurt, but at least he could talk. Seeing the bloodtrail marking the aristocratic vampire's path through the room, he raised his eyes to his employer's haggard face, bracing for a blast of rage. Instead Francesco Borgia sank onto the empty bed and laughed bitterly.

***

Achieving the relative safety of the highway, BC pulled off the road and scrabbled for his mobile. Nervously glancing over his shoulder, he pressed the bluetooth headset into his uninjured ear and tentatively hit speed dial. The screen lit up then the earpiece crackled and he heard a familiar voice, "White Fang! You okay?"

BC smiled wryly, wincing at the renewed stings. "'Okay' is debatable, but I'm in one piece, no thanks to the premature Fourth of July display. What the hell happened?"

Anger came through the distortion of the tiny receiver. "The Ladies' Auxiliary of the IRA. Need I say more?"

"Not a word. I better boogie, Aries. No pursuit yet, but I'm taking no chances, things are hotting up back there in more ways than one. See you down below."

"Sure thing, White Fang."

The transmission clicked off, he stowed the earpiece back in his jacket pocket, pulled back onto the still agreeably empty road and sped for home.

***

The tempered steel padlock shattered like so much papier mâché in Borgia's fingers. Voice weak, he declared, "My son and his friends have won the skirmish, Edgar, but the war lies ahead of us."

Eddie stepped from his former prison massaging his wrists, his neck and head throbbed where the little ninja's kick landed. The last thing he remembered before awaking in the stocks was an extreme close-up of a black crepe-soled shoe. "Boss, you're bleedin'. Maybe we better cut our losses and get outta here before the police — fire department — *whoever* — gets here?"

Borgia rubbed his temples. "*Madonna*, Edgar. You are, as usual, the voice of reason in an insane world. We must be away as quickly as possible!"

Eddie moved to lend support. "Cops or no, Boss, you're bad hurt. We gotta get you outta here and back to the city before we do anything else."

Borgia chuckled bitterly. "Providing Byron has left us transportation." Shaking Michalson off, he gestured toward the hall. "I will survive, Edgar, I am very hard to kill. Release the two idiots down the hall and I will meet you outside after I have . . . freshened up."

Eddie's gaze slipped to his employer's bloody clothing and he suppressed a shudder at the thought of what that blood could do. Without another word, he hurried into the hallway where he nudged JD awake with his toe. Suddenly, the four outside guards burst into the house and charged up the stairs on a collision course with Michalson. He shouted them to a halt, then grateful for the ability to delegate, instructed two to search the upstairs rooms for Dirk and the rest to be sure the cars were still rolling. The others dispatched, he rejoined Borgia. The usually pale face was ashen when he reentered the master bedroom but the voice didn't quaver as the renaissance lord said, "There are kerosene and propane remaining in the storage units, yes?"

Taken unaware, Michalson stammered, "I think so, Boss . . . why — ?" Suddenly comprehending, he said, "First we get you into a car headed back to the city. I'll tie up the loose ends."

Borgia was too weak to argue when Michalson bundled him into a waiting sedan. Eddie watched the taillights disappear around the first bend, then hurried back into the lodge alone. Less than five minutes later, he, JD and Dirk were speeding back toward Chicago. Emergency vehicles intent on the sparking glow in the northern sky raced past them just as the seeping gas in the deserted lodge's kitchen ignited and the night was rent with another blast.

Eddie relaxed against the leather upholstery and motioned Dirk to keep driving. Whatever else went wrong tonight, Mr. Borgia should be pleased with *that* timing.

NINE

Funny, he didn't remember the corridor being so long. The simple act of pulling out his identity card generated a whole new crop of aches in places he didn't know he could hurt. Swearing silently, he fed the plastic card into the slot by the security entrance. He needed a large infusion of blood, and for once, he'd welcome the oblivion dawn brought. As the heavy, sound-proofed door opened, admitting him to the Special Operations offices, distant voices reached his ears. Galen Miller and Jim Nelson. Arguing. As usual. He snorted. Miller and Nelson had a lot of nerve accusing *him* of arguing all the time.

Galen declared, "Just because I have a vampire for a partner doesn't mean I have any experience with witches!"

Jim countered, "I thought your mother —"

"You leave my Mama outta this! Besides, *nobody* in my family has ever done anything like that! All she did was pick up a twig, twirl it in her hands and toss it at the boat, then — *BLAMMO*!"

Ah. Maeve. He tried to warn them.

Jim and Galen were beside the coffee urn intent on their dispute and didn't see him come in. What *he* saw framed between the combatants was the coffee machine. More importantly the hot water tap on the front of the urn and the roll of paper toweling on the table beside it. *Yes*! More than anything else, he wanted the blood off his face. Dried or fresh, his injuries left him too hungry to deal with even his own bloodscent.

Jim exploded, "Oh, *great*. New York is gonna love *this*! 'Suspect's boat was blown up by magic stick' —" He broke off in mid-tirade, as the gruesome apparition edged between them. "Good God, Peale! What happened to *you*?"

Galen gaped wordlessly as his blood-caked partner reached past him, wet a paper towel and began gingerly dabbing at his forehead. Concerned, the big man snatched his own handful of towels, wet them, and pulling BC's hands aside, began cleaning the gory smears away himself.

Submitting to the ministrations, BC muttered gratefully, "Thanks. It's at times like this I regret not being able to use mirrors." Eyes sliding to Jim, he elaborated, "Francesco Borgia and I were in front of the picture window when the fireworks began. I came through it better than *he* did. He took a whopping great chunk of glass through the back."

Nelson paled and Galen seethed, "Too bad it wasn't a chunk of wood, it might've solved a lot of trouble right then and there." His friend flinched. Galen apologized, "Sorry, I know that strikes a raw nerve considering recent history."

BC sucked air making Miller look more closely. "Looks like you still have a little glass in there, pal. Doesn't that hurt?"

With a mixture of incredulity and humor Peale replied, "Of course it hurts! I'm not *that* dead."

Moving in for his own examination, Jim grunted agreement. "Yep, there's glass in there, I'll get Dr. Klotski up here right away. He's gone home by now, but he's the only medical officer with clearance high enough to treat you." Lifting the telephone, he added, "By the way, BC, your ladyfriend is in my office nursing a cup of tea. Why don't you go in and keep her company while we wait for the doc? I'm going to hold the debriefing in there anyway, *and* after what Galen tells me, I don't think I like the idea of her being alone very long."

BC frowned. "I agree wholeheartedly with your assessment, Jim, but, isn't there somebody else you could send? I . . . uh . . . ended the relationship with Maeve quite a while ago. It was a rather stormy finale."

Tossing the reddened toweling into the trash, Galen chuckled evilly. "Yeah, I know. She told me *her* side of the story in the boat coming back. You're lucky you got off with unlife, Buddy. If I'd pulled that shit on Fiona she'd have flat out killed *me*!"

BC started away, remarking, "Hey, I never said I was a nice person!"

Jim called, "Oh, yeah, you might want to tell Ms. Donal that S.I. took the liberty of retrieving her things and paying her hotel tab. Part of our witness protection thing."

Peale paused as the implication of the statement struck home. Nodding, he disappeared into the office.

She stood by the big window, gazing at the city lights, head gracefully tilted to one side. It was amazing how delicate and vulnerable she could appear, even after all these years and painful evidence to the contrary, he felt himself softening — but not much. Though he wasn't particularly quiet, she didn't notice his entrance. Probably still under the influence of the drugs Borgia used on her, he could smell them and her exhaustion across the room. He reeled, tightening his grip on the doorknob. Damn! If he wasn't so hungry! Closing the door more firmly than absolutely necessary to announce his arrival, he stepped in.

Her face brightened and she joyfully ran into his arms. "Byron, m'love! You *did* come for me, I knew you still cared."

Gently extricating himself, he backed away from her enticing aromas. Looking at him questioningly, she saw the cuts and still-oozing blood. Touching the wounds with a feather soft caress, she lamented, "You're hurt! Did Frankie do this?"

Wryly amused, he answered, "No, I happened to be in the line of fire when a plate glass window shattered due to the mysterious explosion of a motor launch."

Her hand flew to her mouth, she recoiled and regarded him with remorseful eyes. Her act was born of anger, and it never entered her mind that anyone would be hurt. Especially Byron. Never mind that she loved him, it was a very dangerous thing to seriously injure a vampire. "I'm so sorry. You've every right t' be angry with me."

"I'm not so much angry as tired. So very, very tired." He sank onto the edge of the desk, and seeing her move to embrace him again, his head snapped up, eyes flashing. Finger stabbing the air for emphasis, he warned, "*And* don't assume that because I helped rescue you, I'm still in love with you."

The gesturing hand tremored, hastily clenched then dropped. Judiciously, she returned to her place at the window. It was a magnificent view, she couldn't understand why Captain Nelson kept his blinds closed. She murmured, "Byron, you *are* angry."

Eyes dropping to the carpet and away from her inviting presence, he admitted, "Okay, I'm angry, but that's not all of it. Y'know what the real pisser is? It's that I honestly can't define how I feel toward you even though I've been thinking on it for a long time." Indigo eyes peeked at her through lashes and hints of mischief played around his mouth as he added, "You told me yourself that vampirism makes for a lot of time to think things over. Remember?"

Unmindful of the risk, she came around in front of him, a terrible yawning feeling in the pit of her stomach. Familiarity told her he was about to say something unpleasant, and bloodscent or no, she wanted to see his face when he did. "Oh? What have you decided?"

"My initial impulse was right."

She sprang at him, right hand wedged for a solid slap, but he moved with the inhuman speed of his kind to catch her arms in a firm grasp. The grip was tight but gentle. Abruptly, she realized he was trying hard not to hurt her. *Another difference between Byron and Francesco* came unbidden to her thoughts.

Pulling free, she stalked to a chair, and put the comforting bulk between them. Digging red-lacquered nails into the upholstery, she furiously searched for a searing comment. Before she could frame anything vitriolic enough, he said, "Look at us, Maeve. I mean that quite literally. No matter how many years — *decades* even — pass between our meetings, they always go the same way. I don't think we're good for each other."

Provoked beyond caring, she burst out, "'Good for each other'? And what is that supposed to mean? You didn't risk your freedom and existence against Francesco Borgia so you could stand and spout touchie-feelie phrases at me, Byron Peale. I *know* you feel for me! We're bound —"

She stopped uncertainly. He was like his sire in that he was capable of making his own use of intimate knowledge, albeit in different, and usually more pleasant, ways. Seeing her dilemma, he came to where she stood and gently placed his hand on her arm. The chill of his flesh through the light sweater on loan from Agent Zoeller, was alarming. The night's activities and injuries had depleted him severely.

His voice was gentler than she'd heard in years. "Don't say any more, I know about it. Borgia told me what happened the night Mario Hernandez tried to destroy me."

She glanced startled questions into his eyes, but he only shook his head. "He didn't tell me how he knew, but since Hernandez' body was dumped outside this building roughly the same time you were abducted, I can pretty well guess. It isn't easy to refuse a vampire's will, especially if one's mind is as weak as that lad's was. Once the tale was told, it would be simplicity itself to link the two events." He stopped with a slight smile. "Captain Nelson's office isn't the proper place for this. Besides, Galen and the others will be coming for the debriefing any minute, we'll finish our chat later."

Suddenly cold, Maeve hugged herself. "You're right, this isn't a good place to talk, but how can I know you'll not disappear on me again? You have t'admit you're prone to it, Love."

His smile became self-mocking, and he bowed in an exaggeratedly courtly manner. "The prisoner pleads guilty as charged. This time, Maeve, I give you my word of honor, I'll not be leaving Chicago for a while to come and we *will* talk later." He suddenly remembered. "Oops. I nearly forgot. Captain Nelson wanted me to tell you Sentry picked your things up and checked you out of the hotel right after we discovered you'd been grabbed."

Maeve wheeled, eyes flashing, then stopped, knowing she could never have returned for them herself. "Had Frankie or his people been through my belongings?"

"I don't *think* so, Captain Nelson didn't mention if they looked like they'd been searched. I believe he would, had it been apparent."

"Did they find a small, brown leather case with brass fittings?"

"Was it hidden? I expect they didn't turn the place over, just removed your things and paid the bill."

"It was on the table by the side of the bed." In sudden urgency she pleaded, "Is there anyway you could find out for sure? There were irreplaceable things in that case."

Sensing her upset was genuine, he lifted the telephone and punched a button on the base. Presently he spoke quietly, "This is Special Agent Peale . . . Oh, hi, Zoeller! Could someone check the list of Ms. Donal's stuff from the hotel for a particular item? It's a smallish leather case, brown with brass trim." A pause. "Hey, great! D'you think you could bring it to the Captain's office? Sure, I'll take responsibility for it. Of *course* I'll sign for it, it's not like I'm trying to nick it or anything, Ms. Donal wants it. Yeah, it's very important to her."

The smile was brilliant as he concluded, "Thanks, Zoeller." Dropping the phone with a triumphant flourish, he turned the thousand watt smile on Maeve. "There. All done."

Tossing red-gold hair, she laughed. "Rogue. You'll never change. And if you're expectin' applause, Mr. Peale, you're out of luck! Thank you for callin' about it, though." Taking a lace handkerchief from her sleeve, she gently swabbed the crimson beads welling from his many cuts, murmuring, "You're still bleedin', Byron."

Taking the scrap of fabric, he dabbed a new trickle he felt rolling from his temple. "I know, there's glass imbedded in places. Captain Nelson has called the staff physician to take care of it." Suddenly serious, he said, "You can't possibly go back into a hotel, you know. It would be frighteningly easy to find you, even in a city this large. Do you have an alternate place to stay?"

Used to his mercurial nature, and more than willing to be hopeful, she responded coyly, "No, M'love, I don't. Are you suggestin' someplace in particular?"

She'd always loved his laugh, and it was especially rich now, even though his words were disappointing. "I *am* suggesting a place, though not in the way you mean. I couldn't make that offer even if I were inclined — and I'm not. I'm sharing digs with Galen Miller, and he was there first, so he has the right of veto. I have an old friend by the name of Jump Veron . . . ."

He got no further. The office door swung open admitting Jim Nelson with the rest of the team, Miller brought up the rear. Nelson carried the brown grip and presented it to his guest. "Curbside service with a smile is our motto. Has our junior partner been annoying you?"

Taking the case, she said, "Not nearly enough t'make it worthwhile. The most he's been doin' is bleedin' on your carpets and stainin' me hankies!"

Marquez grimaced. "Oh, sorry, BC, I should have called to update you on Dr. Klotski. He's out, but his answering service has a message on his beeper. He hasn't checked in yet, but it'll be any time, the doc isn't one of those 'don't-bother-me-I'm-off-duty' types."

"*Wha-at?*" The normal peaches and cream of Maeve's complexion mottled with fury. "Are you sayin' that because one lackadaisical doctor isn't answerin' his page, Byron will have to endure — I'll not have it."

Exasperated, she plunked the small valise onto the cluttered desk and popped the latches. "It's just as well y'brought this, it has all my herbs and ointments in it. I'll treat him m'self while we speak. Sit over here under the light, M'love."

Peale obeyed. From past experience, he knew her medical skill was excellent, besides, the splinters hurt and until they were removed, he wouldn't heal.

Miller said, "I'll get some hot water."

Hu followed him, saying, "You'll need towels, too. I'll get a fresh roll."

Marquez mouthed, "Deserters," as they passed.

Zoeller found herself overwhelmed by unspoken guilt. She stood behind Nelson and Tidrow, watching the graceful Irish woman rummage inside the case. There was no easy way to explain how she was feeling, still the urge to blurt an apology was strong. When she'd been shown a picture of their objective, the photo showed an exquisitely beautiful, porcelain-delicate woman in a low-cut beaded evening dress. Instantly, words like weak and fatuous sprang to mind. *She*, who fought so hard to overcome exactly those stereotypes, had so formed one of her own, that she'd been nonplussed when the china doll transformed into a raging amazon. Amazed, she'd watched as the other woman, spitting in a language she'd never heard before, leaped to drag the unconscious Edgar Michalson into stocks. That had amazed her even more than Peale's revelation that he was an actual factual vampire. It appeared there were a lot of things she still had to learn.

Unbidden, her gaze slid from Peale and Donal to the plate glass window behind them. The blinds were wide open. That wouldn't do, she couldn't abide the feeling of being on display even in an upper story. It was an especially bad idea now that Ms. Donal was a target. She turned to close them, then paused with her hand on the cord, casting a puzzled look behind her. She briefly watched Maeve fuss with jars and BC leaning forward in his seat, curious as a cat, trying to get a peek at the mysterious contents. Glancing back to the glass, she unwillingly verified her earlier observation. The interior lights turned the pane into a sort of mirror wherein she saw Galen and Emily coming back with the towels and water, Mick, Frank and Jim sorting things at the desk, Maeve with her little suitcase and herself standing, holding the curtain cord like an absurd Statue of Liberty. But no Peale. Oh.

She closed the blinds, touched the other woman's shoulder and offered, "Ms. Donal, I've had field triage courses, I might be able to help."

Maeve flexed a set of tweezers. "Thank you, Agent Zoeller, an extra pair o' hands is always welcome." She paused for an impudent glance at her erstwhile patient, then added, "And maybe later, you could teach me that lovely flyin' kick you used on poor Eddie. It looked ever so effective."

Peale ignored the implied threat, and seized the moment to view the unobstructed contents of the case. Leaning in, his sharp eyes glimpsed the edge of a small object tucked into a pouch. Something about it struck a familiar chord. *Be damned!* Faster than the human eye could follow, the pale hand darted into the case and emerged clutching what looked like a tiny photograph. "What's this?"

Maeve snatched at it, but BC stubbornly dove out of her reach. Dangerously rattled, she said, "Leave that be, Byron Peale!"

"*No way!* I recognize this. My brother, James, painted this for our mother."

Behind the desk, Jim Nelson waited, unwilling to breathe lest he upset some precarious balance. Instinct told him Mick, Kim and Frank were similarly immobilized. As one, they transmitted a silent plea for Gae to corral his volatile partner. But Galen, unsuccessfully searching for a place to deposit the water bowl, merely nervously ogled from his partner to the distraught witch, then shot a desperate 'what do we do now' look at Hu, the closest seemingly rational being. Emily was frozen in the act of removing the plastic wrap from a roll of towels.

"It's *mine*! Your mother gave it me herself!" As if the words surprised her more than anyone, Maeve stood, fists clenched against her ribs like a vividly painted Kore. Her eyes never left the slender man and the precious thing he held.

Finding the whole thing inexplicable, Hu stretched past Miller hoping that a better view of the object would clarify the situation. She gasped with pleasure and wonder, then flushed with embarrassment. "Whoops. I guess that was an inappropriate response, but that's a beautiful little picture. I've never seen anything like it."

Curiosity propelled Mick around the desk. "Did you say this was the work of *James* Peale? Could I look at it? I mean, in all the reading I did while checking your background, I kept reading about what a good portraitist James was, but the only illustrations I ever saw were from your oldest brother, Charles." Careful not to address one more obviously than the other, he finished, "If no one objects, that is."

During it all, Peale had never once looked away from Donal. Now, he slowly held the artwork toward her. "Since Mama gave it to you it's your place to decide."

Carefully, as though he'd snatch it back if she moved quickly, she repossessed the painting, then handed it proudly to Lt. Marquez. "It *is* a beautiful piece. All sibling rivalries aside, even Byron praised James' brushwork."

As the room's atmosphere relaxed, Jim started breathing again. He shoved papers aside as Mick placed the miniature on the desk for fear of damaging the old pigments. Leaning in, he saw a wonderful likeness of Peale in eighteenth century garb. "This is really good, BC!"

Galen snorted. "That's high praise coming from Jim 'it-has-to-have-a-horse-in-it' Nelson!"

Happily ignoring the goings-on at the other side of the room, and with a great show of disgust, Maeve shoved the injured vampire back into the chair. Dipping a piece of toweling into the cooling water now resting on the closed lid of the case, she deftly swabbed his cheek and throat. "And *look* at you, you willful rogue! All over blood again, as if you weren't weak enough t' start with."

Byron humbly submitted to her ministrations. "My apologies, tonight has been harder than I'd expected."

Taking up the tweezers, she deftly removed splinters, listening with half an ear to Lieutenant Marquez elaborating on what he'd learned about the "Painting Peales". She bent forward, allowing her lips to brush his hair, her whisper too soft for any but vampire's ears. "Thank you for believin' me, Love."

He responded almost as softly. "I knew Mama did something with it, but she'd never tell what. It was hers to give or keep, and not my decision."

* * *

Roughly brushing Gwen's caresses aside, Borgia made for his private suite. Ignoring her protests, he wrenched the sanctuary door open, and angrily blocking her entrance, slammed it closed. Seething and wobbly from blood-loss, he didn't need Gwen pawing at him. Alone, he dropped onto the bed, falling against the pillows letting pain and weariness break over him.

Feeling black unconsciousness tugging at him, he flung himself upright and forced his eyes open. He couldn't slip under now, there was too much chaos to permit the luxury of oblivion. For something to occupy his mind, he examined his new bedchamber, and frowned. The room was unsatisfactory. He had doubts when it was selected, but then again, that was why it was the *secondary* location, wasn't it? True, it was large, and his antique furnishings fit fairly well into it, but there was something about the proportions he didn't like. It was mildly annoying before, but now with his massive four-poster in place. . . . No need to get upset, there'd be time later to find a permanent location. This would do for now, there were more pressing needs to be seen to at the moment.

The ever pragmatic Edgar sent for fresh blood as soon as he'd returned from Wisconsin. It was proof of his own clouded mental state that he hadn't given the order himself. Borgia would never voice it, but he was grateful Edgar was back to take charge. He was too unstable from his injuries to trust himself with a live victim, and the Hunger was becoming hard to control. He'd realized that when Gwen met him. He had enough control to brief her on the disaster at the lodge before her scent infiltrated his defenses. He knew that was intentional, he needed blood and Gwen was too willing to be the donor. He couldn't permit that, her ultimate price was too high. It was amazing. Eddie feared and hated what his employer was, yet had more understanding of Borgia's nature than did Gwen who professed to love him and wanted to be like him. Perhaps it wasn't so surprising, after all, Edgar had the advantage of sanity and whether Gwen realized it or not, that *was* an advantage.

The welcome aroma reached him through the heavy panels of the door even before Michalson freed a hand to rap lightly. "Hey, Boss, I got your tray."

The stocky Italian swung the door wide and held it long enough for Michalson to enter. Without preamble, Eddie set the tray on the secretary, then backed rapidly and wisely to a spot as far distant from his employer as the size of the room and propriety would allow. He apologized, "It's only cow blood, Boss, but it's as warm as we could manage it. Banged up as you are, it ain't a real good idea for you to go out huntin' — but you know that already. I brought a whole lot, mebbe that kind of thing don't kill you guys, but it sure as hell hurt ya."

Borgia managed a wan smile and chuckled. "*Daverro*, Edgar, as usual you are correct. Sometimes I am undecided as to whether you are my Director of Operations or my nursemaid."

Eddie twitched uncomfortably. "Yeah, well, *somebody's* gotta do it."

As appetizing as the carafe of beef blood smelled, the scent of Edgar's pounding heart'sblood was more inviting. He was a wise man to distance himself from his injured master. Borgia poured the thick crimson into the accompanying goblet, speaking in as measured tones as his raging thirst and lengthening fangs would allow. "Thank you, Edgar, I believe you have other business to attend to. Be certain the door latches behind you."

Michalson didn't need a clearer message. Being close to the Boss when he was in this shape made him sweat bullets, anyway. He bolted, saying, "Right, Boss. Just yell if ya need anything else."

The door shut solidly and Borgia flipped the inner latch into place. Edgar had given him a hurried precis of the final activity at the lodge over the cell phone. The report was necessarily brief and cryptic, neither of them had confidence in the security of that infernal mode of communication. Eddie had done well, *that* was certain. An explosion of the magnitude Edgar arranged, wouldn't leave much evidence for the authorities to sift through.

Dio! Byron and his associates made such a mess of it all! Giving the devil his due, things weren't bad until the first explosion. Maeve, undoubtedly. Curse her lovely hide! It was hard to guess how his discussion with Byron would have ended had she not interrupted. He was angry with his scion, too, though. The boy was so *stubborn*. What was a father to do with such a son? Nothing was ever simple. Gwen wanted the gift, but couldn't be trusted with it and Edgar could be trusted with it, but didn't want it. And Byron? Phaah! The lad enjoyed being nosferatu, but didn't appreciate he who gave the gift.

He downed the strengthening fluid in one gulp and refilled the goblet. He detested the taste of dead blood, but it would work in his body as well as any other.

It pained to admit it, but the whole fiasco was his own fault. He shouldn't have acquiesced to Maeve in the first place. But, the boy was graceful and beautiful enough to be a scion of the house of Borgia. No. He didn't regret the choice of the fledgling, but things would have been different had he taken the lad to himself for training as he should have. What did a witch know of training a fledgling? Not much if one were to take this failure as proof. The woman couldn't control a new-made vampire for even one night.

Conversely, he never confided much about his nature to her. Concealment was an inborn habit, and he successfully kept many secrets from her even in their time as lovers. It was his custom to lock himself away during his daily sleep and so he kept his other secrets as well.

It wasn't too late for the boy, though, he could see that through the bloodbond they shared. *He* felt the tug, so must his son. The depth of his feeling astonished him. He didn't think he'd have that link to contend with, since he wasn't present when Byron first rose and had no hand in his training. Obviously, that reasoning was faulty.

Byron didn't acknowledge the pull, not on the surface, anyway. Perhaps anger at what he perceived as desertion interfered with natural filial reverence. If the boy would listen to reason . . . perhaps that was the answer. He knew where the child was staying. If he arrived unannounced, he could force him to listen to his arguments. He was the sire and therefore the more powerful. He would be victor in a test of wills.

Yes. That would be the best course. He'd allow the boy a few nights to calm down *and* time for him to familiarize himself with the child's habits before he made his move. He'd also need to familiarize himself with the habits of his son's companion, this Galen Miller. That one was very strongwilled.

TEN

The club downstairs was in full swing. Muted, exuberant jazz drifted through the floor blending pleasantly with the conversation. Given the turns unlife had taken, he'd despaired of spending a quiet evening with good friends and good music again. Amazingly, he was even enjoying Maeve's company, a first in several decades. If only he could forget why they were all together in this pleasant place, but even *he* couldn't dodge responsibility well enough for that.

Jump's calming personality pervaded the apartment, making it an easy place to unwind. When he was on the road, this room with its towering bookshelves, stacked records, tapes, CDs and sheet music symbolized home as much as Belridge. Contented, Peale turned back to the conversation flowing around him.

Jim Nelson was engaged in an enthusiastic rendition of Peale's first Sentry medical exam. Judging by the appreciative chortles, it would soon become part of the Special Ops' private legends. "...so then Doc takes a gander at Peale's lily white carcass and there's not so much as a scratch on 'im by this time. He gets his senator look and says, 'I though you said Agent Peale had been injured.' Before I could say boo, he was fiddling with BC's wrist, then went whiter than his patient. I thought he was gonna choke before he gasps, 'Nelson! This man has no pulse!'"

Amid the resulting laughter, Galen chimed in, "I bet that asshole sat through it all looking vaguely amused. Wish I coulda been there."

"You sure you weren't?" Jim let the chuckles fade before remarking to BC, "I suppose I'll get used to this. I've handled special Special Agents before, but never one like you. Or had a witness to protect like Ms. Donal." He frowned. "All joking aside, I'm leery of using an apartment over a night-club as a safe house, especially against someone as tricky as Francesco Borgia. It's not just unorthodox, it's impossible to secure."

Galen rolled his eyes. "Of course it's unorthodox, Jimbo! Name some-thing about this shit that hasn't been."

"I know, I know, and I don't want to be accused of judging by ap-pearances, but I keep looking at little Jump Veron, then thinking about Borgia. Sure Veron's a smart old guy and Benny Glissen could give Gae a run for his money, but can they defend against *that*? I'd feel better if we had a couple of agents in the place, too."

From the depths of the armchair, Peale drawled lazily, "I thought we decided that would only draw attention. From what Maeve heard while she was Borgia's unwilling guest, my association with this club is known, they'll be watching it anyway."

Nodding, Miller finished, "Yeah! Isendamer even scoped the place to get her mitts on BC's picture from the fliers. The appearance of business as usual is the best protection. Why look twice where everything appears nor-mal?"

BC's empathic receptors got a hefty zing from the shudder that rippled Maeve's body. He cocked an interested eyebrow as she spoke.

"Gwen Isendamer. That one makes my skin crawl just thinkin' of her." Maeve's eyes clouded. "Truth t'tell *she* worries me more than Francesco. By Eddie's account, it was a mercy that Francesco killed the Hernandez lad himself rather than leave him to Isendamer. He called her the Ice Em-press and if half the things he told me are true. . . ."

Impressed by the depth of Maeve's revulsion, BC mentally added Ms. Isendamer to the discussion list for later. He'd never known Maeve to be so unsettled by any individual. From the uneasy silence, her words affected the others as well. He interjected into the tension, "Ice Empress notwithstanding, I think the decision to put as few normal humans in Borgia's path as possible is sound. Most precautions won't be very effective against *this* adversary. Besides, Jump is quite capable of taking care of it all by himself."

Maeve blurted, "That he is." Pointedly ignoring Byron's widening grin, Maeve continued, "Not to worry, Frankie sneaked up on me once, but he'll not be given that chance again. I've already set up wards and other even nastier surprises so if the darlin' should come callin' unannounced he'll be rewarded in a way he'll not soon forget!"

Marquez's brow furrowed. "Before anyone jumps down my throat, I assure one and all I'm not questioning anyone's judgment. I'm asking for reassurance, remember, my sister works downstairs. What if the worst happens and Borgia tumbles to what we're doing?"

BC answered, "I understand. I have a personal stake in this, too. Aside from the *other* thing, I have a responsibility to every employee of this club. I'm confident about the arrangements. Maeve was taken off-guard before, not so now. Also, I've known Jump for a long time. Trust me when I say I've seen him do remarkable things." Straightening, he added in a louder voice, "Isn't that so, Jump?"

Bearing a clattering tray of china, Jay Marquez rump-bumped the swinging door wide and held it for her employer. Smiling broadly over a platter of still-warm cookies, Jump entered. "So you have said, *mon ami*. Will anyone have tea? Hot or cold?"

Veron busied himself with the teapot and surprisingly, handed the first steaming mug to Peale. More surprising, the vampire accepted it gratefully and sank back cradling the warm ceramic. "Thank you, Jump. That's marvelous."

Handing the next cup to Miller, Veron explained simply, "He get cold. Especially in the hands."

Jay broke away from the throng around the cookie plate to perch on the arm of BC's chair. Guiltily, she flipped a stray strand of silky gold over her shoulder, and said, "When Benny told me you was up here, I took off a little early 'cause I needed to talk to ya."

Suddenly curious, BC tilted his head toward her oblivious to her brother's hard looks. Still more intent on the chair's fabric than its occupant, she explained, "It's more like I wanted to apologize. When I heard what happened to Mario, an' I thought you done it, I got so mad I couldn't see straight. I mean, sure I didn't know there was another vampire in Chicago, but . . . well . . . I shoulda known *you* better than t'think ya'd do something *that* awful."

Taken aback, he stared in silent wonderment. Many people leaped to the same conclusion, and why not? Lately, he *had* lost it far too often for peace of mind. Even Jump had wondered. Now, *that* stung. But, what hurt more was how many believed he'd hunt Hernandez alone after he'd promised otherwise. He was irresponsible. He readily admitted that, but it was a matter of pride that when he gave his word, he kept it. He squeezed her arm reassuringly. "Believe it or not, Jay, I understand. It wasn't illogical for anyone to assume that if the guy was killed by a vampire, the only known vampire must have done it. I'm sorry Galen and I kept quiet about Borgia."

Mick interrupted, "Now it's *our* turn to say we understand. Sure, Jim and I chewed your ass over it, but that was official. On the personal level? Well, if it was me and I discovered what you discovered, I don't think I'd have taken it as well as you did."

BC smiled. "I'm not sure I've taken it as well as everybody thinks I have."

Galen exclaimed, "You can say *that* again! I didn't know a vampire could do it, but this asshole went out the same night he found out about his parentage and came back at the crack of dawn, stinking, falling-down drunk. Passed out on the living room floor and I hadda drag his ass into his bedroom."

Wide-eyed, Jay cried, "BC! Why — *how* on earth did you do that?"

With a smugness that made Byron want to spit, Maeve interjected, "Alcohol finds it's way into the blood stream quickly, Jay dear, and this blackguard's always had a penchant for pub crawlin' even at the best of times. Lets other folks do the drinkin' then gets drunk as a lord on their blood afterward."

Openly annoyed, Peale glared at the witch and was rewarded with a dazzling smile.

Nelson stifled a snicker and said, "Before we get into a critique of personal stress relief techniques, I want to remind you folks that we still have a lot of ground to cover. Let's get back on track. For starters, I've been wondering if several of us should find new digs for the duration — most notably BC and Gae."

The identical noises of dissent fizzled under Maeve's ominously sub-dued comment, "'Tis true, y'know. If he didn't know before, Frankie knows where you live now because he took Galen's card from me. I was foolish enough t' leave it in m'purse, but I was also foolishly trustin' Francesco Borgia. Silly me, I thought friendship meant somethin' to him."

Undaunted, Peale argued, "But, maybe that's good. I mean that he knows where to contact us. If we leave, the only way he could do that is through Sentry, and I don't believe he'd do that."

Nelson mused, "Maybe we should say: He knows where to contact *you*."

The new agent flinched like he'd been slapped. "Your point, S*ir*?"

Frustrated, Nelson scrubbed at gritty eyes. Must be getting old, late nights never *used* to bother him like this. "Calm down, BC, nobody is ac-cusing you of working with Borgia. Your disgust is far too evident. Dammit, I'm too tired to talk straight, I was trying to say it appears he's more inter-ested in *you* than anyone or anything else we know of."

Thoughtfully, Maeve placed her cup on the tray. "That's true, too, Byron. Francesco changed unbelievably when he learned you were the renegade invading his territory. The term blood bond has real meaning for a parent vampire and the fledgling, and I'm thinkin' it proved stronger than Frankie bargained for."

Nelson affirmed, "So I gathered from our earlier interview, Ms. Donal, but I'm balking at asking anyone to be bait." Turning to Miller, he stated, "I'm even *more* reluctant to ask you, Gae. Peale has special abilities to fall back on plus a certain understanding of the situation, you'll simply be operating on instinct."

"Jim, I didn't sign onto this outfit to play it safe. I've done pretty well on instinct for quite a few years," Miller said.

Nelson laughed. "Why did I know you were going to say that, Gae?" Sobering, he turned back to Peale. "How about you? Ms. Donal raises an interesting point about the blood bond thing. It's possible the connection could give you as much trouble as it does Borgia. Did you feel any kind of tug or sway when he was talking to you?"

"I'm not sure." Peale considered, then shook his head. "All I remember when I think back is this incredible anger boiling up and trying to surge out."

Galen chuckled. "Do tell, Kimosabe. When you first came into the room, Mick, Kim and I were taking bets on how far we'd get before you punched the guy's lights out. Hey! Come to think of it, that might not have been a bad diversion, after all!"

BC sneered. "Maybe I'll try that next time."

Blasting a piercing two-fingered whistle, Nelson said, "Okay, you two, you're on the same side, remember. Now, how about it, Peale? Feel like being bait?"

"Sure. Why not?" With a sudden burst of enthusiasm, he added, "Besides, I just joined an on-line game I'd like to carry on with."

Miller groaned. "You wouldn't believe this guy. I didn't know there were this many social networks and online games out there, but he found 'em!"

"I used to have a lot of fun with those on-line games." Marquez grinned. "I was in several until I got kicked upstairs and got too busy. What kind of game are you in?"

Peale's smile became broader and decidedly more wicked. "It's a role playing game. I'm playing a vampire."

For a few beats, there was confused silence before Marquez threw back his head and enjoyed the first real laugh he'd had in weeks. The laughter was infectious, and afterward the room was easier. With one exception, Jump's guests forgot business and enjoyed a companionable evening of conversation.

Maeve Donal sipped tea. *Hope you're easy in yourself, Francesco Borgia, wherever you are. I swear I'll never forget what you've done an' however long it takes me t'do it, I'll pay you back in kind.*

It wouldn't be easy, in fact, it might be the hardest thing she'd ever done, but for safety's sake, she intended to keep track of her ex-ally. Keeping tabs on a vampire of his age and power was difficult under the best of circumstances and practically impossible if he was prepared. Francesco was *very* aware of Maeve's fury; he'd be prepared. But this time, so was she.

Leaning forward to freshen her cup, she found Byron's penetrating gaze locked on her. She covered her dismay with a coquettish wink over her teacup. Damn the scoundrel anyway, how long was he watching? The intensity of those eyes always made her feel as if he were reading her inmost thoughts like a particularly elementary book. She'd felt that before he was changed, she felt it more now.

Their unspoken communication ended abruptly as Mick Marquez tapped his wristwatch, and Jay grimaced and stood up. "Geez, we gotta go already. Y'know havin' my brother stayin' with me is a real drag, I ain't had t' turn in so early since I was in school."

Gathering her belongings, she paused. "I hate t' sound like a whiner, but I'm kind of scared. When it was only Mario slinkin' around, it made me feel better with Mick stayin' at my place, 'cause I figured that, wacko or no, Mick was more than a match for 'im. But Mario's dead now and — no offense, *Hermano*, but this Borgia guy *really* scares me. I mean, like BC said, the usual things ain't gonna stop 'im."

Mick nodded soberly. The idea wasn't new, he and Jim considered it earlier, but there was more than enough to worry about without it. It didn't take a leap of logic to guess that Borgia knew all there was to know about Jay from that damned Mario. One question hung unasked between them: Was Juanita important enough for Borgia to bother with? The unasked question remained unanswered. Aloud he said, "No offense taken, *Chica*, that's been bugging me, too. Too bad we don't have one of those charms Galen's mom makes." He glanced at his new colleague. "Sounds like they're pretty effective against rampaging undead."

BC winced and gave a convincing shiver. "It was *very* effective. That burn itched for days. By the by, where is the damnable little thing, Galen?"

"I still got it!" Galen said. "When I got home from arguin' with this deadhead, I found it in my pocket. Lemme see. I put it in the top drawer of my bedside table. You want it?"

"*Do I?*" Jay was ecstatic. "That little thingummy will make me feel a lot better." She shot a pleased look at BC. "Not all vampires are gentlemen."

Galen made a derisive noise and dug in his pockets. "BC's got his keys, you take mine so your brother won't have to pick my lock again."

Digging his key ring from his jeans, he lobbed it across the room. Mick plucked it out of the air and Jay relieved him of it, demanding, "Pick your lock? What the hell are you talking about, Gae?"

Galen savored his friend's discomfort as he answered, "I'm sure Magic Mitt Miguel will be more than happy to tell you *all* about it if you ask him real nice."

At the door, Mick shot Galen a withering glare. "*Muchas gracias*, Special Agent Miller, I owe you for this one big time."

Giving her brother a playful shove, Jay commanded, "C'mon, 'mano, haul ass, it's past your bedtime!"

***

Francesco Borgia had never cared for modern apartments. They simply lacked elegance. It was the same in Europe, so he couldn't blame it all on America. He stirred restlessly in the massive leather chair, one of those dreadful recliner things that smelled of beer, popcorn and his son's mortal partner. Perhaps he should put the light on. There wasn't much coming through the small windows. No, it was enough and it was unwise to announce his presence before he was ready. Not surprisingly, he found his mind lingering on his estate in upstate New York. That was the perfect place to take Byron. They'd be alone to hunt and get to know each other. More importantly, it was a place neither Maeve nor the boy's friends knew about.

He'd prefer eliminating Miller altogether, but considering his son's penchant for forming strong attachments to mortals, it wouldn't further his cause. Patience was the game here. It was more dangerous, but better to leave the mortal alive while he used his superior power to spirit Byron away. Once the boy was thinking along the proper lines, he'd allow the child to slay Miller himself. Perfect proof of allegiance to his father.

Displeasure rippled the calm exterior. All plans would come to naught if the lad didn't return to his pied-à-terre before daybreak. He showed a distressing tendency to skate in as the sky was turning light; although that was rare when he was in Miller's company and the mortal was gone, too.

Where was the whelp anyway?

That seemingly simple bit of information eluded him, but not for long. His most trusted employees, armed with copies of the promotional photograph, were watching Byron's usual haunts. Maddeningly, to no avail. Tonight, according to his sources, he was neither at the dismal club where he performed, nor at the at the Sentry offices. Even though that infernal motorcycle and the Volvo sedan were still in their parking spaces, *he* could attest to the fact the apartment was empty. To all appearances, his fledgling and Miller had vanished as completely as Maeve. He suspected if he could find one thorn, he'd find them all.

Murmuring voices drifted down the hall. Sharpening his senses, he heard an unfamiliar man and woman exiting the stairs and continuing up the hall. Blast! They were coming to this apartment, there was nothing else in this part of the building. He tensed, willing them away, wanting no interference when his son arrived. Ideally, they'd knock, and finding the apartment unoccupied, depart. The metallic scratch of a key sliding into the lock abruptly cut short his reverie and sent a jolt of dismay through him. *Damn!*

Bolting from the chair, he stood momentarily irresolute. This was unexpected. Who dreamt someone else had a key? The boy was impossibly trusting. Perhaps he should duck into a side room. *No.* What was wrong with him? He could turn this into an advantage. The tumblers fell and the bolt shot back almost as swiftly as he reached the entry hall. Squinting against the sudden glare, he toggled the overhead lights, and before the mortals on the other side could touch the knob, flung the door wide.

For once this evening, Francesco Borgia was pleased, his visitors figured prominently in the recent surveillance of his son. Standing aside, he bowed courteously. "*Buona sera*, Lt. Marquez. *Buona sera, signorina* Juanita. I am pleased to make your acquaintance at last. Will you not come in and join me?"

Time stopped for Mick Marquez as the door opened. Irrationally, recognizing the man framed against the interior light triggered the thought that Charles and James weren't the only superb portrait artists the Peale clan spawned. Jay hadn't seen BC's eerily accurate drawing, but her brother's painfully tightening grip on her wrist was identification enough. His voice sounded strained and unnaturally high to his own ears as he said inanely, "Francesco Borgia, I had no idea you were here. I think perhaps we'll wait for another time."

Before either Marquez could retreat, Borgia interposed himself between them, and with arms like iron encircling them, propelled them inexorably into the apartment. Exuding old-world courtesy, their captor proclaimed, "Nonsense, you have obviously come for the same purpose as I:

to await the return of my son and his companion. Come inside, we will wait together."

Although the words were uttered in a casually cheerful manner, Mick knew he and his sister were prisoners. Clearly, Jay understood that, too, because she shrank from Borgia's touch like a taint might rub off. Perhaps he could at least win her freedom. He accepted these risks when he'd accepted the badge, Jay never made that deal. With the unwavering conviction this was not a tame vampire, he began truthfully, "Actually, we were on our way home and just dropped in to pick up something Gae lent my sister. If it's all the same to you, we'll grab it and head out. We've both got early days tomorrow"

The forward motion continued unabated as Borgia sighed regretfully, "Then it is unfortunate that I must detain you, but *ecco*, that is the way of it." He released them and gestured grandly to the sofa. "Surely, our wait will not be long. If you have arrived, Byron cannot be far behind. You *were* with him, *sì*?"

Instinctively knowing it was a bad idea to admit it, Mick extemporized seamlessly, "I'm not sure where he and Gae are tonight, but if you'd like, I could call around for them. I'm certain BC would like to know his . . . um . . . father is waiting for him."

"*Grazie*, but no. A handsome offer, Lieutenant, but I had hoped to surprise my son."

In spite of her fear Jay heard herself, "Finding you in his living room will sure as hell do that."

Registering an odd mix of interest and puzzlement, Borgia turned toward the shivering girl. "Such beauty, *signorina*, but such poor use of the voice! What a pity. In my century. . . ." His voice fading thoughtfully, he captured her chin and looked into her eyes. She was a chaotic mix, this Juanita, this courtesan trying to escape into respectability. What a waste. Looking deeper, he savored the radiant sexuality overriding even her intense fear and wondered idly if this was why Byron so enjoyed her company.

Forgotten by the absorbed vampire, Mick swatted the ensnaring hand away. Uncaring for consequences, he drew his shuddering sister behind him. "Sorry, Borgia, but this is the Twentieth century and aristocratic rights have been out of fashion for a long time."

The nobleman recoiled, struggling with animal rage that railed at the cage of self-control. Anger at himself for allowing such weakness overwhelmed the indignity of the slap. What was wrong with him that he should be so consumed by this woman's erotic essence? Had Marquez chosen to strike another way, he would have been unable to defend against it. He resumed the civil exterior. Humiliating as it was, these humans held the key to his fledgling. For the nonce, he needed them. "The time for masquerade is over, Lt. Marquez. Did I not know you to be more soldier than policeman, I would not suffer such indignities lightly." Gesturing imperiously, he commanded, "Be seated. We will talk while we await Byron's return, there is much we may discuss. I know you to be a man of honor, that is a quality to be respected." *Respect, yes, but honor makes poor armor, signor Marquez, rather it affords a chink through which a well-wielded sword may pass.*

Stubbornly, Marquez remained standing. "Okay, masks off. You never had any intention of letting us walk out of here, did you?"

"Alas, it will be impossible until after my son has returned. I suppose I should be grateful to you after a fashion, you will provide much-needed insurance against Byron or Mr. Miller doing anything disagreeable. I deeply regret the circumstances, but such things happen, even though the idea of holding hostages is distasteful."

"Didn't seem to bother you when you were holding Ms. Donal."

How like Lt. Marquez not to see Maeve was an entirely different case. True, he hadn't liked detaining her, but she gave him no choice. She never did. He beamed enigmatically, admiring the brave faces they presented. Masks off, indeed. No matter, he knew how to remove them. Without warning, he thrust the latchkey with its dangling photograph of two smiling children inches from the lieutenant's nose, demanding, "You know where my son is, admit it. If this were not so why would you let yourselves into his sleeping place with a key belonging to Galen Miller?"

Mick blinked at the key. He'd honestly not seen Borgia take it from the lock where he left it dangling in hopes his colleagues would see it as a danger flag. Forcing his face into the stony expression Jim called his Toltec face, he maintained silence. Infuriated, Borgia flung the key chain to the floor. "Mortals! Do you not see that my only interest is in my son?" As suddenly as the anger appeared, it disappeared, the veneer of civility covering it as completely as a lead sheath. It pleased him that though neither told him what he wanted to hear, this minor display upset them both. Good. That was it's sole purpose.

He maintained eye-contact with the lieutenant for a few more seconds, then gestured sharply for them both to be seated, turned and lowered himself onto the arm of Galen's recliner.

The shot took him over the left eye and angled shallowly outward to exit behind the ear carrying with it a gout of gore and splintered bone that hit the wall just before the body did.

***

The unexpected gunshot paralyzed Jay in open-mouthed, ear-ringing shock. It happened too fast to look away as the body slid down the wall in seeming slow motion. She sat, fingernails gouging palms, unable to decide which was worse: the horrific spectacle indelibly printed on her brain or the sublime relief at seeing Borgia fall coupled with the irrelevant notion that there ought to be smoke hanging in the air. Abruptly, relief evaporated with the realization the body was still moving.

Pistol trained on the convulsing form at his feet, Mick shouted, "*Jay!* Snap out of it and call Jim, he should still be at the club. Let's hope Gae and

BC are, too. Tell them what happened and get them over here pronto."

Gulping air in an effort to control her racing heart, she scanned for her purse and cell phone. She found it on the small table bare inches from Borgia's writhing body. Recoiling, she forced speech through a fear-constricted throat. "I can't go near that. I'll use the phone in the bedroom."

Eyes locked on the downed vampire, Mick replied, "Make it quick. From what I've seen of BC's abilities, I can't guarantee how long a wound like that will keep this joker down. I'm gonna need a lot of backup."

She sidled toward the master bedroom in the half-superstitious hope that by keeping her gaze riveted on the enemy, she could assure he didn't rise. It didn't work.

Impossibly, the gruesome thing lunged from the floor, and swatted the troublesome agent and his offending pistol aside. Moving unsteadily, Borgia flung himself at the human with a furious howl. Uttering a tiny shriek of her own, Jay fled for the phone, and fumbling the receiver at first, managed to enter Jump's private number. To her unbounded relief, Jim picked up, she sobbed, "Jim, thank God you're still there! Borgia was waitin' for BC when we came for the charm. Mick shot 'im an' they're fightin' in the other room. Please tell me BC is still there!"

"Whoa, Jay! Slow down, Borgia's at Gae's place right now?"

A heavy thud against the bedroom wall made the pictures shower to the floor and reduced her reply to an inarticulate yelp.

Jim hurried on, "Look, Jay, BC and Gae left here a while ago, they'll be there any minute, they'll take over. Listen carefully, I want you to get the hell out of that apartment. *Now!*"

Welcome as help was, she wondered if BC's arrival was a good idea. Even she could tell the elder vampire was obsessed with him. If Borgia was this nuts now, who knew what would happen when he actually *saw* BC. But there had to be *something* . . . clutching the small table to steady herself, her trembling fingers brushed the brass drawer pull. She suddenly remembered why they'd come in the first place. Decision lent her strength. "Not yet."

Slamming the phone on Jim's protests, she wrenched the drawer open. There, under a wad of credit card receipts, nestled a small linen bag. That had to be it. Clutching it, she raced into the fray, part of her wondering if any of the tenants had called the police yet and how they'd explain everything if they did.

The scene in the living room was as terrible as it sounded. Accustomed to the laid-back and slightly lazy behavior of BC Peale, the raw power of Francesco Borgia was an unpleasant revelation. Battered, but unbroken, Mick Marquez had no intention to go down easily. Rolling for his dropped weapon, he kicked, catching the vampire in the midsection, sending him crashing back and scattering furniture. Chillingly, the undead creature was up before Marquez could regain the pistol. Clinging to the door facing, Jay watched in helpless horror as the maddened vampire tossed her brother across the room as if he weighed no more than a teddy bear.

Mick fell sprawling atop the coffee table that splintered beneath him like so much matchwood. Grunting with effort, he rolled back for the weapon. He twisted to bring the pistol up, and as Borgia leaped again, Marquez emptied the clip. Every slug hit its mark, but the vampire's momentum landed him against the lieutenant, sending them rolling over and over across the ruined carpeting.

Too enraged to stop hitting, Borgia straddled his enemy, his back to Jay. A small voice in the back of her head urged her to move *now*. Breathing every prayer she could remember, she lunged. The solid impact of the charm against the vampire's flesh jarred up her arm into her shoulder. The results were spectacular.

Borgia roared and dived to one side, bloodshot eyes frantic for the new attacker. When the horrible eyes found her cowering and nursing her numbed arm, there was nothing human in them. As he clawed for her, she thrust the charm into his grasping hand. The tiny amulet seared the undead flesh even as it was flung aside. The stench of burning flesh filled her nostrils as she raced to her brother's side.

She made the mistake of looking back and their eyes locked over the fallen body. Contact made, the furious vampire forced his way into her soul. As pure hatred buffeted her, she knew *this* was Evil. Unable to withstand the onslaught, she collapsed, oblivious to the anger of the vampire and only dimly aware of another entering the room.

***

Whether it was good or ill, the pain in his hand gave a much-needed focus to regain control. Unfortunately, with control came the realization of more pain making it difficult to think and even harder to remember what happened. Movement slightly behind him wrenched him from the enticing smell of blood and fear. Pivoting unsteadily, he struggled to lift his head toward the newcomer only to see an elderly woman rushing toward him. How foolish. Ignoring distant alarms clamoring at the edge of consciousness, he charged. He'd barely moved before the termagant flung the contents of a container into his face. Hot, sticky unguent clung to bare flesh, oozed into open wounds and stabbed needles of fire into his eyes. Digging at streaming eyes, he retreated howling fear and pain into the sudden darkness.

***

Cursing her necessarily hasty preparation, Jasmine Miller dug into her bathrobe pockets. The smoothness of a small jar met her questing hand, and edging closer to the bawling vampire, she emptied red powder over his back and shoulders. The unguent was ideal glue for the dust, it caught and hung for a millisecond before bursting into brilliant scarlet flame.

Powerful hands grabbed her from behind, wrenching her away from her target. Furiously, she writhed around intent on landing the empty jar on her attacker's head only to discover at the last moment, it was her own son. She sagged gratefully into the powerful arms until she noticed Byron closing on the pain-maddened Borgia. The boy moved like lightning, aiming a two-fisted sledgehammer punch at the elder vampire. Her eyes widened, knowing the result of that blow, but he was moving too swiftly for her to do more than shout: "*WATCH THE MAGICS, BOY!*"

Everything was in that punch, and he couldn't have pulled it if he wanted to. He didn't want to. Snarling, he aimed for the point of his sire's jaw, reflexively ducking as fiery unguent spattered him. Knowing he couldn't allow his opponent to recoup, he ignored his burns, landing a second blow that brought Borgia to rest near the still-open door. Feeling fresh air against his raw flesh, Borgia broke for the open. Peale flung himself after, bringing to bear all the dirty street fighting moves he'd had occasion to learn in his two hundred-odd years. They tumbled into the hall.

Through swollen eyes, Borgia saw the fury-contorted face of his son. He knew this before he cleared his vision, no mortal could hit with such force. Reeling against the wall, he tried to speak, distantly recalling that was why he'd come, but, impaired by the head wound, his voice was thick and slurred. "*Figlio mio*, let us not contend. I came tonight to speak with you. What has happened was not part of my plans."

"Save it. No one is interested in anything you have to say."

Weaving slightly, the younger vampire tried to wipe the scorching stickiness from his face, but only managed to spread it. For once, he welcomed pain, because it obliterated anger, an emotion he could ill afford. He had a nasty feeling that, even badly wounded, his sire had enough advantages already. Pain couldn't erase what he'd seen as he charged into the flat, though. He wished it could. There'd been no inkling of danger until he reached the top of the stair, where the full force of his sire's fury all but knocked him to his knees.

Dimly, he remembered shouting to Galen, then vaulting to the landing, arriving in time to witness the final moments of the skirmish with Mrs. Miller. The cumulative effect of bloodscent and pain left him in no mood to be polite. Unfortunately, he was also in no mood to be careful. Borgia, seeing an opening, shot forward, and digging a shoulder deep into his scion's middle, slammed him into the concrete block wall. Stunned, Byron collapsed at his sire's feet.

Muttering in satisfied, but incoherent Italian, Borgia attempted to gather his child into his arms, but his tortured body was not equal to the task. His weakened grasp allowed the boneless form to slide back to the floor. At last he fumbled the dead weight onto a shoulder, and straightened preparing to make for home.

"*Freeze, Borgia.*"

Clasping the precious burden, the battered aristocrat turned toward the commanding voice and found himself looking down the barrel of the pistol in Galen Miller's hand. Sneering through blood and unguent, he rasped, "Fool, you dare threaten *me* with that petty weapon. Look upon me, Miller, and tell me why I should fear you."

"Try silver slugs, asshole," Miller lied. "Got 'em from your own runners. Now put my partner down gently and we'll all be happy."

Too unsteady to verify the claim, Borgia snarled, and moving faster than human eyes could follow, flung his burden into Miller with enough force to ram them both into the doorjamb. He fled down the hall and out of the building. Miller slid to the floor beside Peale, counting stars.

***

Where had he disappeared to for so long? Impatiently, Isendamer drummed her fingers against the brocaded chair arm and glared at the bed chamber's elegant furnishings as if they were to blame for her wait. Really, now, it wasn't the first time he'd dashed off without telling anyone where he was going. No, but it was the first since they learned about Francesco's delinquent fledgling. And she, fool that she was, was the instrument of their reunion. Insult to injury. Well, here's to hoping the reunion was not a reconciliation, that wouldn't bode well for *her* plans. She knew Francesco well enough to know that with one scion by his side, he'd see no need for a second.

She plucked thoughtfully at the rich threads. On the other hand, nothing overruled the half-formed plan sparked by Peale's photograph, either. In fact, it might be more plausible. Byron Peale *was* handsome, and by all accounts, charming. Yes. An excellent alternative, but if she went that route, Francesco must be eliminated quickly. He'd be anything but pleased if she joined forces with his son, and he was too powerful to leave to his own devices. How kind of him to share his weaknesses.

The knob on the private entrance rattled. Snapping to attention, she schooled her face against her thoughts as the white-paneled door pivoted slowly inward. At the apex of the swing, a shaft of light fell across the figure there, illuminating not the dignified form of Francesco Borgia, but a nightmare figure of blackened, cracked flesh. Gasping, she tried to press herself through the chair back, right hand automatically seeking the comforting solidity of her pistol. The monstrosity fell into the room, and she released the breath in a piercing scream. Small, but deadly pistol in hand, she sprang up, and weapon trained on the flailing horror edged toward the hall and the henchman posted there. Appallingly, the thing released a pitiful moan that slowly resolved into a word.

It sounded like her name. Against her better judgment, she peered closer. Abruptly abandoning the weapon, she ran forward. "Oh my God! Francesco! What happened? Who did this?"

Aversion forgotten, she steered him to the chair, seized a handful of tissues from the box on the table and blotted at the red-oozing burns. The resulting bellow arched him from the chair and displayed elongated fangs. She bolted to the house phone, then stopped before it parted from its cradle. Heavens! She was so shaken she'd nearly failed to recognize a capital opportunity.

Returning to his side, she knelt, and taking his face in her hands, gazed into his eyes. Was there enough Francesco there to risk it? Who cared. Life was a gamble, anyway. Softly, she crooned, "Darling, you need blood to heal. Why not take mine? You've been meaning to exchange blood with me, isn't this the time for it?" He was listening, she could tell. "Let's do it now, then we'll have others sent up. We can feed together as it ought to be. I'll never leave you, Darling. Not like Byron. Gwennie will be with you forever and for always."

There wasn't much to begin with, but resistance crumbled as she watched. Her words struck the lonely spot in him, the one that ached for his own kind.

Yes. So much easier than worrying with Byron. Gwen's mind was much more like his own . . . a flurry of activity intruded as abruptly Gwen's face was wrenched away and replaced by Edgar Michalson's. The round face was flushed and wore a ridiculously panicked expression as he called, "*BOSS!* Can ya hear me, Boss?"

Something in the frantic demeanor struck home. Red-rimmed eyes in puffy flesh focused just beyond the man's shoulder. Borgia groaned, "Out! Both of you."

Unhesitatingly, Eddie complied. Latching onto Isendamer's arm, he yanked her behind him. The door slammed in their wake and the bolt thunked solidly punctuating the slam with finality. Leaning against the door panels, Eddie called shakily, "Boss? Is there anything I can do? Mebbe there's a doctor or somethin'? Just tell me what an' I'll do it for ya."

A hardly recognizable voice rasped, "I need blood. Get it!"

"S-sure, Boss." The path to the house extension was blocked by Isendamer, exuding a rage more frightening than Borgia's burned flesh. She hissed, "How *dare* you interfere?"

Teeth grinding, he bulled past her. "Shut up, Gwen, you was only gonna make things worse that way."

"What do you mean by that?"

"If you can't figure it out for yourself—Look, I gotta take care of the boss. You stay away from him, ya hear what I'm sayin'?"

Quivering with barely contained fury, she loomed a moment longer, then wheeled and stormed away. Looking nervously after her, Eddie mopped his brow with his pocket handkerchief, wondering how much he was going to regret his intervention. Swallowing hard to steady his voice, he pressed the button for the kitchens.

***

Funny. The club was regularly more crowded, but he never felt this claustrophobic there. But then again, he'd never been at the Inferno so soon after a fight like this one. Come to that, he couldn't remember ever *having* a fight like this one. Fingering the painful places, he concluded that it was a damned good thing. He wouldn't survive many of these.

It was demoralizing how many of the most painful things in the recent past originated with Jasmine Miller. Small wonder Jump was so taken with the lady, they were practically two of a kind. As for himself, he was still in awe of the courage that brought her face-to-face with Borgia. It was certainly nothing *he'd* volunteer for, and, as Jim pointed out, he had certain advantages over so-called normal humans.

Yeah. Normal humans like Mick and Jay Marquez. Careful to not violate Mrs. Miller's stern order to stay on the couch, he wriggled around for a better view of the efficient knot of EMS personnel around the fallen agent. They'd been a damnably long time at it. Tonight, he found cause to curse his enhanced senses, for if the injuries themselves were alarming, the medic's murmured comments were worse. At least Jay was all right. Physically, anyway.

Shivering with mingled guilt and fear, he looked away, and for the first time since awakening to the Millers cutting him out of his smoldering shirt, was grateful for the blanket they draped around his shoulders. Dropping a mental curtain against the disquieting scents hanging in the flat's close air, he huddled deeper into the concealing folds and concentrated on the earnest conference between Galen, Jim and the CPD Officer In Charge. At least he could eavesdrop without moving. The medics were a Sentry team, but with the hellish potion burning and blistering his flesh, he wanted to attract as little attention as possible. He'd leave it to Jim to explain it, that's what commanding officers were for wasn't it?

Tuning in the whispered conference, he jerked to rough attention as he heard Nelson suggesting that the perpetrator of tonight's assault was one and the same as the Vampire Vigilante. As the CPD OIC took notes, Nelson expanded the scenario. The guy was unbalanced and by the looks of what happened tonight, spinning out of control. He explained Galen and BC's involvement by claiming them as informants assisting SI's investigation. The detective wore a slightly dubious expression, but didn't argue.

A gentle weight settled beside him and Peale looked up. To his surprise, he found Jay smiling wanly at him. "They chased me away from Mick, so I come over t'see how you're doin'."

Her palpable concern startled him. After the ill-treatment she and her brother received at the hands of his sire, he figured the last thing she'd want was to look at another vampire. "Um, thanks . . . I'm fine. Really."

She sniffed doubtfully. "Y'don't look it." Abruptly, she gestured across the room, saying, "I jus' knew somebody'd call the cops. 'Specially after the gun went off, y'know? That's Floyd Linzay, the guy in charge? Mick usedta work with him when he was a regular cop. 'Bout time Floyd made detective, he's real good. Mick'll be glad . . . ." The hysterical edge grew with each word until her voice collapsed altogether into a high-pitched whine of suppressed grief. Before he knew it, she was snuffling and sobbing against him. He caressed the quivering shoulders and murmured reassuring sounds.

A shadow fell across them, and BC looked up at a medic fidgeting before them. The man's face was drawn and dark smudges hollowed his eyes as he said, "We got him pretty stable and we're ready to head for the hospital. If Ms. Marquez wants to ride with us. . . ?"

She leaped up. "D'ya have ta ask? I got everything I need, so let's go." Stooping to plant a swift smooch on BC's cheek she added, "Sorry t' blubber all over ya, I jus' . . . see ya at the hospital, okay?"

She darted out in the wake of the gurney. Biting back his own emotion, BC moved to follow. The touch that hauled him back to his couch and blanket was not particularly gentle, but the voice was. "You not goin' nowhere, boy, until I get this concoction washed off you. I got the tisane ready, now, so you just sit still." Mrs. Miller's lyrical voice became gentler still. "I know you want to be with them, I do, too, I was always partial to Mick, but there's nothing either of us can do for him right now. Besides, Galen is with them an' he's gonna call as soon as they reach the hospital. Mind, now, these are powerful things splashed on you, child, they gonna keep right on burnin' until I get them off. Jus' sit still, it won't take a minute."

For a moment, she doubted he was listening, then slowly, he settled back. She relaxed and concentrated on his burns. Knowing how powerful Borgia was left her impressed by the way the normally lackadaisical Byron waded in. Given his usual behavior, self-sacrifice was the last thing she expected from him. Grudgingly, she admitted that Augustine had a point: there was much more to this one than there seemed at first.

His eyes slid away, and her gaze following, she saw Jim Nelson reentering sans the CPD contingent. Diffidently, he approached where she swabbed away the sticky unguent. Deep-down, she was sorry for the obvious discomfort on the part of her son's friend. She'd always tried to hide her dislike for him, but, being a perceptive child, he sensed it anyway. He also knew she held him responsible for Galen's involvement with Sentry, an unnaturally dangerous occupation. In light of what just happened, maybe he saw her point.

Nelson cleared his throat. "We're wrapped up here for now, but I want to seal the apartment until I get a team in here to look for . . . ." He broke off and continued vehemently, "Oh, *hell*! I don't know *what* they should be looking for, and right now I don't *care*. Look, when BC's ready, I'll drive us all over to the hospital."

"Then we can go soon as I get shoes on and this one changes out of those tore up clothes." Wiping her fingers on a linen dish towel, she said, "I kept feelin' something bad wrong somewhere. Wouldn't let me sleep, so I jus' got dressed and started cookin' potions. Wish I'd known what the trouble was, I'd have whipped up something stronger." Pensively blotting the inflamed welts marring BC's ivory skin, she told the shivering vampire, "May be a good thing I didn't after all. What I made worked like it did against that other one because of the deep evil in his soul. You? You a royal pain in the backside, child, but you not evil. More powerful magic would hurt you more, too. The potions worked, that's all we can ask."

He grinned impishly, then clouded, remembering. Standing, he said, "We better get up to your flat, then."

Shaking a finger she proclaimed, "I been puttin' my own shoes on for a long time now and I don't think that Borgia will linger around here. I can run up and get them by myself." Before either could lodge a protest she jabbed a finger at BC. "*And* regardless of what you think, you better change your clothes, too. You're a mess."

As the formidable lady hurried upstairs, he felt a nudge from behind, and found Jim Nelson holding a flask from the fridge. The aroma of beef blood rose from the open container. Jim said, "I think Mrs. Miller has the right idea, BC, you better change those clothes or the docs are going to try to slap you into a bed right next to Mick. You better drink this, too, you look like you could use it. Besides, Galen called. The ambulance has cleared the hospital, and while we're close, Chicago traffic is awful even this time of night, a couple more minutes won't make much difference in our ETA."

Peale glanced doubtfully from the door to his commanding officer. Jim could feel his desire to bolt. He felt the same, but it was worrying to see how shaky he was. More so to look into his eyes. Nelson insisted, "BC, I don't want to make this an order, but as far as I'm concerned, Mick Marquez wasn't my only agent injured in the line of duty tonight." Frustrated, he added, "If this were New York or San Francisco where S.I. has their own medical facilities, *I'd* slap you into a bed. Unfortunately, Chicago doesn't have anything like that, so you'll have to make do with a quick fix."

BC decided against arguing; the blood smelled awfully good and it would serve no purpose for him to be battling his Hunger at the hospital of all places.

***

There were times, Jim Nelson mused, *having VIP privileges was almost worth the stress that went with them.* The parking space provided was next to the elevator doors and the elevator opened directly on the corridor where he'd find the others. He hoped BC and Mrs. Miller had as easy a path when he'd let them off at the front entrance.

The doors parted and he sprinted down the hall only to slow and stop as the demeanor of the waiting group burst upon him. He was too late. Choking a sob of grief and rage, he assumed his officially capable face and resumed with a slower and infinitely more weary step. Just a little over an hour had passed since he and Mick Marquez bade each other a good night.

***

Silent images flashed world events behind Eddie Michalson as he stuffed belongings into a large suitcase. He wasn't sorry to leave Chicago. He'd missed New York since joining Borgia here, and was pleased to be going home, even if the reason for returning was a rotten one. Three of his top people were taken out last night. Blown to hell all at one time. Officially, the Boss was sending him back to look into the problem. That was Borgia-talk for find out who the hell was responsible and give them a taste of their own medicine. That'd be dandy if it was the Columbian Cartel striking back for hijacking their power base like the Boss thought. Eddie didn't think so. He felt the answer lay much closer to home. In fact, he was ninety-nine percent positive the Ice Empress' signature was all over it.

She was crazy-mad when he stopped her moves on the Boss the other night, and was giving him hate looks ever since. Until tonight, that is. Tonight she looked kind of happy, and that usually meant bad karma for people she was pissed with. He wished to God he could tell the Boss what he suspected, but what could he say? Nothing. Better to go to New York like a good little soldier and see what he could dig up there. Besides, the Boss wasn't tracking so good yet. With a full day down and an unbelievable quantity of fresh blood, he still looked wonky. Still, 'wonky' wasn't bad, if he was a normal guy, he would've been dead.

As it was, Borgia didn't remember the fight with Marquez and was genuinely surprised and saddened to learn the man died. Rotten luck. But, if it made him realize how nuts he was getting about the kid, it wasn't a complete loss. Eddie was no psychologist, but he knew enough to see the Boss' style wouldn't fly with a guy like Peale.

The one bright spot was that Gwennie was being sent to Louisiana to talk with their importer. The guy was getting too full of himself and that was bad for business. Eddie didn't like Isendamer, but she was in her element there. If she decided the guy was a liability, there'd be a new man in charge before she left even if she had to dismantle the operation to do it. That might not be a bad idea. It was a goofy setup, and he'd feel better once they were shed of it, anyway.

The flash of a breaking news logo caught his eye, and turning toward the silenced TV, his jaw dropped as he recognized the grainy photograph superimposed in the upper right corner of the screen filled with twisted wreckage of what had been a car. Make that *four* good people. Face in hands, he sank onto the bed moaning softly, "Why does everything have to go to hell at the same time?"